THREE
WIDOWS

BOOKS BY PATRICIA GIBNEY

THREE WIDOWS

PATRICIA GIBNEY

bookouture

Published by Bookouture in 2023

An imprint of Storyfire Ltd.
Carmelite House
50 Victoria Embankment
London EC4Y 0DZ

www.bookouture.com

ISBN: 978-1-80314-739-0
eBook ISBN: 978-1-80314-738-3

In memory of Louis Collins Snr.
Rest in Peace

PROLOGUE

Mud is caked on my hands, clogged beneath my nails and crusted around the cuticles. My fingers have turned a mucky-brown colour. The further I dig, the wetter I get, the darker my hands turn.

Bogs are waterlogged, nutrient-rich patches of land used as a source of fuel, an ecosystem for wildlife and plant life. An ideal site to bury a body on this cold, silent night.

Down my hands dig, the trowel discarded. This is the perfect burial place. I hope the body I plant will take hundreds of years to be discovered. I toyed with the idea of cutting it up to make it easier to transport, but I didn't relish the thought of cleaning up all that blood. Instead, I tied it to a briquette trolley, leaned a plank of timber against the back of the jeep, wheeled the trolley up with its cargo and tipped it in.

I couldn't get the jeep any closer to where I wanted to dig the earth for the burial, so it will be another trek back to the narrow lane to where it's parked. Then I'll have to drag it over the soft peat. All this is something I have to do myself. My work. My crime. My responsibility.

Disposal is a means to an end. To be rid of the body. To

forget all about the misery. To move on while it dissolves in its watery grave.

I am doing what needs to be done.

Ridding the world of an evil person.

I know all about evil. I've lived with it. It took root in my soul. I fought it. Oh, did I fight it, until I could no longer stand to be in the same room. I had to rid the world of this evil person who hurt good people, making me complicit in the crimes.

I get on with my work, conscious that daylight is only a few hours away. I hurry, removing the remaining watery earth. I am possessed with a need. A need to do right after all this time. A need to do it the only way I can, by killing another human being. And let's not forget, I argue about using the word *human* in relation to this person I have murdered.

I concentrate. I dig. I bury the body in the bog.

At that moment, I feel free.

I have no idea that it will be almost a year before someone else is murdered.

Orla Keating stalled inside the door of Fallon's lounge bar as her senses were hit by the odour of beer and fried food. A television droned from one corner. A few tables were occupied and a bored-looking bartender chatted with a guy at the end of the bar.

The first time she'd met the others, she'd expected them to be dressed in black. Widows of old wore black to mourn their husbands, but she didn't think she'd ever met one. At thirty-three, what would she know? A missing husband wasn't a dead husband, even though he'd been gone almost a year. She'd thought it would be beneficial for her to join this group. The guards hadn't found any trace of him. He hadn't boarded that flight to Liverpool. His car wasn't located in any of the airport car parks. To date, neither he nor the car had turned up. She'd convinced herself he was dead. The other widows in the group, Jennifer, Éilis and Helena, agreed with her.

Two of them were seated in the snug when she arrived. These were now her friends.

She ordered a gin and slimline tonic, and waited while the girl dallied over which gin to pour.

'Hendrick's,' Orla said.

'Right so.'

Would she ever hurry up?

'There you are.'

Orla eyed the generous measure of gin before she poured in the tiny bottle of tonic water and paid with her card. Turning, she studied the two women in the snug, heads close together, chatting without anyone to overhear. It was just gone seven in the evening. The afternoon patrons had already departed for home, and the night crowd were still undecided on whether to go out or not. Bottom line, Fallon's was quiet.

Glass in hand, she approached the table.

'Hi, ladies,' she said. 'Sorry I'm late.'

Helena laughed, shaking her copper curls loose. 'You're here, and that's all that matters.'

Éilis said, 'Gosh, you're looking great. Love the skirt. Fab colour. Suits you.'

Orla was sure Éilis knew it was charity-shop fare and was looking down her nose at her, but she let it pass, like she always did. She shoved her bag under the table and sat on the cushioned stool. Clutching the stem of her balloon glass, she willed a smile to her lips to hide her nervousness. She couldn't help it. The coming weekend would see the anniversary of Tyler's disappearance.

'What have I missed?'

'Not a thing,' Éilis said.

Orla had tried so hard to like Éilis, but they were too similar to become real friends. Éilis was no-nonsense, told it like it was. So did Orla. Éilis was the founding member of the Life After Loss group, having set it up on Facebook originally. Her husband, Oisín, was now three years dead, and she was still struggling with balancing their two children and work. Orla knew she had a good babysitter, so why the Mother of Sorrows face all the time? But she herself was neither a mother nor a widow, so how could she have any idea what Éilis was going through?

'Still no sign of Jennifer?' she asked, making conversation about the other member of the group.

'Not a peep,' Éilis said. 'I hope she's okay. It's a month now.'

'Did you call her?'

'Numerous times. Her phone seems to be off.'

'We don't want to pressurise her,' Helena said, swiping her unruly curls out of her eyes before sipping her drink. From experience, Orla knew that Helena was trying hard to pace herself with alcohol, and life in general.

'I suppose we need to give her space,' she said.

'I remember when Damien died, she went off the rails for a while,' Helena said, putting down her glass, 'Losing a husband will do that to you. She will be back to us. She just needs time to process it all.'

'I don't like talking about people who aren't here,' Éilis said, pouting. She hurriedly replaced it with a smile. 'It's good you could make it tonight, Orla. Are you okay for the weekend?'

'The weekend?' Orla looked from one to the other, raising an eyebrow. 'Oh, you mean Tyler. Yes, actually I'm very okay about it.'

'I feel for you. At least we have closure, our husbands being dead and all,' Éilis said. Lowering her voice, she added, 'It must be awful for you, not knowing...'

'I'm getting used to it.' Dropping her eyes, Orla stared at her nails. 'It's the loneliness that gets me, with just the four walls for company.' She hoped her expression projected sorrow, because she actually enjoyed the quiet house.

'That's so sad.' Éilis smoothed her dark hair behind her ear, flashing the largest emerald Orla had ever seen. It matched her clothes. Loud and colourful. All for a Thursday night in Fallon's?

'How long is it again since your husbands died?' Orla directed her question to both women.

Éilis was first to speak. 'Three years since my Oisín, and Helena, your Gerald, when was it?'

'Oh, it must be three, no, four years now. Seems like yesterday.'

Orla waited for tears, but there were none. There never were with Helena. Jennifer, though, she was like a burst water balloon. Cried over everything. Her dead husband; her job; a toasted sandwich with the wrong cheese. It never took much for her to switch on the tears.

'Like I've said numerous times, I'm so sorry for you both.' Orla eyed her gin without taking up the glass. 'Do you think we should look for new members? Other women who have lost their husbands.' Seeing the look of horror flash across Éilis's face, she added quickly, 'I don't mean that we kill off husbands so we have more widows...' What *was* she trying to say?

Éilis clapped her hands and laughed. 'You're hilarious. This group is for women who understand what it is to lose someone, be it through death, separation, divorce. Not lost in that they can't find them. Oh, I'm sorry. I didn't mean you lost yours like—'

'It's fine. It's a clever joke.' Orla grimaced.

'I wasn't making a joke of your situation. I'll shut up before I put my foot in it again.' Éilis delicately sipped her drink, as if it might be laced with poison.

Helena lashed into her pint of Guinness, seemingly at a loss for words. A pint! Where is your class? Orla wondered. She was dressed in dark navy jeans with a black satin blouse cut low. No bra, but she probably wore tapes on her generous curves. And her hair was haloed by those magnificent auburn curls. She must have the new Dyson curler.

'Do you think we should organise an outing?' Orla asked. 'Like the day we went to the zoo. Maybe a trip to the Hugh

Lane gallery in Dublin?' She knew Éilis would like that. Helena? Not so much.

'I don't think so,' Éilis said with a blush when Helena's jaw hung open. 'It was a bit of a struggle at the zoo last time, with Roman and Becky.'

'Of course. Sorry.' Jesus, it was like being at a wake for your worst enemy.

Éilis regained her equilibrium, her green eyes flashing. 'I know they upset you that time, Orla. The kids. I don't want it to happen again.'

'They didn't upset me. I'm just not used to being around little ones. I'm more of a cat person.'

'Oh, you never mentioned you had a cat,' Helena said. 'What's it called?'

Orla had no cat. Could she say she called it Pussy, or would that be a step too far? 'George is a ginger, like Garfield.'

'My Noah loves Garfield. Didn't I tell you we have a dog? Mutt. Gerald, my husband... late husband...' a sorrowful droop of Helena's eyelids made Orla want to throw up, 'Gerald named him.'

'Good name for a dog.' Orla faked a smile. This conversation was boring the tits off her. 'Éilis, how is your little fellow?' Her Instagram feed was cluttered with photos of a white dog that might be a terrier.

'Mozart is perfect in every way.'

'I'd say your kids love him.' Orla leaned forward, feigning interest. Éilis's son was eight and her little girl was five. The perfect family, with their perfect dog. Ugh! 'Did your husband name him?'

'I got him after Oisín died. My therapist told me that having a dog in the house would be good for the children.'

'To replace their dad?'

The looks on the women's faces told Orla she had gone too far. 'I'm kidding. Sorry. No offence.'

'That was a little insensitive, if I'm honest,' Éilis said, straightening her back. 'You wouldn't like me to talk about your Tyler that way.'

Orla fiddled with her glass and sipped her gin, willing tears into her eyes. 'I'm so sorry. It's just with Saturday being the anniversary of his disappearance... We talked about this before.' She didn't want to talk about it now.

'It will help to talk about your life with him,' Éilis said.

Was that a knowing glint in her eye? Orla wasn't sure. Helena kept her head down. Probably wondering who was going to the bar. Her glass was empty.

'You know we were married five years, and I'm sorry if I come across as insensitive to your situations, but I've been so confused since he disappeared, I've lost my social niceties. This is my only outlet, and it's great to be with women who understand.'

She forced a tear and urged it to snake down her cheek, hopefully dragging mascara with it. Faking sorrow was a pain in the arse.

Helena reached over and took her hand. 'You are one of us, Orla. Aren't we glad to have her?'

Éilis opened her mouth slightly, as if the effort was too much for her, and said, 'Sure we are.'

And like that, Orla knew she was off the hook. 'Another Guinness, Helena? And what's that you're drinking, Éilis? Vodka?'

Éilis's expression was like she had sucked an egg and it had lodged in her throat. 'God, no! Nothing so vulgar. I'll have another Chilean Sauvignon. White wine,' she added, as if Orla was a total novice where alcohol was concerned.

She drained her gin and went to the bar. Relieved.

Entering her renovated split-level house, Éilis slipped off her shoes. It was chilly outside and the underfloor heating travelled from her feet up to her knees, warming her instantly. She paid Bianca, the sitter from next door who doubled as a nanny from time to time even though she had a summer job in Dolan's supermarket. After the girl left, Éilis locked the door and fastened the safety chain in place.

In the kitchen, she plugged in her phone to charge and dropped her keys in the dish on the counter. She threw another log on the wood burner in the living room and shut the glass door quietly. There wasn't a sound from upstairs. Roman and Becky were asleep.

She sat on her yellow two-seater couch and plumped up the orange and white velvet cushions. Colour soothed her and the house was dotted with pops of it. She used the remote to dim the lights and settled her legs beneath her, but feeling her eyes droop, she decided to go to bed before she could uncork a bottle of Sauvignon. That would be dangerous. She didn't want to go down Helena's route. She closed the damper on the stove and headed upstairs.

With her foot on the soft striped carpet of the top step, she paused. Was that a noise downstairs? Listening intently, she heard it again. The logs settling in the stove, perhaps? She'd locked the front door. Had Bianca locked the back patio door? She hadn't checked. It was possible the teenager had gone out to the garden for a smoke.

'Damn,' she muttered, and headed back down the stairs.

Switching on lights as she moved through her red-painted galley kitchen, she walked into the open-plan extension with its high ceiling. She had never been one to conform to the sedate, so the walls pulsed with colour from a clutter of abstract paintings. If your life was dull, inject brightness into it, was her motto. Being an interior designer helped.

Tugging at the sliding glass door, she found it unlocked.

'For God's sake, Bianca.'

She locked it and stared at her reflection in the glass. A squeak behind her caused her to swing around on the ball of her foot. The gaping room was empty.

That was when she remembered she hadn't seen or heard the dog since she'd arrived home.

'Mozart?' she called softly, not wanting to wake the children.

The dog didn't come running like he usually did. Had Bianca let him out to the garden? He didn't like the dark. He'd have come straight back in. She thought of bringing her phone upstairs, but it was still charging. She switched off lights as she went.

She heard it again. Upstairs. Roman and Becky!

She took the stairs two at a time, almost falling over as her dress tangled around her legs. Fear gathered like a fluff ball in her chest, and without a thought for waking the children, she crashed into Becky's room and flicked on the light.

The little girl sat up suddenly, squinting in the brightness. 'Mammy?'

'It's okay, sweetie. Go back to sleep.'

She kissed her daughter, tucking the duvet up to her chin, turned out the light and headed to Roman's room. Putting her head around the door, she allowed the hall light to spread into the room. Her son was fast asleep. She pulled his door shut and slid to the floor, relieved, listening to her heartbeat pound in her ears. The noise had unnerved her. Where was Mozart?

Wearily she stood, tucking the hem of her dress in her hands, and entered her own room.

There he was, sleeping on her bed. The little dog knew he wasn't allowed there. She was about to wake him and shoo him down the stairs when she felt the negative energy in the room. It was too late to run, and she stood frozen as a figure stepped out from behind the door.

She made to scream, but a gloved hand covered her mouth, dragging her backwards against the wall.

'Don't say a word or your kids die.' The voice was muffled behind the mouthless black hood covering the face.

She couldn't scream or shout. The hand was clamped firmly on her mouth, almost covering her nose. She took a few frantic breaths, kicking her feet back against her assailant's legs. The hand on her mouth clamped tighter, blocking her nose completely.

She tried to draw back an arm with the intention of hitting out, but she was getting weaker by the second. Her terror was such that she felt her bladder opening, powerless to stop the warm flush down her legs. It didn't deter her attacker. The hand tightened again. Fear was a bomb in her chest ready to explode.

Her children.

They'd already lost their daddy; they couldn't lose her too. Then she wondered why Mozart wasn't barking.

With no choice, she allowed her attacker to walk her down the stairs and out the front door. She felt herself being bundled into a vehicle. Something sharp dug into the side of her neck.

No matter how hard she tried to prevent it, she was going to pass out.

She couldn't form a coherent thought; her brain was fuzzy. She was powerless to stop the darkness blotting the colour from her life.

———

A film of death slips over her eyes; dying ponds watered with tears. She is no longer able to widen them, to silently plead for freedom. When it suits me, I will give her the release she craves, but never freedom.

I can't hear anything she might want to say, because layers of tape are stuck over her mouth.

The frog-like croaks that rise from the depths of her throat no longer escape her shuttered lips. The sound is like a mouse squeaking. Annoying the life out of me. Grating on my nerves. Raising tension in my muscles.

I like a little resistance from my prey, enough to mount a weak challenge. Weak being the operative word. They are all weak. I eye my second conquest, sleeping, but not for long. Just long enough to give me time to dispose of this one.

Walking barefoot around the room, I sense gravity pulling me towards hell. I don't mind. I gave up on heaven a long time ago. The carpet beneath my feet was once soft, but now it is coarse and worn, hidden beneath the plastic sheeting. I idle at the mantelpiece and eye the bronze ornaments standing there, crafted locally in Ragmullin. I've owned others over the years, but I dropped them into a charity shop in town. I kept these two. For a reason.

I pick up the ornament of the little girl sitting on top of a pile of books. I assume she is unable to read, because she has no eyes. Where her eyes should be, there is just smooth bronze. Was the sculptor making a statement? See no evil? It is something I ponder in solitary moments. I replace it on the circle where it stands surrounded by dust.

Turning away from the mantelpiece with its unlit fire, I see her sitting there, skeletal, tied to the chair. She has served her purpose. Time for me to get dressed for the final act. I pick up the plastic pack containing the white forensic suit. It's the last one, and as I tear it open, I mentally put it on my list next to duct tape. I know I'll be needing them. I have another target in my snare. That excites me even more.

DAY ONE

At the roundabout, the driver hit the indicator signalling he was bringing his articulated lorry to the left. There wasn't much traffic at six a.m. He shifted the vehicle into gear and headed towards the distribution depot. Further on to his right, Bay 13 was open and ready.

'Unlucky for some,' he muttered.

Before turning into the compound, he looked to his left over the mini roundabout to make sure the way was clear. Ragmullin was plagued with bloody roundabouts. Some smart-arsed council engineer must have thought they'd be great for a laugh. Graham Ward wasn't laughing. He'd had to negotiate four after he left the dual carriageway.

He glanced towards the waste ground on his left. Something had caught his eye. A flag of yellow shimmering in the early-morning breeze. Probably stuff left over from the carnival. That had been a nightmare week. Caravans and trailers had lined the narrow road towards the depot. Twice he'd tipped the rear of the lorry against a caravan as he'd driven round that narrow fart of a roundabout.

He backed his vehicle up to the bay door, jumped down

from the cab and lit a cigarette. It wasn't his job to load or unload, so he wandered across the road and stood at the fence. Dragging heavily on the cigarette, he caught sight of what had alerted him while he was driving. He blew out a smoke ring.

What was it? Something yellow with black on top? It looked like material. He blew more smoke from his nostrils. A hacking cough squeezed his chest. Two crows rose from the yellow mound and circled before flying off.

Graham stubbed out his cigarette and stared. The air was still, the only sound the hum of traffic out on the dual carriageway and the whirr of the hydraulic lift at Bay 13.

'Dammit,' he muttered, and lifted his leg over the thin wire fence.

Underfoot the ground was soft, and tyre tracks from the carnival vehicles had left ruts an inch deep in places. Rain had been incessant for the duration of the carnival, and though the weather was fine at the moment, the clouds bulged ominously.

As he neared the object of his interest, another crow swooped low, cawing loudly. He shooed it off by waving his hands. The closer he got, the more laboured his breathing became, and he felt a finger of fear track a line down the nape of his neck. It couldn't be, could it? No. He wanted to turn and run back to his lorry, drive home to Dublin and leap into bed beside his girlfriend. Maybe the heat from her body would dispel the ice-cold fear that nestled at the base of his skull, causing the hair to stand up on his neck.

His hand was reaching for his phone in his back pocket as he came to a halt. Long red hair fanned out around her porcelain face, which he could see had been damaged badly. The birds? Her arms and legs were at awkward angles, as if she'd fallen from a height. He couldn't see any blood, but that didn't mean it hadn't been spilled. He just wasn't close enough, but still he felt too close for comfort. Young. Around his own age maybe? Graham was twenty-seven, and this unfortunate creature looked no older than that. But he'd heard that death returned your youth.

The yellow he'd seen from the cab of his lorry was her light cotton dress. Thin straps, halfway down her arms. Her feet were bare. Dirty, as if she'd run through mud. Or been dragged? Then he saw the small round hole in the side of her temple.

'Sweet Jesus,' he muttered, and hit 999 into his phone, his trembling sweaty fingers sticking to the screen.

'Hello? Yes. The name is Graham Ward. I found a dead woman. I think she was shot.'

The clouds opened, and rain spilled from the sky in big fat drops.

Lottie Parker woke at five a.m. After a quick shower, she dressed, wondering what the weather would be like. She glanced out the window. It looked like rain, so she pulled on a pair of ankle boots, just in case she had to hit a muddy crime scene. Best to be prepared for the worst.

Her mother, Rose, was in the kitchen.

'Mother! What are you doing up at this hour?'

'I put in a wash. I know how busy you are.'

'I did the laundry last night.'

'I had to do my own sheets. They should be finished by now.'

Lottie watched her mother ambling over to the machine, taking out a sheet, duvet cover and pillow cases. Sopping wet. She'd used the wrong setting. Now Lottie would have to put them through a long spin.

'I'll finish them off,' she said tetchily.

'I know how to wash a few sheets!'

'Why don't you make a pot of tea? I'll put them in the dryer.'

'I'm able to hang them on the line, missy.'

Lottie hated being called missy. 'Fine.'

She couldn't mask the annoyance in her tone, because she *was* bloody well annoyed. It was 5.30 in the morning – her *me* time – and she hated confrontation, especially this early.

'If you want to do it that badly, you can.' Rose dropped the basket.

As Lottie picked it up, she realised there was no fresh smell. 'Did you put in detergent?'

'Oh, so now you think I'm stupid as well as losing my mind. Give it here.' Rose snatched the basket and marched out the back door.

Snapping on the kettle, Lottie leaned her head against the wall cupboard. She couldn't figure out if her mother's mind had deteriorated further, or if it was her own lack of patience that fuelled the tension between them. Whatever it was, work could only be better than conflict at home.

Abandoning the idea of making coffee, she swiped up her bag and phoned Boyd on her way out the door.

She sat with Detective Sergeant Mark Boyd in the car outside Millie's garage. The windows were fogging up as the rain began to beat mercilessly down. So much for the washing her mother had hung on the line.

'What did you get in your sandwich?' she asked, with her mouth full.

'You're not having any, if that's what you're after,' he said.

Swallowing, she shook her head wearily. 'Can I not ask anyone anything this morning without my head being bitten off?' She rolled up the crusts into the greasy wrapper and threw it into the footwell. 'And you're like a hen on an egg since you got back from Malaga.'

He stayed silent.

She looked at the raindrops streaking down the glass. July

had been brutal weather-wise, and it was now mid August and not much better. Two days of sunshine, three days of rain. It was typical to experience four seasons in one day in Ragmullin. Frustrating.

Leaving the house in a huff earlier, she'd swiped one of Sean's sweatshirts from the hook. When she'd pulled it on in the car, she was horrified to see it had a Batman image on the front. She couldn't go around with her arms folded over her chest all day, so she'd just have to suffer the comic remarks. It was worse for Boyd, because she knew he'd be called Robin. She smirked for a second, then felt the seriousness of the energy in the car weigh heavily on her shoulders. Boyd was miserable, and having her mother living with her was making her grumpier than him. A right pair.

What they needed was a big investigation. Something to get stuck into. To have the team working diligently and concentrating hard. They were all sick of administration and paperwork. If she saw another Excel column of an unbalanced budget, she'd scream. An investigation would give her a bona fide excuse for not having the returns completed and distract her from her home life. Superintendent Deborah Farrell was grouchy as hell, and that mood had wended its way right down to the desk sergeant.

She glanced at Boyd, and read the irritation written on the hard line of his jaw. It took a lot to irritate Boyd. Maybe they needed a holiday together rather than a new investigation. But her life was complicated. And it was even more complex since Boyd had arrived home from Malaga with Sergio, his eight-year-old son. He'd only found out about the boy a few months before he'd met him for the first time in June. She was sure she knew what was eating him. She wanted him to admit it. That wasn't looking likely any time soon, so she decided she'd be the one to say it.

She twisted around to look at him. 'It's Jackie, isn't it? Have you heard from her?'

'My ex-wife has nothing to do with anything.'

'Of course it has to do with her. I'm not stupid. Talk to me. Please, Boyd.' He was as thin as ever. The subtle tan that had given him a healthy glow had faded. His jaw was sharp and unforgiving. His sticking-out ears had turned red. She struggled with how to comfort him.

Placing his uneaten sandwich back in its wrapper, he folded the paper around it neatly and fastened the sticker back in place. 'You can have it if you like. I only took one bite.'

'Stop using diversion tactics.'

'You're such a head wreck, Lottie Parker.'

She took the sandwich from him and placed it on the dashboard. Grabbing his hand, she squeezed it. 'Talk to me when you feel comfortable doing so.'

He extricated his hand and stared out at the rain. Silence washed over them before he spoke.

'She's coming to Ireland.'

'Feck! Ah, shite, Boyd.'

'Just when I have Sergio settled with me. You and your family have been amazing with him, especially Chloe and Sean. I couldn't do it without you. And now this bombshell.'

With her daughter Chloe caring for Sergio during the day while Boyd worked, Sean, her seventeen-year-old son, had come out of his box, as her mother had put it.

'The kids enjoyed the carnival last week,' she said, 'and Sean even brought Sergio to his hurling training the other evening. First time in ages he's trained. They're good for each other.'

'They got drowned in the spills of rain,' Boyd pointed out.

'Bet Sergio was happy.'

He smiled. 'He thought it was hilarious, traipsing water all over my matchbox apartment. Our life is just getting settled, and my ex-wife pops up like the proverbial bad penny.'

Lottie grinned back at him, but shivered inside. A nugget of anxiety had taken root. She was afraid to ask, but she had to know. 'When is she arriving?'

'No idea. Got a text that said, "Can't wait to see my little boy soon." She probably has her flight booked and could appear at any time.'

'Try not to let it get to you. She can't take him away from you.'

Boyd twisted in the seat and faced her. 'That's just it. She can, and she will.'

'But you have the DNA test to prove he's yours.'

'What judge will take a boy away from the mother who's raised him for eight years? Sergio's been with her since the day he was born. I didn't even know of his existence until a few months ago. What does that demonstrate? What type of father does that make me?'

'A good one. Your ex has a history of cavorting with criminals, and as soon as she revealed Sergio's existence, you flew to Spain to meet him.' This was a flimsy argument, but she had to calm him somehow. 'Stop worrying. I bet she only wants money.'

'Where will I get money? I'm trying to buy a bigger apartment – and don't say I can move in with you again. You have Rose to contend with now, along with your own three and your grandson.'

'Intergenerational blended families are all the rage.' She forced a hopeful smile.

He shook his head without a hint of levity. 'Thanks for the offer, Lottie, but you have enough on your plate.'

Leaning back, she folded her arms and stuck a foot on the dashboard like a grumpy kid.

'It's hard to believe we were nearly married, and now we can't even conduct a normal conversation.' She hadn't meant to sound sharp, but it had to be said.

'Maybe that makes us like a real married couple.'

'God knows, we argue enough.'

'I'm sorry, Lottie. Let me sort this out on my own. Can you do that for me?'

Could she? The pressures of her home life deepened daily. She wanted to have Boyd by her side at home as well as in work, but that didn't seem like it would be happening any time soon. It had taken her long enough to accept that she loved him, and now she was in danger of losing him. All because of his bloody ex-wife.

She opened her mouth to let fly with a rant, but was saved when the garda radio burst into life.

———

Early-morning yoga class normally offered headspace to Orla Keating. Today, she hoped it might rid her of the pain pinging behind her eyes.

As she walked from her home on the cemetery road towards the studio at the other end of town, she kept glancing back over her shoulder. The hairs stood up on her neck. No one behind her. Few people were out and about at this hour of the morning. She liked walking. It helped clear her mind of the things she'd rather not be worrying about. It was a chance for her to use all her senses.

She breathed in and out as she took a detour along the canal path. She had plenty of time. She looked at the sky, then at the flowers and weeds in the hedgerows. She marvelled at the sound of the water rippling and the birds twittering in the trees. Stopping for a moment, she touched the reeds and leaned in to smell the freshness – and then the heavens opened. She pulled up her hood and continued up the incline, over the bridge and onto the street.

Passing Millie's garage, she noticed two people sitting in a car, eating. How could they eat garage food, especially at this hour? As she walked down Friar's Street, she once again looked behind her.

Stop! No one was following her. Still, she couldn't shake the uneasy sensation. Orla knew she was astute and sensitive. So if she felt this way, there had to be a reason.

Shuddering, she moved her yoga mat from one shoulder to the other and straightened the small rucksack on her back with its towel and water bottle. Despite her headache, she felt good this morning in her purple Lycra gear and her new Asics runners. Tyler would have made her send them back because of the price tag. But Tyler wasn't the boss of her any longer. Today, that didn't give her the satisfaction she knew she should feel.

That was when she felt it again. Eyes on her back. Swinging around quickly, she thought she saw a shadow pull into the alleyway behind her. Should she stop and wait? Have a look? Should she run? No, she was done with running. That had got her nowhere.

Sirens blared. She watched as two squad cars shot past, splashing through the gathering puddles.

Someone was dead.

She was certain of it.

She felt that tumbling motion in the pit of her stomach that she'd felt the day Tyler had disappeared.

He'd been standing at the sink in their tiny kitchen with his back to her. His shoulders were hunched and she knew his phone was in his hand.

'Who are you texting at this hour of the morning?' She'd glanced at the digital cooker clock: 4.05 a.m.

He swung around, his face shrouded in the shadows cast by the dim light bulb hanging from the ceiling. She had forgotten to get a higher wattage.

'What I'm doing is not your business. And if you want to know, I'm confirming my flight time.'

Cringing, she flicked on the kettle.

'Did you even check if there's water in that?' He glared before turning his back once again, texting one-handed.

The kettle barked and she realised he was right. It was empty. Should she turn on the tap, or would that infuriate him further? Did she even want a cup of tea? No, was the answer to both questions. She could creep out, leaving him to his myste-rious texting. Or stand her ground. She shivered and back-stepped towards the door.

'Are you going to fill it, or leave it?' He turned slowly. 'I don't know why you're even up. I never made a sound.'

'I was just going to make a cup for you before you left.'

'And have me stopping on the motorway for a piss? Go back to bed and leave me alone. I'll see you in a few days, and you better have this house sparkling. It's a tip. You wouldn't make a dog live in this filth.'

She silently gulped down her tears, a feat she had mastered over the last five years of living with Tyler Keating. The house was shining. Not a thing out of place. Not a mote of dust. She knew all that, but she would still wash and polish and scrub while he was away. There was no point in not doing it. The thought of the consequences was too frightening.

She didn't say goodbye or safe trip, just backed out of the kitchen and silently made her way up the stairs to the bedroom. Lying on the bed, she wished away the minutes until she heard the front door close and the scream of the engine as he sped away.

Now she wondered if that had all been a manufactured memory. Was that really what had transpired that morning?

Shivering, she quickened her pace, knowing it was impos-sible to outrun the past.

5

The hangover from hell had taken hold, and Kirby couldn't lift his head from the pillow. He tasted stale whiskey at the back of his throat and wondered how he could get a drink of water without having to get out of bed. Impossible.

He reached for his phone on the night stand. As his fingers scrabbled around for it, he knocked it to the floor. Leaning over the edge of the bed, he squinted with one eye; it was too painful to open both. The phone had landed beside a shiny black shoe. Both his eyes shot open. A second shoe came into focus, along with a white lacy bra.

'What the...?'

Each word thumped behind his eyes like an amateur banging at typewriter keys. Agony. As he fell back on the pillow, dizzy, he felt a hand snake over his rotund tummy.

'Hi. You're awake,' she said.

In the few seconds since it had registered that he'd brought a woman home, he'd half hoped it was the lovely Garda Martina Brennan. But he knew he would never be so lucky. Detective Sam McKeown had his claws well and truly dug into Martina, despite his wife finding out about the affair.

Turning, he stared at the top of a blonde head, face down on the pillow beside him. Slowly she looked up at him.

She was fucking gorgeous!

Kirby shook his head, causing more shooting pain.

'Good morning,' he managed.

'You don't remember last night, do you?' A little smirk curved her butterfly lips, and he immediately wanted to kiss them.

'Remember it? Of course I do.' He was lying. He hadn't a notion how he came to have her in his bed.

She laughed and buried her face in the pillow again. Her outstretched hand was doing terrible things to him. Not terrible, awesome, except he felt he might throw up any minute from the booze he'd consumed. The taste rose in his throat. Whiskey! After all the promises he'd made to himself, he'd gone out and drunk bloody whiskey.

He needed to use the toilet. How could he extricate himself without offending her? He didn't want her fingers to stop their magical trails, but he really needed to pee.

'Hey, I have to go to the bathroom. Can you... you know... wait here until I get back?'

She laughed again, and the sound was so musical he could dance, if he wasn't dying.

'I'm not going anywhere yet.' She turned onto her back and pulled the sheet up to hide her nakedness.

He suffered a frightful flash of awareness. Were the sheets even clean? How could they be? He hadn't been to the launderette in ages. And where were his underpants? No way was he waddling his naked fat arse across the room.

'Don't be worrying,' she said. 'I saw it all last night.'

She turned away anyhow, preserving some of his remaining dignity.

In the bathroom, he peed, flushed the toilet and washed his

hands. He found a pair of boxers on the floor and quickly pulled them on before glancing at himself in the mirror. The flabby red face staring back at him was his all right, and his bushy hair for once lay flat in sweaty curls against his scalp. Time for a quick shower? No, she might disappear on him.

He ran a toothbrush over his teeth, splashed cold water on his cheeks and rinsed sleep from his eyes. After drying his face, he rooted in the cabinet for something nice to spray on himself. He needed to get rid of the stale odour of alcohol, sweat and sex. Finding a bottle of Old Spice that he'd forgotten he even had, he doused himself liberally and returned to the bedroom.

He had only been gone two minutes, but she was dressed, sitting on the edge of the bed, tying up her hair.

'Don't leave yet,' he said. 'We can go somewhere for breakfast. Would you like that?' Feck the job.

'I've to get to work, and if your phone is anything to go by, you have somewhere to be too.'

He felt the blood drain from his face. Had she been snooping? Not that he had anything to hide, but all the same, he liked to be able to trust people.

'And I didn't check it, if that's what you're thinking. It's vibrating like a clucking hen somewhere under the bed.'

'God, no, I didn't think that at all. Head's just a bit woozy.' The phone could wait. He didn't trust himself to be able to stand back up if he stooped to retrieve it.

'It's okay, Larry. It was good to meet you.' She held out her hand.

For a minute he thought she was asking for money. He hadn't been *that* stupid, had he? Then she moved towards him, wrapped her arms around his waist and leaned up to kiss his chin. God, she was tiny. No wonder she needed the stilettos he'd seen on the floor.

'Where are my shoes?'

He pointed, then blushed seeing her bra on the floor beside them. She picked it up and bunched it into a tiny handbag that was lying beside the leg of the bed.

'Will I see you again?' he asked.

She shouldered her handbag and slipped her feet into the shoes. 'You invited me out to dinner, Saturday night. Remember?'

'Actually...'

'Don't worry. We were both pretty wasted. I have your number.'

'How?'

'You forced me to put it in my phone last night. I hope it's the right one; I'll feel a proper tit if I phone some other guy.'

He grinned. 'Did you give me yours?'

'Yes. I'll text you later today.' She moved to the door. 'In case you've forgotten, I'm Amy.'

Kirby sat on the edge of the bed for a good five minutes after she'd left, trying to dredge up some memory of the evening. Flashes came and went. Fallon's bar, Danny's and Cafferty's. Then the Brook Hotel. Dancing. Drinking. So much drinking. On a Thursday night, too! He'd be skint for a week. After that, it was an alcoholic blank. Definitely time to ditch drinking whiskey.

The state of the sheets told him there was yet more to remember, but he needed to check his phone and get to work.

'What time is it anyway?' he mumbled, holding his head and dragging the phone from under the bed. 'Jesus Christ!'

Seventeen missed calls and nine text messages.

He was in the shit now.

But then he smiled. He could handle anything that was thrown at him today.

He lay back down on the bed, made his pillow comfortable and closed his eyes. For the first time in ages, maybe since his girlfriend Gilly had been murdered, Kirby was close to what he'd call happy. And all due to this little whisper of a woman named Amy.

6

Ballyglass Business Park was home to glass-plated car showrooms, fitness gyms and the largest supermarket retail distribution depot in the country. To the right, as you looked in, there was a patch of wasteland caught up in a planning dispute. This was the designated location for circuses and carnivals when they came to entertain the citizens of Ragmullin.

The rain was easing, but Lottie felt her boots sinking in the churned-up earth. Then she spied the stepping plates placed by the SOCOs and quickly jumped onto them before anyone noticed her mistake.

Grainne Nixon was in charge of the SOCOs. Struggling under the weight of a steel case containing her forensic tools, she walked up behind Lottie.

'Morning, Inspector.'

'Hi there, Grainne. You won't believe this, but I was wishing for something to relieve me from spreadsheet head-wreck week. I honestly didn't wish for someone to be murdered, though.'

'I've just arrived. Is it definitely murder?'

'Unofficial report says gunshot wound to the head.'

'Shit.' Grainne put down her case on one of the plates and shoved her wild red hair under her hood. She fixed her mask over her mouth. 'Is Detective Boyd with you?'

'He's pulling on his whites. After you.'

Lottie stood back to allow the SOCO to enter the tent. It had been hastily erected over the body in an attempt to preserve potential evidence from the rain. Bit late for that, she thought.

Another SOCO stood at the dead girl's head, awaiting instruction from Grainne. The only sound was the patter of rain against the canvas.

'She wasn't killed here,' Grainne said immediately.

'Because there's no blood?' Lottie asked.

'Yep.' Grainne knelt on the plastic sheeting.

'Could it have been washed away?'

'Maybe. It rained during the night, and then there's this most recent shower, though I'd still expect to see some discoloration of the soil.'

Lottie leaned over Grainne's shoulder to study the victim. The young woman's face was pretty in an understated way. Not an ounce of spare flesh on her frame. Bone thin. Her neck was long and slender, and bruised. They might get lucky with DNA from that area. Her dress was low-cut, and it was obvious she wasn't wearing a bra. Her red hair put Lottie in mind of Grainne's locks. They could be sisters, the two women.

She let her gaze linger on the victim's damaged face. Birds had pecked at the pale skin, and it seemed both eyes had been plucked from their sockets. She felt a rush of bile, and quickly swallowed it back down.

'Early to mid thirties, I'd estimate,' she said. 'God, this is horrific. She's someone's daughter, sister, partner or wife. Could even be someone's mother.' She mourned for the unnamed woman whose family was about to be plunged into a tortuous nightmare.

'Gunshot. Left temple. If I'm not mistaken, both arms and one leg are broken.'

Lottie had noticed the awkward angles of the bones, and the torn flesh. 'Did she fall from a height? Or was she thrown? Pushed?'

Grainne glanced at her. 'Wait until the state pathologist—'

'Yeah, I know.' She was impatient to learn more. 'One thing's for sure, she didn't walk out here and lie down on the ground while someone shot her in the head.'

'Her feet are scratched and torn,' Grainne said.

Hunkering down, Lottie squinted at the small, delicate feet, probably a size four. Grainne was right. 'Is it possible someone walked her here, then broke her limbs and shot her?'

'Like I said, there's no visible blood. She could have been dragged here. But the ground's turned into a mud bath, and after the carnival vacated the site, they left behind a multitude of tyre tracks.'

'What's that around her mouth?' Lottie scrutinised the sticky black substance on the victim's lips and cheeks.

'I'd say she was bound with tape. Possibly duct tape, but the black makes me think it could be insulation tape. We might get lucky and be able to lift fingerprints from the residue.'

About to turn away, Lottie said, 'The dress looks like light cotton.'

'A party dress?' Grainne said.

'A summer dress.' Boyd entered the confined space. 'Shot somewhere else?'

'Looks that way,' Grainne said, opening her case to begin work.

Lottie left the tent. Pulling off her mask, she breathed in the damp morning air to unclog the scent of death.

Boyd joined her. 'There are security cameras on the depot over there, but all the showrooms with the high-resolution cameras are on the other side of the retail park.'

She ducked her head back inside the tent. 'Grainne, any idea how long she's been dead?'

'Maybe five or six hours, and she's been out in the open long enough for the birds to disfigure her. The pathologist will give you a more definite answer.'

Lottie walked with Boyd back along the stepping plates. 'We need to establish who she is. That will give us a starting point.'

'Why dump her here?' he said. 'Does it hold some significance for her murderer?'

'She wasn't killed here, that much is obvious. Someone went to the trouble of transporting her body and leaving it out in the open to be found. Why?'

'Wait for the post—'

'Yeah, yeah.' Lottie walked to the edge of the cordon. 'But it strikes me that she was posed and left to be found. Who does that?'

'An arrogant son of a bitch.'

She took off her overshoes. 'Where's the guy who called it in?'

Boyd pointed to a man sitting in the passenger seat of a squad car, door open, smoking a cigarette. 'Graham Ward, aged twenty-seven. Lorry driver. He drove straight here from the docks. Arrived at six twenty. Parked in Bay 13 and walked over for a smoke.'

Lottie approached the car. 'Mr Ward, I'm Detective Inspector Lottie Parker. Can you tell me what led you to discover the body?'

'Just having a smoke. There were birds on top of her. They flew off when I got a fit of coughing. Never seen a dead body before and don't want to ever again. It was the yellow material, you know. I saw that from my lorry as I drove in. And the birds...' His body convulsed in a long shiver. 'Just wandered over to see what it was. Never expected... you know...' He gulped. 'Sorry.'

The tremor in his hands was so bad he let the cigarette fall to the ground, where it sizzled in a puddle.

'See anyone else around?'

'Just the lads operating the lift at the bay. They began unloading the lorry and I left for my smoke.'

'Do you know her?' Lottie asked.

'The dead woman? I never saw her before in my life. Was she shot? It looked like a bullet wound to me.'

'And you'd know a bullet wound, would you?'

'Not a real one like that. Just what you see on the telly. You can't think I have anything to do with it?'

'Not at all, but we will need a formal statement, fingerprints and a DNA sample. Elimination purposes.'

'I never touched her. I couldn't do anything like... like that. Her arms and legs... God, it's brutal.'

'I know, Graham,' Boyd said. 'It's a shock to the system. We'll get you to the station for that statement.'

'What about my lorry?'

'You'll be dropped back here.' Boyd turned to the garda driver and instructed him to bring Ward to the station.

When they were alone, Lottie said, 'He didn't do it.'

'I figured that. What's your rationale?'

She shrugged, looking around her. 'The depot cameras will have recorded him arriving. Once we have time of death, and confirm his movements, we'll know for sure. Get the footage and have McKeown examine it.'

Detective Sam McKeown was their go-to CCTV guy. A pain in the arse, but he was good at his job.

'Where's Kirby this morning?' Boyd asked.

'That's just what I was wondering,' Lottie said.

———

It's interesting to stand and watch the aftermath of your crime. I'm a fair distance away from the army of law-enforcement stooges descending on the small patch of waste ground.

Fantastic location to dump a body. The idea came to me when I drove by last week. Hundreds, if not thousands of people trekking through the site. Adults and kids. Trailers, caravans and camper vans. Monstrously heavy equipment. A forensic nightmare. Plus, I wanted to display my work. To give them a puzzle as they try to figure out my motive. I am way too clever for their ant-sized brains.

I'm standing at the far end of the business park in a garage forecourt, walking around admiring cars I don't want. It's not yet open, but still, there are a few others here, so it's easy to blend in as just another prospective buyer having a snoop.

With one eye focused on the guards and the forensic people, I wonder when they will realise they are up against a genius.

I have my reasons for killing. Will they ever work them out?

I have a great location for killing. They will never find it.

I already have my next target in captivity. I hope they discover she has been taken before they find her body. It's much more exciting to be hunted while I do my hunting. Class act.

But my most immediate task is to identify the next dumping ground.

I might not find a place as forensically compromised as this, but I will do my best.

7

'Look what the cat dragged in. Good of you to join us, Amy, for part of the day at least.'

Amy was in no mood for Luke Bray. Who did he think he was? Twenty-two going on forty. She knew she was late. She'd had to go home, shower and change into Dolan's supermarket uniform. She was sick to death of wearing black trousers and T-shirts, but at least it saved her own clothes.

She unlocked her till. With a smile, she released the aisle barrier.

'Good morning, Mr Rodgers,' she said, scanning his newspaper and a carton of milk. 'Anything else today?'

'Two-euro scratch card. Nice to see you happy, Amy.'

'I'm always happy.'

'Told you to call me Kenny.' He winked.

She knew his name was John, so she smiled. Before last night, she'd thought she must only be attractive to eighty-year-olds like Mr Rodgers; now, she couldn't help the warm glow inside her body. It must show on her skin.

'Who's the lucky gent, then?' He had a twinkle in his eye as he tapped his bank card. Yes, it shows, she thought.

'You wouldn't know him, Mr Rodgers.'

'He's a lucky man. See you tomorrow, Amy.'

'Lucky?' Luke leaned over from his till. 'It's you who's lucky, not the dope you hooked.'

'Shut up, will you?' She could never figure out why he had to be so abrasive. He was a dick.

'Did I offend you, contrary boots?'

One of the girls had lodged a complaint against Luke for using inappropriate language in her presence. Obviously he was trying to cover his arse now, but he hadn't changed one iota. That girl now worked in the office. Perhaps complaining was a cute move.

'You have a customer, Luke.'

She wasn't about to allow that twit to dim her glow. As she scanned a basket of groceries, she wondered what Detective Larry Kirby was at. It wasn't an idle thought. She really wanted to know.

———

'Inspector!' Grainne called from the tent. 'Need you back here for a minute.'

Lottie put on a fresh pair of overshoes and hurried back across the slippery plates.

'What is it?'

'The victim is a small build. Height five one; shoe size four; dress size I'd estimate eight.'

'Agreed,' Lottie said.

'The dress she's wearing is a fourteen. Three sizes too big. It's been pinned at the side to make it fit.'

'Maybe she borrowed it.'

'I just thought it might be important.' Grainne's eyes were downcast with disappointment.

'You're right to bring it to my attention. Make sure Gerry

photographs everything before her body's moved.' Lottie glanced at the dead woman. 'Did you discover anything to identify her?'

'Nothing. No handbag. No shoes. No nothing. Sorry.'

As she sat into the car with Boyd, Lottie said, 'The body was dumped here to confuse us.'

'Because the carnival was based here last week?'

'Yep. Ground is torn up. Litter scattered around. Makes it difficult to know what's truly evidence and what was already here.'

'Forensics will be able to determine time scales and—'

'That takes too long,' she interrupted. 'I believe we're dealing with a very clever and arrogant murderer.'

'Whatever about the arrogance, you're cleverer.'

'I'm not sure if that's a compliment, but let's get to work.'

8

Kirby wheezed into the incident room for the morning briefing and Lottie could see he was hoping no one would notice him. Some hope.

'You look totally hung-over,' Garda Martina Brennan said in a loud whisper. She passed him a mint lozenge as he sat next to her. He smiled his thanks.

'Good of you to join us, Detective Kirby,' Lottie said before pointing to a photo of the victim lying where she'd been placed by her killer. 'We need to identify this woman. Did anything show up on the missing persons database, Detective McKeown?'

'No one fitting her description on our files. I extended the search nationwide. Nothing so far. Early days.'

'She looks to be in her thirties. From her initial assessment at the scene, Jane Dore, the state pathologist, suggests the gunshot wound to the head is the likely cause of death. A full post-mortem should confirm it. The victim suffered a severe beating, and there's evidence she had been restrained at her wrists and ankles, possibly by a thin nylon rope. Nothing like that has been recovered on or near her body so far, but a search of the area is ongoing.'

McKeown grunted, wiping the top of his shaved head with a lazy hand. 'After a week-long carnival there, it'll be a massive job determining what's relevant and what's not.'

'I'm aware of that.' She wondered when, if ever, he'd lose the plank weighing down his shoulders. He was at loggerheads with every member of staff with the exception of Martina Brennan. He was convinced one of his colleagues had informed his wife of their affair. Detectives Maria Lynch and Kirby were his main suspects, but it hadn't stopped him carrying on the affair.

'Her mouth had been sealed with tape at some stage. We might get lucky and extract DNA from the residue.'

'Don't hold your breath,' McKeown said.

'We don't know her eye colour. Both eyes had been... you know...' She found it so disturbing, she stumbled over her words. 'It's possible that birds destroyed her eyes along with pecking at her flesh.'

'That's horrible,' Kirby said, looking like he was about to throw up.

'The security footage in the area has to be checked. I want to know when her body was dumped there. Your job.' She nodded towards McKeown.

'Could she have been killed where she was found?' Kirby asked.

'SOCOs say not.'

'Why?'

'If you had answered your phone, you'd have been there and you'd know there was no blood found despite the gunshot wound.' Lottie bit hard on her tongue. It pained her to be short with Kirby, but he had let them down this morning.

'Sorry, boss. Phone was on silent.' He blushed to the roots of his damp unruly hair.

She immediately felt sympathy for him. Kirby was one of her most loyal detectives. Still, she couldn't help adding, 'It might be no harm investing in an alarm clock.'

McKeown sniggered.

Lottie glared.

'The yellow dress may not have been hers. It's three sizes too big. Find out where it was bought and we might be able to find... Yes, Martina?'

'I thought I recognised it from the photo as a Zara dress, so I did a search. It was available online, on sale, so I doubt it will help us.'

'Investigate it further. She had no shoes or handbag, so where are they? The entire site needs to be searched for them. We need to find out who she is and then trace her movements, which may lead us to her killer.'

'Was she drugged or maybe drunk?' Garda Lei asked.

Lottie admired the newest recruit to Ragmullin garda station, part of the cycling patrol unit. From Longford, his father was second-generation Chinese. Lei was short and lean and brimming with enthusiasm for the job. She wondered how long it would take for that to be knocked out of him.

'Toxicology will take time. Jane's initial estimate is that she was dead no longer than six hours before her body was moved to the site. That means sometime after midnight. The post mortem later today should provide us with a more accurate time of death. This woman was held somewhere. She was beaten before being shot and her body dumped. She couldn't have been there too long.'

Boyd piped up. 'The fact that we can't find anyone fitting her description on the missing persons database suggests she may have been taken only last night. No one has noticed her gone yet.'

Lottie considered that. 'Or she may have lived alone with no one to miss her. We can put out an appeal based on her physical features, saying we need to locate her.'

Garda Lei raised his hand. 'Erm, sorry, but will that not give the media ammunition? They'll run with a story that either she's the dead woman or she's the killer we're looking for in connection to the death. It will need to be a carefully worded press release.'

'I agree with Garda Lei.' Superintendent Deborah Farrell marched to the front of the room. 'I will work with the press office. We can do without a media feeding frenzy. Find out who she is as soon as possible. Anything else to add, Inspector?'

Lottie hadn't noticed Farrell enter the room and momentarily withered under her stare. She quickly regained her self-control. 'Just what I said. She was beaten, shot dead and dumped on the waste ground. Two broken arms and a broken leg. Post-mortem will confirm any other injuries. The assault was vicious and sustained. She was restrained. We know she was dressed after being shot, because there is little blood on the dress, and said dress is likely not hers because of its size.'

'What about the guy who found her?'

'According to the distribution centre log, Graham Ward's lorry arrived at six twenty a.m. Detective McKeown will check the security footage to confirm it. We are in the process of securing all other footage from the area.'

Superintendent Farrell fixed her clip-on tie and faced the group. 'I want a fully committed team on this one. Work as quickly as you can with your SIO.' She glanced at Lottie, with a look that said it was against her better judgement to make her senior investigating officer. 'We will make an appeal online this morning and I've called a press conference for three this afternoon. Bring me something before then. And I don't want to see that death photo on the internet.' She flashed a warning look around the room before leaving.

Lottie groaned inwardly. Did her boss think she was a bloody magician? She said, 'I want everyone focused on this case. Now get to work.'

As the room emptied, she turned to the board and studied the photo of the dead woman. 'Who are you? Why were you targeted? Where were you held? Talk to me.'

'The dead don't talk,' Boyd said from behind her.

'Jane is like a ventriloquist, she can make them speak, but the post-mortem won't be even started by three. What can I offer Farrell for her press conference?'

'She can make a plea for people to check on their family and friends. Hopefully someone will come forward with the victim's name.'

'There must be someone out there who doesn't yet know their loved one is dead. A husband, mother, friend.'

'She didn't have a ring.'

'What?'

'You mentioned a husband, but our victim wasn't wearing a wedding ring.'

'That doesn't tell us anything definitively.'

She watched Boyd study the victim's photograph.

He said, 'No jewellery at all, even though her ears are pierced. If she was on a night out, wouldn't she wear jewellery?'

'I know I never take my studs out.'

'I reckon you only have the one pair.'

'I lost everything when my house burned down. What are you getting at, Boyd?'

'The fact that the dress might not be hers and she had no jewellery, shoes or bag, and the evidence that she was restrained makes it's plausible that she was held somewhere for a time. If that's the case, why has no one missed her?'

'Good point.'

'You know that gut feeling you talk about, Lottie? Mine is

telling me this woman has been missing for more than one night.'

'I hope you're wrong, because that will make our job all the harder. Let's grab a coffee and a proper sandwich, then we have to find out who she is.'

The appeal went out on social media and elicited an immediate response.

'Boss, we might have something here.' Detective Maria Lynch tapped her keyboard. 'Call came in a few minutes ago from a Frankie Bardon at Smile Brighter Dental Clinic. After seeing the news and our appeal, he says he's worried about one of his former employees, a dental nurse called Jennifer O'Loughlin. A month ago, she posted her resignation letter to the office, which he thought was a bit unusual. He said she hasn't been in contact with any of his staff since.'

'Did he follow it up with her?'

'Don't know. He gave us her address: 171 Riverfield Road. That's close to the cemetery, isn't it?'

Lottie leaned over Lynch's shoulder, trying to read the report on the screen. 'Phone him back. See if he has any more information.'

'Will do. He also provided her phone number.'

'Try it.'

Lynch dialled the number and shook her head. 'Seems to be dead.'

Lottie turned to Boyd. 'Fancy a trip over to Riverfield Road? Hopefully Jennifer O'Loughlin is fine and it'll be a wasted trip, but you never know.' She straightened her back.

'I could go,' Lynch said.

'I need you to keep monitoring the call information as it comes in. Set up a meeting with this Frankie Bardon for me in case Jennifer O'Loughlin turns out to be our victim.'

She grabbed her bag and jacket from her office and nudged Boyd to follow. She caught him giving Lynch a sympathetic eye. With a small shake of her head, she kept walking. No point in going soft in her old age. Lynch was good on the computer, like McKeown was good at analysing security footage. She needed her team to utilise their skills in the best possible way.

'Where has Kirby disappeared to now?'

'Don't know,' Boyd said, shrugging his arms into his jacket.

'He's been acting odd recently. His moods go from high and loud to low and silent.'

'He's fine.'

'He's drinking too much, and that's from one who knows all about engaging in that destructive pastime.' Lottie wondered how she could approach Kirby to talk about what was wrong. 'Boyd, would you—'

'No, I won't talk to him. It's his own business. If it affects his work, it's your job to have the chat, not me.'

She bit her tongue. No point in arguing with a grumpy arse. Still...

'Just a quiet word. Friend to friend.'

'No way, Lottie. Come on, I'll drive.'

Lottie scrolled through her phone on the way over to Riverfield. If Jennifer O'Loughlin had had any social media accounts, she'd deleted them at some stage. Nor did she appear to have an online footprint. If she turned out to be their murdered woman, she'd get Gary from their technical unit to have a look.

The house was a detached red-brick affair, situated on what seemed to be a settled estate. The houses had been built only thirty years before and the area appeared quiet, with no children out on the footpaths. The lawn hadn't been mowed in a while and was at odds with the neighbouring gardens, which looked slick and trim. The red door was solid and all the window blinds at the front of the house were closed. A silver Toyota RAV4 hybrid stood in the driveway.

Boyd admired the car. 'Nice set of wheels.'

'Cool,' Lottie said.

Boyd raised an eyebrow. 'Exactly what Sergio would say.'

She grinned and leaned on the doorbell. It echoed from inside, but otherwise all was silent. Tried again. Same result. 'Her car's here but no one's home.'

'She might be out for a walk or in town. We can quiz the neighbours if you want, but if we'd checked her out before we left the station, maybe we'd know if she has any friends or family.'

Lottie didn't respond as she headed around the side of the house. The wooden gate opened easily and led to an overgrown back garden. A set of wicker furniture stood on a raised patio. The concrete underfoot was green from the weather. Potted plants dotted around were in serious need of weeding. Like the front of the house, the rear window blinds were pulled down.

Peering through the frosted glass panel on the back door, she couldn't make out a thing.

'She's not here,' Boyd said. 'Let's go.'

Before she moved away, Lottie depressed the chrome handle, almost falling over as the door opened inwards. She threw a quizzical look towards Boyd.

He shook his head. 'We have no legal reason to enter.'

'Her car is out front, the door is open, she hasn't been seen in a month and we have an unidentified murder victim. In the circumstances, I feel justified.'

She stepped into a large utility room, kitted out with high-end electrical appliances. A row of hooks held only one coat, a navy waterproof, and a pair of boots with dried mud on them stood on the floor beneath it. She opened the internal door and entered a drop-dead-gorgeous kitchen, complete with white quartz worktops and duck-egg-blue cupboards.

'We should go.' Boyd shifted from foot to foot.

'Calm down. Door was open.' She wasn't leaving until she'd had a good snoop. 'We have reason to believe Jennifer O'Loughlin might be our dead woman. Gloves.'

He handed her a pair of gloves and tugged on his own. 'Okay. Two minutes, then we're out of here.'

He headed to the hallway and up the carpeted stairs. Lottie made her way into the living room and flicked on a switch.

The room revealed vivid furniture that took her by surprise. Everything was soft and colourful. The wall hangings were nothing more than abstract splashes of paint on canvas that her grandson Louis could have done, but she reckoned Jennifer might have paid a fortune for them. The couch was an invitation to lose yourself, and the low chrome-legged table with its glass top held a stack of what she'd call coffee table books. Not to be read, just admired. A beautiful room, but it didn't have the feeling of being lived in. There wasn't a single photo to be seen.

'Find anything useful up there, Boyd?'

He came down the stairs.

'Everything seems very impersonal to me. Not much to tell you what the woman is like.'

'Minimalist is the new fashion.' But she had to agree with him.

Back in the kitchen, she opened a few cupboards and drawers. No letters or bills. She checked the refrigerator. It held a bottle of wine, a two-litre bottle of sparkling water and a carton of milk.

'It's like she packed a bag and left,' Boyd said.

'Look at the milk carton. No, don't smell it! It's dated four weeks ago.'

'Maybe she put the house on the market.'

'Check online to see if it's listed for sale.'

While he fumbled for the phone in his pocket, she opened the pantry cupboard. Only non-perishable foodstuffs. Apart from the garden, the place was like a show home.

'It's not for sale that I can see,' Boyd said. 'We need to talk to the neighbours. They might know where she's gone and when she left.'

'Any clothes in the wardrobes? Cosmetics in the bathroom?'

'Some.'

She ran upstairs to see for herself.

The wardrobes held an eclectic mix of clothing. High-end fashion, to complement the style of the house. It was obvious that Jennifer would not be seen out in a sale dress three sizes too big. Something was off. There was no way of knowing if a handbag or shoes were missing. Or what Jennifer was wearing when she left, and whether she was indeed their murdered woman.

She noticed a range of expensive branded cosmetics on the dresser. The bathroom had deeply coloured wall tiles depicting a jungle scene. The taps on the shower and sink were black chrome. Pristine. In the cabinet, she made no significant discovery. Paracetamol and some sort of herbal anti-anxiety pills. Toothpaste and a battery-operated branded toothbrush. Smile Brighter. Wherever she was now, Jennifer either had a spare toothbrush with her or she'd left without one.

. . .

After a quick knock on the neighbours' doors, they met back at the car. It was really a job for uniforms, but Lottie needed to know one way or the other, and quickly, if Jennifer O'Loughlin could be the dead woman.

'Anything?' she asked Boyd.

He switched on the engine. 'Not many people at home this time of day. Those I did speak to hadn't seen her around for a few weeks. No one could pinpoint exactly when they last saw her. It appears she told no one that she intended to head off. Not that anyone chatted with her much. How did you get on?'

'The only noteworthy thing I learned is that she's a widow. Her husband died two years ago. One neighbour told me that Jennifer had the house completely refurbished just a month after his death.'

'That seems a bit quick.'

'Grief affects everyone differently.' She knew how Adam's death had affected her, and felt an affinity with Jennifer.

'What age was the husband when he died?'

Lottie checked her sparse notes. 'According to one neighbour, Damien O'Loughlin was around thirty-five years old when he died from oesophageal cancer.'

'Do you think this O'Loughlin woman is our victim?'

She scrunched up her eyes against the sun, squinting at the empty house. 'It's possible. But if so, where has she been for the last month?'

'Good question,' Boyd said.

'And why was her back door left unlocked?' Her phone vibrated in her bag. 'What's up, Lynch?'

'Our victim is definitely Jennifer O'Loughlin. Frankie Bardon just emailed over her photograph from her personnel file. Hair colour's different, but there's no doubt she's our dead woman.'

'See what you can find out about her and her husband,

Damien. He died two years ago.' She hung up and looked at Boyd. 'We need to get SOCOs out here.'

'You could have thanked Lynch.'

'Are you saying I've an attitude problem?'

'No, but you need to hone your people skills.'

'Why don't you hone your fuck-off skills?' She folded her arms in a huff.

At thirty-three years of age, it wasn't the first time Helena McCaul had woken up disorientated on a floor. She glanced through splayed fingers to get her bearings before sitting up. She was in her son's room. Panic gripped her chest and squeezed like a vice.

As she pulled herself onto her knees, she spied the vodka bottle, and the reality of her situation came swirling back to her like an unstoppable tornado. Exhaling, she picked up the bottle and shoved it behind the Winnie-the-Pooh bear on top of the wardrobe.

She'd had a bad nightmare, recalled the harsh breathing in her ear. Had she taken vodka on top of everything else? She checked the bottle again. Three quarters full. That meant a quarter was gone. Maybe that was from another night. Her memory failed her. At least she was relatively okay. She needed to wash the stale, sweaty smell from her body and brush her teeth for at least five minutes.

Under the cold jet of water, she shuddered. She turned the switch around to full heat and waited for the stream to dispel her goosebumps. A memory flooded to the surface of her mind.

Had she been that drunk that she'd hallucinated someone grabbing her, choking her, blocking her airway with a hand? Her mother, Kathleen, was forever telling her she had an active imagination, that she was delusional. Maybe it was true.

Unable to dredge up any other significant memory of the night, she recalled having the light on in the room, and then it was suddenly dark. She'd blacked out. She really needed to get a grip on her life, otherwise these fleeting episodes could become the norm.

Stepping out of the shower, she wrapped a towel around her body and wiped the steam from the mirror. Her hair dripped and frizzed into curls as she stared at herself. There were no telltale marks on her skin except for heat blotches. It had been a hallucination. She needed to go back on her meds. That meant she couldn't drink, and she needed to drink to dull the pain.

With wet feet, she stomped back into the room. Grabbing the bottle from its hiding place, she took it to the bathroom and poured it down the toilet. Enough was enough. She had to take control of her life or, worst-case scenario, she would die from alcohol poisoning. Sometimes that was what she wished for. Shaking off her morbid thoughts, she worked out her plans for the day.

She had to talk to Éilis.

There was no way she could continue the Thursday-night sessions with Éilis, Jennifer and Orla. It had been good for a while, helping her to forget. She drank too much on those evenings, but she told herself it was only one night in the week, so what harm was it doing? But then she found herself drinking at other times to obliterate the memories. Thursday night morphed into Friday and then the weekend. The only days she was actually sober were Monday to Wednesday, and even then she was anxious for Thursday to arrive. That meant that for four days out of seven she functioned in an alcoholic fugue. It had to stop. No longer could she use a crutch to blot out the past. She had to face it, and if that meant revealing the widows' secret, then so be it.

Hurriedly she dressed in her best underwear and a blue cotton dress adorned with yellow butterflies. She tied up her hair to hide the frizz and slipped her feet into her comfortable NeroGiardini sandals. They added two inches to her five-foot-three height. Once she was ready, she had an overwhelming desire to have a drink before she left. Not water. Not coffee. She craved a tumbler filled to the brim, one hundred per cent proof.

Helena McCaul had shrouded truth in delusion for so long, she wasn't even sure if she had a serious alcohol problem or not.

11

Éilis Lawlor's children, eight-year-old Roman and five-year-old Rebecca, sat at the table. Kellogg's Sugar Puffs were scattered across the surface. Milk had dribbled to the floor after Becky spilled it while trying to pour it from the carton onto her breakfast.

'Roman, where is Mammy?' Becky said.

Her brother groaned. He didn't want to worry his sister, but why wasn't Mam around? 'I don't know. Will I ring Bianca? She might know where she is.'

'She never stays out all night. She always comes home.'

'Stop sniffling. Eat your breakfast, then I'll call Bianca.' He looked around, wondering where he would find the babysitter's number. He saw their mother's phone charging on the counter. He leaped up and unplugged it. He knew her PIN code. She'd told him it in case of an emergency. This felt like an emergency.

'That's Mammy's phone!' Becky yelled. 'Why is it here when she isn't?'

'She probably forgot to bring it out with her. Give me a minute.'

Roman turned his back to his sister. No point in worrying her further. He walked to the sliding glass door and looked out at the sun shining on the wicker patio furniture. His dad had put down the patio. Roman remembered the day was so hot and his daddy had made him wear a floppy sunhat. Gross. He didn't think Becky was even born then because he had no memory of her being around, moaning like she always did.

He scrolled through his mam's contact list and found Bianca's name. He was about to tap her number when he thought of something. Turning to Becky, who had Sugar Puffs stuck in her hair, he said, 'Where's Mozart?'

She dropped her spoon and jumped off the chair, shouting for the dog. 'Mozart! Where are you? Mozart?' Then she turned to Roman, her little mouth downturned and her eyes big pools of tears. 'I don't know where he is.'

'He's probably with Mam. Hold on.' He tapped Bianca's number and kept his fingers crossed. 'Hi, Bianca. Do you know where our mammy is?'

'Is that you, Roman? You're ringing off her phone. Isn't she at home?'

'The phone was on the counter, but we can't find her or Mozart.'

'She probably brought him out for a walk to the shop to get milk for your breakfast.'

'We have milk. We're eating our breakfast.'

'Right. I'll ask my mam if she knows where yours is. Then I'll call over. Okay, sweetie?'

He usually hated it when she called him that, a name for babies, but in this moment Roman felt as helpless as a baby. 'Don't be long. Rebecca is scared.'

He hung up and sat at the table. 'We better finish our breakfast and clean up the table. We don't want Mam to be mad when she comes home with Mozart.'

'Roman? She never brings Mozart to the shops.' Becky burst into tears.

Little flutters of fear trickled along the hairs on his neck. He leaned over and held his sobbing sister in his arms. He had a bad feeling. A very, very bad feeling.

12

Kirby went out to the yard at the back of the station and lit his cigar. After a few quick drags, he coughed loudly in the smoky haze and debated sending a text to Amy. He wanted to meet her this evening. He needed an ally, and she would be the perfect antidote to a bad day at work. Then he realised he didn't know where she worked. Knew absolutely nothing about her. The euphoria of waking up with her by his side had all but disappeared.

He topped his cigar and shoved it into his stained shirt pocket, then took a deep breath of air before heading inside. Hopefully no one would notice him sneaking back in.

As luck would have it, Sam McKeown was the first person he bumped into. He was standing in front of the photos tacked to the incident board.

'She was stunning,' McKeown said.

'You don't have to talk about her physical appearance. It denigrates her.'

'You're turning into a grumpy old man, Kirby. You need to get laid.'

Kirby smirked. If McKeown only knew. 'You're one to talk.

You aren't satisfied with your wife and kids, so you have to target the young women who work here.'

'I can't help it if you're jealous of me and Martina.'

'And what about your wife? Ever stop to think what you're doing to her?'

'That's the problem with you, Kirby, you can't deal with the fact that I have two beautiful women fawning over me while you can't get anyone.'

Kirby turned on his heel to leave. The conversation was travelling one way – downhill – and he wasn't in the humour for fisticuffs. He feared he might blurt out about Amy. No way was he going to let McKeown belittle her with his narrow-minded standards based entirely on looks.

At the door, though, he couldn't help himself. 'You need to watch out, McKeown. You can only ride your luck so far, and you're fast running out of a clear road ahead.'

McKeown's shaved head blazed and his mouth flattened in an angry line. He swallowed his lips as he spoke through his teeth. 'Take this advice for nothing, Kirby. Watch your back. I wouldn't be too clever around me if I was you.'

Feeling the flush rise up his cheeks and his chest tighten, Kirby scrunched his hands into fists. One good punch and he'd land McKeown on his back. But McKeown was taller and fitter, and Kirby would certainly suffer the worst of the battle. Instead, he left the room, banging the door so hard he heard the windows rattle. He needed a strong coffee. Three shots. Nothing less.

———

Orla had ended up skipping yoga. The sound of sirens and the screech of vehicles racing through town had put her on edge.

She'd walked as far as Ballyglass Business Park, where the emergency vehicles had headed, and then back into town. She'd mooched aimlessly through a few shops before entering Fayne's café. Sitting on a stool by the window, she'd thrown her yoga gear at her feet and stared out at the day stealing away from her.

Sipping her strong coffee, she felt the presence of someone beside her. She nodded to the man who questioned with his eyes for permission to sit. He was burly and sweating but smelled okay. She knew him, though it was obvious he hadn't yet recognised her. Or maybe he was just distracted.

'Turned out nice after all the rain,' he said, and slurped his black coffee.

She remained silent. He seemed to get the message. Side-eyeing him, she noticed that he was scrolling on his phone with stubby fingers. A pearl of sweat fell from his bushy hair onto the screen, and he swiped it away.

'Are you all right?' she couldn't help but ask. 'You're not ill or anything, are you?'

'Hung-over,' he said, with a smile.

He actually had a lovely smile; it lit up his face, but she recognised the effects of alcohol in his eyes. Bloodshot.

'Same,' she said. 'I backed out of my yoga class this morning. Actually, I know who you are.'

'If you were in any of the pubs last night, you might have bumped into me.'

Here was the bloody detective who had worked on her husband's case, and he didn't even remember her.

'Do you recall the disappearance of Tyler Keating?' she asked

He scrunched his lips up to his nose and squinted as if trying to dredge up a face. Then he seemed to get the connection. 'Of course I do. You're his wife. Orla, isn't it? Your husband disappeared... twelve months ago now? Left home to go to the airport and hasn't been seen since.'

'That's correct.'

'I'm afraid there's no news. We never found his car and he never boarded the plane. We did all we could. I'm sorry.'

'Looks like he slipped down your order of priority.'

'The file is still open.' His hands flailed in the air and he almost sent his coffee flying.

'Seems Tyler is just another statistic for you.' She hoped she was convincing, because she didn't want to reveal that her life was an awful lot better without her domineering husband.

'Like I said, the file is still open. If we get anything new, it will be prioritised. I take it you don't have any news of him?' He put a hand on her arm, and she looked down at it. He promptly removed it, shifting further away from her.

'No news,' she said. 'Not a thing.'

'Honestly, we turned over every stone searching for him. There was no evidence of him to be found anywhere. It's a total mystery.'

'Do you think he's dead?'

'Logically it's the most likely scenario, but where is his car? If he – and pardon me for saying this – if he took his own life, we'd at least have found his car. He'd have left a footprint somewhere. If he was abducted or kidnapped, we never received any communication from anyone.' He turned, and she held his gaze as he studied her. 'What do *you* think happened to your husband, Mrs Keating?'

'I don't know what to think. He might be living it up in some exotic country.'

'We checked airlines and ferries. No record of his passport being scanned.'

'He might have got a fake ID. Tyler was resourceful. The car? He could have dumped it somewhere. Sold it to a breaker's yard under the table. You know what I mean?'

'I do. Had he any reason to do a flit?'

'No.'

'I seem to recall you telling us you had a happy marriage. Was that true?'

'We got on just fine. He never gave me any hint of wanting to leave. I know I said he's probably living it up somewhere, but in reality, I think my husband is dead.' She forced a few tears to the surface of her eyes, then hastily swiped them away. 'It's a year tomorrow since I last saw him, and I just want closure. You never gave me that.'

'Look, Mrs Keating—'

'Orla, please.'

'Right, Orla, I'll pull his file when I go back to the station. I'll have a fresh look at it and let you know.'

'I appreciate that. Thank you.' She smiled sweetly. 'I better get going. Oh, by the way, what was all the commotion earlier this morning? Sirens going off like there was an incoming missile.'

'We found a woman murdered out by Ballyglass Business Park.'

'That's awful. Who was she?'

'Don't know yet.'

'How did she die?'

'It's early days in the investigation. I better be going too. I have a killer to find.'

Orla slid off the stool and shouldered her belongings. 'I hope you have better luck finding your killer than you had with finding my husband. Goodbye, Detective.'

13

At Bowen Solicitors, Madelene Bowen paced her office. Having just turned sixty, she prided herself on her smartly cut suits and silk blouses. Hours in the gym helped maintain her figure and boost her strength. She loved her shoulder-length hair, which she figured was unintentionally in vogue. Platinum styles were the latest fad with the younger set.

Tapping her jacket pocket for her vape, she found it and inhaled greedily. Caramel flavour. She'd give her right arm for a Benson right now, but her health was more important. Why did she bother? After all that had happened? Really?

She glanced around her office and went to stand at the window. It looked out to the rear of apartments and shops. Walls and cement. She was bricked in metaphorically and physically. A knock on the door brought her out of her musings.

'Ms Bowen, there's a call for you.' Her PA waved a yellow Post-it. 'I was trying to put it through... Oh, the phone is off the hook.' She made her way to Madelene's desk and lifted the receiver then replaced it. 'I'll put it through now.' She left as quickly as she'd entered, without waiting for a reply.

In less than ten seconds, the silence was shattered by a shrill ringing.

Madelene let it continue for a bit before moving from the window and answering. No matter how low she felt, she had to work. She needed to work. For her sanity.

'Good morning, Madelene Bowen speaking, how can I help you?'

'It's Orla Keating. I'm wondering how to go about having my husband declared dead.'

Madelene settled into her chair, puffed on her vape and listened intently.

———

The scent of spices and herbs welcomed Helena into her shop. She wrapped her red curls in a bobbin and stood inhaling deeply, soaking her senses. But the usual relief she experienced was absent. Nausea tumbled around her stomach. She was an hour late opening up, but there'd been no one waiting on the path outside as she'd rolled up the shutters and unlocked the door.

Every step she took across the floor synced with the thumping in her head. She flicked on lights as she moved, blinking at the brightness. Her shop was small; she loved the intimate atmosphere it created. It had always been her dream to own her own shop, and Herbal Heaven became her haven. An escape from the darkness that had clouded her life. She checked the float in the till, but all she saw was an image of her son, Noah, and her husband Gerald.

She was grateful for her mother's help, despite the long-term tension between the two of them. Kathleen suffocated her at times, and at others was so distant as to be invisible. Helena didn't know which type of mother she needed. She only knew that without Kathleen's money she wouldn't have her shop.

That kept her awake at night. She wasn't generating enough income to sustain the business. She needed it to ground her in reality; to keep the nagging demons away. So what would she do today?

The dates on the perishable stock had to be checked. The wheaten bread and goat's milk. But somehow everything seemed a bit too much for her. If no customers arrived by midday, she vowed to lock up and go home to sleep until teatime.

After making her decision, she felt even more exhausted. Folding her arms on the counter, she rested her head on them. One minute, she told herself. Just one minute and then she would start work.

———

Kathleen Foley's thoughts were consumed by her daughter. Helena was being a handful again, and the way she was acting, anything could happen.

Buttering a slice of toast, she searched beneath the stack of newspapers on the table for a spoon to stir her tea. The kitchen was cluttered and warm. After the earlier rain, she thought it was likely the day would turn into a scorcher. Maybe she could begin clearing her living space. That seemed like too much work to her overloaded brain.

Giving up on her watery unstirred tea, she was munching the toast when she heard the letter box slam. On the inside mat she found a familiar-looking plain envelope. No name. No address. No stamp or postmark. She unlocked the door and peered outside. No one around. Whoever had made the delivery had left quickly.

In the kitchen, she opened it and extracted a photograph.

She had been horrified on receiving the first one, but time had faded the memory and the horror had waned. No question had been posed with the photo. It was a statement that someone knew what had transpired.

Should she have burned it? No. It was a reminder of her actions. She looked at the photo she'd just received. Same scene. She placed it in the old biscuit tin and slammed the lid shut.

She was surprised that she was no longer shocked that someone had gone to the trouble of taking the photographs and delivering them to her. She had yet to figure out if they were a threat.

14

Detective Maria Lynch had pinned the headshot photograph of Jennifer O'Loughlin to the incident board. It had been emailed over from Smile Brighter Dental Clinic, where Jennifer had worked.

Lottie studied her petite, childlike features before turning her attention to the death-mask photograph. No doubt in her mind that it was the same woman, despite the intervening years and the change of hair colour. Jennifer had been fair-haired originally, but had at some stage dyed it a reddish auburn. And she had brown eyes. Lottie shivered as she stared at the eyeless face.

'I'm going to talk to this Frankie Bardon in person. Find out what you can about Jennifer's life, if she had any enemies. You know the drill.'

'Sure, boss.'

'Boyd, fill in the team about her house and neighbours. Get uniforms knocking on doors for statements.'

She was doing a quick check of her emails before she left when the phone rang. Jane Dore.

Without preamble the state pathologist said, 'I got to work

straight away on the body. I left word with the station, but it seems you didn't get the message.'

'I'm sorry, I was out trying to identify the victim. I have a name. Thirty-one-year-old Jennifer O'Loughlin. A dental nurse here in Ragmullin.'

'Ah, that's why her teeth are in excellent condition. About the only thing that is, really.' Jane paused, and Lottie wondered what was coming next. 'She was severely malnourished and dehydrated. Not a morsel of food in her stomach. I'd say she hadn't eaten in at least five days, and very little in the weeks before that.'

Possibly four weeks, Lottie thought, horrified. 'It could mean she was abducted and starved. What else can you tell me?'

'It links in with another fact. She was tied up, and for a considerable period of time. Her wrists and ankles bear witness to that. I found microscopic nylon fibres ingrained in her wounds. Also, some sort of insulation tape had been stuck across her mouth for a time. It was wound around her head. There's evidence of hair loss at the back of her skull. That could have occurred when the tape was ripped off.'

'Bound and starved. The poor woman.' Lottie wondered who could behave towards another human being with such callousness. She found it difficult to imagine what the victim had gone through. 'You'd be locked up for treating a dog that way. I'm nearly afraid to ask the next question.'

'There is no evidence of sexual assault.'

'Good. Did you recover any fibres besides the rope?'

'Some on the inside of the dress. I've sent them to the lab to be identified and analysed. Look like carpet fibres, but don't quote me until the analysis is completed.'

'SOCOs are at her house,' Lottie said. 'There was carpet on the stairs. I'll arrange for a comparison with what you have.'

'You should also know that before her limbs were broken,

she was badly beaten, possibly with a piece of timber. Maybe a four by four. The backs of her legs are in ribbons, and that's not a technical term. I found tiny splinters embedded in the muscle.'

'What kind of bastard are we dealing with here, Jane?'

'Someone without empathy.'

'Anything to point me to where she was held?'

'Somewhere cold for a time. She had frostbite on her fingers and toes.'

'Like a freezer?'

'Or a cold storage room.'

'Was she killed, then frozen before being dumped?'

'I don't think so. I think she sustained the gunshot wound shortly before she was put on that piece of ground.'

'Crap. What about the dress she was wearing? Did you get anything from it besides the fibres?'

'It was new. I've sent it for further tests. Can't tell you anything else at the moment. Oh, and after she was shot, her body was washed before the dress was put on her.'

'Shit,' Lottie said.

'Not washed very well, but it will reduce the chances of getting the killer's DNA from it.'

Lottie pondered that for a moment. 'The gun. What was it?'

'Glock. Nine millimetre. I retrieved the bullet from her brain. Lottie, before you go... I've held off the worst till last. Her eyes.'

'Her body was being pecked by birds when she was discovered.'

'I've seen the pecking made by the birds on her flesh. It wasn't birds that took her eyes. They were surgically removed.'

'Holy God! This is one sick bastard I'm looking for.'

'I'll do my best to find evidence to help you nail whoever did it.'

'Jane, I'm half afraid to ask, but was she alive when her eyes were...'

'No, she'd died from the gunshot shortly beforehand.'

'Thanks. Send on your preliminary findings as soon as possible.'

Lottie hung up and pondered the call.

Eyes surgically removed.

That added a whole new level of depravity, and it sickened her to her stomach.

15

Frankie Bardon was so far removed from what Lottie knew of dentists that it took her a moment to compose herself. Over six feet tall, sun-kissed blonde hair and a smile she reckoned must have set him back upwards of twenty grand. Though now that she thought about it, he probably got it for nothing.

'Apologies for keeping you. I had an orthodontic brace to fit on a child, and it was awkward. The child didn't want it but the mother insisted. You can imagine the scene.'

'The only braces I knew of growing up were those holding up my dad's trousers.' A lie, but she had decided on small talk to ease into the purpose of her visit. 'You didn't get that tan in Ragmullin.'

He laughed. 'No, I spent a few years in Australia. The sun helped with a skin disorder, and now I have a sun lamp at home that helps with my psoriasis flare-ups.' He removed his spectacles and seated himself on the edge of the desk, folding his arms. Defensive? 'How can I help you?'

'I'm here about Jennifer O'Loughlin. You phoned the station to say you thought she might be the woman in our appeal.'

'Did you find her?'

'I'm sorry to have to tell you this, but she was murdered.'

'Oh God. How? Why? I can't believe it. Was she that woman I heard about?' He moved to sit behind the desk, knocking against a stack of boxes, which wobbled but remained upright. 'When I made the phone call, I never contemplated that she might be dead. It was just the description in your appeal that clicked.'

'Tell me about Jennifer.'

'Believe me, there are things I wish I'd done differently when she resigned. I have regrets, but I admit I was a little relieved when she left.'

'Why is that?' Lottie studied him more carefully. Had he held a grudge against his former employee?

'Now that she's dead, I feel bad talking about her.'

'Don't feel bad. I need all the information I can get.'

He nodded. 'Jennifer was difficult at times. I suspect she was struggling with grief. Her husband died, you see, two years ago. I don't think she could deal with it. I think of myself as a sympathetic person, but she didn't do anything to help herself.'

'Did *you* help her in any way?' Lottie recalled her own struggles after Adam had died. No matter how much people tried to be there for her, she had closed them out, until Boyd broke through her defences.

'We weren't close friends, if that's what you mean. I suggested grief counselling, but she ignored my advice.'

'So she didn't attend counselling?'

'I don't know for certain, but if she did, it didn't do anything to help her. Her timekeeping deteriorated and her work suffered.'

'You told my colleague, Detective Lynch, that Jennifer was on a warning before she resigned.'

'True. She hadn't been in a good place for quite some time,

though I thought she'd turned a corner when I heard she'd joined a group for widows.'

'A group for widows?' Lottie was a widow, but she'd never heard of such a group.

'I think it was for women in similar situations to meet and share their grief. When Jennifer told me about it, I genuinely thought it would help her. But whatever they did on those nights turned her morose, and she usually failed to turn up for work the following day. To paper over the cracks, I changed her work schedule.' He paused, staring at the ceiling, before returning his gaze to Lottie. 'Recently she seemed to have lost all interest in her job. Made a few mistakes with clients. I had a serious talk with her a couple of months back; issued a verbal warning. Then her resignation letter arrived.'

Lottie watched Bardon as he ran his index finger between his eyebrows. Was he stressed or trying to keep his story straight?

'You said you didn't hear from her for a month. Why didn't you call her, visit even, or report her missing?'

'She had resigned her job. I didn't know she was missing until I read your appeal online this morning. I phoned her then, but it seems her phone's dead.'

'What would you do differently, given the chance?'

He put on his spectacles, then removed them again. 'I followed correct procedure, but maybe I'd offer her time off to sort herself out. I have a business to run, Inspector, so I did what I could until I could do no more.'

'Was she friendly with any particular member of staff?'

'Not really. Feel free to talk to them.'

'I'll arrange interviews today. I'd also like to see your client list and talk to those Jennifer would have been in contact with over the last year or so.'

He shook his head vehemently, blonde hair catching in his eyes. 'Sorry. No can do. That information is protected by—'

'Spare me the data protection babble. I can get a warrant. But you could lighten my workload by offering me the names of anyone who might be able to help my investigation.'

He stood and stretched his legs. He was so close to her, she felt uncomfortable, so she stood too. He leaned an elbow on the precarious stack of boxes and scrunched his eyes before speaking.

'I can email you her personnel file, but unfortunately not our client list.'

She'd have to settle for that, but chanced a last play. 'Need I remind you that one of your staff has been brutally murdered?'

'Jennifer was no longer a member of my staff. I'll email the file and a scan of her resignation letter.'

'I'd like the actual file.'

He sighed. 'You are a bit of a ball breaker, if you don't mind me saying. I hope that doesn't offend you.'

'Not in the least.'

He went to a cabinet, pulled out a file and handed it to her.

Lottie had half hoped it might be bulkier. 'Can you tell me a little more about Jennifer. What she was like as a person?'

'She was like a wounded bird. A little bird with a damaged wing. She'd forgotten how to fly and wasn't in the mindset to learn again. Do you get me?'

His words surprised her. 'I think so.'

'Her husband's death hit her hard and she hadn't the will to help herself. I really thought that group would help her...'

'Go on.'

'She brightened up at first when she joined it. Then she found she could obliterate her pain with alcohol. Pity. I had to cover for her mistakes countless times.'

'Why would you do that?'

His smile turned sad and he sat back down. 'I too lost someone dear to me. I know how it can tear your world into ribbons and you get to that stage where you can't envisage how to put it back together. I leased out my practice and moved to Australia on a work visa. Visited India on my way back. Best thing I ever did.'

'If you covered for her mistakes, you must have felt something for Jennifer.'

His expression turned mournful, lips downturned. 'It might be my fault that she left. I told her she needed a change of scenery; to get out of Ragmullin. Told her to find peace for herself somewhere else in the world. She was haunted by memories. Everywhere she shopped, had a drink, every street and footpath carried Damien's imprint. I knew she'd never escape from her heartache if she stayed here. She had to leave. That was my advice, and when she resigned, my first thought was *good for you, girl.*'

Lottie wasn't convinced. She prodded him with a direct stare. 'To have had that impact on a grieving soul, you must have been her friend. Did you meet her outside of work?'

He appeared uncomfortable, shifting his weight on the swivel chair. 'A couple of times. We walked and talked. Along the canal, mostly. I find water soothing.'

'Did these walks develop into anything more?'

'Definitely not. I was trying to help her.'

'You don't seem too heartbroken about her death.'

'Of course I am, but I'm also happy that she's free at last.'

Lottie didn't know what to make of this man. 'Surely you wouldn't wish her dead?'

'God no, but Jennifer was so troubled, and now she's no longer in pain.'

Finding his argument unsettling, Lottie asked, 'Did you help her on her way?'

His eyes lost their blue depth and seemed to cloud over. 'I'm speaking about her soul. Her soul is now free.'

'Are you religious?' This guy had single-handedly made himself her number one suspect for Jennifer's murder. If he'd been so concerned about her welfare, why hadn't he visited her? Conversely, if he had harmed her, why had he phoned in to confirm the name of their victim? It made no sense.

'I'm spiritual. I spent six months in an Indian ashram on my way home from Australia.'

'What's an ashram?'

'I hear your cynicism, Inspector. It is a spiritual place. You meditate, practise yoga and learn about the meaning of your life.'

'Right so.' She'd need a lot longer than six months to figure out *her* life. 'Were you ever in Jennifer's house?'

'No.'

'Why didn't you visit her after she resigned?'

'I gave her the space she needed.'

'When did you last see her?'

'She was working the week before she handed in her notice.'

'So you pushed her to leave a good job with a steady income? Why?'

'I can't make anyone do anything.'

'But why even advise it?'

His eyes darkened and she sensed a fury pulsing beneath his skin.

'She had lost her way. Those women she met with were damaging her health and her mind. They were not helping her.'

'What can you tell me about the group?'

'I only know she joined it.'

'Who else was involved in it?'

'She once mentioned someone called Helena. She runs a herbal shop in town.'

Lottie made a mental note of this. 'Did you see Jennifer outside of work, before she resigned?'

'We met at the harbour one evening after I finished work and walked along the canal. She wanted to go into the cathedral. Light a candle and implore her God to help her.'

'And instead *you* became her God. Is that right?'

'I can sense animosity oozing from your pores. Your beef should not be with me. I wouldn't harm another living thing. Especially not Jennifer.'

'She lit a candle, what then?'

'We walked around the cathedral grounds. I told her about my experience at the ashram and she seemed excited by it. She said she would look into it. We returned along the canal path and said goodbye. Then she got into her car and drove off. That was the last time I saw or spoke with her.'

Lottie knew there was no way to prove this. 'Are you willing to hand over your phone to me?'

'Why would you want it?'

'To confirm the last time you texted or phoned her.'

'That's ridiculous. If I'd wanted to contact her, couldn't I have used the office phone here?'

'You're refusing so?'

He moved to the door and opened it. 'You're wasting my time now. You should talk to the women in that group.' And he marched off like a man possessed, his affable demeanour disappearing with the slap of his shoes on the highly polished floor.

'Well, you've certainly given me food for thought, Frankie Bardon,' Lottie said. He had pushed through the swing doors and was outside before the last word left her lips.

For a guy who preached about ashrams and yoga, there wasn't a shred of calm about him now.

16

Bianca Tormey stood on the step waiting for Roman Lawlor to open the door. She was fond of the Lawlor kids, they were no trouble, but she really wanted to be in town with her friends. Friday was her day off from her part-time summer job at the supermarket. Éilis was calling on her more and more lately. If she wanted a nanny, she should pay for one, not be depending on Bianca for cheap labour. But she had to acknowledge that Éilis was a good mother, always fawning over her kids, dipping in and out of her garden office to check up on them, ensuring they were fed and watered. Or maybe that was the dog.

She pressed the bell again.

At sixteen, Bianca was lean and tall, and she knew of at least three lads who liked her. She excluded Luke Bray at work, because he was a leech and she avoided him like the plague. He wouldn't shut up about her tattoos, saying he would get one to match hers. He could feck right off.

She loved her tattoos, though her mother had almost had a coronary when she'd got her first ink. Since then she'd kept them hidden at home. Life was too short to listen to the tirades. She couldn't wait for the day when she could ink her neck and the backs of her hands. It comforted her to know what lay beneath her clothes.

Not much fazed her, but when Roman opened the door, the look of terror in his eyes caused her to pause.

'Don't know where Mammy's gone, but we found Mozart,' he said, leading her to the kitchen.

'Where was he?'

'Upstairs. We were searching everywhere for Mammy and we found him under her bed. I think he's asleep. He never sleeps this long and we were shouting. Do you think he's okay?'

'Let's have a look at the little fellow.'

Her bangles jangled as she took the stairs two at a time and headed into Éilis's bedroom. Too many vivid pinks and reds for her liking; she was more into monochrome. On her knees, she peered under the bed. The little white dog's fur was rising and falling. Catching hold of his collar, she dragged him out. He was out cold. How? Cradling him, she turned to find the two kids staring at her, wide-eyed and open-mouthed.

'Don't worry, kiddos, he'll be fine. Might be a virus or something. Which vet does your mam use?'

'Animal Love,' Becky said.

'Okay. Let's go back downstairs and phone the vet, and then we can call your mam's friends. They might know where she is.' Though when she'd asked her own mother, she'd had no idea.

Carrying the sleeping dog in her arms, Bianca followed the two children down the stairs. A trickle of worry pricked beneath her skin. Where was their mother? From what she knew of Éilis, she never left her children alone. She worked from home on her interior design business, and would ask Bianca to watch the kids even if she was just popping to the corner shop.

She phoned the vet first and was told to give the dog water and a little food and if there was no change to phone back.

'Who's your mother's best friend?' she asked.

'I only know of Helena and Jennifer,' Roman said. 'They're

in her Thursday group. That's where she went last night.' He handed over his mum's phone.

Bianca couldn't help curling her lip. The famous widows. On more than one occasion she'd had to stay until three a.m.

'Okay, let's see if I can find their numbers.' She scrolled through Éilis's contacts, relieved to see that the women were listed under their forenames; Roman was so agitated, it was doubtful he'd remember any surnames.

Settling Becky on her knee while Roman cradled the dog, she called Helena first. Waiting for the pickup, she said, 'Stop sucking your thumb, sweetie.'

A voice answered the call. 'Hi, Éilis? All okay?'

'Hi, Helena. It's Bianca, Mrs Lawlor's babysitter. I'm wondering if you saw her this morning? She's not at home and her kids are worried.'

As she listened to Helena, Bianca felt her hands sweating and wished she hadn't the little girl on her knee. Becky could hear every word.

———

Helena shook herself to wake up as she answered the phone. How long had she been asleep at the counter? Twenty minutes if the time on the old wall clock was correct.

'Bianca?' she said. 'Éilis talks about you. Says you're great with the kids. No, I haven't heard anything from her this morning. Did she get home okay last night?'

'Yeah, she did,' Bianca whispered. 'Any idea where she might be now?'

'Maybe at the shops or out for a walk with the dog. But it's odd that she wouldn't take her phone with her.'

'The dog is here. Her purse, too.'

'Are the children okay?'

'Just worried. I'll give Jennifer a call. She's in your group, isn't she?'

'We haven't seen her for over a month. It was just myself, Éilis and Orla last night. We left the pub around eleven. Maybe Éilis went somewhere after. You know... met someone...' She hoped Bianca could fill in the gaps.

'No, she came home. She paid me and I left. But the kids say she wasn't here this morning. Any idea at all where she could be?'

Helena felt a cold tongue of dread lick its way down her spine, swallowing up her hangover. 'Shit, Bianca, I don't know. Should you phone the guards?'

'I thought of that, but if she's only gone out for a walk and arrives home to find it's like a scene from *CSI*, I'd look a right eejit.'

The girl was correct, but Helena couldn't help the prickling sensation on her skin that something bad had happened. Her sensory powers, dulled by alcohol, now fizzed through the follicles on her arms, sounding alarm bells.

'Phone the guards, Bianca. I'm working and can't leave yet. Call me the second you have any news. Okay?'

'Okay.'

'And stay with the children.'

'I'm not stupid.'

'Sorry. I know Éilis trusts you.'

As Bianca killed the call, Helena stood up from the stool and moved around the shop, biting at the skin around her nails. Stop! Worry never solved a problem. Not for her, anyhow.

Deciding she needed to keep busy in order to put a halt to her irrational thoughts, she began clearing a shelf of vitamin D. When she had all the tubs on the floor, she sensed someone watching her. She swung around so quickly she crashed into the tower she'd created. She watched helplessly as it toppled.

Luckily the tubs had childproof lids, or she'd be sweeping up pills for a year.

She thought she saw something moving along the floor by the magnesium and sleep therapy products. A shadow? Footsteps? Had someone come into the shop while she'd dozed by the till? She scanned her eyes all around. No, there was no one. It must have been her imagination. Then she thought of the door behind the tiny storeroom where she mixed her herbal remedies.

That was when she heard the back door slam shut and the roller door at the front of the shop crashed to the ground.

She screamed.

Then she thought: how stupid. No one can hear me in here.

She was all alone.

Maybe she was alone now, but had she been a moment before?

17

Opening Jennifer's personnel file, which she'd brought from the dental clinic, Lottie pulled on gloves and extracted the resignation letter. She slipped it into a clear plastic sleeve, photocopied it and pinned the copy to the board. Then she asked Lynch to send the original for forensic analysis.

'We need to know if Jennifer wrote it herself,' she said. 'We found no laptop or computer in her house. No sign of her phone. A hand-written letter in this day and age is unusual.'

'Maybe it was her way of being final about it?' Lynch said. 'Written in longhand, stamped and posted, with no trace left behind like you'd have with an email.'

'If she even wrote it,' Boyd said.

'You're right,' Lottie agreed. 'We need to match the writing with something of hers.'

'Her colleagues should be able to do that for us,' Boyd said. 'Was there any bad feeling at work? What about with her boss?'

'Frankie Bardon is a bit of an enigma to me. On the surface he appears to be a genuinely nice man. But he gave me a weird vibe. He went for a walk with her the week before she resigned. Did he force her? I had a quick chat with some of the staff on my way out, and not one had a bad thing to say about him or Jennifer.'

'The fact that she refurbished the house a month after her husband died is a bit bizarre,' Boyd said.

'Grief does funny things to a person,' Lottie said wistfully. 'Sorry, funny is the wrong word. Destructive, more like. Self-destruction was my vice following Adam's death. Arrange for the dental clinic staff to be formally interviewed. If Jennifer was intending to leave town, we need to know where she was planning to go.'

'I can talk to the staff,' McKeown said. 'They might be more open with me, a friendly face.'

Lottie ignored his smirk. 'We have to find her next of kin. Someone needs to be informed of her death. They might be able to give us a hint as to why a killer targeted her.'

'Might be an opportunistic murder,' Boyd said.

'I don't think so. It smacks of planning to me. What about this widows' group?' she said.

'I'll research it,' Lynch said.

'Do that.' Lottie looked up as Kirby waddled in. 'Where were you this time?'

'Having a sneaky smoke by the smell of him,' McKeown said, half under his breath.

Kirby threw him a death stare. 'I needed fresh air. I'm here now.'

'Hangover and cigars.' McKeown raised his voice. 'A great combination for a heart attack.'

'That's enough,' Lottie said, and waited while Kirby sat. That battle was for another time. Turning to McKeown, she said, 'We need to trace Jennifer's movements from when she was last seen until her body was found. Someone put it there. A brazen act. I don't like it one bit. Have you found anything on the security footage you've been looking at?'

'Nothing to help us yet. The garage showrooms are on the

other side of the business park, and the cameras on the warehouse distribution centre are trained on the loading bays. Confirms Graham Ward's arrival time, though. The waste ground is a fair distance from the main road, so dashcam footage will be useless.'

'She didn't drop from a parachute,' Kirby said.

Lottie groaned. 'I need to know how the body got there. SOCOs are at Jennifer's house now. Hopefully they'll find something to help, but she wasn't killed there.'

'Do we know what type of gun was used?'

'A nine-millimetre Glock. Most likely illegally held and impossible to trace. But dumping her body was the killer's last act. What he did before that is conjecture until we can find clues and evidence.'

The desk phone rang. Lynch picked up. Everyone waited. When she'd finished the call, she said, 'It appears we might have a missing woman.'

18

Lynch brought Garda Lei with her. She itched to switch on the siren to block out his incessant chatter.

'We really should be following up with interviews now that we know the victim was Jennifer O'Loughlin,' he said. 'What if her killer has taken this woman too?'

'I sincerely hope not.' She parked outside a house with wild roses creeping up around the porch.

'She's not even missing forty-eight hours yet. I don't think—'

'I don't care what you think. Lei. You have a lot to learn. You're hardly here a wet week, swanning around on your BMX like a kid, and—'

'It's not a BMX, and I'm here since—'

'Enough. Go on and ring the bell.' Giving him something to do might keep him quiet for five seconds. Wrong.

'And I don't swan around.' He pressed the bell. 'It takes skill to ride the bike at the speed I have to. The cycling unit is gaining in popularity with the powers that be, so...'

He shut up as the door swung open. A teenager stood there. She had hoops in her ears and a multitude of bangles on both arms.

'You must be Bianca,' Lynch said gratefully.

'I'm relieved you came,' the girl said. 'The little ones are so upset. Yes, I'm Bianca Tormey, and this munchkin is Becky.' She pointed to the girl holding her hand tightly. 'Roman is in the living room on his iPad. Little madam here won't leave my side. Have you any news on Éilis?'

Lynch's head swam. Bianca and Garda Lei both talked nineteen to the dozen. 'This is a beautiful room.' She couldn't help herself commenting on the kitchen decor as she tried to lighten the sombre mood. She looked at the dog in the child's arms. 'And who is this lad?'

'Mozart,' Becky said. 'He's tired.'

Catching Bianca's side-eye glance, Lynch gathered she wasn't to go there. 'He's cute.'

'Do you want to sit down?' Bianca said. 'Sorry the table is a mess. The kids fed themselves and I haven't had time to clean up.'

'Don't worry about it.' Lynch sat awkwardly at the glass table. Garda Lei followed suit. Bianca sat with Becky on her knee.

'Becky?' Lynch said. 'Would you like to go play with your brother while I talk with Bianca?'

'He won't let me play with him. I want Mammy.' The child bit down on her lip and failed to stop the tears falling. 'Where is she? Will you find her? I'm afraid.'

'Don't be afraid, petal. Myself and Garda Lei will bring her home. When did you last see her?'

'She put on the light and woke me up. She gave me a kiss and told me to go back to sleep, and now she's gone.'

Bianca rubbed the child's arm. 'Shush now, Becky. No need to cry.' Looking directly into Lynch's eyes, she said, 'Éilis was home around a quarter past eleven last night. I was babysitting the children. They were as good as gold. Both asleep by nine. She paid me and let me out the front door. A little while ago,

Roman rang me from her phone.' She glanced at the counter. 'I put it back where he found it.'

'Do you know the PIN?'

'Roman knows,' Becky said.

'Will you get your brother for me?'

The little girl slid off Bianca's knee and ran from the room.

'Her bag is here too.' The teenager leaned back and took it from the counter. 'Bank cards and cash. I checked. It doesn't make sense.'

Lynch nodded. 'Are her keys here?'

'Yes, they're in the dish where she always leaves them.'

Lynch got up to look at a wedding photograph on the wall. 'Is this her husband?'

'Yeah, Oisín. He died three years ago.'

Returning to the table, she said, 'Could Éilis have gone out for a run and got delayed somewhere?' The woman in the photo struck her as someone who worked out regularly.

'I've never seen her out jogging. She does yoga, though. I babysit for an hour on Monday and Wednesday evenings when she goes to her class.'

'What's it called?'

'I haven't a clue.'

'Did you check with any of Éilis's friends to see if they'd know where she might be?'

'I called her friend Helena. They were out together last night. Fallon's bar, I think. Éilis probably got a taxi home, because she didn't bring her car with her. It's still outside.'

'Has she any other friends?'

'I only ever heard her talk about the women she meets on these Thursday nights. Jennifer was another one of them, but Helena said she hadn't been there for over a month.'

Feeling the prickle of anticipation on her skin, Lynch asked, 'What group is this?'

'It's some sort of a social gathering for widows. Éilis set it up after Oisín died. A support group, maybe? They sometimes go to the cinema. They even went to the zoo once. Usually it's drinks and chats at Fallon's, though. Sounds boring to me, but I'm only sixteen and they're ancient, so what do I know?'

Masking her grin at what the teenager considered ancient, Lynch said, 'Do you know the names of any of these women?'

'There's a Jennifer, and Helena mentioned an Orla. That's Helena McCaul. She has the herbal shop across from Dolan's supermarket, where I work part-time. I phoned Jennifer too, but it sounded like her phone's dead.'

Lynch flinched. 'Do you have Jennifer's full name?'

'Éilis's contact list just gives her first name. Helena would know.'

'Could it be Jennifer O'Loughlin?' She caught Bianca's shrug and added, 'Don't worry about it. I'll contact Helena, and I'll talk to the neighbours to see if anyone saw Éilis leave this morning. Can I have a look at her room?'

Bianca fidgeted. 'She's not up there.'

'I need to see if anything is out of place.'

'Okay. I hope I'm not being silly, it's just the kids were so upset...'

Becky ran in dragging a gangly-looking boy with her. He bit his lip and eyed Lynch suspiciously when she asked for the PIN code, but then called it out.

Lynch wrote it down and smiled at him. 'That's a great help, Roman. Will you play with your little sister for a few more minutes? I want to have a look in your mam's room.' She caught Bianca's eye, and the teenager took Roman's hand.

'Let's make pancakes,' she said.

Lynch scooted out the door, leaving Garda Lei looking lost.

In the living room, she couldn't help admiring the vibrant colours. Éilis had a good eye and excellent taste. The room was soothing yet invigorating. She could do with something like that in her home. Cost a fortune, though. Money she didn't have.

Upstairs in the kids' bedrooms, she found the duvets bunched up on the beds. Everything else was tidy, despite there being more toys than either could ever play with.

She pushed open the door of the main bedroom. The double bed was made up and a beautiful patchwork quilt lay across the yellow duvet. It either hadn't been slept in or Éilis was super-efficient and had made it when she got up. She noted a few creases on the quilt and a scattering of short hairs. The dog had lain there.

The wardrobe door was open. She glanced at the vast array of clothing, knowing she wouldn't be seen dead in anything so bright. Looking around, she decided that nothing seemed out of place in the large room.

As she turned to leave, she noticed a damp patch on the carpet by the bed. She got down on her knees and stared. Had the dog peed? Wrinkling her nose, she shuffled backwards and stood.

Everything else in the room was pristine, but right there, near the stain, she noted scuff marks on the blue carpet. Was she reading more into it than she should? Had the kids been play-acting in their mother's room? She'd ask them.

As she descended the stairs, she couldn't shake off the feeling that something sinister had happened in this house. The fact that it was probable that Éilis Lawlor knew Jennifer O'Loughlin made it even more suspicious.

Helena couldn't stop the shakes, though she'd found no evidence of anyone having been in the storeroom. The back lane was empty too. She'd checked. At the front of the shop, she discovered she hadn't locked the roller door. That was why it had fallen down. She pressed the mechanism. Once the door was securely in place, she took the key from her pocket and made sure she locked it this time.

Back inside, she found that the usual sanctuary her little shop provided had evaporated. Disturbing vibes rattled around in her chest. She made herself a nettle tea and sipped the hot liquid. Her hands were still shaking.

'I'm never drinking again,' she vowed.

The bell over the door tinkled. Maybe a customer would alleviate her uneasiness. She walked out holding her mug.

'Oh, it's you,' she said, relieved.

Orla Keating stood there holding a yoga mat and gym bag, dressed in leggings that Helena could only dream of fitting into.

'How are things?' Orla stared at her. 'You look as rough as I feel.'

'Very rough. You seem to have already got some exercise in.'

'I backed out at the last minute. I dropped by to see how you're doing today.' She pointed to the floor. 'What happened here?'

'Damn, I forgot about that. I never finish what I start.' Helena put her mug on the counter and bent down, picking up tubs and putting them back on the shelf.

'Let me help you.'

'Honestly, it's fine. I need to keep myself busy.'

'Two pairs of hands are better than one.'

Unable to protest without appearing ungrateful, she said, 'They go on this shelf.'

Orla joined her, kneeling on the floor. 'I enjoyed last night. Paying for it today in a big way.'

'I'm a bit fragile myself.' The sound of tubs slamming on the shelf echoed in Helena's head. 'Did Éilis mention anything to you last night about her plans for this morning?'

'No, why?'

'You walked with her to the taxi rank. I wondered if she might have said something.'

'Nothing that I can remember. I left her outside Danny's to wait for a cab. I couldn't be bothered hanging around for God knows how long, so in my drunken state I decided to walk home. I needed fresh air after the pub. Why?'

'No reason.' Why was she reluctant to share Bianca's phone call? Narrowing her eyes, she glanced surreptitiously at the other woman. Orla's clothing matched, in an unmatched way. Éilis would approve. Feck it. She told Orla about the call.

'Holy shit.' Orla sat back on the floor. 'That's odd.'

'I told Bianca to call the guards.'

'Not that they're much good, and I speak from experience.'

'I'm sorry.'

'Don't worry. But really, what mother goes off and leaves her kids alone voluntarily? Éilis has never struck me as that type of person.'

Helena felt her head fill with static guilt. Memories (were they even memories?) melted into white noise. Was she that type? After Gerald, she had floundered around.

'You're right. Éilis isn't like that. I'm worried.'

Orla stood, placed her hands on her hips and admired the stocked shelves. 'That looks better. Do you want me to do anything else for you?'

'No thanks. This is great.'

'You look like you could do with a strong coffee. Can I make one for you? Or will I run out and fetch one?'

'Honestly, I'm fine. I had a nettle tea.'

'Ugh. How can you drink that stuff?' Orla blushed. 'But I do love your shop. The oriental smells. Reminds me of a nice Indian restaurant I went to on my honeymoon.'

'You were in India?'

'God, no. It was in London. Tyler had a work thing that week. Said he couldn't get out of it. I spent my honeymoon in a London hotel, mostly alone.'

'That was a bit pissy of him. Sorry, I didn't mean... I have a habit of putting my foot in it.'

'No worries. It was just his way. He put himself first in everything. It's only since he's been gone that I can truly be myself. I don't know why I'm spilling my guts to you today. You know all this already.'

Helena smiled. 'Shouldn't you be working?'

'I'll be at it soon. I've been neglecting my home office and I have a few client accounts that need finalising. Boring. At least I haven't Tyler breathing down my neck. Shit, that sounded awful.'

Back at the till, Helena sat on the stool, hoping it would stop her head swimming. 'Any news on him?'

'No. I actually met a detective in town this morning and asked him for an update.'

Helena felt her heart flutter like a host of butterflies were trying to escape. 'Was that wise?'

'What could I do? He sat beside me.'

'You need to be careful. *We* need to be careful.'

'I'm well aware of that. Look, if you're okay, I better head home and change out of these clothes. They make me look like an elephant.'

'You look amazing.'

'Ah, thanks. But after last night, I'm so bloated I could float.'

'Could have fooled me.'

'Has your mum still got your son today?'

'My son?' Helena blinked rapidly, feeling confused by the quick change of topic.

'You mentioned last night that she was minding him.'

'Oh, right. Yeah, she's great. He stayed there last night and today.'

'We're lucky Éilis set up the group. It's good to talk.'

'It's so lonely when your husband dies.' Helena realised what she'd said. 'I'm sorry, I meant when you lose someone... Oh, I'll shut up.'

She noticed Orla's eyes narrowing, and a darkness descended on their silvery blue like storm clouds gathering over the lake.

'Helena, we *need* to keep quiet. Are you sure you can do that?'

'Of course.'

Orla walked around in a small circle. 'The thing is, if one of us talks, we all might die. Remember that.'

20

In her office, Madelene couldn't concentrate. Word on the street was that the body found in Ballyglass Business Park was Jennifer O'Loughlin, Damien's widow. She couldn't find anything online yet. News reports just mentioned an unidentified female. But her know-all PA had heard the name.

She unlocked the old filing cabinet to her right and extracted Damien O'Loughlin's personnel file. It was too voluminous for his ten years' employment. But then Damien hadn't been an exemplary solicitor. Far from it. As she went through the file, Madelene worried that the gardaí would come looking for it. If they found no reason for Jennifer's murder, would they turn their attention to her late husband? Was that even rational? But she knew nothing was rational about murder and murder investigations. The guards would be all over this like rabid dogs.

What she kept on her computer files was slim, but the physical file... this could create a whole world of problems for Bowen Solicitors. She closed the cover and slapped her hand on top of it, trying to think of a reliable strategy. Was there really anything to think about? She knew what she had to do, even though it went against everything she stood for. It was unethical. But there was nothing ethical about Damien's time with them.

She could still hear the slam of the door as he'd left her office following their disastrous argument. Four months later, he was diagnosed with oesophageal cancer. He'd died within two months. Though she had liked the young solicitor, Madelene was relieved. She'd believed that all her problems had died with him. Then Tyler Keating had gone missing and Jennifer had arrived asking questions.

Without thinking further about the consequences of her actions, she slipped Damien's file into her black leather briefcase, locking it firmly before settling it at her feet under the desk.

She desperately needed to see Kathleen. Her friend was the only one who could ease the tension crippling her shoulders.

21

Lottie stared at the email containing the pathologist's prompt preliminary report. Eyes surgically removed. Broken bones. Gunshot. Frostbite. She was dealing with a monster.

Boyd knocked and entered her office.

'I organised a full door-to-door of Jennifer's neighbours, the entire estate. And going by the reports coming in, not one person has seen her recently.'

'If she hasn't been seen for a month or more, does that mean she was held captive that long? If so, where? Jane said she had frostbite, so it could be a cold storage room. To find out what happened, we need to strip her life down to the last bone.' She recounted what else Jane had found at the post-mortem. The starvation. The beating. The eyes.

He shook his head. 'God, she went through hell.'

'This bastard left her body out to be found. No attempt to hide her. What's he playing at?'

'It might be someone she met online.'

Rubbing her chin, Lottie said, 'Jennifer isn't on social media. Could be a client from the dental clinic.'

'Maybe.' Boyd was pensive for a moment. 'Or one of her colleagues?'

'Anything is possible. As we have so little to work on, I think that's the best place to start. And then there's this support group for widows that she belonged to.'

'We should locate the other members and talk to them.'

'Yes, definitely,' Lottie said, feeling relieved that they had something practical to do at last. 'I wish there'd been such a thing available when Adam died. It would have been good to talk to others in the same situation.'

'You could have gone to counselling.'

'I tried that. Anyhow, you were better than any counsellor. See if Lynch is back from that missing woman's house. Get her working on the members of this widows' group.'

'Right, boss.' He smiled, the first genuine good humour she'd seen on his face today.

As he turned to leave, he was almost upended by a flushed-faced Lynch bustling in.

'That missing woman, Éilis Lawlor, she was the founding member of the widows' group that we think Jennifer O'Loughlin was part of.'

Lottie jumped up, dragging her bag from the floor and unfurling her jacket from where she'd thrown it under the desk. 'Who's at the house?'

'I left Garda Lei there. I know it's not the required forty-eight hours, but we need to open a missing person file and issue alerts.'

'Do that. I'm heading round there to see for myself. Boyd, you're with me.'

In her rush to leave, she missed Lynch's surly expression at once again being left out.

———

They're staring at me. Two white orbs with their brown irises. Are they losing their colour? They shouldn't be, because I sourced the formaldehyde online and thought it would do the job. Now, I'm not so sure.

I'd love to have been up close to the guards when they discovered the corpse was sightless. She was dead, so of course she was sightless. It was ingenious to remove her eyes. Give them a puzzle they will struggle to figure out.

I turn away from the glass jar and begin to scour the cold room clean. Jennifer was a pushover. No fun at all. Breaking her bones was exhilarating, but I still felt a little let down. This one won't cheat me out of my fun. As I scrub, I wonder what clues I might have left behind at her house. The kids slept soundly. The dog? Who calls their dog Mozart? I couldn't harm an animal, I'm not that heartless. A little chloroform helped him to la-la land. I hope he wakes up. He was so small, it was hard to calculate the amount to give him.

A rattle echoes along the pipes.

She's awake. Good.

Dropping the scrubbing brush into the bucket of bleach, I leave it there to soak and strip off my Marigolds and apron. Time to have some fun.

But then I remember.

I have some people to see to first.

22

Kirby was in two minds about answering the call flashing on his phone screen, but he was out the back again, having a quick smoke, so he did.

'How's the head?'

Her voice was soft and soothing. It made his stomach flutter.

'Hi, Amy.'

'Are you having a good day? Head okay?'

'So I did give you my number?'

'You sure did,' she laughed. 'Couldn't let the day pass without checking up on you.'

'Are you stalking me now?' Shite, why had he said that? Despite a series of Tinder dates, he still hadn't learned to keep his mouth shut, to clamp down the gabble that invariably found its way out.

'Maybe I shouldn't have called.' Her voice quivered. *Damn*.

'Oh shit, sorry, Amy. I shouldn't have said that. Long day so far. Busy day. Big case.'

'Sounds tiring. Are you all right?'

'If I make it to bedtime in one piece, I'll have managed just fine. All okay with you?' That was better, he thought.

'Today is a bit of a shitshow if I'm honest. I only called to see if you want to meet for a drink later. After work. Or whenever suits you.'

The thought of another drink caused Kirby's stomach to roll in protest. Though come to think of it, a drink might cure his head. Then again, one could lead to another and then another. So maybe it wasn't the best course of action.

'I'd love to meet up,' he found himself saying. Then qualified it by adding, 'Only coffee for me.'

'Famous last words.'

'I know. I'm a glutton for punishment.'

'Meeting me is punishment?'

'God, no. I didn't mean that at all. Honestly, I—'

'Stop it, Larry, I was joking. You take everything so seriously.'

'It's the job.'

'No worries. Does Cafferty's suit you?'

'Perfect. When?'

'Why don't you text me when you finish up there?'

'I will. And Amy, thanks for calling. You've made my shitty day a whole lot better.'

He killed the call and wondered how he could run out on his colleagues this evening. It was the beginning of a murder investigation, when all hands on deck meant just that. Long hours and adrenaline-fuelled brains. The critical time. But this was also the first time in ages that he'd felt good about someone. About himself. He sensed he was a bit lighter on his feet. Knowing his weight, that was a miracle.

Topping his cigar, he stuffed it into his shirt pocket and headed inside, his brain swirling with excuses to leave early. Until then, he would keep his head down and work diligently.

His stomach rolled again, and he only just made it to the toilet in time.

'I'm never having another drink,' he muttered as he washed out his mouth with a handful of water from a dripping tap.

23

Standing in Éilis Lawlor's living space, off the quaint galley kitchen, Lottie repeated all the questions Lynch and Lei had asked of the teenage babysitter.

Unable to discover anything new, she said, 'Would you be able to take the children to your house for an hour or two, Bianca?'

'Sure, my mum can help. But why?'

'I'm worried about their mother. I don't want to frighten them further, but I want my forensic team to have a quick look around the house. Garda Lei, will you accompany them?'

'Sure,' he said.

'Becky and Roman?' Bianca said. 'Want to come to mine while this lady contacts your mum?'

The children were reluctant, but eventually they took her hands and left.

Lottie put in the call to SOCO.

'Are you being a bit premature with that?' Boyd said when she finished the call.

'I don't like the feeling I'm getting about this. Our murder victim, Jennifer, was part of this social group for widows that

Éilis Lawlor apparently founded. And now Éilis is missing. I hope I'm wrong, but...'

'She might have gone out for a walk and bumped into someone. Maybe they got chatting and she didn't realise the time.'

'She has a neighbouring teenager to mind the children. She'd at least have asked Bianca to come over to sit with them.'

'She might have forgotten to call her. She forgot her phone, after all.'

'And her wallet and keys? Come on, Boyd. It's past lunchtime. No way a mother *forgets* her young children that long.'

She opened the patio door with gloved hands and stepped outside. She made her way to the wooden cabin nestled in the corner of the garden. The door was unlocked. She stepped inside.

It appeared at first glance that no one had disturbed the inside of the woman's workspace. An Apple Mac computer stood on the desk. She admired the shelving unit with its neatly ordered sample books. Wallpaper, fabric, wood, floor coverings. She peered at the square pieces of carpet pinned to the wall, thinking that one or two looked like remnants from the seventies.

A drawing-board-type desk stood in the corner with a sketch taped to the worktop. A ground-floor design with lots of colour. Lottie liked it. She could only dream. Living in an ancient ramshackle home didn't give her many options. Lack of funds gave her no options. It frustrated her and she tried not to think about it.

She tapped the mouse, but the computer was switched off. If it came to it, Gary from tech could have a look at it. There was an A4 notebook on the table, the pages bulging with scraps of photos and material. She photographed it *in situ* with her phone camera, then took it with her to look through later.

Not finding anything out of place or disturbed, she returned to the house.

'Anything?' Boyd asked.

'Not at first sight, but SOCOs can check.'

'What do you think happened?'

'The link to Jennifer raises questions I don't have answers to yet.' She held out the notebook. 'It's her work notes.'

'Bit old-fashioned, isn't it?'

'Probably the best way to examine ideas with her clients. She has a desktop computer. I'll get Gary to check it out. Kirby or Lynch can contact her clients. Best-case scenario, Éilis had a consultation she'd forgotten about and rushed off without organising Bianca for the children.'

'Her personal belongings are here and her car is still outside. She'd have had to walk.'

'True. Someone has to have seen something, unless she left in the middle of the night. Or was taken then. But let's be optimistic.'

As Boyd went off to organise a canvass of the neighbours, Lottie stared out at the garden, gathering her thoughts. Despite what she'd said, she didn't feel optimistic. Her gut was telling her that either Éilis Lawlor had been frightened of something that had made her leave her home, abandoning her children. Or, more realistically, that she had been abducted.

Then an awful thought struck her.

What if Éilis had been involved in some way with Jennifer O'Loughlin's murder? What if she'd heard about the discovery of the body this morning and decided to flee, leaving behind anything that could be used to track her?

It was a possibility she could not ignore.

———

Kirby felt buoyed by his chat with Amy. He had a date. Life was looking up for him. Yes!

'I haven't seen you this chirpy in ages, Kirby. What has you looking so happy?' asked Garda Martina Brennan as she deposited a pile of door-to-door from Jennifer O'Loughlin's estate on his desk.

McKeown raised his head, scowling. 'He's probably been prowling the dark web for someone to take out his lack of sexual gratification on.'

'What are you talking about?' Martina snapped angrily, and slapped the remaining questionnaires on top of McKeown's precious iPad.

'Hey! Look where you're throwing those,' he snarled.

Kirby couldn't take much more of McKeown. Shuffling out of his chair, he moved to the man's desk, glad to see the untidy pile of paper littering it. 'That's no way to speak to your colleague.'

'What's it to you?' McKeown stood.

Kirby felt dwarfed. 'You're a chauvinistic pig, thinking you're superior to all women.'

'Too right,' Martina said, folding her arms.

'Ganging up on me now? What is it? Are you going behind my back?' he snarled at the young garda.

'That's rich from someone who's used to sneaking around behind his wife's back,' Kirby said. 'Not everyone lives by your lack of morals.'

'You are a mouthy fat fuck.' McKeown's spittle landed on Kirby's cheek and his hands turned into fists.

Kirby wiped it away. He wasn't afraid of the shaven-headed hulk. On the contrary, he would welcome McKeown punching him. Best way to get rid of him.

'Stop!' Martina cried.

Lottie arrived at the office door. 'What's going on?'

Kirby held his ground and McKeown unfurled his fist. 'Nothing.'

'Didn't look like nothing to me. I want an explanation from the three of you after I meet with the super.'

Martina backed away from Kirby and let go of his sleeve. 'It's fine, Inspector. A misunderstanding.'

'Is that right, Kirby?'

'Ask him.' Kirby drew in his neck and returned to his desk to shuffle the questionnaires.

McKeown remained silent.

'This can't continue,' Lottie said. 'We have a murdered woman and another missing. I don't need this carry-on behind my back.'

'Won't happen again, boss,' Kirby said.

McKeown rooted for his iPad in silence.

'It better not. I'm watching you, Detective McKeown, every step you take. And I do not like where it's taking you.'

'Not my fault if he wants to start a row.'

'For heaven's sake, will you all just grow up.' She flung her bag and jacket on her desk and left the room.

Kirby wondered if she would tell the superintendent. In a way, he hoped she would.

24

No way was Lottie going to be accused of withholding anything to do with this investigation. She'd got in enough trouble during her previous major case.

She knocked on Superintendent Farrell's office door.

'Come in.'

Inside her boss's office, she refrained from rolling her eyes. The super had moved the furniture around again. It was something she did to relieve her anxiety. But it didn't seem to quench her thirst for narkiness.

'You better be here to tell me you've arrested that woman's killer.'

'I'm afraid not, but I suspect we also have a missing woman.'

Farrell slapped a hand to her forehead; a little too hard, Lottie guessed, noticing that she flinched.

'Do you even know how to take on a murder investigation without making it more complicated than finding the origins of life? Hand over the missing woman case to another team.'

'The thing is... she hasn't been missing for the required forty-eight hours yet.'

'Christ Almighty! Haven't you enough to be doing with the murder investigation without inventing another case. Do you thrive on confusion and chaos? Because I think you do.' Farrell unclipped her tie and opened a button at the neck of her shirt, before clipping the tie back on.

'With all due respect—'

'Don't *all due respect* me, Inspector Parker. I told you what to do. I expect you to follow orders.' Farrell stood, shoving her chair back with her legs. It hit the wall with a thump.

'Éilis Lawlor,' Lottie persisted, 'the woman who may be missing, has a connection to the murder victim.'

'Did they meet for a coffee once upon a time?' Farrell mocked. 'Or did they attend the same college together ten years ago? Played under-eights camogie? A woman has been murdered and I have the commissioner sniffing around my arse like a bloodhound. The locals are not far behind him. There's talk of candlelight vigils for the victim. I need a suspect, not another victim. Do you get it?'

'I do, and I'm sorry, but we have to explore all aspects of Jennifer's life and—'

'You haven't even found her next of kin yet, Detective McKeown informs me.'

'Bastard,' Lottie murmured under her breath. 'About Detective McKeown, is there any chance you can redeploy him? Back to Athlone, or somewhere more suitable than here.' She didn't spell out what she meant. Somewhere like Siberia.

'You want to deplete your team when you've just told me you have another possible victim?'

Why did the woman talk in questions? It did Lottie's head in. 'He's disrupting the team dynamic.'

'I'll give you team dynamic if you don't bring me the killer's head on a plate. Today!' Farrell sat down heavily. 'You're going to give me a heart attack. A fucking heart attack!'

'I'm sorry.' Trying to contain her anger, Lottie marched to the door, where she turned back. 'You know what? I'm not sorry. I have the highest success rate at solving major crimes in the entire country. I know what my team are capable of. But McKeown... he doesn't fit in. He disrupts everyone with his domineering attitude, his snide comments and...' She was going to mention his affair, but stopped herself. 'Superintendent Farrell, I am formally requesting that you take him off my team. I'll put it in writing.'

She turned on her heel and left before she could witness Farrell's anger erupting as she rummaged in a drawer for her anti-anxiety pills.

'Still no sign of the missing woman, Éilis Lawlor,' Boyd said as he knocked on the jamb of Lottie's door.

'That's not what I want to hear. We have enough to deal with as it is. Anything from the Riverfield Road door-to-door?'

'Garda Brennan collated the questionnaires,' Boyd said. 'Kirby and McKeown are going through the information, but it looks like all we've gathered so far is that Jennifer kept to herself. Didn't mix or get involved with the residents' association. Her late husband did his bit, but she stayed in the background. One neighbour said she'd been almost invisible since her husband died.'

'Maybe she felt isolated, and joined the widows' group for the company of like-minded women. It gives us a connection to Éilis. Has Lynch sourced any more information on the group?'

'Not yet.'

Lottie looked at the ceiling, failing to hide her exasperation. 'What about Jennifer's work colleagues? What do they have to say?'

'McKeown and Garda Brennan interviewed them.

Confirmed that it is her writing on the resignation letter. She was quiet, kept to herself, good at her job and cordial to everyone. No complaints.'

'But she was on a warning.'

Boyd shifted from the door, ready to leave.

'Just a minute. I wonder if Éilis Lawlor has ever attended the Smile Brighter Dental Clinic. Find out for me while I have a look through her work notes.'

'Do you want to treat the two investigations as being related?'

She rested her chin on her hand, thinking before speaking. 'Éilis hasn't been missing for the required forty-eight hours, though I have a feeling she didn't leave her home voluntarily. But is she connected to Jennifer's murder?' She shrugged. 'The only thing linking the two women is the widows' group. Why don't you go and talk to...' She searched her notes for the name Bianca had given her. 'Helena McCaul. Jennifer's boss mentioned her too. And find out if there are any other members we should know about.'

Once Boyd had left, she pulled on gloves and took Éilis's notebook from the plastic evidence bag, along with the woman's phone. Until they gained access to her computer, she hoped there might be something in the notebook about her clients. A list of phone numbers would help to save trawling through her phone.

'Bingo.' Éilis was old-school for a young woman. Inside the cover she had created a list of clients complete with alphabetical index tags.

Carefully she read down through the names and was rewarded when she came to the 'O's. Jennifer O'Loughlin was listed. She checked Éilis's phone and found a series of texts about meet-ups. The notebook contained an itinerary of appointments between the two women. These matched with most of the texts. The first contact was twenty-three months previously. A month after her husband died, Jennifer had hired an interior designer. Éilis Lawlor. And another month after that, there was the first text inviting her to join the new widows' group.

25

Boyd hunched his shoulders and pushed open the door to Herbal Heaven. A bell tinkled over his head, and he almost cracked his skull against the lintel.

He inhaled the oriental spice aroma and glanced around. The shop was small and appeared disordered, but as he wandered around examining the shelves, he noticed a logic to the way the products were stacked.

'Can I help you?'

A woman appeared from behind the counter, her dress fluttering as she moved. He felt his breath catch in his throat. She was startlingly beautiful. Her hair was tied up, and escaping curls accentuated her porcelain skin, soft lips, and tiny ears sporting massive silver hoops. He drew his gaze to her penetrating brown eyes.

'Oh, hello,' he said, trying not to gush. 'Helena? Helena McCaul?'

'That's me.'

He held out his hand. 'Detective Sergeant Mark Boyd. Ragmullin garda station.'

Her grip was sweaty and fleeting. 'You're here to ask about

Éilis.' She dropped her eyes and set her mouth in a fine line. 'Have you found her?'

'No, not yet. We aren't even sure she is missing. I believe you were with her last night. Is that correct?'

'Yes, I was with her. Do you mind if I sit?'

She turned and wended her way back behind the counter, where she plonked onto a high stool. Boyd followed. The aroma of the shop was intoxicating; he actually felt a little light-headed.

'What do you want to know?' Her voice was lyrical, though slightly out of tune. He suspected she might have been crying.

He couldn't help being struck by the woman. He figured she was in her early thirties. There was something about her that made him want to comfort her, to ease her pain. Irrational thoughts, he told himself, but Helena McCaul came across as a vulnerable human being.

'Start with last night.' He regained his composure. 'We can work from there.' He found his notebook in his inside jacket pocket. She handed him a pen as he opened it.

'Sometimes we go out for a meal or to the cinema, but last night was much the same as most Thursday nights and we met in Fallon's pub.' She told him about the group Éilis had set up to help women who had lost their husbands through either death, separation or divorce.

'Who else is in the group?'

'Well, Jennifer O'Loughlin was one of Éilis's first members, but she stopped coming about four, maybe five weeks ago. Then there's Orla Keating, she's our newest member. We're a small group.'

He would return to talking about Jennifer after he got the information on Éilis Lawlor. 'Bianca, the babysitter, thinks Éilis arrived home in a taxi. Was she alone?'

'I had assumed she'd shared a taxi with Orla. They left the pub together. But Orla called in here earlier and told me she left

Éilis at the taxi rank by Danny's pub. She walked home to clear her head.'

'The name Orla Keating is familiar to me. Wasn't it her husband who disappeared a year ago?'

'Yes. A year ago tomorrow.'

'Right.' He wondered if this was important. 'Can you remember anything unusual about last night? Anything that sticks out in your mind as not quite right? Anyone taking an interest in your group?'

'Not at all. It was low-key enough. Orla was a bit uptight. I can understand, with Tyler's anniversary...' She paused. 'Look, we've all suffered loss in one way or another. We understand each other and our grief. But it's not all doom and gloom. We talk about kids and pets.' She laughed wryly. 'Plus it gets me out of the house one night a week. With Jennifer we had an even number and went out for meals together.'

'How do people find out about your group?' He was still parking his questions about Jennifer.

'Éilis set up a Facebook page. I can't stop worrying about her.'

'What did you talk about last night? Anything out of the ordinary or different?'

Helena seemed to hesitate. 'Just the usual. I really should have left with them.'

'Why didn't you?'

'I was a bit tipsy. I went back inside and got another quick drink. Then I left. Got a taxi at the post office. There were none outside Danny's by then.'

'Was Éilis in a relationship?'

Helena's jaw dropped and her eyes widened. 'You think she met someone and did a flit, leaving her kids behind? No, that's not the Éilis I know. After Oisín died, she lived for her kids. She even moved her office from town to her house. She wanted to be on hand at all times.'

'Except Thursday nights.'

'We're widows, Detective, not dead.'

He felt an embarrassed flush flood his cheeks. 'I apologise. I didn't mean anything by it...'

She reached out and touched his hand. 'I can feel that you're stressed. Very stressed. I have something that will help. Wait there.'

He watched her make her way through a door at the back of the shop, her dress swirling around her tanned legs, gold glittering on her sandals in the shard of light streaking in from the front door. She returned almost instantly with a small brown paper bag.

'What is it?' He opened the bag. A fine green powder nestled in the bottom.

'Nettles. I pick them myself and grind them. You'll need to use a strainer. Try it. I guarantee it will ease your stress.'

'Only thing that would ease my stress is if my ex-wife would disappear in a puff of smoke.' Shit, why had he said that?

'You're funny, Detective.' She must have seen the serious glint in his eye, and added, 'Be strong in the face of opposition. That's what my husband, Gerald, used to say to me whenever I hit a brick wall with my business. Another health food shop, one of those franchise chain affairs, opened up in town a few months after I had plunged every cent I possessed into this place. Thank God, my little haven has survived against the odds.'

'It's good to know your business is successful.' He waved the brown bag. 'What do I owe you for this?'

'Not a thing. It's on the house.'

Boyd felt he had strayed so far off the reason for his visit that he was at a loss to know how to bring it back on track. The only information he'd secured from Helena was that Éilis had left the pub with Orla Keating, whose husband went missing a year ago. And he still hadn't mentioned Jennifer.

'What's the name of this Facebook page?'

'Life After Loss. Not very original. It's a closed group, with Éilis as the administrator. Oh feck.'

'We will find her.' He braced himself for what he was about to say. 'Helena, there is another reason for my visit. Did you hear about a murder this morning?'

Her hand flew to her mouth. 'It's not Éilis, is it?'

'No. Unfortunately the body of a young woman was discovered out at Ballyglass Business Park. We believe it to be that of Jennifer O'Loughlin.'

'No. No. You're mistaken. Please, tell me it's not true?' She wobbled back onto the stool again.

'I'm afraid it is. Can I get you a drink of water?'

She shook her head, and more strands of hair flew loose from their mooring. 'It's just a lot to take in. Éilis is missing, and now you tell me Jennifer is dead. God!'

'You said Jennifer hadn't been to meetings in a month or so. Did she give any indication why she wouldn't be attending?'

Helena bit her lip tightly, as if she was trying to prevent words from spewing out. At last she seemed to trust herself to speak. 'I can't think. She was closer to Éilis... Oh my God, this is awful.'

'Did she ever mention something she was worried about, or anything that concerned you?'

'What do you mean?'

'Anything she might have said about someone wanting to harm her?'

'N-no. No, not at all.'

'What did she say about leaving her job?'

'She never said anything about that.'

'I know it's upsetting, but I need something to give me a starting point to investigate her murder.'

Helena rubbed her eyes with the back of her hand. He noticed there were no tears.

'Are you sure she was murdered?' she said.

'Why do you ask?'

'She was still depressed, even two years after Damien's death. They were close, devoted. He got cancer. Died quickly. She found it hard to cope. Éilis provided some decor inspiration on her house. That's how they met. Detective, I... I honestly can't talk about this right now. It's such a shock.'

'I understand. Here's my card. Call me when you've had time to think.' He waved the little brown bag with the nettle tea. 'Thank you for this. I'll be sure to try it.'

She took a sticker from a roll and pressed it to the bag, her fingers brushing his. 'My number is on there. Let me know when you find Éilis.'

He shoved his notebook into his pocket and nodded his thanks. The little bell tinkled as he let himself out of the shop with his bag of nettle tea.

And he couldn't help thinking that Helena McCaul, despite her distress, real or not, had shed no tears over the news about Jennifer's murder. She had asked no questions about how or when or where.

Helena was hiding something from him.

26

Éilis woke on a chair, drooling. Confusion shot through her. How could she have fallen asleep? It didn't make sense. Where was she? Where were Roman and Becky?

Anguish gurgled in her stomach like a wave in a storm and rose as bile to her throat. With something approaching clarity, she recalled what had happened last night. An intruder in her home. A threat against her family if she didn't do as she was told. Being walked to a car. Then passing out.

Were her children safe from this monster who had taken her? Why, though? What had she done that had led her here? And where *was* here?

Turning her head around, she figured she was in some sort of padded room. The walls looked like they had been crudely covered with various shapes and sizes of cushions and mats. Soundproofing?

What else could she see through the dimness?

It had once been a sitting room. There was a stained and faded orange carpet on the floor. An old-style fireplace. A whistling sound came down the chimney, even though there was some sort of packing blocking up the grate. She could just about discern two ornaments standing on the mantelpiece, the only nod to decoration or sentiment in the room. Did they hold some memory for her abductor? Could they provide her with a hint of who had taken her?

In the distance she heard what sounded like bolts being drawn back. A surge of hope caused her heart to beat erratically. She held her breath. Hoping. Praying. She dared to believe she might see her children soon.

The door opened.

An antiseptic smell and a weak light preceded her abductor as he entered the room. She thought of the abductor as a he. There was no way she could imagine a woman doing this to another woman. She could be wrong.

The light was coming from a small head torch. Her abductor was dressed head to toe in a crinkling white suit, similar to those she'd seen forensic people wearing on television at crime scenes. She looked up at his face. It was almost entirely covered with some sort of balaclava under the hood of the suit, and his eyes were hidden behind black-rimmed goggles.

Maybe this was a good thing, she thought. If he was concealing his identity, was it logical to assume that he didn't want her to be able to identify him when he released her? That she would survive this horror? Her moment of hope was short-lived.

Under one arm was a roll of thick plastic sheeting. It had to be heavy because it weighed him down on that side. In the other hand he held a long piece of timber. He dropped the sheeting to the floor and began to unfurl it over the already stained carpet, one-handed. As he did so, the beam of light lit up the piece of timber in his hand. Was that dried blood on it?

Unbridled fear replaced her moment of hope.

She tried to scream, but could only croak.

She struggled to twist out of her restraints, but she could not drag her eyes away from her captor as he worked in deathly silence.

Once the sheeting was close to her chair, he stopped his task. All she could think of was her children and what they would do if she died. She couldn't die. She had to get home to them. They had no one else, only her. She had to survive this. *Roman and Becky, I'm not going to let this monster take me away from you.*

She stared at her abductor. Stared so hard she felt tears burn her eyelids. He held her gaze. It was as though the eyes of the devil were looking straight into her soul, their darkness draining all the colour from her life.

Then he lifted the timber high above his head.

27

Lottie found Lynch working in the incident room.

'Maria, we should focus on this Frankie Bardon who owns Smile Brighter. Find a way of getting his phone records without a warrant.'

'That will be difficult but I'll see. Boss, the widows' Facebook page is a closed group. You have to request to be admitted, but Éilis is the administrator so I've hit a brick wall. I'll have to hand it over to Gary. He should get in quicker. Why do you want me to concentrate on Bardon?'

'It's likely he convinced Jennifer to resign, and he appears to have had no time for this widows' group.'

'Could he have had anything to do with Éilis Lawlor's disappearance?'

'Maybe. I feel he's too good to be true. I don't know why, but he is top of the shit pile for now.'

'Gosh, he really rubbed you up the wrong way.' Lynch shook her head before going back to work.

'He'd certainly know his way around a surgical implement. Ever heard of an ashram?'

Lynch looked up, appearing put out at the constant interruptions. 'Sure have. It's some sort of meditation place.'

'I'd never heard the word until today. I need to widen my horizons.'

Standing before the incident board, Lottie stared at Jennifer O'Loughlin's death mask photograph. They were dealing with a depraved killer, but also someone who was highly organised and cunning. Someone who might go back to the scene of the crime, perhaps? She whipped up the phone from the desk and called Grainne.

'Gerry recorded a video at the crime scene this morning, didn't he?' she asked without preamble

'Yes, he did.'

'Tell him to email it to me. Now.' Annoyed at her misplaced anger, she added, 'Please.'

'Certainly.' Grainne cut the call.

Staring at the full-length photo of Jennifer's body, Lottie wondered aloud, 'What's with the big yellow dress?'

She sat at a spare desk, the computer fired up, and waited until her email pinged. She opened the link for the video the SOCO had taken that morning. She found it hard to believe it was still the same day.

Leaning forward, she pressed play. Gerry had scanned his camera over the entire area encircling the body as he initially approached.

'Why leave her body there?' Lottie said. 'What significance has that piece of waste ground got for you?' She wondered if Jennifer had been left there by design or necessity. Had the killer been in a hurry? Or had it been a carefully chosen site? If so, it was probably because it had been compromised by the previous week's carnival traffic.

The video rolled on, but instead of concentrating on Jennifer's body, Lottie studied the area around and beyond the victim.

She could see the glass-fronted car showrooms in the distance and the distribution centre as Gerry panned his camera around again. She studied the victim as he moved in closer. The yellow dress rippled in the morning breeze. Again she wondered if she was missing something.

———

The office was quiet when Boyd returned from Herbal Heaven and his chat with Helena McCaul. Kirby was at his desk. No sign of McKeown. Good.

He punched Orla Keating's name into the system and called out to Kirby when the file appeared.

'Hey, bud, you investigated a missing man last year. Tyler Keating. Remember that case?'

Kirby's head shot up. 'It's weird you should ask.'

'Your favourite word,' Boyd smirked. 'Why is it weird?'

'Believe it or not, I met his wife this morning. She asked me for an update on her husband's disappearance, which was a year ago tomorrow.'

'You were talking to Orla Keating this morning?'

'Yes. Why are you asking about Tyler?'

'I was searching the system for his wife, not him. She was with Éilis Lawlor last night in Fallon's. Both women went to the taxi rank. I've asked Garda Lei to check with the taxi drivers to see if we can identify who brought Éilis home.'

'But the babysitter confirmed she got back safely. Her bag and phone are there.'

'The driver may have overheard something. A phone call, maybe? She might have left the house later to meet someone.'

'Her phone has been checked. It hadn't been used since six forty-five yesterday evening, when she phoned for a taxi to bring her out. No other calls after that, until her son rang Bianca this morning.'

'Anything else turn up on the phone?'

'Gary's working on it.'

'Back to the cold case. What do you think happened to Tyler Keating?'

Kirby filled Boyd in, which saved him trawling through the file.

'It's a mystery. No body. No car. No evidence of foul play at the house or his office. He never got on the flight to Liverpool. No activity on his credit cards. You know the score. The man disappeared into the ether.'

'You think he's dead?'

'He must be.'

'He could have had a second passport and got a flight from somewhere else.'

'We trawled the airport security footage. He didn't go through Dublin airport anyway.'

'What about Knock or Shannon? Cork? The ferries, even?'

'All checked. Nothing for that day, or any day for weeks after his disappearance.'

'He might have been gone before he was reported missing. Says here his wife didn't call us till five days after his supposed flight.'

'She thought he was in the UK at a conference. It was only when he failed to arrive home that she started to worry.'

'She never tried to ring him in that time?'

'Her phone records showed she called a few times but got no answer.'

'And his phone? Did you track its GPS?'

'I'm not an eejit, Boyd. We did all the checks. His phone was dead. Last place his GPS registered was the long-term car park at Dublin airport. But we didn't find him, his phone or the car there. Or anywhere else, for that matter.'

'Did you suspect his wife at all?'

'Number one suspect. Boyd, there's no point raking it up

again. She was questioned multiple times. Said she talked to Tyler before he left and then went back to bed.'

'But you only have her word that he went to the airport *that* morning.'

Kirby ran a hand through his bushy mop of hair. 'We carried out a full and thorough investigation.'

'Did she have an alibi for all five days?'

'She worked from home. She was there all week.'

'How did you check that?'

'Jesus, you're like a dog with a bone.'

'Humour me.'

'Gary looked at her computer. Her phone. We talked to the neighbours. She went nowhere further than Tesco that week.'

'I think you should review the case all the same.'

'Why?'

'I find it odd that the very day we find a murdered woman, Orla Keating wants an update on her husband who disappeared a year ago.'

'It was an accidental meeting.'

'Maybe she had something to do with Jennifer's murder. What if her missing husband is still alive and was involved with the murder too?'

'That's the weirdest theory I've ever come across.'

'I think you need to come up with a new vocabulary.'

'Feck off, Boyd, and let me think.' He took his cigar out of his shirt pocket and twirled it between his fingers, dead ash fluttering to his desk, before returning it to its safe place.

'I'm calling out to her to have a word. Want to accompany me?'

'If you don't mind, I'll pass.' Kirby lowered his voice to a whisper. 'I have a... I mean, I have to meet someone this evening and need to finish up stuff here first.'

'Don't let the boss hear you.' Boyd thumped him good-naturedly on the back.

'What am I not supposed to hear?' Lottie walked into the office.

'Nothing,' they said simultaneously.

Boyd added, 'I'm about to go talk to Orla Keating. She's a member of that widows' group and she was in Fallon's last night.'

'The woman whose husband disappeared last year?'

'Yeah.'

'I'll go with you. By the way, Kirby, you need to find middle ground with McKeown. He's staying for the foreseeable and I need a motivated team, not one with you all at loggerheads every time I turn my back. Got it?'

'Sure, boss.'

'What about the information I asked you to find about the site where Jennifer O'Loughlin's body was discovered?'

'I started it, then I got sidetracked. I'm on it now.'

'You better be.'

'Boss, what time do you think we can knock off this evening?'

'Got somewhere important to be, have you?'

'Well, not exactly, but—'

'Then keep at it until you do what I asked you to do.'

Kirby didn't look too happy, Boyd noticed. And he himself was anxious to see Sergio. At least Kirby had a date later. That could only be a good thing for his friend, as long as he was able to escape on time. With Lottie in her current humour, he wouldn't place any bets on it.

The Keatings' two-storey cottage was located just outside town, close to the cemetery. A row of three sat on their own plots with a vast housing estate behind them. It was evident that the adjoining fields had been snapped up by developers. The cottages were situated a little in from the main road, surrounded by overgrown hedges. A foil against the expansion around them.

Boyd parked outside the house and Lottie stepped onto the gravel driveway, noting dandelions and thistles sprouting through the stones. The cottage too appeared in need of repair.

Orla Keating opened the red-painted door. Dressed in jeans, sharp shoulder bones protruded from a floaty white shirt with pockets in the sides. She wore thick-soled black sandals complemented by smears of black polish on her toenails.

She led them through a narrow tiled hall into a kitchen at the back of the house. Lottie found herself standing amongst a clutter of clothes hanging on a rack and on the backs of chairs, and magazines discarded around the floor. But her eye was drawn through the window to the garden. Flowers were blooming in a raised stone circle flower bed, the lawn was cut, the perimeter bushes neatly trimmed. Beyond, she could see the expanse of the housing estate. It was a big garden, and she thought the kitchen could have been extended. There was barely room for the three of them.

She turned to find Boyd sitting at the small round table and Orla shifting mugs from it to the sink.

'You have a lovely home,' Boyd said. Lottie raised her eyebrows.

'It's small, but it's mine,' Orla said. 'Or rather, it's mine and Tyler's. Would either of you like something to drink?'

'No thanks,' Boyd said.

'Water would be good,' Lottie said. She pulled out a chair and sat on top of an old *House & Home* magazine.

Orla placed a tumbler of tap water on the table and sat on the last remaining chair. Definitely not much socialising, if any, went on in this house, Lottie thought.

'Sorry for the tight squash, but it's always been just me and Tyler here. Now that he's gone, I've been thinking about moving away, but what if he comes back and can't find me?'

'Do you think he will come back?' Lottie said. There had been no sorrow in the woman's tone.

'His body hasn't been found, so it's possible he's still alive and will return one day.'

Lottie noticed Orla shake with an involuntary shiver. 'Would you be happy if he came back?'

'Inspector, what are you implying? That I don't want Tyler home where he belongs?'

'That's not what I meant at all.'

'I'm still worried about him. Only this morning I asked Detective Kirby for an update. Every day Tyler is missing, I fear he will never be found.' Orla stared hard, and Lottie found herself wondering if she hoped, rather than feared. She continued, 'Not knowing is worse than knowing. Are you here because you have new information on his case?'

'I'm sorry,' Boyd said, 'that's not the reason for this visit. We have a few questions for you.'

Her expression lost some of its tightness. 'Go ahead.'

Lottie noticed that the woman's eyes were pinned to Boyd's face, totally ignoring her. All the better to study her then. She'd let Boyd take the lead.

'You were out with Helena McCaul and Éilis Lawlor last night,' he said. 'Is that correct?'

'Yes. We met up in Fallon's. I think I stripped my stomach lining with the amount of gin I consumed, but it's worth it to meet up and talk.'

'You don't get out much?' Lottie couldn't help herself.

'Not really. Not socially, anyhow. I work from home and my only outlet is yoga.'

'You're an accountant, isn't that right?' So much for letting Boyd take the lead, but something about this young woman spiked a reaction in her inquisitive antennae. And it made her impatient to find out what that was.

'Yes. I've worked from home since I married Tyler. He said we didn't need the expense of an office in town.'

'And you're a qualified accountant?' Lottie pressed.

'You make it sound like you're surprised.'

'Just clarifying.' In reality, the house didn't give off the orderliness vibe she'd expect from an accountant. Not that she'd know, never having had enough money to require the services of one. 'Have you a large client list?'

'Enough to say I'm good at my job.' Orla's tone had an edge now.

'That's great,' Boyd said before Lottie had an opportunity to antagonise her further.

She was a bit disappointed. Her gut was in overdrive in this quaint, untidy little cottage.

Orla said, 'Has Éilis not returned home yet? Helena told me she'd had a call from the babysitter this morning. Where do you think she is?'

'If we knew that, we wouldn't be here,' Lottie said, before realising she had uttered the words aloud. She shook her head as the woman's mouth fell open.

'You seem hostile towards me, Inspector.' Orla laid her hands flat on the table, palms down. Lottie noticed the absence of a wedding ring, and a half-hearted attempt to remove her dark nail polish.

'It's been a long day.'

'Tell me about the taxi,' Boyd said.

'It's all a bit of a blur. Alcoholic haze, I imagine.' Orla smiled sweetly at him, as if she had found a kindred spirit. 'We walked down to Danny's but there was only one taxi there. I told Éilis to take it. She said we could share, but I needed the walk to clear my head and help me sleep. Alcohol keeps me awake.'

'Do you know anything about the taxi she got into?'

'I've no idea. They all look the same to me and I rarely use them. I mainly walk where I can.'

'Did Éilis say anything to you?'

'Like what?'

'Was she due to meet anyone today? Something that could give us a hint to where she might be.'

'Sorry, she only talked about her kids. Worried that she'd wake them when she got home.'

'What was the conversation about in the pub?'

'This and that.'

Lottie snorted. 'We need to know exactly what you talked about.'

'Look, we meet once a week for a few drinks. Helena and Éilis talk about kids and work. I listen and talk about yoga. That's it.'

'And when Jennifer was in the group, what was the conversation like then?'

'Jennifer? She stopped coming weeks ago. Éilis said she'd tried ringing her a few times. She's probably gone on holiday.'

'Did she contact you to say she was going away?'

'No. We're not BFFs. She probably needed to clear her head or something.'

'In this Life After Loss group, what did Jennifer talk about?'

'Nothing much that I can remember.'

'Had she problems at work?'

'I don't know. Maybe.'

'Like what? Did she discuss her boss, Frankie Bardon?'

Orla's cheeks coloured. 'I'd like to know why you're asking these questions.'

'Did you know she'd quit?'

A loud crash sounded from somewhere inside the cottage, and Lottie jumped.

Orla smiled. 'It's the radiators. The ancient boiler and piping needs replacing. Whenever the heat kicks in, it's like a bomb going off.'

'I thought it might be your pet,' Boyd said.

'What pet?'

'I'm sorry, I must have picked Helena up wrong.'

A shadow crept over her eyes before she brightened. 'Ah, I think I know what she meant. They were talking about their pet dogs, and I said I had a cat just to be sociable.'

Lottie wasn't convinced by her recovery. If she could lie about a pet, what else might she lie about?

'So you created an imaginary pet. What else did you talk about last night?' she said. There was something going on behind those eyes and she'd love to know what it was.

Orla's face hardened. 'The more we drank, the more they went on about their kids and dead husbands. I felt a little excluded, as I have neither.'

'Do you not believe your husband is dead?'

'I don't know what to believe,' she said earnestly. 'I wish I knew one way or the other, and then I could get my life back on track.'

'You still joined a group for widows, though?' Lottie said.

'It's not exclusive to widows. Look at the details on the Facebook page. Life After Loss, it's called. It's for divorced or separated women as well.'

'But you aren't any of those.'

'My husband is missing. They didn't turn me away.'

'Can you offer any explanation for Éilis disappearing?'

'Wherever she is, it has nothing to do with me.'

'Still, your husband disappeared and now a woman you know has dis—'

'How dare you!' Orla stood up abruptly, causing the chair to skid backwards and the clothes that were hanging on the back of it to fall to the floor.

'It's okay, Orla. Sit down, please,' Boyd said, patting the table like she was an upset puppy.

Without a glance at Lottie, she picked up the clothes and sat, bundling them up on her knee.

'Did you hear about the woman who was found dead on waste ground this morning?' Lottie said, lowering her tone a little.

'Oh God, it's not Éilis, is it?'

'No, but it is someone you both knew. Jennifer O'Loughlin.'

Orla's face showed its first real emotion. She looked stricken and terrified as she dumped the clothes on the table and began wrapping the sleeve of a blouse around her hand. 'It can't be Jennifer. She must be on holiday or somewhere.' Her skin turned deathly pale. 'Do you think I'm in danger?'

'Do *you* think that?'

'It's just... I don't know. Éilis is missing. Tyler is missing. And you're saying Jennifer is dead.'

'Did you ever feel threatened because you'd joined the group?'

'Not until you just planted the idea slap-bang in the centre of my consciousness.'

Lottie felt like she was up against a seasoned negotiator. Orla had a question or an answer for everything. She leaned over the small, cluttered table and stared into the woman's eyes, hazel flecked with black streaks. 'How well did you know Jennifer O'Loughlin?'

'Not that well. What happened to her?' Orla grimaced, and Lottie noted her straight white teeth.

'We are in the early stages of our investigation,' Boyd said.

Lottie said, 'She worked at Smile Brighter. Do you have your teeth done there?'

'Yes, I do. Frankie Bardon usually treats me. He's big into his meditation and yoga. He said I should take it up. I find it helps clear my mind.'

'What's the name of the studio you go to?'

'Why do you want to know that?'

Jesus, but Orla Keating was hard work. 'Did Éilis or Jennifer go to—'

'SunUp studio. I know Éilis does.'

'Thank you.' Lottie stood, and felt the perspiration pool in her bra. She waited for Boyd to follow suit. Was it the little kitchen giving her claustrophobia, or its owner? Something definitely was.

Boyd loitered as she made her way through the narrow hallway to the front door. She heard him chatting with Orla, and crunched her hands into fists before shoving them into her pockets. Out of trouble.

'Thanks for your time,' he said. 'Here's my card. Mind yourself.'

'You are so kind, thank you.'

Lottie caught the flirtation in Orla's words. So much for her fear and horror at the death of someone she knew.

And if Boyd was the good cop, she must be the bad one.

29

At the station, Lottie found the state of her office less intimidating after the chaos of Orla Keating's tiny kitchen. She kicked off her shoes, settled behind her desk and clicked into Gerry's file to watch some more of the video he'd taken that morning at the scene where Jennifer's body had been discovered.

'What do you hope to find?' Boyd asked, lounging at the door, eating from a tub of ice cream. He was making her hungry, and she realised she was actually starving.

'I won't know until I see it. If I see it.'

'I need to pick up Sergio. Your Chloe is working tonight. You should call it a day.'

He knew more about her family than she did herself. 'I don't know what time it is, so how can I call it a... Look at this.'

He unfurled his long body away from the door jamb, dumped the carton in the bin and stood behind her, knocking over a tower of files that were stacked on the floor.

'Don't even think of picking them up,' she warned.

'I think my OCD might be cured.' He grinned as he leaned in beside her. 'Probably the Sergio effect.'

She loved how Boyd could laugh at himself.

'What am I looking for?' he said.

His warm breath on the back of her neck where she'd tied up her hair made her skin tingle, and she had to shake herself to concentrate on the screen. 'Gerry scanned the camera over the entire area, including those showrooms you can see on the periphery.'

'With you so far.'

'See that one? There's someone standing there looking straight over at the activity around Jennifer's body.'

'Rubberneckers are not unheard of.'

'I am well aware of that.'

She felt a chill on her neck as he pulled away.

'It's too pixelated to identify anyone.'

'But they look out of place just standing there staring.'

'I beg to differ, but I'm too tired to argue.' He winked and rubbed her shoulder.

'Feck off, Boyd,' she said with a smile, glad of his touch. 'You know what that does to me. Before you leave, call the showroom and find out who was there this morning.'

'McKeown's got all the security footage from those garages. He found nothing unusual on them.'

'He was checking for someone dumping the body, not someone looking at us doing our job.'

'It'll have to be tomorrow. I have to go pick up Sergio, and it's time you went home too.'

'What are you now, my mother?'

'No need to be a pain in the arse. I'll tell McKeown to contact the garage in the morning.' He turned her towards him and kissed her on the lips.

She extracted herself from his embrace and glanced out the open door to make sure they were alone. 'Why not call the garage now?'

'Because it's seven p.m. and they'll be closed.'

'Is that the time? Shit.'

She found she was talking to a void. Boyd was already making his way out of the outer office.

Maybe it *was* time to leave. She needed to check on her mother. It wasn't fair leaving her kids to look after a woman the doctor had recently diagnosed as suffering from the start of dementia.

She forwarded the video to Gary in the tech team, with a request to enhance the specified image as best he could. Enough for one day. Hopefully tomorrow would bring some answers.

30

'You aren't as feisty as Jennifer was at the beginning. Pity. I like a bit of fight, you know.'

'Wh-what about Jennifer? D-did you take her?' The stench of the room was overpowering now. It smelled like a butcher's abattoir. Surely not. She banished the thought and tried to concentrate on getting the hell out of this situation. She struggled against her restraints, uselessly.

'Ah, now you fight back.' The figure moved around the room clutching the timber.

'Tell me what you want. I'll do anything. Just let me go. I won't tell anyone.'

'Too late for that. You and those other interfering biddies. Thought you were hiding your secrets. But it turns out you weren't hiding them well enough. One of you talked out of turn.'

Shit, she thought. 'I... I h-have no idea what you m-mean.'

The crack of the timber smashing against her leg caused the most excruciating pain she had ever experienced, and the sound of her scream echoed like thunder in the room. Her mind blanked with savage agony before the haze lifted, and in a moment of lucidity, she wondered if this was all down to what Jennifer had discovered. The reason they had set up the group, to have a mask over the reality of that secret. Was that why she was here? Was the explanation that simple?

Her abductor left the room, and Éilis tried to recall through the pain that conversation from two years earlier.

'Can you believe it?' Jennifer had said.

'No, not really.' Éilis had tried to concentrate on the measurements. 'I think shutter blinds would work well in this space.'

'But if it's true, what should I do?'

'Or maybe venetian? Do you have a preference? I can price them for you.'

'Are you listening to me?'

Éilis had turned from the window. Jennifer looked so minute in her large bare kitchen. After her husband had died, she had hired a skip and in a fit of madness that was really grief had thrown out most of the furniture and appliances. Now, standing in the midst of nothing, her hair was as wild as her eyes, and her top and jeans were dust-covered. Her feet were bare, and Éilis worried that she might cut her feet on shards of plaster.

'Jennifer, don't take this the wrong way, but I don't want to get involved. I think you need to take time to grieve. Leave well enough alone. That's my advice.'

'I told Damien about what I overheard in the clinic, and he said he would discuss it with his boss to see what could be done. I don't know if he told her, and now he's dead and it's eating me up.'

Éilis's head was mithered. 'Jennifer, you don't really know what you heard. I say leave it alone or it may come back to haunt you.'

'I'm haunted as it is. Éilis, if it's true, it's a terrible crime and it should be punished.'

'Let it go. It could destroy your career.'

'I don't care. I hate my job at Smile Brighter. And Frankie Bardon is such a fraud. I have to tackle him about this.'

'Don't do anything hasty.'

'I'm going to talk to Orla Keating. If she doesn't already know about this, I think it's time she did, don't you?'

Éilis took her A4 notebook from her satchel. 'Can we discuss the blinds now?'

'You don't care, do you?'

With a sigh, Éilis looked at Jennifer and noticed tears flooding her eyes. She put down her notebook and approached her. 'You're going through a particularly rough time. It's not easy when you lose the person you love. Take time out. Time for yourself. Then, if you're still worried, we can talk about it.'

'I really think I should tell someone.'

'You've told me, and that's enough for now. I'll have a think and come up with a plan. For the time being, I really think it should remain between the two of us. Now, can we get back to blinds?'

That horrible truth Jennifer had overheard at the dental clinic. She wouldn't let it go. Éilis had formed the widows' group as a means to meet and talk. She knew Jennifer needed counselling, but she refused to acknowledge her grief. In the end, Éilis had agreed to help her. Wrong move, Mrs Lawlor!

Their meddling had caused her to be here, she was sure of it, and it was the most terrifying experience of her life. And what about Jennifer? She hadn't seen her for weeks. Had this monster taken her?

She rested her head on her shoulder and cried, unable to wipe away her tears as she was still bound tightly. In a moment of clarity, she realised she might never see the outside of this room or her children ever again. And that was even more terrifying than any physical pain.

31

Cafferty's bar was gloomy, though a streak of light filtered through as Kirby opened the door and settled on the dusty optics behind the bar. He glanced at his watch. Just gone half seven.

He was disappointed not to find Amy waiting for him. He had sent her a text half an hour ago and she'd sent back a thumbs-up emoji. He'd presumed that meant she was okay to meet him.

'Pint, please, Darren,' he told the barman. After a few seconds' hesitation, he added, 'And a small one.'

Darren placed a shot of whiskey in a tumbler on the counter and went about pouring the perfect pint of Guinness. A few old-timers sat beneath the television, chatting over the garbled sound. Two women were in one of the snugs and looked like they were discussing business, with a laptop open on the small round table. Otherwise the bar was empty.

Taking his whiskey, he dipped his head under the low arch and entered the lounge. Amy was sitting in the corner, scrolling on her phone, a cup of tea or coffee on the table. He remembered the glass in his hand. Shit.

She looked up and smiled, slipping her phone into her bag.

He sat down before his knees buckled. She was gorgeous. Her butterfly lips and deep brown eyes gave her petite face a movie-star look, and her hair was like a halo.

'Amy,' he said, and coughed. His voice was too high with emotion. 'I see you bought me a coffee. I got you a whiskey.'

She grinned. 'You are a scream, Larry Kirby. I couldn't stomach any more alcohol. I used up my monthly quota last night. You look a lot better than you sounded on the phone.'

'I died a thousand deaths all day, but I feel a lot better now. How are you?'

'Fine, thanks.' She eased back into the leather upholstery and held her cup in one hand.

He groaned inwardly. Get a grip, he warned himself. He'd already slept with her, seen her naked. Not that he remembered much. Fuck. She'd seen *him* naked. He felt the blush roast his ears.

'What's up? You've turned beetroot.'

'Ah sure, I'm just happy you didn't stand me up.'

'Liar. You were thinking about last night.' She took a sip of her coffee. 'What you can remember, that is.'

'Got me in one.'

'We were both wasted.' She grinned, and his gaze lingered on her mouth.

'I can't argue with that.'

'It was a good night.'

He blushed even harder. *Goddammit, grow up.* He was acting like a teenager.

'Do you want to start again?' he said. 'Get to know each other first.'

'We did kind of put the cart before the horse, didn't we? My name is Amy Corcoran. I'm thirty-five. I used to work in an office but now I'm in Dolan's supermarket. I was in foster care as a child and I don't talk about it. I was once in a serious relationship. I don't talk about that either. No kids. Work is a bore. One of my colleagues is a pain in the proverbial, but the customers are great. Your turn.'

'Larry Kirby. Married once. Not any longer.' He glanced over and found her nodding her head. 'Work is hectic and stressful. My boss is a tough nut but nice behind it. One of my colleagues is also a pain in the arse. My best friend recently found out he has an eight-year-old son. Now that he's preoccupied, I worry about losing his friendship.'

He was saved from more personal revelations as Darren placed a perfect pint on the table.

'Thanks, Dar.' Kirby handed the empty tumbler to the barman. So much for never drinking whiskey again. A few pints, then home to bed. To sleep. Nothing else.

'I never could stomach Guinness,' Amy said.

Safer ground. 'You don't know what you're missing. Great source of iron.'

'I'll stick to G&T.'

'Oh, sorry, I never asked. Can I get you a drink? A real drink.'

'I'm fine, thanks.'

A silent void eased in between them, and Kirby struggled with what to say next. Amy clasped her hands on her knee and stared straight ahead.

He gulped down half the pint, set the glass back on the table and wiped his mouth. 'It's good. Best pint in Ragmullin.'

'Larry, can I ask you a question?'

'Fire ahead.'

'Can you tell me about that dead woman who was discovered this morning?'

'Ah, I can't, Amy. It's early days, and details of the investigation have to stay confidential.'

'Is that the party line?'

'It's the truth, but you can get the bones of it on the news. Check it out on your phone.'

'I did. That's what has me worried.'

'Don't be frightened. It's a one-off. Must be someone she knew. Usually is.'

She leaned over and put her hand on his. 'The thing is, I think I knew her.'

He involuntarily startled. 'Why would you think that?'

'A description was issued when you were trying to identify her. Small build. Five foot one. Shoe size four. Reddish hair. Pale skin. People were asked to check on their family and friends to see if anyone was missing.'

'That's right.' He eyed his drink on the table and licked his lips. His mouth felt dry, and he had a feeling he wasn't going to like what Amy said next.

'Let me show you what's trending on Twitter.'

'What has that got to do with Jen... I mean, the dead woman?'

She sat up straight and slapped a hand on her knee. 'I knew it. It is her.'

'Who?'

'The woman I'm thinking of is called Jennifer O'Loughlin.' She took her phone from her bag. 'Give me a minute and I'll find it for you.'

'Amy, please, stop. I shouldn't have let that slip.'

'It's all over Twitter, so don't worry.' She returned her gaze to her phone. 'There! Told you. It's up already.'

Kirby took her phone and looked at the screen: #hernamewasJennifer. 'Shit. I don't understand. How...?'

'Her name might have come from someone you interviewed. Or maybe a guard was overheard in a bar or coffee shop. It can't be avoided nowadays.' She took the phone back and scrolled through the feed. 'Poor woman. How did she die?'

Kirby watched as she slipped the phone back into her bag and turned her head towards him in anticipation.

'Honestly, Amy, don't ask. I'm sure you'll read about it soon. I'm sorry.'

Her shoulders relaxed. 'I'm the one who should be sorry. I understand about your job, but I do want you to share things with me. Only when you're allowed to do so. Is that fair?'

'Sure is.' He kept his gaze focused on the near-empty glass in his hand. Something about the conversation had dimmed her sparkle. Mustering what he hoped was an engaging expression, he said, 'So tell me, Amy Corcoran, who is this work colleague who's hassling you?'

She laughed then. 'I barely mentioned it and you pick up on it.'

'That's why I'm a detective.'

'So tell me,' she repeated his words, 'what are you going to do? Clamp Luke Bray in chains and waterboard him?'

'If that's what you want, I'm your man.' He couldn't stop his grin. Maybe Amy would be good for him. God knows he could do with someone in his life to make him smile.

Kicking off her sandals after she came home from her shop, Helena made her way into the sitting room and threw herself down on the couch. Should she have swung round by Éilis's house to check if she had returned home? No, she could ring her once she'd had a long, cool shower. First, she needed a glass of wine. The comfortable cushions seemed to swallow her, and she couldn't find the energy to move.

The doorbell shrieked through her brain and she realised she'd fallen asleep. She hauled herself up from the couch and went to answer the door.

In the hall, she saw a face peering in through the glass panel. She let out a shriek and the face pulled back, but the shadow remained. With the security chain in place, Helena opened the door a crack and then slumped with relief.

'Jesus, Orla, you scared the heart out of me.'

She shut the door, undid the chain and let the woman in. This was only the second time ever that Orla had been at her home, and she tried not to think of the first time. They'd all been here then. Six months ago.

'I'm sorry for turning up unannounced. I didn't know who else to talk to.'

'Would you like a drink?'

'Yes, whatever you're having. I can't believe Jennifer is dead.'

'It's terrible.' Helena looked for two clean glasses and fetched the wine from the fridge, then led her guest to the sitting room.

'I love this room,' Orla exclaimed. 'It didn't look so big with all of us here last time.'

'Éilis designed it for me.' Helena poured the wine and settled back on the couch. 'Orla, what do you think about Jennifer?'

'It's too awful to imagine. Listen, two detectives came to talk to me about Jennifer and Éilis. And they quizzed me about Tyler.'

'Why would they ask about him? Were they following up because it's a year since he went missing?'

'I suppose that's part of it, but it got me wondering. What if he's still around?'

'Why would you even think that?'

'I don't know, but Jennifer is dead and Éilis is missing. We know Jennifer started all this, and maybe that's why Tyler disappeared when he did. Maybe he wanted to remain hidden, but what if one of our group talked and he's back doing damage.' Orla took a long drink and Helena realised what she was getting at.

'You think Tyler could have killed Jennifer? That's ridiculous. Did he even know her?'

'I know he used to go to Smile Brighter, where she worked. I think he might have known her. She never said. Maybe I'm making a mountain out of a molehill.'

Helena's wine sloshed over the rim of her glass and she took a large swallow before speaking. 'You are. The guards will ask all sorts of questions. Don't worry about it.'

'But the thing is, I *am* worried. Tyler could be... He was a control freak. I was scared of him. What if he faked his disappearance only to come back to torment me? What if he's looking for revenge? We know why he might be, don't we?'

'This is ridiculous, Orla. If he was still around, someone would have seen him. The guards would have found him. Stop worrying and drink up.'

'Poor Jennifer.'

'It's so upsetting. Do you think we should have done more when she stopped contact so suddenly?'

'Maybe. I don't know.'

'And Éilis is missing still.'

'I'm scared, Helena.'

'Me too.' She couldn't help wishing that Orla would leave. She didn't want to talk about this. Orla was too intense. She just wanted to enjoy a drink in peace and fall into bed. Things would look better tomorrow.

'Is Noah not here?'

'He's with my mother.' She was about to say she was alone for the night, but something in Orla's eyes caused her to lie. 'She'll be back with him any minute. I really miss him.'

'I don't miss Tyler. I wish I knew for certain that he was dead, then I could rest easy.'

'I'm sure you don't mean that.'

'I do mean it. Every night I pray his body will be found.'

'Oh.' Not knowing what else to say, Helena stood. She wanted this woman out of her home, out of her life. The vibe coming at her was not pleasant. It was... She searched for the word. When it came to her, she shivered. Was Orla really malevolent?

'Give me a call at work tomorrow if you like. I need to get some order on this house before my mother arrives. She'll have the hoover out in a second and I'll never get rid of her.' She attempted a laugh, but the sound that came out was like a strangled cat.

'Thanks for the wine.' Orla stood, and placed the glass on the coffee table. 'I'm sorry for imposing on you. Be careful, Helena. Be extra vigilant. Make sure you lock up your lovely home. If my husband is out there somewhere, I wouldn't put anything past him.'

Once Orla had gone, Helena double-checked that every door and window was securely locked, then rushed into the utility room and fetched a fresh bottle from the wine rack. She let the corkscrew slip as she frantically tried to open it. Then the bottle crashed to the floor and she fell to her knees to scoop up the broken glass. When she thought she had it all in the bin, she got out the mop. That was when she noticed blood pouring from her little finger. And in her rush to get to the sink to wash it, she slipped on the spilled wine and felt tiny glass shards bite into her bare feet.

The air seemed to have been sucked out of the room and her throat tightened. She dragged herself to the counter and leaned heavily against it, looking out the window. She screamed at the reflection before realising it was her own terrified face.

There was no way she was imaging the mysterious sensation of goosebumps popping up on her arms. And she wished she wasn't alone in the house for the night.

33

'So you don't like this Luke fellow?' Kirby said.

'Not really. He's probably harmless, but he freaks me out a bit,' Amy replied. 'He's twenty-two and acts like a fifteen-year-old schoolboy at times.'

'That's not a crime.'

'I never said it was,' she said sharply. 'He's... I don't know... maybe a little weird.'

'Weird in a world where *everyone* is slightly weird.'

'I suppose you're right.'

'What is it specifically that freaks you out, as you say?'

She bit her lip as if debating telling him anything at all.

He said, 'I want to hear why this little fart has upset you.'

'It's not that he's upset me as such. It's the constant snide remarks that wear me down.'

'Tell me about it! There's a dope from Athlone working with me and I swear to God I'll level him with a punch one of these days.'

She smiled at that, but only briefly.

'Some of Luke's comments are... well, a bit sexual. It makes me uneasy.'

'I take back the little fart observation. He sounds like a prick.'

'He probably doesn't mean any harm, but you'd think he'd have got the message that that type of talk is no longer acceptable.'

'Did you discuss it with your manager?'

'I don't want to make a fuss. I'm applying for every job that comes up. I want out of there.'

'You should report him.'

'I have no proof. It would be *he said she said*.'

After thinking for a moment Kirby said, 'Record him secretly.'

'Isn't that illegal?'

'At least you'd have proof. Or arrange for someone to over-hear him. A colleague you trust, or what about a customer? Any you like or trust?'

'There's old Mr Rodgers, but he's eighty if he's a day.'

'All he has to do is be a witness to this Luke shithead talking to you. In the meantime, I'll see what I can do.'

'I don't want you getting in any trouble on my account.'

'You would be the best reason for me getting into trouble.'

He noticed her looking at her hands to hide a blush. Then he caught her glancing up under her eyelids at him. She took his hand and drew him close and kissed his lips.

And Kirby though he just might burst with happiness.

———

As they drew away and sipped their drinks, still looking at each other, neither of them was aware of the lounge door opening.

Of someone slipping in, walking under the arch and into the bar.

Of that person sitting at the counter, where they could watch uninterrupted and unseen.

34

Farranstown House looked like an old ruin, Lottie thought as she drove up the avenue. She drew her eyes away from the house to take notice of the dimming sun showering sparkling diamonds on the lake. The leaves in the trees fluttered in the evening breeze, and as she got closer to her home, it revealed itself in all its decay. The house was ancient, and despite the fact that she now lived in it with her children and grandson, plus her mother, Rose, she hadn't the time, energy or money to repair it. It was crumbling before her very eyes and she could do nothing to prevent it.

'How was your day?' Rose said without looking up from whatever she was doing at the kitchen table.

Pausing with her hand on the refrigerator door, Lottie said, 'It was hectic.' She caught sight of what Rose was at. 'Are you making a sandwich?'

'Isn't that what it looks like?' Rose snapped.

Moving towards the table, Lottie eyed the small tub of Lidl custard. It still had its orange price reduction label stuck to the side. Besides the fact that it was out of date, it was not butter.

'Erm, Mother, that's custard.'

Rose paused with the knife in her hand, custard dripping onto the table, glassy-eyed but daring at the same time. Daring Lottie to interfere?

'Well, I like it.' She resumed her task, scooping up more custard and lashing it on the bread.

Lottie stood open-mouthed.

Rose picked up a chunk of cheese, edges hard as rock, and placed it on the second slice of bread. Please God, don't let her put it on top of the other slice. But she did just that.

'I really think you should throw that out and—'

'I'm well able to make my own sandwich. Your father will be home soon. Set the table for him.'

Lottie's heart sank at the thought of her dead father. Her mother was getting more confused by the day, and it scared the shit out of her. She had no idea how to deal with it.

Placing her sandwich on a plate, Rose marched out of the kitchen.

Shaking her head, Lottie cleared the mess from the table and dumped the offending custard tub into the bin. Her own hunger had vanished, and she washed the cutlery in the sink before wiping down the countertops. Chloe had been great with the housework for a time, but now she cared for Sergio during the day and worked nights at the pub. Once again, the house was being neglected.

A knock on the back door brought her out of her musing. It opened without invitation, and she smiled when Sergio rushed in.

'Hello, Lottie. Is Sean here? Chloe told me he'd fix my Nintendo.'

'In his room. Go on up.'

'Thank you.' The eight-year-old smiled widely and flew up the stairs.

Boyd followed him in, a bottle of red in his hand. 'He kept on about his Nintendo the whole way home after I'd picked him up. Nothing for it but to come back. Sorry about today. We were both on edge.' He kissed her on the lips and waved the bottle. 'I stopped in the shop on the way. Okay if I have a drink while I'm waiting?'

'I'll join you,' she said, deadpan.

'Shit. I'm a dope. I never stopped to think. Just thinking of myself and—'

'Will you stop?' she laughed. 'I'm fine. Well, I would be if my mother would stay out of the kitchen. She's a danger to herself.'

'Hope she didn't do too much damage. Where's the corkscrew?'

'That's a screw top.'

'So it is.' He opened and shut cupboard doors until he found a tumbler.

Lottie said, 'I've no idea where I've put the wine glasses, or if I even have any.'

'I'd drink it out of a shoe this minute.' He poured some of the red liquid and gulped a mouthful before refilling the glass, slowly this time.

Her eyes watered as the aroma wafted towards her. What she wouldn't give for a quick swig of anything containing alcohol. She was distressed over Rose, but Boyd was also cause for concern. She couldn't remember the last time she'd seen him this rattled, or seen him drinking like *she* used to.

'Sit down and tell me what's really bothering you.' She flicked on the kettle, having to make do with a coffee. 'It's not all Jackie, is it?'

He stared at her, bottle in one hand, glass in the other, and leaned against the counter. 'It's just... Oh, I don't know... Parenting is hard work.'

'Is Sergio dropping his clothes all over the apartment again?' Lottie smiled, knowing that Sergio was wrecking Boyd's compulsive tidying gene.

'Ah no, I got over that. He's a good kid. I can't get a school to admit him. The rules of entry are so bloody antiquated. Did his parents attend this school? Is he living in the catchment area long? No, he lived in Spain for eight years because his mother didn't inform me of his existence. Has he a sibling already attending? No, he hasn't any siblings. None that I know about, but I wouldn't discount it, knowing Jackie.' His shoulders relaxed as the alcohol took effect.

She moved closer without touching him, though she dearly wanted to smooth the worry creases from his forehead with a kiss. 'I hate to be the one to say this, but when Jackie arrives—'

'Don't go there.' He jumped, sloshing wine down his shirt, which he uncharacteristically ignored. He paced around the kitchen. 'I want him enrolled in a local school. I want him kitted out in a uniform with a bag full of school books. I want him settled. I don't want to make it easy for my ex-wife to take him away from me.'

The kettle whistled and she busied herself spooning coffee into a mug. She poured in the water and milk. At the table, she pulled out two chairs and sat, waiting until he joined her.

'I think you'll have to work things out with her,' she said, 'Jackie is his mother. She reared him from the day he was born.'

'I wasn't given a chance to rear him. She never told me about his existence until it suited her.' He put down the glass and turned to her. 'I don't know what to do.'

It was a long time since she had seen Boyd so vulnerable. Not since he'd received his cancer diagnosis. 'I'd go easy on that stuff for starters. You have to drive home.'

'Or I could get drunk and stay the night with you.'

'That would be nice. Not the drunk bit, mind. But now you have your son to think of, and I don't relish putting him in Sean's room for the night. Sean is a night owl and doesn't sleep until near morning. Bad example for your little boy. And I still have my mother sleeping in the sitting room.'

'Didn't you give her your room?'

'I did, but she got a bee in her bonnet and insisted on setting up a bed downstairs. I can't argue with her. She's impossible.'

'Has she asked to go back to her own house?'

'Yes, but she can't live on her own. I honestly don't know what to do any more.'

'Seems like we're both in awkward situations.'

'Awkward is an understatement. Can I have a sip of that?'

'Drink your coffee, Lottie.'

'Yes, Dad.'

When he put his hand on her shoulder and drew her to his chest, she welcomed the safety of his arms. If only the feeling could last for ever. But she felt she didn't deserve to be happy. So many attempts had been thwarted that she could not envisage ever enjoying pure happiness again. She was willing to accept every brief second where possible, and right now was one such second. No one knew what the future would bring, least of all her. And then there was murdered Jennifer and missing Éilis.

Boyd pulled away. 'Your mind is on the case.'

'We need to find Éilis Lawlor. She has two young children longing for her return.'

'Tomorrow,' he said.

He lifted her chin and pressed his lips to hers. She leaned against him and allowed the beat of his heart to soothe her racing mind. One moment is all I ask for, she thought, just as Sergio burst in the door.

'It's fixed!' The boy skidded around the table waving the console. 'Sean is a genius.'

And the moment was lost.

35

Boyd loved Sergio, the son he hadn't known about until earlier in the year. But he was living under the constant threat of his ex-wife returning to Ireland. It was a certainty that she would try to take the boy away from him.

Sergio was eating a bowl of cereal in front of the television. Boyd yawned. He could do with another glass of wine, but he'd left Lottie's without the bottle and he only had a few Heinekens in his refrigerator. He didn't relish mixing beer with the wine he'd already drunk. And he couldn't sneak off to bed, because he was sleeping on the couch. He'd given his bed to Sergio, and the aches in his hips and back were testament to the uncomfortable arrangements. His one-bedroom apartment was no longer suitable.

'Is it nearly over?' he asked hopefully.

Sergio hit the remote. 'Twenty-three minutes left.'

He could survive twenty-three minutes. Couldn't he?

'You can have your own bed, Dad. I don't mind sleeping here.'

'And watch television all night? Don't think so, son.'

'Okay.' Sergio spooned more cereal into his mouth and

settled his head against Boyd's arm. That small gesture filled him with love.

Once the twenty-three minutes were up, he had Sergio tucked up in bed and the couch set up with a duvet and pillows for himself. Then he thought of the nettle tea he'd got from Helena McCaul. Maybe it would take the edge off. Worth a try.

He boiled the kettle and spooned in the finely ground leaves. Hadn't she said to use a strainer? Too late. He poured the grainy concoction down the sink and rinsed out the mug before drying it. When the kitchenette met with his approval, he lay on the uncomfortable couch, hoping sleep would come quickly.

Some hope. An hour later he was still awake.

————

The fire was down to dying embers when Kathleen Foley heard the key turn in the front door. She hadn't needed a fire, but it made the room a bit more homely. If only she could get it tidy.

Her visitor rushed across the room and Kathleen fell into her warm arms.

'I thought you'd be in bed.'

'I thought you'd be here earlier.'

'I got here as soon as I could escape from work.'

The two women kissed.

'I hate this secrecy,' Kathleen said.

'I've explained my views on going public.'

'Coming out, you mean?'

'I can't do it, Kathleen. My reputation would be ruined.'

'Years ago, perhaps, but not nowadays.' Kathleen wriggled out of the embrace.

'It's okay for you, at home all day with nothing to think about except your delusional daughter. I have my business to consider. I couldn't live with the shame.'

'Shame? You're ashamed of me?' She couldn't mask her anger at the put-down. The receipt of the latest photo was fresh in her mind.

'You know what I mean. We agreed. It's a contract you cannot break.'

Kathleen slumped onto the armchair. 'I don't think I can do this any more. I've so much going on. You know Helena is out of control. I'm terrified she'll do damage.'

'To herself or someone else?'

'Both, really.'

'I can have a word...'

'I can handle my own daughter, thank you.'

'Can you, though? You can't keep lying for her.'

Kathleen stood. It was pointless having this ongoing argument. 'I'm going to bed.'

'I can't stay tonight.'

'That's okay. I'm tired. Call me tomorrow.'

She was pulled into another warm hug, the woman's jacket soft and luxurious.

In her ear, the woman whispered, 'Don't even think about telling anyone.'

Kathleen pulled away, speechless. Shaking violently, she watched as Madelene Bowen walked away.

36

Jackie Boyd wanted to surprise her ex-husband. He had no need to know she was on her way to Ragmullin. She'd booked the one-way flight from Malaga. She needed time to work on him. To see how she could wangle her way back into his life so that she could stop running. She knew it would be difficult. There was no longer any love between them. She had never believed in love anyhow. Without regret or conscience, she knew she used people to satisfy whatever need she had at a particular time. And she'd used Boyd to give her son safety and protection.

The Spanish police had been happy with her work as a CI, a confidential informant – a snitch according to the criminals. That was until she had to disappear when her cover had been almost blown. That was the reason she'd had to tell Boyd about his son.

Maybe now she could help the gardaí and put the smile on the other side of Lottie Parker's face. She grinned as she drove the rental car up the slip road off the M50 and onto the M4, settling it into cruise control.

She couldn't wait to see her little boy, but she was even more excited to see the look on her ex-husband's face when she presented him with her ultimatum. The package deal. She grinned, thinking about her scheme. If he wanted Sergio in his life, she had to be part of it too. Sergio plus her, or Mark Boyd would never see his son again.

She let down the window and laughed into the darkening night air.

———

I can't believe it. How can this be happening to me?

The dumb bitch has gone and croaked after a few whacks of the plank. It might have been a heart attack, or shock from her broken bones. I'm no doctor, but I know she's dead.

I have to reel my plans into one night. I had so much laid out for her. The time in the cold room. I wanted to watch her teeth chattering, her eyes widening. Making her think I was about to let her go, then smashing up her arms to match her broken legs. I'm astounded at how much pain the human body can withstand before succumbing to death. But this bitch has denied me all that. She's cheated me. I can't contain my rage. I take her hands and stamp on them with full force. Bitch.

There is one last thing I have to do. I take the scalpel and bring it close to her face. With a gloved finger, I peel back the eyelids and stare into her dead eyes. Another pair to make a set.

Once I have them sitting in a jar with the lid tightly closed, I know I don't have much time to do what must be done.

Looking at the blood streaked plastic sheeting, I think about the site I picked to dump her body. Will it still work with no time to prepare it properly? One thing is certain, I can't keep her here. Already I can smell the decay seeping from her orifices. Soon the room will be suffused with toxic gases. The human body is such a vile thing. She is a vile thing.

The cold room? No. Nothing for it but to dispose of her body.

Then I'll watch the stupid guards flounder around like pigs in shite. I laugh at the analogy. I am too clever for them.

All the annoyance with this one just means I have to speed things up.

My next victim is already in my sights.

DAY TWO

37

Helena hated waking up alone. The walls seemed to whisper their secrets; she strained to hear what the house was keeping from her. She rubbed her eyes and her fingers came away with streaks of mascara. She'd gone to bed without taking her make-up off. Again. A veil of despair descended, and she shivered, even though the rising sun streamed heat through the window.

Shuffling onto her elbow, she glanced at the clock before gingerly lying back on the pillow. Could she leave the shop closed today? But if she didn't go into work, she'd just lie in bed all day, drowning in her anxiety.

She wanted to talk to her friend. It wasn't like Éilis to leave her high and dry. She thought of Jennifer. Éilis had set up the group after meeting her. When Helena joined, she had felt like a third wheel. For no apparent reason, she seemed to be blocked out of certain conversations. Things were being whispered behind cupped hands. It wasn't until Orla arrived that Helena had been brought into their confidence. To be part of what they came to call the deadly secret. More like a red destruction button, when she thought about it.

Now Jennifer was dead and Éilis had gone AWOL. Did

that mean she was in danger? A slowly climbing trail of fear inched up her spine.

The sound of a bird twittering on a branch of the tree outside her window roused her from her self-pity. She had to get up, get dressed and get out. Life waited for no one.

If she didn't keep her shop going, what else did she have?

Nothing much, she concluded.

38

When Boyd arrived at Farranstown House to drop off Sergio, he felt like he had walked in on a breakdown in UN negotiations.

'It's a belly top, Gran,' Chloe said, stamping barefoot across the concrete kitchen floor.

'Your poor father would turn in his grave if he saw you going out like that.' Rose slapped the table repeatedly with a tea towel.

'I'm not going out, am I? It's eight o'clock in the morning and I wouldn't even be up yet if I hadn't to look after Sergio, and you're making such a racket, you'd wake the dead. Will you stop doing that, Gran?'

'In my time, young ones didn't go around half naked at any time of the day.'

Boyd stepped into the kitchen with Sergio. Leave or stay? He was already late for work and there was no one else to mind his son.

'Good morning, ladies. Hope I'm not interrupting anything.'

'Hi, Sergio,' Chloe said quickly.

Boyd noticed she was working hard to fake a smile. 'Are you sure it's okay to leave him with you?'

'I'm absolutely certain.' She gave Sergio a hug, took his hand and brought him out to the hall. She indicated for Boyd to follow. 'What am I going to do about Gran, Boyd? It's so sad, but if I hadn't agreed to mind Sergio, I'd have volunteered to work at the pub day and night.'

'It's a tough one,' he said. 'Have patience with her. It isn't her fault. It's the way her brain is wired at the moment.'

'I know all that, but it's so hard to watch. Do you mind if I take Sergio into town today? Just to get a break from this house.'

'No problem. I packed his swimming gear in case you or Sean want to bring him to the lake later.'

'Great idea!' She smiled, and he saw her father in her eyes.

'Make sure someone stays with Rose. Will Katie and Louis be here?'

'I'll check. Don't worry, I won't abandon Gran. Though sometimes...' She grinned and gave him a hug. 'Thanks, Boyd.'

'For what?'

'For trusting me to mind your son. He's a dote.' She pulled away and ruffled Sergio's hair. 'How about toast and orange juice? Later we'll go on a little trip.'

Sergio seemed reluctant. 'Only if you're sure. I don't want to be a burden.'

Boyd smiled weakly. Sergio had heard the interchange between Chloe and Rose. His son definitely took after him.

And now he was late for work.

———

Jackie had stayed in some terrible rooms, so she was delighted to get a nice clean one in the Joyce Hotel. While compact, it was comfortable. The window looked out over the street and the hum of the early-morning traffic below woke her, despite the late hour checking in.

She spent fifteen minutes in the shower with the hot water

drumming open the pores of her skin. Refreshed, she dressed in white jeans and a white T-shirt and slipped her feet into soft leather pumps. Spanish leather was one thing she'd miss if she moved back to Ragmullin. And the sun, of course. It looked fine outside, but she was well aware of the sharp breeze that blew in from the lakes, so she pulled a navy blazer out of her case and admired herself in the mirror.

Her tanned skin saved her a fortune on the fake stuff. She'd had her hair cut and it was almost bleached. Satisfied with her look, she picked up her bag and checked she had her wallet and cigarettes before leaving the room.

She wanted to scout around town before she met up with her son and her ex. God, but he was in for a shock.

Exiting the hotel, she couldn't help the conspiratorial smile that curled her lips.

39

Neither Boyd nor Kirby had turned up for work by the time Lottie decided to have a chat with Éilis Lawlor's kids to see if she could learn anything further. Their mother still hadn't come home, nor had she been found.

She parked outside the house and quickly checked her phone for emails. The initial results on the stain found on Éilis's carpet were in. Urine. Human. Not the dog, so. It was fast work by the lab, but there was no report from SOCOS at the site where Jennifer's body had been found. Time was against them while the killer was still free and another woman was missing.

About to enter the Lawlor house, she received the dreaded call. A body had been discovered at Ladystown Lake.

She sped out there and parked in the car park. Pausing to gather her wits, she gazed out over the vast expanse of water. A family of swans nestled by the shore, oblivious to the horror in the trees behind her. A warm breeze skirted over the reeds and a smell of late summer hung in the air. She shook herself into work mode.

Skirting the outer cordon, a hundred yards from the shore, she found her feet slipping on the muddy terrain. There hadn't been much rain since yesterday morning and she wondered why it was soggy underfoot. Making her way through the trees, she reached a tarmac pathway and could walk without sliding. Maybe she should have entered via the gate in the car park fence, but it was too late now.

The inner cordon was alive with activity as SOCOs set up. She saw Boyd talking earnestly with Grainne Nixon.

She dipped under the tape and approached them. 'What have we got?'

Grainne pointed a little further up the path, where a tent was being erected over a large wood carving. Lottie had been out here during the summer, walking with her grandson, Louis, and knew there was a series of life-sized carvings from felled trees along the pathway, representing Irish mythological figures.

'The body is draped over the Fionn Mac Cumhaill statue,' Grainne said.

'I want to get closer to see who it is.' Lottie glanced up through the leafy canopy above her head, praying it wasn't Éilis. She donned gloves and a mask, and pulled booties on over her muddy footwear before falling into step beside the SOCO, with Boyd behind them.

As they neared the clearing, her heart rate raced. She had to see this for herself and make her initial assessment. The tent was in the throes of falling apart, and Grainne took charge of her team while Lottie stood in front of the carving. She couldn't see much of the statue because a woman's body was indeed draped over it, as Grainne had warned.

It was as if the dead woman was asleep, her arms around the statue's neck, her head resting on one shoulder and her legs out behind her. The skirt of her yellow cotton dress fluttered in the breeze and a white feather floated downwards from an over-hanging branch to rest in her hair. Lottie glanced up, but couldn't see any birds.

Returning her attention to the body, it was evident, even

without further investigation, that both legs had been savagely broken. Bones protruded though flesh.

'Same killer?' Boyd said. 'The dress, the legs...'

Lottie shrugged.

She couldn't see the face, none of them could, but the nausea rising in her stomach told her it was Éilis Lawlor. She visualised little Becky and Roman's sweet faces in anticipation of their mother's return. 'Goddammit. I told two children I'd find their mother.'

'You've found her,' Boyd said softly.

'Not the way I hoped. This is awful.' She took a breath of fresh air to compose herself. 'I need a closer look.'

'Best to pull on the full gear then.' Grainne rooted in her large steel case and drew out a white overall.

Once she was suitably attired, Lottie made her way forward, walking on the stepping plates.

Grainne said, 'She's in rigor. Dead over two hours; no longer than six, maybe eight. Two broken legs are the obvious injuries. Possibly her right arm too, for it to be in that position.'

'Post-mortem injuries?' Lottie hoped.

'Can't say.'

'No blood that I can see.'

'She was killed elsewhere. And before you ask, I have no idea how she died.'

'I want to see her face.'

'We can move around to the back of statue.'

As Lottie was about to follow Grainne, she yelled, 'Stop! She moved. Fuck, she moved.'

'What do you mean?' Grainne stared from Lottie to the body. 'It's just the breeze.'

'Her arm moved. Look. Not the one around the neck, the arm that's around the statue's waist.'

'It's in the same position.'

Lottie squinted. 'Now that I look at her, I think it might have been the strap of her dress that moved.'

'Another dress too big for the wearer.' Grainne continued her journey around the body. 'Stay there, Inspector. It's mucky over here; the plates are sinking.'

'Can you see her face?' Lottie resisted the urge to follow the SOCO; she didn't want to be the one to contaminate a crime scene, even if the crime had occurred elsewhere.

Grainne shook her head. 'She's facing into the statue and will have to be moved in order for us to identify her. Can't do that until the state pathologist arrives.'

'I need her on site now.'

'Why don't *you* phone her then?'

Lottie bit her tongue before saying, 'Any sign of a bullet wound?'

'I can only see what you can.' Grainne examined the body from a distance before making her way back to Lottie. 'Sorry for being rude, but this job gets to me at times.'

'Don't worry about it. I know the feeling.'

'Have you a photo of the missing woman? Any identifying marks or tattoos?'

'Only head and shoulders. Hair looks similar. Why?'

'There's a small scar on the index finger of her right hand. It's like she had a mole removed recently.'

'I'll check that out. Anything else?'

'All her fingers are broken.'

'Jesus Christ! What kind of a sick fuck are we dealing with?'

'Initial guess, we're dealing with the same *sick fuck* who killed Jennifer O'Loughlin.'

'The minute you have anything for me to go on, I want to know.'

'Sure thing. And please ring the pathologist. I need to move the body to see if her attacker left any evidence on her or the statue.'

The dress fluttered again and the strap fell further down the inert arm.

'What's that mark on her side?' Lottie said. 'Up under her arm.'

Grainne moved a little closer, careful of the sinking plates. 'Looks like another scar. From an operation, maybe?'

'Okay. Something else to go on. Thanks.'

Lottie returned to Boyd, who was talking to a flustered young woman with a child in a buggy.

'I really have to leave,' the woman said. 'You have my number if you need to ask me anything else.'

'That's fine, thanks for all your help.'

As the woman scurried away towards the outer cordon, Lottie raised a quizzical eyebrow. 'Witness?'

'Yeah. She stumbled on the body. She's a school teacher, on the last few days of her summer holidays. Very calm.'

'I always say teachers have the patience of saints.' Lottie looked up. Grainne was calling across to her. 'What is it?'

'I've been wondering why the ground is so wet around here when we had no rain last night.'

'I thought that too.'

'We found a hose over there on the grass under the bush. It's been gushing out water for some time. Might be no harm seeing what's on the other side of this clearing.'

'I will.' Lottie made to move forward.

'No, Inspector, head back around and look at it from outside. I can't allow any more foot traffic here.'

Once she was outside the cordon, Lottie brought Boyd with her to investigate the water source, keeping her protective clothing on. The site where the body was located backed onto the car park. Peering through the trees, she could see the SOCOs in their white suits working like a colony of ants.

A concrete structure of three walls about four feet high housed a cold-water tap attached to a wooden stand, for visitors to the lake. A green hosepipe was screwed to the tap. With a fresh pair of gloves on, Lottie turned off the tap and sent word to the SOCOs to examine it and to follow the line of the hose for any clues left behind by the killer.

'We are dealing with someone very determined and very smart,' Boyd said. 'They literally covered their tracks.'

'Whoever it is, they are extremely vicious.'

At the car, she tore off the outer clothing and stuffed it into an evidence bag. Then she followed Boyd's car back to the station, wondering why he hadn't confided in her the reason for being late that morning. She needed him at his best. Since he'd found out he was a father, his attention was definitely not on the job. Something had to give.

Kirby ambled over to Lottie's office door after she had updated the team about the discovery of the body at the lake.

'Boss? I wonder if it's okay for me to examine the Tyler Keating cold case?'

It took her a few seconds to understand what he was saying. 'I spoke with his wife yesterday and she sure has an attitude against us.'

'I wouldn't blame her really. We never did find her husband. I think maybe I should take a fresh look.'

Lottie moved like a panther around her desk to face him.

'In case you missed the memo, Kirby, in the last twenty-four hours we have two dead women, a shitload of paperwork, and now you want to examine a file on a man who disappeared a year ago? Why in God's name would you even entertain that idea?' Breathless, she sat heavily on the desk, knocking a container of pens to the floor. How did she even have a container for them? Boyd and his compulsive need for neatness, she assumed.

'I only asked because his wife enquired if I had an update.

And then I learn she's a member of this Life After Loss widows' group. I just need a yes-or-no answer.'

'Simple answer is no. The department budget is shot to pieces, but don't let me stop you if you want to work on it in your spare time. Seems to me you might have an awful lot of it in the not-too-distant future.'

Kirby scratched his head and dandruff flew into the glimmering light. 'What do you mean?'

'You've been late for work two days in a row. Please don't continue in that vein. It will end up outside my control and you may well be suspended.'

'That's unfair, so it is.'

'Is it? You're better than that, Kirby.'

'Sure, boss, whatever you say.'

She watched his shoulders hunch over and his head droop as he walked back to his desk, wheezing like an old man. He needed to get a hold of his life. It was Boyd she was annoyed at, but Kirby was taking the brunt of her anger. With a shake of her head, she followed him, forcing merriment into her tone.

'You could start yoga or meditation. Seems like everyone's at it nowadays.'

He drew out his chair noisily, the wheels catching on sheets of paper that had spewed from a file on the floor under his desk.

'Goddammit to hell and back.' He looked at her, his blood-shot eyes watering. 'I need yoga like I need a nail in the head.'

'It was just a suggestion.'

'I'll do it when I see you doing it.' He gave her half a smile.

'That'll be the day.' She grinned back at him.

'See? It's not for everyone after all.'

'We need to find out if Éilis Lawlor had any identifying marks or scars. We can talk to the babysitter Bianca, and her mother. Or the friend, Helena McCaul.'

Boyd came over. 'I talked to Helena yesterday. Want me to follow this up? I can give her a call.'

'Face to face is best. I'll go with you.'

The bell tinkled over Lottie's head as she entered Herbal Heaven.

'Wow, this is a little gem,' she said. 'I've passed this way so often, how have I not noticed it?'

'Hello.' A woman came out from behind the counter, her silver skirt floating around her legs. A skin-tight white top accentuated her figure, while the hair piled up on her head exposed her clear skin and highlighted her round, tired eyes. 'Can I help ... Oh, it's you again, Detective.'

Was she flirting with Boyd? Lottie glanced at him and found him smiling. Feck.

She introduced herself, keeping an eye on the woman's reactions. Helena McCaul seemed to deflate.

'Is there somewhere we can talk?' Lottie prompted.

'I'm on my own here. I don't employ any staff.'

'It's important.'

'I'll lock the door for a few minutes if you like.'

'That'd be great. Won't keep you long.'

Once she was back at the counter, Helena leaned against it as if she needed propping up. Boyd took up sentry beside Lottie. Helena directed her question to him.

'Have you found Éilis? I still can't believe she'd go off somewhere without her kids being looked after.'

Before Boyd could answer, Lottie said, 'We wanted to get a few more details about your friend. I believe you met through the Life After Loss group, is that correct?'

'Yes.'

She needed more information on Éilis to conclusively identify the body. 'Has Éilis any distinguishing marks or scars?'

Helena shook her head. 'Why are you asking that? Is she—'

'What about the index finger on her right hand?'

Helena scrunched up her eyebrows, thinking. 'Oh, that. She had a mole on her finger. Her doctor burned it off. Said it was safer in case it was cancerous.'

'And was it?'

'She never said. I know she was terrified at the time that her cancer had come back.'

'She had cancer?' Lottie glanced at Boyd, who had his full attention on the woman's nutmeg eyes.

'Way before I knew her. A few years before Oisín, her husband, died. He had a genetic heart defect. She got the kids checked out and they were fine. Is Éilis okay?'

'What type of cancer did she have?' Lottie persisted. If she'd had breast cancer that had needed a mastectomy or lymph node removal, that might account for the scar high up on their victim's side. And then Helena confirmed it.

'Breast cancer,' she said. 'She told me she had a mastectomy.'

'It could have left a scar,' Lottie said, half to herself as she turned towards Boyd. He acknowledged this information with a slight nod.

'You've found her, haven't you?' Helena looked from one to the other, her face paling.

'We found the body of a female, but we haven't been able to identify her.' Lottie wished they'd been able to turn the body, but Grainne had insisted on waiting for the pathologist. However, she had little doubt now. Éilis Lawlor was dead.

'Oh my God,' Helena cried. 'That's terrible.'

'We need a formal identification.'

'Who can do that? Surely not her kids... Please don't ask them to look at a body that might or might not be their mother.' There was horror on Helena's face. It was as clear as if she'd got a Sharpie marker and written it in words.

'Don't worry, we're not that callous. Has Éilis any family?'

'A sister. She lives in Dubai. A teacher, I think. Can't even remember her name.'

'Right. Do you think *you* would be able to do the identification?'

'What? Look at a body that could be my friend? No! No way. Can't you use a photograph? Or... Oh no! Is the body so bad that you can't identify her?' Helena looked around wildly, as if there was something in her little shop to help her. Not finding anything, she said, 'Okay, I'll do it, if you think it's important.'

'Thank you,' Boyd said, and put a hand on her arm to stop it flailing about.

Lottie said, 'It might be later today, or maybe tomorrow. Does that work for you?'

'I'll make it work.' Helena's eyes clouded over, and Lottie thought the woman had gone into a semi-trance until she spoke again. 'Mam can hold on to Noah.'

'Noah?'

'My son.'

'Okay. Really appreciate you doing this for us, Helena.' Lottie felt bad at foisting it on her, but she had no other choice.

'That means you believe this dead woman is Éilis, doesn't it?'

Lottie sighed. Helena was persistent, she had to give her that. 'We suspect so, but please don't say anything to anyone yet.'

'First Jennifer. Now Éilis. What's going on? How did she die?'

'We can't divulge that at the moment.' Lottie couldn't divulge anything because she didn't yet know.

'Where did you find her?'

'You'll read about it online soon enough,' Boyd said softly, 'so we might as well tell you. The body of a female was discovered this morning at Ladystown Lake.'

'She drowned?'

'Not as far as we know,' Lottie said. 'Is there anything else you can tell us about Éilis that might help us?'

'You think she knew her killer, don't you? You don't believe she was murdered by some psycho on the prowl.'

'We need to investigate every angle. You also knew Jennifer O'Loughlin. What can you tell me about her?'

Helena's body slumped as if someone had dropped a weight on her shoulders. But her eyes had darkened, and this puzzled Lottie.

'Jennifer was as quiet as a mouse. Wouldn't hurt a fly. Soft-spoken and gentle. Éilis was more vocal and outgoing. Poles apart and they generally moved in different circles.'

'From our information, Jennifer hardly moved in any circles apart from the Life After Loss widows' group.'

'What I meant is that Éilis works... worked for herself. Jennifer worked in the dental clinic. From the little she let us know, I took it that it wasn't a particularly nice place to be. I could be wrong.'

'Was anyone upsetting her there? Did she feel threatened?'

Helena paled again. 'No, no. She didn't say, but then why did she quit without having another job? Doesn't make much sense to me.'

'When did you know she quit?'

'I... What?'

'Did she tell you?'

'When she stopped coming to the group, I phoned Smile Brighter. Someone there told me she'd left. I assumed then she just wanted to be left alone and she'd tell us in her own time.'

'Anything else you can tell us?'

'No. Jennifer was closer to Éilis,' Helena said, and Lottie could see the confusion dropping like a blind over her eyes.

'How much closer?'

'Éilis did some decor designs for the renovation of Jennifer's house. That's how they met.'

Helena had already told Boyd about this so Lottie changed direction. 'I heard Éilis did yoga. Did Jennifer do it also?'

'I don't know about Jennifer, but Éilis went to SunUp.'

'And you have no idea why either of them might have been murdered?'

Helena gulped loudly before speaking. 'Am I in danger?'

'I don't know is the honest answer. Is there anything else you want to add?'

Helena lowered her eyes, silence filling the small shop as if it was visible. 'If I think of anything, I'll let you know.'

'Thanks for your help, Helena.'

Lottie turned and made her way to the door, surprised when Boyd stayed behind. She headed outside and waited for him.

'What was that about?' she asked when he joined her, her tone thorny as a cactus.

'Nettle tea,' he said.

———

When the door closed behind the detectives, Helena's legs gave way. She sank to the floor and rested her head against the coolness of the wooden counter behind her until her breathing returned to something approaching normal. The silence was total. She closed her eyes to the work she needed to do in the shop and tried to rationalise what was going on.

Jennifer had been found dead yesterday, and now it seemed like Éilis was dead too. Things were gathering pace, and if she wasn't careful, she might lose total control of her senses and her main aim; the aim she'd had when she joined the widows' group. There was no way she could let her focus shift.

She wondered if she should have told the detectives more

about Jennifer. How she had been consumed by a secret. How she'd suffered in silence until she met Éilis. How Orla had warned them they might die if they didn't keep quiet. That had incensed Jennifer. But now two of them were dead. Had someone talked? Was that the reason? Had Orla been right all along?

Shoving her fear way down her chest, she made her way to the storeroom and boiled the kettle. Ground nettles rested in the bottom of the mug and she thought of Detective Boyd. What was going on with his boss? It was obvious there was something there, but she had enough to do without thinking about them.

She emptied the mug and rinsed it before pouring in a good finger of vodka from the bottle she'd stashed in the cupboard. She swallowed the liquid before the water had even boiled. At last the trembling in her fingers abated.

The alcohol didn't clear her head, and she felt woozy. Her overriding feeling was one of confusion. She couldn't understand what was going on, and more importantly, she had no idea what her role was in all of it. Had she done or said something to make these horrors happen? Was this because of her? Was it something to do with the times she'd blacked out and lost time?

No, it had to be someone else, and now that she thought about it, she had a good idea who was at fault.

41

The office personnel thinned out as they were allocated jobs. Kirby couldn't help himself: he brought up the Tyler Keating file on his computer. He read while opening the tub of chicken salad he'd bought in Wholesome Pantry, having vowed to change his lifestyle. He would start with his eating habits. Bye bye, McD's. Hello, greens. It wasn't too bad if he closed his eyes. If he used his imagination, he could pretend it was deep-fried chicken nuggets.

Tyler Keating was a thirty-nine-year-old accountant with an MBA, and a part-time lecturer at the college in Athlone. He'd been due to attend a conference in Liverpool the day he had disappeared. His wife had reported him missing five days later. It had bugged Kirby at the time and now it bugged him again. Why the wait?

He scanned his eyes over the reports and interviews. Nothing jumped out at him. Everything had been done by the book. But they still had no clue as to what had happened to the man or where he might be one year on. The file was still open, just not active. No new leads. Not a thing had turned up in the intervening twelve months, despite a full investigation followed by intermittent appeals. Tyler had a sister and brother in Mayo, and they'd phoned at the beginning, but they seemed to have accepted what Kirby believed: their brother was dead.

If that was so, where was the body? If he had killed himself, or had an accident, his car would have been found. It had not been taken on a ferry, and to date it had not been sighted or recovered. That was the mystery. Was someone else involved?

They had suspected his wife, Orla, for a time. She'd been checked out, but nothing had been found to support that suspicion, despite the delay in reporting her husband missing. Phone records showed she'd called him but he hadn't returned any calls. If she had killed him, she might have brought the car to a dismantler's yard and had it destroyed. They'd gone down that avenue and hit a brick wall. Tyler's bank cards hadn't been used either. But they hadn't been checked in a while. He'd call the bank and see what was the position with the missing man's accounts. And after that? He felt the hopelessness that came when he had no idea where to turn.

He needed to know definitively that Tyler Keating was dead. He also had to accept the fact that some people just didn't want to be found.

42

Boyd headed through the station door, letting it bang shut behind him. Lottie watched from the car, unable to understand why he was being so moody. She had one more place to visit before she returned to her desk.

Hill Point was a sprawling apartment complex built during the highs of the Celtic Tiger. The white-painted walls now looked sad and grey, but she knew there wasn't a spare room to be had in any of the apartments above the commercial units.

She parked, and entered the SunUp studio. It was marketed as high-end deluxe on their website, and never having set foot in a yoga studio before, Lottie found the decor matched her imagination. She felt she could relax here. As if she'd ever have the time to indulge in relaxation and mindfulness.

Green-leafed plants, which on closer inspection proved to be plastic and dusty, were draped all around the tight foyer. The chairs were orange felt and chrome. Through the glass at the lower end of the reception desk she could see the long legs of the startlingly beautiful woman seated there. In her frayed jeans, black ankle boots – she couldn't find her shoes when leaving the house – and Sean's Batman hoodie once again tied around her shoulders over a greyish-white T-shirt, Lottie felt like a Z-list actor who'd walked onto the wrong film set. And she couldn't help thinking that SunUp was desperately trying to be something it was not.

She flashed her ID badge. Up close, she noticed that the woman's face was caked in thick foundation. If you peeled it off, you might find a different person buried underneath. She blamed Instagram celebrities with their beauty collaborations. Even her daughters fell victim to the hard sell.

The woman opened her crimson-glossed lips and bared her veneers in a tight smile. A flat accent emerged from her mouth. 'You'd be wanting to speak to Owen, would you?'

'I must do. Is he here?'

'Where else would he be? This is his *paradise lost*.' She made air quotes.

Lottie vaguely remembered reading an excerpt from Milton's poem for her Leaving Cert a million years ago. The fall of mankind brought about by Adam and Eve? Mmm.

The PA pressed a button on her console. 'There's a detective here to talk to you, Owen. Yeah. Grand, so.' She hung up and pointed to a door. 'He's in there. Be warned.'

'What?'

'He's in a pose.'

Lottie knocked on the door and entered without waiting for a reply. Inside, a man wearing black leggings and a sleeveless gym top was upside down in a handstand against the wall.

'I'll be thirty seconds,' he said.

Lottie listened to the soft pan-pipe music as she glanced around. A phone lay on the floor beside him, and from her angle she couldn't make out his features. She counted to thirty in her head, and he must have been doing likewise, because he suddenly folded over, let his feet fall to the floor and stood upright.

He held out a sweaty hand. 'Owen Dalton. How can I help you?'

Lottie introduced herself, adding, 'I want to ask you about a client of yours. Éilis Lawlor.'

'I have a huge clientele, so I don't know everyone personally. I'll have to check the members list.'

'I'd appreciate that.'

He moved smoothly around a narrow glass desk to sit on an inversion chair. She recognised it as one used by people with back trouble. So much for the yoga, she thought.

As he brought up a document on a silver-backed MacBook Pro, Lottie noticed his thin, almost gaunt face crease with a frown. He had a goatee beard and dark curly hair. His long fingers ceased tapping. He looked at her. Blue eyes so light they were almost transparent quizzed her without a word. She waited him out, and at last he broke the silence.

'Can I enquire as to why you're asking about Mrs Lawlor?'

'She hasn't been in contact with her family for over twenty-four hours. I believe she is a member here. When was she last at a class?'

'Don't you need a warrant for that information? At the very least, I need to have her permission.'

'I haven't time for this. I believe Éilis is dead. Murdered.'

'Oh God, that's terrible. And I heard Mrs O'Loughlin was found murdered yesterday. What's going on in this town?'

'Was Jennifer a member here also?'

'As she is no longer with us, I can confirm she was a member, though I don't think she'd attended for some time.'

She noticed how he talked about the women formally. She preferred to call victims by their forenames. It made their deaths more personal. She figured Owen Dalton was aged anywhere between twenty-five and forty-five. No lines on his face, but with Botox and other such therapies trending, that didn't mean a thing.

'When did Jennifer last attend a session?'

He bent his head of sweaty curls and tapped the screen. 'Her membership runs out at the end of the month. It's six weeks since she was here. What happened to her?'

'When was Éilis Lawlor last here?'

He gulped. More tapping of keys. His initial reluctance to divulge information seemed to evaporate. 'Monday. The seven-thirty class.'

'Morning or evening?'

'Evening.'

'Who's her instructor?'

'I am.'

'And were you also Jennifer's?'

'Yes.'

'How many instructors do you employ?'

'I have three freelance. I'm full-time. This is a deluxe service and—'

'So two women from your classes have—'

'Sessions, not classes. My studio is exclusive, expensive and beneficial for my clients. Believe me, I value my business too much to do anything bordering on unethical.'

'You think abduction and murder is bordering on unethical?' She couldn't help her sharpness. He was too bloody calm.

He opened his mouth, then shut it again. He bowed his head and stared at his manicured nails. Lottie hid her own bitten ones in her pockets.

'Listen, Owen, I am not accusing you of anything. All I need is information.'

'I can't tell you anything other than that both women were members here. GDPR and—'

'Yeah, okay. Were either of them friendly with other members?'

'Not that I noticed.'

'Ever see them talking to each other?'

'No, but that doesn't mean they didn't.'

'Is Helena McCaul a member?'

He glanced at whatever list he had open on the screen. 'No.'

'Orla Keating?'

'Yes, she is.'

She stood. 'Can I have the names of your freelance instructors?'

'Why do you need to talk to them?'

'I just do,' she said irritably. He was really pissing her off. She eyeballed him; he shrank under her stare, then started tapping at keys. She heard a printer hum behind him and he waited for the paper to emerge.

'There you go. But I must be breaking the law by giving you these names.'

'And *I'm* known to break balls, so don't try my patience again.' She made to leave, then turned back. 'Can you tell me where you were Thursday night until this morning?'

'Do I need a solicitor?'

'For God's sake...'

'I was here until late on Thursday doing meditation, and here all day yesterday and late last night. Then I went home. I had my dinner and went to bed.'

'Anyone verify that?'

'If needs be, I can get verification.'

'That would be desirable.' She gave him her card and left.

Standing at her car, she ran through the conversation she'd just had. Then she sat in and started the engine. For the life of her she couldn't figure out what made her uneasy. Either she'd missed something, or there was something relevant that he'd not said. Shaking her head, she drove back to the station. It struck her then what she hadn't been able to figure out earlier. SunUp was marketed as an exclusive deluxe facility, but it seemed to be a failing enterprise.

43

McKeown felt his head swell with the heat pulsing through the office. He'd been interrogating websites and calling the Companies Registration Office, and now he was on the phone to the revenue office in Athlone. Twenty-five minutes on hold and his patience was as thin as his angry lips. He almost killed the call just as someone came back to him.

'Detective? I might have something for you under Jennifer O'Loughlin's maiden name, Jennifer Whelan. But I believe I need a warrant to give you the information.'

Who was he talking to? Anne, Annette? 'As the person I am enquiring about is now deceased – murdered, I may add – I don't think you have anything to worry about. It's just a line of inquiry, Anne.'

'It's Annette. Okay, if you say so. I'm emailing it to you now. Please don't get me in trouble.'

'Don't worry at all. I really appreciate all your help.'

'Thank you, Detective McKeown. You know, I know a McKeown woman and—'

Shit. 'Have to rush, sorry, but thanks again, Annette.'

He hung up and stared at his computer screen, hitting refresh every five seconds. At last the email appeared.

'Got it!' He turned around and found he was alone in the office. No one to share his success with. He made sure the details were on his iPad and went off to find Garda Martina Brennan.

'You should have got someone else to come with you.' Martina was like a coiled spring on the seat. Though he loved women, not counting Lottie Parker, he didn't understand them.

'You and I are a team, gorgeous.'

'I'm not a detective and I know I'm far from gorgeous, so I'm not falling for your bullshit. If you wanted a lowly guard to stoke your ego, you could have asked Garda Lei.'

'His mouth isn't as cute as yours, princess.'

'You're full of shit.'

He shifted uneasily as he turned the car out of the station and drove past the cathedral. 'What's eating you?'

'You're a player, Sam. I told you before, I don't like how you treat your wife and kids.'

'My family has nothing to do with you.'

'Yes, they have. I'm the cause of how you treat them.'

'Don't get up on your high horse. If it wasn't you, it'd be someone else.' Fuck! Now he'd gone and put his size twelve in it.

She twisted ninety degrees on the seat and he could feel the heat of her stare burning the side of his face. He didn't dare take his eyes off the road.

'We are done, Sam. Finished. Finito. I'll do this search with you and then I don't ever want to be alone with you in a car or the office or anywhere else for that matter. Your attitude makes me sick. I really don't know how I could have been so blinkered.

I was warned often enough. Just drive, and don't talk or even look at me.'

He remained silent, desperately trying to put a damper on his temper. Someone had got to her. It wasn't his wife, because as far as she knew, the affair was over. It had to be Kirby. He would beat ten shades of shite out of him. He clutched the steering wheel so tight, his knuckles turned white. The silence dragged on as his boiling anger threatened to consume him.

'Where are we going, anyhow?' she asked eventually.

He didn't trust himself to answer.

The building was the smallest of three located on a square plot of land just outside Ragmullin. It was less than two kilometres from where Jennifer's body had been found on the waste ground at Ballyglass Business Park. Two of the units housed a furniture showroom and a shop selling plants and garden accessories. The one he was interested in was used as a lock-up. He eyed the roller security door and wondered where he could source a key to enter.

Martina flung off her seat belt and exited the car before he had the engine switched off. He sighed, unfolded his long legs, and followed her into the furniture shop.

She was speaking to a man at a desk inside a small glassed-in office.

'And you haven't seen Jennifer O'Loughlin around here in how long, Ted?' she asked.

'Oh, must be two months now. But I don't see all the comings and goings around here. That's the wife's forte,' he chuckled.

'Do you have keys to her lock-up, by any chance? We need to search it.'

McKeown stood back and let Martina work her charm. He

felt miffed, because he was the one who had sourced the address in the first place.

'Jennifer gave me a spare key in case the alarm went off when she was at work or away. I'll have to look for it.'

As he started to mooch through drawers, McKeown stepped forward. 'Did Jennifer go away often, Ted?'

'Don't know. I never had to respond to an alarm for her, anyhow. It could be one of those dummy alarms. To put off would-be burglars.'

'When did you last see her?'

The plump man, who looked over seventy, wheezed as he searched. 'I've already told your colleague it was more than two months ago. Didn't think it'd be the last time I'd lay eyes on the young woman. Do you have any idea who killed her?'

'I was about to ask you the same question,' McKeown said.

The man stood bolt upright, rage threading the veins on his cheeks. 'That sounds like some sort of accusation. I barely knew her.'

'No need to get all defensive. Was anyone bothering her? Did she ever confide any fears?'

'We hardly spoke. She must have been here in the evenings. Don't think I saw her much during the day.'

'It must be very dark out here in the evenings.'

'All the units have sensor lights on the outer walls.' The man kept rummaging, pulling out docket books and screwdrivers. 'Damn nuisance with foxes and badgers. That garden centre next door attracts all sorts of animals.'

'It's the two-legged sort we're interested in.' McKeown twisted his hands into fists in his pockets to stem his impatience. 'Any sign of that key yet?'

'If I'd found it, I wouldn't be still searching, would I?' Ted looked up before opening another drawer. 'Ah. This is what I wanted.' He took out a small tin box. It was locked. 'The missus might have the key to it. I'll give her a shout.'

'Give it here.' McKeown walked into the cramped office. He snapped the box from Ted's hand. Grabbing one of the screwdrivers, he jimmied the lock and it flicked open.

'You'll have to reimburse the missus for that.'

The box was full of old keys. 'Which one is it?'

'How would I know?'

'Jesus, you're some help.' He lifted up a bunch of keys and searched through them. 'Show me the one you use to open your shop. Jennifer's key is probably similar.'

Ted obliged. After another minute of looking, McKeown was certain he had the right key, and he headed out towards Jennifer's unit, leaving Martina to placate the furniture man.

'Thank God,' he muttered, when the key worked and the roller door began its slow ascent.

'You didn't have to be so rude,' Martina said, joining him.

'He didn't have to be wasting so much time staring at your chest.'

'You're such an arsehole, you know that?'

'It's been said before.' He waited until the roller shuddered to a halt above his head before he pushed in the wooden door behind it. No alarm. No key required. That was a blessing, as he would have strung Ted up if he'd had to watch him shuffling through any more drawers.

It was dark inside, except for the light coming through the door behind him. Searching the wall, he found a switch. Two fluorescent light tubes hanging from the ceiling buzzed and crackled before the place lit up.

'Oh fuck,' Martina exclaimed behind him.

McKeown said nothing. He was struck dumb at the sight before him.

44

With no customers, and unable to concentrate on work, Helena shut up the shop and left. Walking to her car she wondered if it was okay for her to drive. It had only been one vodka. But on top of what she'd had over the last two nights, it might be a mistake. Indecisive, she stood beside her car, keys in her hand.

'Hi there, Helena!'

She jumped and turned quickly. 'God Almighty, Orla, you shouldn't come up behind people like that.'

'Oh, I'm sorry. You'd think it was the middle of the night the way you reacted. Are you all right? You look peaky.'

Peaky? She looked positively shit. 'I'm a nervous wreck. Did you hear the news?' She leaned against the car to get her equilibrium back. Maybe she was still drunk.

'What news?'

She thought Orla looked wary, her hands stuffed in the pockets of a long black blazer, her eyes darting around the car park.

'The guards think they've found Éilis. They asked me to identify a body.'

'What? Oh my God! She's dead too? Helena, this is serious.'

Orla took her by the elbow. 'Do you want me to go along with you?'

'Thanks for the offer, but I'd say it won't be for a while. They're still running down leads.'

'What leads?'

'I don't know, but they seem sure they have her body. This is a nightmare.'

'You need a stiff drink and we need to talk. Let's go across to Fallon's.'

'It's the middle of the day, Orla.'

'I don't care what time it is. We have to discuss this. We could be next. No argument. I'm buying.'

Against her better judgement – what judgement? – Helena allowed herself to be led through the car park and up the road to the pub. She barely had time to wonder why Orla had appeared out of nowhere, before she was on her second drink of the day and it wasn't yet lunchtime.

———

Jackie glanced over quickly, then stared. Her eyes were not deceiving her.

She couldn't believe she was looking at her son walking on the opposite footpath. He was with a tall teenage girl, his hand clasped in hers. The girl's blonde hair, tied up in a tight ponytail, swayed as she chatted with him. She looked familiar. Then it struck her. She was one of Inspector Lottie Parker's daughters! Her ex-husband had really gone and done it now, entrusting the care of her son to that lot.

Pressing the button on the crossing, she waited for the traffic to stop so that she could follow them. She wanted to hug and kiss Sergio. To whip him away from the Parker family, away from grotty Ragmullin, and never have to set foot in the town again.

She paused.

That'd be rash, wouldn't it? She needed to do this correctly. If she crossed any lines, invisible or not, she might lose her son for ever. Her past would cloud any judge's decision if it came to a court case. And given that Mark was under Lottie Parker's influence, this could very well end up in court. Jackie did not want to enter any courtroom. With Lottie in the picture, he would never accept her deal. She wanted her son, but she needed safety. Mark Boyd could guarantee both.

Waiting until the traffic flowed again, she watched them entering a pub. How was this allowed? An eight-year-old boy and a teenage girl walking into a pub in the middle of the day. She should take a photograph. It might help to have proof of Mark's ineptitude as a father. Once again she mentally kicked herself, like she had done every day since she'd told him about the existence of his son, even though it had been necessary at the time. She had been under pressure, her cover almost blown in her quest to bring down a drug gang in Malaga, and she couldn't place Sergio in further danger. She'd taken the step she'd avoided for eight years and contacted her ex-husband. She'd thought it was for the best at the time, but the threat to her life hadn't surfaced, and now she was back in the town she hated, having to rectify a problem of her own making.

Making up her mind, she followed them into Fallon's pub.

———

Chloe fetched two bowls of soup and brought them to the table. The light shining in the window gave the pub a brightness that wasn't there when she worked behind the bar at night. It seemed like a different place.

'You'll need to blow on it, squirt. It's hot.'

'That's not my name.'

He was so serious, it was cute. 'If you drink all your soup and eat two slices of bread, guess where I'll bring you later?'

'Papa told me this morning. You are bringing me to swim in the lake.'

'It'll be fun. Now drink up. Soon as we're done here, it's the lake for the whole afternoon.'

She watched as he paused with the spoon halfway to his mouth. 'Why are you rushing? Do you not like me, Chloe?'

'Of course I like you. You're like a little brother.'

'But you have a little brother. Sean isn't that little because he's taller than you, but you're older than him, so that makes him your little brother. Isn't that right?'

She grinned. 'Sean isn't as much fun as you are. We'll have such a good time at the lake, you'll sleep like a baby tonight.'

'I don't want to be like a baby.' He slurped a spoonful of soup. 'Do you really work here?'

'Yeah, for my sins.'

'What sins?'

'It's a figure of speech.'

She was about to explain the turn of phrase to him, but he nodded. The kid was bright, but way too serious. Just like his dad. Not like *her* dad, who'd had a funny bone and liked to find hers by tickling the life out of her. She smiled at the memory.

The pub was pretty full for lunchtime. Her eyes landed on two women nestled in the corner snug, heads close as if they were discussing a conspiracy. Hadn't they been in the other night? At the widows' thing? She'd read online from an anonymous source that the woman found murdered had been part of that group. With her curiosity piqued, she drank her soup without noticing and kept her attention glued to the pair.

'Do you know those women?' Sergio asked.

'Nope.'

'It's not nice to stare.'

'Are you finished? We should get a move on while it's still warm enough for the lake.'

She waited while he slurped down the last of his soup, then told him to sit tight while she brought the dishes to the bar. She caught sight of a woman seated at the end of the counter, her eyes fixed on Sergio. What the hell was Jackie Boyd doing back in Ragmullin?

Chloe tapped her card on the machine and rushed back to the boy. She had to get him out of there before Boyd's ex-wife pounced. She wondered if she should tell Boyd, but knew in her heart that she'd rather not.

45

The unit rented by Jennifer was constructed of bare concrete blocks with a galvanised roof. An array of canvases were stacked against the walls. That wasn't what had stopped them in their tracks, though.

'What the hell is that?' McKeown said.

'Do you think maybe it might be a car?' Martina said.

He turned at her sarcasm. 'Really? Here was me thinking it was a fucking bus.'

She had her phone out taking photos of the vehicle. 'The only car registered to either Jennifer or her husband is parked outside her house.'

He walked around the car and peered in the window on the driver's side. 'How did Jennifer get this white Hyundai in here?'

'Gloves,' Martina said, and handed him a pair.

'Why?'

'It might have been involved in a crime. It's been hidden in a lock-up for a reason.'

'True,' he conceded. 'Anything show up on the registration number?'

'I'll have to radio it in.'

'Wait a minute. I want to have a look around first.' McKeown marched around the car and moved towards the rear of the building. 'There's a big rolling security door here. The car was driven in this way.'

'Will we look outside?'

'In a minute. I want to see if the car is unlocked, and if there's anything in it.' He tugged on the gloves and depressed the handle. The door opened.

'That's a stroke of good luck.' Martina leaned over, trying to see around him.

McKeown inhaled her sweet perfume before another odour invaded his senses. 'I smell bleach.'

'There's only one reason someone would clean a car with bleach.'

'To cover up something. A crime?'

He tapped on the torch on his phone to have a better look. The upholstery looked pristine, but the odour was coming from the footwell.

'We'll need to call SOCOs. There might have been blood in here.'

He opened the other doors and looked in at the rear seats. A stronger smell of bleach. No papers, wrappers or dirt of any kind was visible.

'A body in the boot?' Martina said.

'Doubt it.' All the same, he moved carefully around the car and pressed the boot. It popped up and he peered inside.

'No body.' The inside looked and smelled similarly clean. He shut it again and checked the tyres. No mud or debris caught in the rims or grooves. He shone the torch underneath. 'A new car wouldn't be this clean.'

'It has a 2014 registration.'

'You know what I mean.' He stood. 'Why has it been cleaned so meticulously? And what the hell is it doing in a lock-up rented by Jennifer O'Loughlin?'

'We need to find out who it's registered to.'

'Radio it in now. I'm going to have a look outside.'

As Martina got busy, McKeown walked the perimeter, which was lined by hedges. There was a concrete yard either side leading to a paved space at the rear. Easy enough for someone to drive a car round and into the unit. The security door was similar to the one at the front. The rear was used to bring stuff in and out. Was the car there before Jennifer rented the unit, or had she rented it for this specific purpose? When they found out who owned the car, they might have an answer.

Turning, he bumped into Martina. He knew from her flushed face that she had the name of the vehicle owner.

'You won't believe this,' she said.

'Try me.'

'It's registered to a man who disappeared a year ago. Tyler Keating.'

'Really? I wasn't here then, but I heard Kirby talking about it this morning.'

'The thing is, like Jennifer, Tyler Keating's wife Orla is a member of the Life After Loss widows' group.'

46

Jane Dore, the state pathologist, had just arrived back at Tullamore hospital from her preliminary examination of the scene at the lake when Lottie reached her on the phone.

'Hi, Lottie. The body isn't here yet.'

'Did you get to have a look at her face? I need confirmation that it's Éilis Lawlor.'

'Garda Lei showed me the missing woman's photograph. It's her.'

Emitting a long, low sigh, Lottie said, 'I knew it was, but it's still a shock. Her poor kids.'

'I'd hate your job, having to tell them.'

'Yeah, but I wouldn't swap with you. Shares in Vicks VapoRub would sky-rocket. What can you tell me?'

'Not much until her body arrives. Similar injuries to your first victim. I could see splinters of timber snagged in her wounds. Her eyes have been removed.'

'Good Lord. Was she killed by a gunshot?'

'No, and I didn't see any sign of what did kill her. You'll have to wait for the post-mortem.'

'How long has she been dead?'

'The weather has been warm and we don't know how long she's been outside. Maybe six hours, but don't quote me. From visual inspection, I didn't notice any frostbite.'

'Are you saying it might not be the same killer?'

'I can't answer that, Lottie. The physical injuries that I could see suggest she was killed by the same person who murdered Jennifer O'Loughlin, but I can't confirm it until I do the post-mortem.'

'That's fine. Thanks, Jane.'

After hanging up, Lottie stared at the wall in her office. All she could think of was the worried faces of Éilis's children. She hated her job at times like this. She would wait for Helena to identify the body before breaking the terrible news to Roman and Becky. And, she hoped the media didn't go public with the story before that.

She needed to talk to her superintendent. For that, she needed support.

'Boyd. You're with me.'

Superintendent Farrell stood at the window, her back to them. She turned around and fixed Lottie with a sharp glare.

'What is your rationale for requesting a security detail for this Helena McCaul?'

Lottie's update hadn't panned out the way she'd expected. The super was latching on to one aspect alone. 'Both of the dead women were members of this Life After Loss group, and so is Helena. She could be next.'

'You think so, do you? You should investigate the group a bit more. Maybe our killer is someone with a grudge against the women. Find out who else is involved in it. I'm sure there are others besides this McCaul woman.'

'Jennifer was the first to die, but it was Éilis who established the group. Taking your point logically, she should have been killed first.'

Farrell walked into Lottie's space and looked up at her. 'Logic? There is nothing logical about anything you have told me.' She took a step back. 'But I'm also aware that to a sane person, there is very little logic to any murder. I believe I am sane, even though you push me to the limits more times than I can count.'

'Is that a no?' Lottie glanced at Boyd, and was glad to see he looked as confused as she felt.

'Yes, but it's not a definite no.'

'What is it then?' Lottie asked, totally bewildered.

'Talk to the McCaul woman and get as much information as you can about the group, including its past and present members. Build up a profile. Then talk to me again.'

'There's another woman involved in the group that we know about. Orla Keating. Her husband went missing a year ago. Never found.'

'Are you thinking that this missing man, who is more than likely dead, has risen from his unknown grave to kill all around him?'

'No, that's not what I said. I'm only—'

'Just warn the women to be careful. Dismissed.'

Outside the door, Boyd shook his head. 'I have absolutely no idea.'

'Neither have I, but we need to check up on Orla Keating and talk to Helena again.'

'We talked to her earlier. It might spook her if we get back to her so soon.'

'When the body is ready to be formally identified, it will be a genuine excuse to contact her.'

'I'm with you on that.'

'At least we can agree on one thing.'

'What's that supposed to mean?'

'You need to get back to playing ball, Boyd. You're distracted. And with two dead women and a killer on the loose, I need you totally focused.'

'And *you're* always focused, are you?'

'I do my best.'

'You're accusing me of below-par work? That's unfair, Lottie.'

She noticed that his ears appeared to stick out more when he was angry. 'Just concentrate, okay?'

'Fine!' He pushed past her and rushed down the corridor, banging the office door behind him.

'Have it your way,' she muttered. Running her hand through her badly-in-need-of-a-wash hair, she wondered if she had burned her last remaining bridge with him.

Her phone chirped in her pocket. Chloe. Probably about Rose. She couldn't answer it until she calmed down. She rejected the call and wondered if Jane would once more succeed in getting the dead to speak to her. At least the dead couldn't talk back to you or bang doors in your face.

Before she could make the call, McKeown's name lit up her screen.

47

She met McKeown at the top of the stairs and walked into the office with him.

'Fill me in.'

'With the discovery of artwork in the unit and the fact she isn't on social media, I figured Jennifer must have had a website.'

'And?'

'I found it under her maiden name, Whelan. She rented the lock-up under that name too.'

'She rented it before she was married, then?'

He shrugged. 'Think I'll need a warrant for that information unless someone can tell us.'

'Maybe she forgot to change the name over. It's a dead end, McKeown.'

'Not quite.' His face held a grin that she thought was a bit uncalled for, with two murders on their books. 'There's a white Hyundai parked inside the lock-up. And the car stinks of bleach.'

'What the hell?' Lottie tried to get her head around what the detective was saying.

'I called in a couple of SOCOs to examine it. I left two uniforms on security detail there.'

'Do you know who owns the car?'

McKeown looked like the cat that had got the cream. 'Belongs to Tyler Keating. He went missing a year ago.'

Kirby shot up from his chair. 'That's the cold case I mentioned to you, boss. Tyler's wife is Orla Keating. She's part of the Life After Loss group, like the two dead women.'

'So you're the numbskull who was running that case?' McKeown smirked, unable to contain his delight.

'You weren't even based here back then,' Kirby shouted, and Martina moved to stand between the two men.

Lynch appeared at the door. 'What round are we on?'

'Shush, don't wind them up,' Martina said, in an effort to restore peace.

'Calm down, lads,' Lottie said. 'We need analysis on that car. It might help to unlock the two murders.' She could almost smell the testosterone levels in the room as she spoke. She looked at Kirby. 'You asked for permission to reopen the case this morning. Because of this new information, I want you to set up a small team to investigate it. Take Martina with you. Go over everything, including Tyler Keating's bank accounts and financials. And find out how Jennifer O'Loughlin is connected to him.'

She turned to McKeown. 'I need to know everything about Jennifer. Why was she missing for over a month without anyone noticing or reporting it? Where was she during that time? Helena McCaul suspected there might have been rancour at the dental clinic. She also said Éilis and Jennifer were the first members of the widows' group. See what you can find. Then cross-reference all the information you find with Kirby.'

'Certainly.' Then, as if he realised he should be annoyed that she had allocated Martina to his nemesis, he said, 'As

Martina has been with me on this today, I'd like to hold on to her.'

'I'm sure you would,' Kirby snapped.

Lottie glared. 'Will you pair stop? I've said what I've said, so get to it.'

As she made her way into her own office, she heard McKeown mutter to Kirby, 'Let's see how far you get with her. She isn't your type.'

'And what type would that be?' Kirby snarled.

'The type that sits in a window in Amsterdam.'

———

The atmosphere in the Keating house had always been electrically charged whenever Tyler was around. Now, when she stepped through her front door, Orla couldn't help the smile that spread over her face and the flush of warmth flooding through her heart. She felt safe. No one could touch her or shout at her. She relished the peace.

She opened the refrigerator to get some juice, and shuddered at a memory dredged from the depths of the past. She could almost hear Tyler's voice barking at her.

'I don't know why you have to buy the expensive stuff. Lidl do a perfectly acceptable own-brand orange juice'

'Sorry. I like this one.'

He'd snapped the Tropicana carton out of her hand and shoved it back on the shelf. 'In future, I'll do the grocery shopping.'

She'd nodded, knowing there was no point in arguing with him. She still had her own wages, so at least he couldn't snatch those from her.

'You really are stupid for a woman who is meant to be intelligent.'

'I suppose I am.'

'No supposing about it.'

'But we're not short of money. There really isn't a need to skimp on food.'

He'd slammed his hand against the fridge door, causing two ceramic magnets to fall off and smash on the floor.

'Who said anything about skimping? I merely pointed out there is no need to waste money when there are perfectly suitable alternatives. Compounds my theory about your stupidity.'

Time for appeasement. Swallowing her pride, she said, 'You're right, Tyler. Sometimes I can be so stupid. I'm lucky to have you to point it out to me.'

Stepping closer, his spittle landing on her face, he snarled, 'Are you mocking me? Yes, you *are* stupid. You need to know your place in our marriage.'

'I do. Honestly, I do.'

She'd tried not to cower away from him, knowing it gave him fuel to torment her. And she had to hold her tongue. She couldn't incite him further or she might blurt out what she had learned about him. If she did that, it would surely result in a burst lip, or even worse. One of the reasons he had insisted she work from home was to conceal the bruises he regularly meted out. They were becoming more vicious and more frequent. But that was only one reason. The other was more deadly.

The knowledge she had would land him in jail for a very long time. But she had to bide her time before she took action.

She drew herself back to the present with a shudder of her shoulders. Even though he'd been gone a year, she felt him stalk her like a shadow; his voice a whisper in her ear she couldn't dislodge. It would take more time, but she didn't have the luxury of time. With Jennifer and Éilis dead, there were few left who knew the truth. She was one of them. Helena thought she knew too, but Orla knew different. Helena! Shit!

She rushed back outside to the car.

48

Helena McCaul's shop was closed, the door locked.

'Do you have her home address handy?' Lottie asked. She needed to take the woman to identify Éilis's body, and then she could start seriously questioning her.

'Sure,' Boyd said.

They drove on, silence shrouding the atmosphere in the car. He pulled up outside a large detached house on a relatively new estate. 'No sign of a car. It looks deserted.'

Lottie went to the door and lifted the chrome knocker, letting it fall back with a clunk. When no one answered, she opened the side gate and went around the back. The garden was a little overgrown, but it had the trappings associated with a child. A small Spider-Man bicycle lying against a play sandpit.

She hammered the back door before looking in through the window. No sign of life.

'Didn't she say something about her mother minding her son?'

'Yeah,' Boyd said.

'Maybe Helena is with her, but we don't have the mother's name to look up her address.'

Back in the car, Boyd got on the radio and made enquiries. 'Think this is her. Kathleen Foley. She lives in Ballinisky.'

Lottie watched him scribble down the address. 'Why were you late today?'

Pulling out of the estate, he said, 'Your mother and Chloe were in the middle of a row when I arrived.'

'Oh shit.' Lottie closed her eyes, trying to block out the image. 'I'm so sorry you had to witness that. Christ, what am I going to do, Boyd?'

'It's a tough one. But you need to be patient. It isn't Rose's fault.'

She twisted in the seat and looked at him earnestly as he drove. 'I know that, but she is so different from the woman I knew. Her body is even shrinking as well as her mind. It's so sad.'

'It's called ageing.'

'And it's difficult to understand.'

'Don't even try. Give her time and space. Can you imagine how she feels?'

'She is in this zone that no one can penetrate, especially me, and she wants to go back to her own house. She can't live there alone, Boyd. I'm scared for her.'

'You need support. Are there agencies you can contact?'

'Most have a six-month waiting list.'

'Register with all of them.'

'I want to help her, Boyd, but she repels me at every inter-vention and I end up upset and angry.'

He drove in silence and she berated herself for offloading her problems on his already weighted shoulders. Before she could say anything further, he had parked the car outside a brightly painted house with a modern lime-green door sporting black chrome accessories. The garden could do with better maintenance.

The door was opened by a tall woman. As she stood out

onto the step, her long hair shone with a reddish hue under the sun.

'How can I help you?' she said, once Lottie had made their introductions.

'Is Helena here?'

'Helena? God, no.' The woman glanced at her watch. Lottie figured she was in her fifties. 'She'd be at work at this time of the day. I don't know how many times I've told her to give up that loss-making venture, but she won't listen to me. Girls and their mothers, ha!' Her laugh was strained, and Lottie heard pain behind her words.

'When did you last see your daughter?'

Kathleen's face paled. 'Is she in trouble?'

'Not that I'm aware of. We need her to identify her friend's body.' On seeing the look of horror falling across Kathleen's face, Lottie added, 'She agreed to do it.'

'Whose body? Not that poor woman they're reporting on the news this morning, is it? Or is it the woman you found yesterday?'

'I can't confirm the victim's identity. That's why we need to talk to Helena.'

'I haven't seen her for over a week. She doesn't call that often. Her shop takes up all her time.'

Lottie glanced at Boyd, who shrugged, looking mystified.

'Let me get this straight, Mrs Foley,' he said. 'You haven't seen Helena for over a week, but aren't you caring for her son and their dog at the moment?'

'Her son? You must be mistaken. Ah, now I'm thinking you're looking for someone else.' Relief flooded the woman's face. 'Helena doesn't have a son, or a dog.'

Boyd stepped forward. 'She definitely mentioned that you were caring for her son while she was out on Thursday night, and while she was at work.'

'No, you're wrong.'

'Why would she say that?' Lottie scratched her chin, perplexed by this information. 'I can understand that she might still be grieving for her husband, but why would she make up a story about having a son?'

'Now I'm convinced you have the wrong person. Helena's not married.'

'But she said... she told us...' Lottie floundered helplessly.

Boyd said, 'She said her husband's name was Gerald.'

'My daughter isn't married and has no children. I think you both should come in and have a cup of tea. We need to talk about Helena.'

49

Having to witness McKeown's performance in front of the boss churned Kirby's stomach. The angst didn't mix well with his recent chicken salad, and his tummy rumbled loudly, craving its normal fat intake.

'Will I fetch you something to eat?' Martina asked.

'No thanks. I want to look at that car you found. Will you do me a favour? See if you can uncover anything to connect Jennifer O'Loughlin to either or both of the Keatings.'

'No bother.'

'Read over the file. It's open on my computer.'

He grabbed his jacket and shuffled his arms into it. Leaving Martina looking happy with desk work, he made his way outside and sent a text to Amy. He hoped she might be on her lunch break, then they could grab soup and Cafferty's house-special sandwiches.

He decided to walk for the exercise and was heading towards Dolan's supermarket when her reply pinged on his phone. He read it and swore.

'Dammit to hell.'

Another hour before her lunch break. He kept on going,

breathing heavily as he laboured with the heat of the day. Why was weight so easy to put on and a bloody nuisance to shift?

Amy was standing at the self-scan checkout and her face lit up when she saw him. He felt a warm glow, like he felt after a Big Mac Meal.

'Hi there,' she said. 'Did you not get my text? I'm stuck here for another hour.'

'No bother. I needed to pick up a few things. For tonight, not for now.' Shit, he was making a bags of this. 'How's your day?'

'Same old, same old.' Her smile was infectious.

'Where's this Luke bloke who's giving you a hard time?'

'Shh. Don't make a scene.' She glanced around as if to ensure no one was watching them. Was she embarrassed by him?

'God, I'd never do that to you,' he said.

'Okay, but don't make it obvious. Over your left shoulder, the guy talking to the security guard, that's Luke.'

'I'm going to look at the bananas. I'll be back.'

Smiling at her warmly, though he really wanted to give her a hug, he wiped his brow with a tissue, then turned and moved towards the fruit and vegetable section. Luke was standing close to the security guard.

Kirby picked up a punnet of strawberries and casually glanced at the dude. He appeared to be early twenties, and was gesticulating wildly, talking about some football game. A mop of dark hair flopped over his forehead, with the sides shaved. A fade, Kirby supposed. A new name for short back and sides. Luke's skin was clear and pale, with an eyebrow piercing and train-track braces on yellowing teeth. He was dressed in the all-black supermarket uniform, and Kirby thought it made him look sinister.

He could bide his time, but he wasn't sure he could stem his anger. This pumped-up prick was making life hard for Amy.

'Excuse me, are these fresh?' He wandered over and lifted a bunch of Fyffes bananas.

'The date is on them,' Luke said. He moved away from the security guard and snatched them from Kirby's hand. 'This sticker is the best-before date.'

'Ah, thanks. Didn't see that.'

'Should have gone to Specsavers,' Luke said, and Kirby caught the sneer in his tone.

'Are you making fun of me?'

'It's a joke. Get a life, old man.'

That did it. Kirby reached out and grabbed Luke's wrist with his free hand, tugging the lad towards him.

'You need to mind your manners, pup. I'm a detective and I don't like how you talk to people.'

Luke's lip curled towards his nose. 'What's your problem? Can't take a joke?'

'As well as annoying your customers, I hear you're harassing members of staff.'

The macho smirk faded from Luke's face, and he took a step back.

Kirby held on tightly and drew him closer. 'Stay away from Amy Corcoran, or I'll have your balls for breakfast. Got it?'

'You can't talk to me like that.'

'And you have no right to intimidate your colleagues. Am I making myself clear?'

'You need to make up your mind. Which is it I'm supposed to be guilty of? Harassment or intimidation?' Luke twisted his arm to dislodge Kirby's grip.

Amy arrived, flushed and flustered. She tugged Kirby's sleeve. 'What's going on?'

Luke looked from one to the other, then pulled himself free from Kirby's grasp and laughed. 'Is this your dad? He was warning me off you, as if I'd even consider someone like *you*.'

'That's enough,' Kirby said. 'That's not what I meant and you know it.'

'Larry, give it up,' Amy pleaded. 'Please go, and I'll talk to you later.'

Luke snorted with laughter. 'Oh, now I get it. He's the guy who has you up to ninety. God, Amy, you could have picked someone your own age.'

Kirby raised a fist, but she snatched his arm away.

'Larry, give it a rest.'

He knew she was attempting to defuse the situation. He wanted to land the young prick into the middle of next week, but a muttering crowd had gathered at the checkouts, all staring across as if a half-price sale had been announced for fruit and veg.

'Can you take your break now?' he said. 'I want to talk to you.'

'Go on,' Luke said, still smirking with glee. 'He might have a heart attack if you don't.'

'Piss off, Luke.' She pointed to the door. 'Wait outside, Larry. I'll be a few minutes.'

Shouldering his way out by Luke, Kirby went to stand outside, feeling like he had been the naughty one and got blamed for something he hadn't done.

She was with him in five minutes, just as he'd made up his mind to leave. She shook her head angrily and dragged him away from the shop.

'You've made things worse for me.'

They sat in Cafferty's with two bowls of untouched soup and towering sandwiches. Both were staring unseeing at the television over the bar.

'He's a smug little bastard. He needed taking down a peg or two,' Kirby said.

'That may be so, but I have to work with him and now he'll be relentless.'

'Report him.'

'I can manage, and I don't need you interfering.' She ran a hand over her forehead. 'I shouldn't have said anything to you about him.'

'I thought I was helping.'

'Well, you weren't.'

They lapsed into an awkward silence, and Kirby wondered when – or if – he'd ever get to understand women.

50

A feeling of claustrophobia engulfed Lottie once she was in Kathleen's overcrowded living room. It was similar to how she'd felt in Orla Keating's home. *Hoarder* was the word that sprang to mind. A pot of tea and three mugs appeared on the table with milk in a carton and sugar in a white bowl. She was grateful for the tea to clear her head a little. But she still had no idea why Helena had lied to them.

'Why did she join a widows' group if she hadn't a husband in the first place?' she asked.

Kathleen sipped her tea slowly before putting down the mug, her hand shaking. 'Helena is an only child. She found it difficult to make friends, and when she did, she found it hard to hold on to the few she had. She was always lonely as a child, and I think she sought comfort in imaginary friends. She had no luck with boyfriends. In her thirty-three years on this earth, she's struggled in relationships. But to answer your question, I have no idea why she joined this widows' group.'

'The group is called Life After Loss. Could she be mourning the fact that she's lonely?'

'Maybe. It's hard to understand how her mind works. But it's inconceivable that she would make up a child for notice.'

Lottie thought the same, but Helena might be inventing a life she had yearned for. Why join in with women who were mourning, though? It didn't make sense. Or did it? Was it sympathy she craved?

'She called her husband Gerald and her son Noah. Do those names mean anything to you?'

'What? Don't think so.'

'What else can you tell me about her?'

Kathleen was silent for a moment. 'Helena's biological father cut his stick when I told him I was pregnant. Left me as an eighteen-year-old unmarried mother to fend for myself. Told me to head to England for an abortion. Even if I'd wanted to take the boat to Liverpool for the procedure, he never gave me a penny to fund it. I never laid eyes on him after that.'

'You told Helena this?'

'Yes.'

'Maybe she invented an imaginary husband to right her biological dad's wrongs,' Lottie said, trying to make sense of it all. 'Then she had him die and became a fictional widow.'

Kathleen looked horrified. 'It sounds preposterous.'

'Do you think it's possible?'

Lifting her mug, she held it in both hands, still shaking. 'I suppose so. She was also devastated when my husband, her stepdad, died.'

'And you have no idea where we might find your daughter?'

'No, but she disappears for days at a time. You see, Helena developed a love affair with alcohol. She had a stint in rehab, and I'd hoped she had turned that metaphorical corner when she got the shop, but I was wrong.'

'And you can't give me any clue to where she might be now or how to find her?'

'No, I'm sorry. If she contacts me, I'll let you know.'

'I'd appreciate that.' Lottie finished her tea and stood. She handed over a card with her contact details.

Boyd remained seated. 'Kathleen, despite her problems, Helena is doing her best to make a success of her business. Don't be too hard on her.'

Kathleen smiled weakly. 'I fund her business. Again and again, I've dug her out of a financial hole. It's the only way I can keep her onside. I hate to admit this, but Helena is a pathological liar and she can be volatile. She's threatened to cut me out of her life on numerous occasions, and only calls me when she runs out of money.'

'You said you saw her a week ago. What was her mood like when you met her?'

'She was asking for money, per usual. Brought me a concoction of herbs and God knows what.'

'Did you give her what she asked for?' Lottie said.

'Are you a mother, Inspector?'

'I am.'

'Then you know I would give her the shirt off my back if it would make her happy.'

'What did you talk about?'

'The shop, mostly.'

'Did she talk about her friends, Éilis or Jennifer?'

'You have to understand, Helena only knows how to talk about herself.' Kathleen dropped her head before raising it with tears nestled in her eyes.

At the door, Lottie looked back over her shoulder. 'We were at her house. There are children's toys and equipment in her garden. Would she go to those lengths to convince herself she has a child?'

'I don't really know. I haven't been to her new house at all, even though I have a key in case of an emergency.' Kathleen bowed her head again. 'Maybe she wanted to convince someone else. I've given up trying to rationalise the things she does.'

In the car, Lottie and Boyd sat in silence for a few minutes before turning to one another and shaking their heads.

'What do you think?' she said.

'I don't know. But lies will complicate our investigation.'

'You can say that again.'

'Lies—'

'Don't, Boyd, don't. Just drive.'

51

When Madelene Bowen looked up from studying a particularly difficult affidavit on her laptop, she was surprised to find someone standing there staring at her.

'What are you doing here? How did you get past my PA?'

'I told her you specifically wanted to see me in private and didn't want to be disturbed.'

'You didn't have to come here, you know. We could have had a conversation over the phone.'

'I need to look you in the eye when I ask you the question.'

'And what question might that be?'

'Ah, Madelene, you know right well. Why do we have to do this dance around the issue?'

The solicitor glanced at the closed door behind her visitor, then at her phone on the desk. She could call out or hit 999. No need. She was certain she was safe in the confines of her own office.

'You want to know what I know about Damien O'Loughlin, is that it?'

'For someone who's supposed to be so clever, you really take a while to get to the point.'

'I haven't time for this. I have circuit court to get ready for.'

'Thought the courts took the month of August off.'

'The first of September is next week. I have a lot of work to do before then.'

Her visitor pulled out a chair, crossed legs and folded arms. 'I can wait.'

'What is it you want exactly?'

'Jennifer O'Loughlin is dead, and I believe Éilis Lawlor is also dead. Both murdered. Tell me what I want to know or else give me the file.'

'The file is destroyed.'

'That's a lie. I know you wouldn't do that. You need it as backup in case you're blackmailed. Oh, don't paste that horrified mask on your face. I know all about Damien and your firm's involvement. I will get it myself.'

Standing, the visitor walked to the filing cabinet, drawing a finger down the labels until it reached M-N-O. Tugging the drawer, they looked back at Madelene.

'It's locked. Open it.'

'I can guarantee you there's nothing in it to concern you.'

'You know the file I want. Open it.'

Reluctantly Madelene took the bunch of keys from her desk and opened the cabinet. 'Be my guest.'

'*Be my guest.* That's so like you. Sarcastic cow.'

Madelene sat back down and nudged her briefcase containing the offending file further under the desk. Out of sight, out of mind.

The slam of the drawer lifted her out of her musings.

'Where is it?'

'I told you, I destroyed it.'

'You should not have done that.' The visitor came to stand behind Madelene's desk, leaning over, hand on the back of the chair, and spoke into her ear. 'Two women have been murdered. Does that not scare you? It scares me, I can tell you.

You may not know how many you are putting in danger by your silence, but I guarantee it's a lot more than the two who have already died.' Straightening, they moved to stand in front of her. 'These murders are on your head, and I can guarantee if the guards zero in on me, I won't hesitate to drop your name right into their investigation.'

'Is that a warning?'

'It's a threat. You have until the end of the day to get me that file.'

Madelene braced herself for the door to be slammed, but the visitor slipped out of the office as silently as they had entered. Only then did she let out a long, relieved breath.

She needed to read that file again. Then she would destroy it. And after that she'd ensure there was absolutely nothing left on any computer or server that could implicate her firm.

Someone had talked and awakened a murderer.

52

Kirby was accosted by a man who introduced himself as Ted the furniture man.

'Do you have CCTV here, Ted?'

'I hardly have the money to put a lock on the door.'

'Notice anyone around Mrs O'Loughlin's unit recently?'

'I mind my own business. I'm not a busybody.'

'Thanks, anyway.' He made to move off.

Ted tugged him back. 'You might want to talk to the missus. Nothing gets past her.'

'Is she here?'

'Gone up the road to the garage for a sandwich. She'll be back soon. That's if she doesn't bump into someone willing to listen to her gossip.'

'I hope she doesn't spread the word about what's going on here.'

'No one told her not to, and even if they had, it wouldn't make any difference. My missus listens to no one, and that includes me.' He stomped back into his shop.

Kirby scratched his head, trying to make sense of Ted's

words, then smiled to himself. He headed to the lock-up and met Grainne as she was handing over to a member of her team.

'I've to return to the lake,' she said.

'We need you here. This could be a crime scene.'

'There's no evidence of blood or criminal activity in the work space. Just the car, which seems to have been deep-cleaned. I've ordered it to be brought in for further examination. You might be able to download something from its GPS.' She snapped her case shut and looked up at him. 'Get one of your tech team to do it.'

'Has the car been there long?'

'I've no way of knowing. Tyres are dry. No caked mud or dirt that I can see on the doors or underside. It's spotless.'

'Did you swab for fingerprints, blood and the like?'

'I know my job, but the problem is that someone else knows it too. They used bleach on the inside, the tyres and the under-side of the car, and on the rear shutters of the unit. I'm leaving a couple of the team here, but I really have to get...'

'...back to the lake. A current case takes precedence. I understand.'

'A current case with a murder victim in the morgue.'

Grainne was driving out the gate when Kirby saw Ted staring at him. He escaped inside the lock-up, pulled on a pair of gloves and approached the car. There had been no mistake. It was Tyler Keating's. He'd sent out enough alerts about it previously to recognise it and the registration number. Who had driven it in here? When, and why? Nothing he could do until SOCOs had finished, though.

Letting them get on with their work, he glanced at the canvases propped up against the wall. He flicked through them. Blobs of paint that made no sense to him. As he reached behind the largest, at the back of the stack, he pursed his lips in a silent whistle.

Three banker's boxes.

Quickly he moved the paintings to the opposite wall, sweat bubbling like raindrops inside the collar of his shirt with the exertion. The boxes didn't appear to have labels or markings to identify what might be inside. Why were they hidden in here, though? He lifted the lid on one of them. A conglomeration of small trophies and scrolled certificates. He unfurled one. Leaving Cert student of the year awarded to Damien O'Loughlin. He counted seventeen rolled-up certificates. Each one would have to be examined to see if they provided a clue to Jennifer's murder. But it was obvious that this was where she had stored her dead husband's personal belongings.

He replaced the lid and moved to the next box. A flutter of anticipation turned to excitement when he saw what was inside. Bulging buff-coloured files. He flicked through one. They appeared to be solicitor's files. Damien had been a solicitor. Were these copies of work he'd been involved in? Or had he stolen them?

The last box contained more files. He needed to get them to the office immediately. They might mean nothing for the investigation; then again, they might mean everything.

After making the arrangements to have the boxes transported, he went outside and headed to the garden centre to ask the staff it they'd seen Tyler Keating's car being driven in. He learned nothing of consequence.

The car, like the boxes, was a bloody mystery.

53

Lottie called a team briefing after leaving Kathleen Foley's house. When she arrived in the incident room, she was relieved to see the team seated and waiting. She knew what she needed was a shower and a change of clothes, but she hadn't had time for lunch, let alone personal grooming.

'We need to locate Helena McCaul. She's not at her shop, her house or her mother's. She knew both the murdered women. How do we find her?'

'She could be anywhere,' McKeown said. 'Might have gone shopping in Dublin, for all we know.'

'She could already be in the clutches of the killer,' Kirby sniped back. 'But first, boss, I have to tell you about the discovery I made at Jennifer's lock-up.'

'Hey, I'm the one who found the car, so feck off, Kirby.'

'Enough of that,' Lottie said.

Undeterred, Kirby blurted, 'Behind her paintings, there were three cardboard banker's boxes. Two of them contain files. The other holds personal effects of Damien O'Loughlin.'

McKeown leapt up. 'For fuck's sake. You have to poke your fat nose into—'

'Sit down!' Lottie waited as the tall detective did as he'd been told. 'Where are these boxes now?'

'On their way back here,' Kirby said.

'Good. And the car? Any idea how it came to be in that particular lock-up?'

'No, but it was bleached thoroughly. Grainne thinks maybe the GPS could give us a clue.'

'Keep me informed, and I want to know the second those boxes arrive. Back to Helena McCaul. Any ideas where she might be?'

'She could be anywhere, but maybe we should check the pubs,' Boyd said. 'Her mother mentioned she'd had issues. She must have taken Éilis's death hard, following so quickly after Jennifer. I know I'd hit the pub if it were me.'

'Me too,' Kirby said.

'Right,' Lottie said. 'Boyd, arrange a few uniforms to quietly canvas the pubs. I'm worried for her safety.'

'That's ridiculous,' McKeown muttered.

'There must be at least thirty-two pubs in town,' Kirby said.

'Counted them on a pub crawl, have you?' McKeown shot back.

Lottie despaired of the two men ever seeing eye to eye. McKeown *had* to be transferred back to Athlone.

As if he'd seen whatever had flashed across her face, he donned a serious expression. 'I agree with what Kirby said earlier. Helena might have been taken by the killer.'

He'd voiced the concern swirling around in the pit of Lottie's empty stomach.

'I hope not, but we can't rule it out. We need to track her movements since we spoke with her earlier today.'

'Maybe she just slipped out of her shop for a carton of milk and is already back there,' Boyd said, taking out his phone.

After a few moments of unanswered ringing, he said, 'I'll try her mobile.'

Same result, which meant no result. Lottie couldn't remember Helena giving Boyd her number.

'Try Orla Keating. Both women are in that widows' group.'

'I'll call her,' Kirby offered. After a moment, he said, 'No answer.'

'It's too soon to get a warrant on Helena's phone, but I'm extremely worried for her safety and her mental health.' Lottie brought the team up to speed on what Kathleen Foley had told them about her daughter's delusions.

'A pathological liar?' McKeown scratched his head. 'Are we sure *she* isn't our killer?'

'The only thing I'm sure of at present is that two women are dead, so let's talk about the murders.' She pointed to the notes on the whiteboard. 'I'm confused about the choice of location. He's chosen waste ground and a wooded area of the lake. Why these random sites? Are they important to him, or is he playing games with us?'

'Are you certain it's the same killer?' Lynch asked.

'Jane hasn't yet commenced the post-mortem, but Éilis has broken limbs, similar wounds to Jennifer.'

'Éilis wasn't shot,' Lynch insisted.

'Agreed, but both victims had their eyes removed.'

'Shit,' Lynch exclaimed. The others gasped.

'Why take the eyes?' Kirby said, nervously twirling the butt of a cigar around his fingers. 'It's—'

'Why break their bones?' McKeown cut in.

'The killer is telling us something,' Boyd said. 'I think we could do with a psychological profiler.'

'And which budget should I raid for that?' Lottie paced up and down in front of the board. 'We need to use our heads on this one. The victims might lead us to the killer. Lynch, tell us what we have on Jennifer O'Loughlin.'

Lynch consulted the copious notes she had collated from the interviews to date.

'Jennifer worked at Smile Brighter Dental Clinic up until a month ago, when she posted in her resignation. After she joined the Life After Loss group, her boss, Frankie Bardon, said her timekeeping became an issue and he had to juggle her roster.'

Lottie nodded. 'He told me he encouraged her to leave. We know she did yoga at that SunUp place. The head guru there, Owen Dalton, made me feel uneasy, and I left feeling I had missed something. Did anything turn up on the other yoga instructors?'

'None live in Ragmullin, and they can all account for their whereabouts over the last few days, but until we know exactly when she was murdered, we can't pin down alibis.'

'True. And until Éilis's post-mortem is conducted, we won't have her time of death. We know she was last seen alive by her babysitter, Bianca Tormey, on Thursday evening. And her little girl claims she woke up to see her mum during the night, but that's unreliable. She might have been dreaming. Éilis lived in a fairly upmarket area; did you get any security footage from the surrounding houses, McKeown?'

'A few have doorbell cameras and fake cameras, but most houses are covered by phone alarms. I found nothing to indicate who might have abducted Éilis or when it happened.'

'Back to Jennifer. She had a sideline as an artist. We need to pick over her financials. Anything on those?'

Kirby said, 'Haven't got them yet, but I was looking at Tyler Keating's, and—'

'The missing man whose car was found in Jennifer's lock-up. Go on.'

'His wife has access to his accounts, so it's impossible to say if it's her or Tyler who's been using them.'

'Ask her.'

'Will do.'

'Sometime after her husband died two years ago, Jennifer joined this group that Éilis set up. And then Helena joined it, followed by Orla Keating within the last year. Is there anything else to link the women?'

Garda Brennan put up her hand.

'Yes, Martina.'

'I've had a quick look over Tyler Keating's case, and I think we should ask Orla if she or her husband did accountancy work for Jennifer or her husband. That might link them.'

'Good point. If she refuses, I don't think a judge will issue a warrant for her records without proof of wrongdoing. Any other way of finding out?'

'Detective McKeown is on good terms with someone in Revenue,' Martina said, giving him a side-eye before looking back at Lottie. 'Maybe he could ask them?'

McKeown had the decency to blush before he said, 'I'll see what I can find out. Jennifer rented the unit in her maiden name, which is a bit odd.'

'See what you can find out about it. And Kirby, those files belonging to Damien ...'

'Yeah, I'll go through them as soon as I get them.'

'When will you know about the car GPS?'

'I haven't had time to—'

'We need to work faster. Who else had keys to Jennifer's lock-up? Was the car there before she disappeared or put there afterwards? Someone has to know. I want information, not excuses. Am I clear?'

'Crystal,' Kirby said.

She hoped he wasn't being sarcastic, though it sounded like he was. 'I want Helena McCaul found. And now I have to go tell two children their mum is dead. Boyd, you're with me.'

'But I've to organise uniforms... the pubs...'

'Garda Brennan, that's your job now.'

'I have to look at the Tyler case and—'

'Garda Lei can help you.

Lei cut in. 'Sure, boss. It's not a problem.'

Lottie's T-shirt was sticking to her skin as she sidled out by her troops to breathe in the relative coolness of the corridor. Her team seemed to be at loggerheads with each other. Was it her fault? She had to sort it out before it spiralled out of control. If they were not at their best, someone else was going to die.

———

Sometimes you had to begin at the end to figure out how you got there. She had come to learn this over the years. But what if you really had to begin where it all started? Would that help, or would it only compound the errors you'd made? She had to try and figure out what she'd got herself involved in.

The meeting with Madelene Bowen hadn't helped. She really needed that file. She felt it was the key to everything either going belly-up or resolving all her issues.

As she settled into her car and turned on the air con, she thought of Jennifer and what had started all this. Had what she overheard really been true? If it had, then Tyler Keating was a worse bastard than she'd suspected.

The woman beside her moaned in her sleep so she started the car and drove off.

54

Mrs Tormey, Bianca's mum, closed the door behind them as they left her house. Lottie drew a long breath, and blinked tears from her eyes as she headed towards the car.

'I never want to have to do that again, Boyd. The heartache on the faces of those little kids...'

'True, but you can't really be serious about contacting social services about them, can you?' He unlocked the car and they sat in.

'I know Mrs Tormey has no objection to Roman and Becky staying with her until Éilis's sister arrives from Dubai, but I have a duty to inform the state agency.' She paused and brushed hair from her eyes, stuck there with tears. Only someone with the hardest heart could fail to be moved by the Lawlor children's fate. 'Oh, I don't know what to do.'

'Let me tell you something.' He turned to look at her. 'You're so busy with two murder investigations, you haven't time right now for anything else, and you might just forget to make that call. And before you know it, the kids' aunt will be here.'

She smiled weakly. 'Maybe you're right.' Shrugging one shoulder, she asked, 'Do you have any cigarettes?'

'No, and you don't need one.'

'Do you think Mrs Tormey should have accepted our offer of a family liaison officer?'

'Her feeling is that it's better for the children not to have any more strange faces around. I tend to agree with her. They'll be going through a tortuous time as it is. They're lucky in a sense that Éilis had such a good neighbour. I can't believe there are no other friends crawling out of the woodwork to help the family.'

'That bothers me too,' Lottie said. 'Neither Jennifer nor Éilis seemed to have any close friends.'

'Éilis worked from home, so I can understand it with her, but what about Jennifer's colleagues at work? Anyone there admit to being close to her?'

'Not a one, unless you count Frankie Bardon. He gave the impression that he had her best interests at heart. He advised her to resign. He even went for a walk with her the week before she submitted her resignation.' She went over the conversation in her mind, but found some gaps in what she could remember. 'He said something to me that I'm sure is important, but I can't recall it.'

'You have your notes from the interview, don't you?'

'I went there on my own and scribbled a few things when I got back to the car. I'll have a look later and see if anything jogs my memory. But I can't get my head around Helena.'

'We need to find out more about that group. Are there even other members?'

'Maybe someone got pissed off with them and left with a grudge?'

'Do you think Life After Loss is exclusive to females, though?' Boyd said.

She hadn't thought of that. 'Widowers and divorced or separated men? Hmm. I'd assumed it was for women.'

'You know you should never assume?'

'Yeah, and we've also been assuming the killer is male. It could be a woman.'

'I agree, except there is one thing to consider. To get the bodies to those two locations, they had to be carried some distance. That makes me believe that we're looking for a man.'

Lottie sat up straighter. 'They could have used some sort of trolley. The water around the statue where Éilis was found. What if that was to wash away wheel marks? And Grainne noticed tracks close to Jennifer's body.'

'The site at Ballyglass Business Park had a carnival there a week ago, so there was a multitude of tracks and ruts all over the place.'

'If SOCOs went back to both sites now, knowing what they're looking for, we might hit lucky.' She suddenly felt excited.

'It's worth a try.'

'Definitely worth a try.' She fished her phone out of her bag. 'I'll call Grainne, and then we need to find Helena. Alive.'

'After you talk to Grainne, we should go back to Orla Keating. She needs to be told about her husband's car being found. Let's see what her reaction is.'

'Do you think he's still alive?'

'Maybe.'

'Let's take it one step at a time and see where we're led.'

She tapped Grainne's number and made the call.

She felt Boyd's gaze on her and turned to him.

A smile woke up his tired face, and he started the car.

———

Jackie Boyd sipped her third cup of coffee, trying to come up with a plan for her next move. She'd decided not to follow the Parker girl, who appeared to be minding Sergio. She wanted to reach out to her son, to hug him. Lottie Parker's kids knew her. Hadn't she once been instrumental in providing information that resulted in one of the girls being rescued from a murderer? And then Lottie Parker paid her back by snaring Mark. Rage bubbled just beneath the surface of her skin.

Her attention had been caught by the two women huddled in the corner. She'd seen them in the mirror behind the bar and thought they'd looked pretty intense for the middle of the day.

They were an unlikely couple, if that was what they were. One was like a wounded bird, her bones sticking out at her shoulders, elbows and ankles. The other had wild red hair and her clothes were a little too out-there for Jackie. Her floaty silver skirt and tight top were more like you'd see on the Costa del Sol rather than in Ragmullin.

They'd gathered their bags. The bird-like woman had left notes on the table to cover their drinks, then arm in arm they'd left the pub.

Jackie turned her thoughts back to Sergio and the Parker girl. She might have to change her plans.

55

At the Keating house, Lottie's insistent knocking went unanswered. She rang Kirby to ensure it had been searched at the time of Tyler's disappearance.

Driving away, Boyd said, 'Neither Orla nor Helena is answering their phones and we can't find them. Does that strike you as strange?'

'Logically speaking, they're probably out shopping or having food somewhere. They might be together, or maybe not. I'm more worried about Helena, though. From what her mother told us, I reckon she could be unstable. It's as if something seems to have broken inside her, and her mother has given up hope of trying to fix her.'

'That's sad.'

'Yep.'

'Mothers and daughters,' Boyd said.

'Fathers and sons.' They lapsed into silence as Boyd indicated to turn up the street towards the station. 'Didn't Kathleen Foley say she has a key to Helena's house?'

. . .

After securing the key from a reluctant Kathleen who reiterated that she'd never had cause to use it, Boyd sped across town to Helena's house.

They made their way up the front path. No one came to answer their knocking, so he opened the door with the key and stepped inside.

'Helena? It's Inspector Parker and Detective Boyd. Helena?' Lottie's voice echoed in the silence. 'She's not here.'

She welcomed the coolness of the hall after the heat outside. It was clean and clear of clutter, with no coats clogging the banister. That was never going to happen in her house, where the stairs resembled a nightclub cloakroom on a wintery Friday night.

She followed Boyd into the open-plan kitchen, with a living room looking out on the garden. As she made her way across the floor, she came to a sharp halt.

'Don't move, Boyd.'

'What?'

'Stay where you are for a minute.' She crouched down and looked at the stain that had caught her eye. Scanning the floor, she saw there were more stains all around her. 'It's blood.'

'There's some here by the counter too.' He glanced around, tracking the trail with his eyes. 'It leads to this door.'

'The utility room? Feck. I hope she's not—'

'Stop, Lottie. We have to call this in, before we disrupt anything else.'

'She could be lying injured or... I have to look.' Taking careful steps, she backtracked and made her way around the breakfast bar to the door Boyd had indicated.

'Gloves,' he said, and handed her a fresh pair in a packet he'd taken from his jacket pocket.

'Bit late now.' But she tugged them on over her sweaty hands with some difficulty and depressed the handle.

'It's a utility room all right, but it's empty. More blood here too. I'll have a look upstairs. You call it in.'

Without listening to his protestations, she backed out, careful to walk only where she'd already done so. At the top of the stairs, she found four doors.

The bathroom door was open. She glanced inside. Nothing to note. The box room seemed to be used as a storage space. The next door was shut tightly, and when she tried to enter, she found it locked. Interesting. She moved to what she supposed was the biggest room, which looked out over the front garden. A large double bed, unmade. Clothing littered the floor. A bloodied cloth was scrunched up in a bin under the dressing table. It was hard to tell if a struggle had occurred, such was the disarray around her feet.

Standing outside the locked room, she called to Boyd. 'Need you up here.'

'Find anything?'

'Nothing much other than an untidy bedroom with a bloody cloth in a bin. Can you open this door?'

'We need probable cause to break it down.'

'We got a key from her mother to enter the house. We believed Helena might have been taken by someone who has already murdered two women. With the blood downstairs, we have more than enough cause to enter this room.'

He huffed, and she knew he wasn't happy.

'Just do it. Please.'

He moved back a few steps, then hefted his shoulder against the light wooden door. It crashed open with negligible resistance.

She found herself in a child's room. Toys, cartoon quilt on the bed and Winnie-the-Pooh decor on the walls. And a half-empty bottle of vodka on the floor at the foot of the bed.

'Didn't her mother say she had no child?'

'Something weird is going on in this family,' Boyd said.

'One of them is lying. This room is obviously a child's. The garden also has stuff relevant to a child. Why the lies?'

'We need to find out. And it's likely Helena is injured.'

'Try her phone again.'

He did. 'It's dead.'

They left as Lynch turned up to take control. A meticulous search of the house got under way while SOCOs examined the blood.

'Fuck, Boyd,' Lottie said. 'I don't like this one bit.'

56

Kirby had taken the call from Lottie about the Keating house, and he cursed the amount of work he had piling up. He banged the photocopier lid in irritation and wandered over to Martina, who was tapping loudly on his computer keyboard.

'Who does she think I am?' he grumbled. 'Of course the house was searched.'

'She's just being thorough, now that we've found Tyler's car in a lock-up used by a murder victim.'

'I can't figure out why the car is there, or for how long.' He moved away and sat at Boyd's desk, marvelling at how his friend kept it so neat and clean.

Martina added, 'It wasn't there since the day he disappeared, because Jennifer only rented the unit eleven months ago.'

'How do you know that?'

'I sweet talked the woman at the letting agency and got the leasing documents.'

'Who rented it before her?'

'Give me a minute.'

He waited while she made the call. Taking a few pens out

of the holder, he scattered them on Boyd's desk. He saw her beckoning him over, her mouth forming an O. He extracted himself from the desk and stood in front of her.

'What?' He tapped the desk. Could she not hurry up?

'Wait,' she mouthed. 'Okay, thanks a million. Email me the details.'

She called out her email address and hung up.

'What did you find?' Kirby shuffled from foot to foot and fought the urge to shake the information out of her.

'You won't believe it.' She was really dragging this out.

'Martina! Don't do this to me.'

'Okay, keep your hair on. That unit was previously rented by none other than Damien O'Loughlin! Jennifer's husband. The letting agency is emailing me the details.'

'Okay, but I still don't understand it. Does this mean that Jennifer knew the car was there all along? And what was the relationship between the Keatings and the O'Loughlins?'

'Maybe she knew Tyler,' Martina said.

'Wasn't McKeown supposed to do a background check on Damien O'Loughlin? Don't answer that. He probably has his head stuck in useless CCTV.'

'Look, I have to go. I'm supposed to be checking out the pubs for Orla and Helena.'

'And why aren't you?' Kirby asked.

'Garda Lei wanted to take the lead, so I let him.'

'Good. You're better utilised here than doing a pub crawl, as McKeown called it.'

Kirby took his cigar out of his shirt pocket and stuck it between his lips. He had no intention of lighting up in the office, but holding it helped him think more clearly.

'Has this lock-up even got anything to do with Jennifer's murder? We have Éilis Lawlor's murder to bring into the equation.' He scratched his head, thinking.

'Yeah, I know. But this rental and the boxes found there

means we need to have a look at Damien O'Loughlin's life. As if we weren't snowed under already.'

Kirby slouched around the office as uniforms arrived with the three banker boxes. 'Might as well start with these. Hopefully we can find something to help us.'

'Like what?'

'Don't know, but there has to be a reason why they were hidden away.'

'Are they originals?'

He flicked open one of the files. 'They seem to be copies.'

'Do you need a hand?'

'Two, if you're offering.'

After a half-hour, Martina held aloft a file. 'Tyler Keating used Bowen Solicitors for his house purchase.'

'How long ago was that?'

'Six years.' She flicked through the thin file. 'Why did Damien O'Loughlin have a copy of this?'

'We're investigating murders, not crooked house deals.' Kirby tapped a pen against his nose. 'All it tells us is that Jennifer's husband would have met one or both of the Keatings. Jennifer didn't work at the firm, so we're back to square one.'

'It's another piece of the jigsaw, anyhow.'

'Or it might be a piece from another jigsaw, just to fuck with us. I doubt it has anything to do with the current investigation.'

'Or it might have everything to do with it.'

He really needed to go outside to light up. He wondered if he could sneak a text or a call to Amy. He felt the heat rise in his cheeks as he remembered her kiss at lunchtime. Was it wrong to fall for her? What did they even know about each other? Not much, though she could probably google him and find out a fair bit. The thought of googling *her* sprang to his mind. No, that was what you did when you were trying to catch a guilty person. He had to stop being a detective where she was concerned. It was one sure way of losing her before they'd even started a relationship.

He glanced over at Martina. What had gone wrong between her and McKeown, besides the fact that he was married? He decided that wasn't any of his business either.

She had abandoned the box of files and maximised Tyler Keating's cold-case file on Kirby's computer.

'I don't think you'll find anything in that,' he said.

'I disagree. I noticed something odd earlier and I'm trying to find it again.'

He groaned. 'I hope it's not something to give the boss rope to hang me with.'

She gave him a side-eye and tightened her lips in a grimace.

'Ah, Martina, please don't do this to me.'

57

It all started with Jennifer. The way she retold the incident is vivid and still fresh.

Jennifer unbuttoned her jacket and kicked off her shoes.

'Where are you?' she called out.

'Sitting room.'

From the doorway, she watched her husband as he sat on the sofa surrounded by files and a yellow legal pad, furiously writing notes. Leaning down, she kissed his cheek and mussed his hair. 'Are you still working? What happened to nine-to-five?'

'That was just a movie.' He put the work to one side and pulled her to his lap. 'You smell good. Where have you been?'

She knew his words were not a test, but she still bristled. She had nothing to hide, had she?

'It's just mouthwash.'

'Hey, only joking,' he said catching her expression.

'I know, but...'

'Come on, Jennifer, tell me what's bothering you.'

She extricated herself from his embrace and stood. 'You're

working too hard. You're grey in the face. I'll have a shower, then I'll start dinner.'

'I took a casserole from the freezer this morning before I left for the office. It's in the oven now. Another half-hour should do it.'

'What did I ever do to deserve you?'

He smiled his lopsided smile that she always thought made him look like a teenager, his fair hair falling into his eyes. 'I hounded you until you had no choice but to accept my proposal.'

True, she thought, but the idea that someone like Damien O'Loughlin would want her, never mind marry her and worship her daily, had filled her with confidence .

'I'm waiting,' he said, closing his notepad and slotting it into the battered brown leather satchel that he used as a briefcase.

With a sigh, she succumbed to his pleas and sat beside him.

'It can't be that bad.' He took her hand in his.

'I overheard a conversation at work today and it got under my skin. I was passing a cubicle and... Look, I don't want to say who it was yet. I know, I know.' She held up a hand to halt his protestations. 'I trust you, but it might be just gossip. Then again, if it's true, it's disturbing.'

'Must be, to have you in such a tizzy.'

She pondered holding back, but since she'd overheard it, her mind was in overdrive. As the words spilled out of her mouth, his hand grew cold in hers and he shifted uneasily before jumping up.

'Who have you told about this?'

'No one. Only you.'

'Please keep it that way.'

'But shouldn't I go to the gardai?'

He shook his head vehemently. 'No way. It's just hearsay. You have no proof of any wrongdoing.'

'Damien, I can't sit on this.'

'You have to. Look, This information... it could get you killed.'

Jennifer felt the blood drain from her face and her hands shook uncontrollably. 'You can't mean that?'

'I'm serious. If this is true, God knows what is going on. Just forget it.'

'Can't you do something about it? Maybe talk to Madelene? She could advise me on what's best.'

'I know exactly what Madelene Bowen will say.'

'And what's that?'

'Same as I said. Hearsay. No proof.'

'What if I got proof?'

'You can't put yourself in harm's way. Let me think about it.'

'Are you okay, Damien? Your colour...'

'I actually feel a bit sick. I... Give me a minute.'

He rushed from the room and she heard him retching in the downstairs bathroom. This wasn't the first time in the last few weeks that her husband had been ill and tried to hide it. She needed to park her own anxiety and get him to a doctor. That was her priority. Then, once she knew he was okay, she could decide what to do with the information she'd overheard. Gossip or not, it had her rattled.

I cringe at the memory of her words to me. Her actions thereafter started my mission. And there are more to die yet.

58

At the station, Lottie bumped into Garda Lei in the corridor as she headed for the toilets. Her bladder was ready to burst and she knew he took ages to get to the point.

'Can it wait until I come out?'

'Of course, sorry, it's just, you see, Fallon's pub... Sorry. I'll wait.'

At the mention of Chloe's workplace, she immediately forgot about going to the toilet. 'What about Fallon's?'

'Right. Sure. The barman... barperson... sorry, I don't know the right term...'

'Get on with it, please.'

'She said it was an unusually busy lunchtime. But two women came in before the rush and sat in a corner for nearly an hour. She remembers them because one of them kept ordering for the other and she needed the table. From her description, one of the women could be Helena McCaul.'

'Two women on their own?'

'That's what she said. She also said your Chloe and a little boy called in for lunch.'

Lottie opened her eyes wide at this news, surprised that

Chloe would go anywhere near where she worked, especially with Sergio. She hoped Boyd wouldn't be angry over it.

'Fallon's has security cameras. Go back and ask for the footage from when those women entered the pub.'

'I'll head back there straight away. Sorry. I should have... you know... sorry...'

She shook her head as Lei disappeared at a sprint. Did she have to draw a map for them all? Enough with the questions, she thought. She needed bloody answers. Right after she had a pee in peace.

———

McKeown was of the opinion that the security footage on the two DVDs that Garda Lei had dumped on his desk would be useless. Everyone and their father knew pubs installed security cameras to watch their staff rather than the customers. He'd had no luck finding anything on the tapes from Ballyglass Business Park, where Jennifer's body had been found. The additional garage forecourt footage that the boss had requested had thrown up nothing of interest. The idea of trawling through the pub's grainy images filled him with boredom. But just to be thorough and not give the boss anything else to beat him with, he decided to rush through the DVDs.

And he got lucky. The first was from a camera trained on the toilet doors at the end of the bar, but captured the table to the left of it. There they were. Two women seated at a small, round table, heads close, apparently in deep conversation. Definitely Orla Keating and Helena McCaul. He fast-forwarded until they stood up and moved out of sight.

He shoved in the second DVD. This showed the alcove at the front entrance, and he caught sight of them as they stepped outside the door. He figured the camera was positioned just above their heads. Probably there to catch antisocial behaviour.

He kept his eyes on the women as they moved out onto the footpath. He noticed Orla Keating's hand on Helena's back. Was she pushing or steering her? The image was too grainy to be sure. They turned left as they exited the pub. Helena's shop was close by, and the car park was that way also. He phoned the council office requesting all footage from the car park within the relevant timeline.

'I need it like yesterday,' he told the bored woman on the phone; then, softening his tone, he tried his charm. 'We've had two murders in two days. You don't want that to happen to anyone else in Ragmullin, do you?'

He hung up after getting a promise of the footage as soon as she could obtain it from the council databank, and a possible coffee date.

The charm still worked. Kirby was welcome to Martina. McKeown was already moving on.

The woman at the council emailed the footage within an hour.

It was grainy and difficult to locate the women, but squinting at the images, he eventually spotted them getting into a car. He checked the registration number. It belonged to Helena McCaul.

Orla Keating sat into the driver's seat. Neither woman looked coerced or too inebriated, but he couldn't be sure.

As the vehicle exited the car park, he noticed someone loitering at the fence. Were they watching the car? Was the figure male or female? They were dressed all in black and it struck him it could be someone in the supermarket uniform. The supermarket was next to the car park. But what made him think it was suspicious was that the instant the car disappeared from the camera view, the person did too. They didn't enter the car park or walk along the fence in the direction they were facing. They had to have turned and gone back the way they'd come.

Could he be sure the person was watching the two women? Or was it just someone on a break from work having a smoke? Or had they been going to their car and then changed their mind?

He groaned and ran his hand over his shaved head, then tugged at his chin in irritation. It was likely irrelevant. His job was to find where the women had gone. He'd have to alert traffic cams and trawl more footage to track their journey. To tie up the loose end with the unidentified watcher, he'd need to trace security footage up along the footpath to the car park and back again. Maybe he could keep his mouth shut and ignore it. Who would even know?

He was considering his dilemma when his phone rang.

The woman from the council.

He smiled and answered the call.

59

With the investigations at a stalemate, Lottie headed home after telling her team there would be a debrief meeting at seven the next morning.

Kirby had filled her in on his initial glance through the solicitor's files found in Jennifer's lock-up. They were related to property transactions, including the purchase of the Keating house. Why keep copies of work files hidden? Why have them at all? She didn't want to get caught up in something that might have nothing to with the murders, but she'd still have to call on Bowen Solicitors tomorrow to see why their files had turned up in a murdered woman's lock-up.

She drank in the glorious sight of the lake down the field from her house, realising how lucky she was to live in such a beautiful location. If only the house wasn't falling down around her ears.

An owl, or maybe a pigeon, hooted in the trees; a dog barked in the distance; the grass rustled around her feet, and the scene became a shrouded backdrop to the horror she encountered in her job. With a sigh, she made her way inside.

Hanging her jacket on the banister, she felt bone weary. It was the dead ends that lowered her mood. She kicked off her boots, removed her socks and massaged her feet. An emptiness lodged in her stomach, a craving hollowness. The urge to have an alcoholic drink was immense. Why now? Was it from the stress of her mother living with her? Rose's constant repetitive questions? Or was it Sergio? It was no lie that he had taken over Boyd's attention. She couldn't be jealous of an eight-year-old, could she? Whatever the reason, it was hard to adjust to this new way of living.

A drink would ease the turmoil in her brain. A small one. No one need know. A sip, maybe? It couldn't do any harm, could it?

'Nana Lottie! Why are you sitting on the stairs?'

She smiled as Louis ran to join her. He nestled in on the step and put his head on her arm. 'It's cold out here, Nana.'

She hugged him tightly, rousing herself from her musings, hoping the little boy could somehow fill that gnawing void inside her.

'Where's your mammy?'

Lottie knew that Katie had a new boyfriend, Benji or something like that. She was probably upstairs plastering make-up on for her first night out in months. She was pleased for her daughter. She deserved happiness after all the heartache she'd endured so far in her young life.

Louis raised an eyebrow quizzically. 'Mammy is painting her face with a brush. She won't let me use it. Not fair.'

She couldn't help but smile at the child. 'Come with me and we'll see if there's any cheese strings in the fridge.'

'Yes!' The little boy clapped his hands, then jumped up and ran into the kitchen ahead of her.

Rose was sitting at the table, frantically buttering bread. She was working methodically, creating a tower of buttered slices.

'What are you doing, Mother?'

'Making sandwiches,' Rose said.

'You don't need all that bread.' Lottie picked up the bread wrapper. Only the two heels remained.

'Are you telling me I don't know how to butter bread?' Rose threw the knife onto the table. It hit a plate and fell to the floor. Butter everywhere.

'I'm simply saying you don't need so much bread.' Lottie fetched a cloth and began wiping up the mess.

'You think I'm useless, don't you?'

She couldn't help thinking her mother sounded just like Louis.

Rose continued, 'I want to go home to my own house. I'm not staying here a second longer.' She folded her arms like a child and her bottom lip quivered. 'You're so mean to me.'

Louis closed the refrigerator door and climbed up on a chair to sit beside his great-granny. He handed her a cheese string. 'Will you open this for me, Nana Rose?'

'What in the name of God is that?' Rose turned her nose up and her lips down.

'Cheese!' He thrust it towards her.

'Get it away from me,' Rose snapped, and slapped the table as if swatting a fly.

Louis got down from the chair, his bottom lip quivering. 'Nana Lottie?'

'I'll do it for you, pet.' When she had the wrapper peeled off, she handed him the cheese. 'Louis, go and find Sean. He might let you play a game on his PlayStation.'

'Yeah!'

She watched him scamper off, wishing she could escape too.

'Why do you allow that child to run everywhere?' Rose said. 'Has he forgotten how to walk?'

'He's only three years old.' Lottie rinsed the cloth under the running tap. Cold. 'I'll kill Katie for using all the hot water.'

'In my day, children were seen and not heard. He charges

around like a bloody train. It's getting on my nerves. Where's my coat?' Rose stood, abandoning the tower of bread.

'Sit down, Mother. I'll make you a cup of tea.'

'Don't you dare speak to me like that, Charlotte Fitzpatrick. Wait until your father gets home and then you'll be in big trouble, missy.'

She wandered out of the kitchen. Lottie leaned her forehead against the cold rim of the sink and wrapped her hands around her head. She wished her father was still alive; to hold her and kiss her wounds better, like he'd done when she was little; to take care of her mother. How was she going to manage this phase of her life, with Rose deteriorating, now that Boyd was preoccupied?

The front door banged, rousing her out of her self-pity.

'Mother?' she called as she ran to the hall.

Rose's coat was hanging on the hook, but there was no sign of her. Opening the door, Lottie saw her marching down the avenue, wearing only a light cotton dress and slippers.

'Come back inside,' she yelled, taking off after her. 'You'll get pneumonia.'

'As if you care,' Rose spat back. She stopped walking, swung around with her hands on her hips. 'You'd like me to die so that you can steal my house from under me. That's what you're up to, missy. Well, listen to me, I won't let you! I'm going home to my own house. Right this minute, you hear?'

'Sure, fine, whatever you want. We can talk about it inside. I'll make you a cup of tea.' Lottie remained frozen in place, pleading with her mother.

Rose's shoulders slumped. She gazed around with vacant eyes. 'It's so cold.' She lifted her dress, feeling the thin material. 'Why have I no coat? Where am I going? A cup of tea would be nice, if you're making it.'

Taking her mother by the elbow, Lottie hugged her gently

before steering her towards the door. She had no idea how they would get through this. She felt powerless.

And she was powerless to stop her tears breaking free and rolling down her face.

60

Kirby stood under the shower for a good ten minutes, scrubbing his skin until it turned red. He washed his hair in the expensive shampoo and conditioner he'd bought on the way home. Then he switched off the water and dried himself thoroughly in the old towel that hung on the back of the door. Time to throw out the old and get in the new, he thought. No matter what he did with his hair it refused to flatten down, so he just ran his fingers through the curls and decided they had won that particular battle.

He took new boxers from the bag of clothes he'd purchased in Wilfs, along with what he thought was a white shirt but now found to be a light shade of pink. At least it was new, with fresh creases. Amy would think he had ironed it specially for her. The black trousers were a perfect fit, and he'd been delighted in the shop to find he'd gone down a waist size. He conveniently ignored the fact that well-made clothes fitted differently to what he was used to buying in Primark. The new outfit was outside his budget, but Amy was worth it.

He'd booked Amber Chinese restaurant for their dinner. Martina had recommended it, saying the ambience was as good as the food. He'd thought she looked put out when he told her he had a date, but she'd rebuffed him so many times, he didn't feel any regret.

Suitably attired, he cringed at the state of his bedroom. His overspent budget hadn't stretched to new sheets, but he made the bed and picked the clothes up off the floor. It was passable.

Arriving early, he ordered a bottle of white. He'd have loved a pint of Guinness, but decided this was one night where he should be civilised. His life was due a dramatic shift, and Amy was the driver.

He'd finished half the bottle and two rounds of prawn crackers before admitting she wasn't coming. He felt his whole demeanour deflate as he checked his phone for what seemed like the millionth time. No messages. No missed calls. No nothing. He'd been a fool. An idiot. He'd been stood up, plain and simple.

The petite waitress was at his table again, and the look of pity on her face almost did him in. He might as well eat. After he'd placed his order for curried pork and garlic fried rice, she still hovered.

'Will you be eating alone, sir?' she asked, almost apologetically.

'No, he won't.'

He peered around the waitress. Amy stood there, still in her supermarket uniform, her face flushed, hair askew.

'I'll have whatever he's having, and bring another one of those.' She pointed to the wine bottle in the ice bucket and the waitress poured her a glass.

'I don't know what to say.' She shuffled out of her gilet and slumped onto the chair opposite Kirby. 'I got held up. Hadn't time to call you. It was Luke, he... Ah no, forget it. I don't want to talk about him. I hadn't even time to go home to shower and change. And look at you. You've gone to so much trouble and I'm like the wreck of the *Hesperus*. I'm so sorry.'

She shook her head before taking a long swallow of wine. 'I needed that.'

Kirby smiled with relief. 'You look beautiful.' And he meant it. Her eyes were so bright, the hazel flecks glinted like gold from the light of the centrepiece candles.

'Bet you say that to all the girls.' She grinned wickedly and he let out a belly laugh.

'Amy Corcoran, you are good for my soul.'

They lapsed into silence as she dived into the fresh basket of prawn crackers the waitress brought with the second bottle of wine.

'Tell me about Luke,' he said when they were alone again. 'What did he do this time?'

'He's just a jumped-up little prick. You know, he probably has a little one and all.'

Kirby laughed and it felt good. Then he became serious. 'Was it because of me at lunchtime?'

'He doesn't need an excuse to be a bollix.' She wiped her hands on the cloth napkin and sat forward. 'I was telling one of the girls that I had a date and he overheard. Started making fun of me. Then this huge order of baked beans arrived and suddenly the boss tells me I have to stock the shelves. We'd run out during the week and we were waiting for the order. Mr Rodgers – he's a customer – was doing all our heads in. He must live on beans on toast. Anyway, I reckon Luke told the boss that I'd stock the shelves because he had this grin from ear to ear like the fucking Cheshire cat.'

'He's a wrong one, that Luke. Why didn't you tell them all to take a running jump?'

She shook her head slowly. 'I couldn't do that. I need this job. I've been begging for extra hours for ages, and the one time I get them, they don't suit me. What could I do?'

'You should have sent me a text.' He bit his tongue once the words were out of his mouth. Her face dropped and she sat back in her chair. He wouldn't blame her if she got up and walked out on him. He quickly tried to rectify his error. 'But it doesn't matter. I'm here and you're here. I don't know about you, but I'm bloody starving.'

'I could eat a horse.' Her face brightened up and he felt he had rescued the situation; maybe even saved the night.

'I want to know more about you, Amy. Tell me about yourself,' he said, aware that she knew more about him than he knew about her.

'Do we have to do that?'

A darkness shrouded her face, and he looked around, half expecting to see the waitress standing there with their food.

'No, we don't, but I'd like to know a little, so that I don't put my big foot in it again.'

'Like you did with Luke? Sorry, we've drawn a line under that.' She took up her glass and stared at the glowing liquid. 'I told you I was once in a long term relationship. It didn't work out. He's gone. A messy break up and it tore my heart out at the time.'

'Oh shit, Amy, I'm sorry. I've had one of those too. Mine was a messy divorce. Are you over it?'

'He wasn't a nice person. But I can't put all the blame on him. There were two of us in the relationship, one playing off the other, and that was only going to end one way.'

'Did he physically hurt you?'

She tightened her lips. 'I really don't want to go there. Safe to say, I often wished he was dead. The funny thing is, once we finally broke up, I missed him. I thought I was to blame for all the things he'd said and done to me.'

'Please, Amy, don't blame yourself. You're free of him now.'

'But am I truly free, Larry? I spent the best part of my twenties in that relationship, and I feel I'm damaged for life.'

He didn't know how to respond. Then the food arrived.

'This looks good,' she said. 'I don't even know what you ordered.'

'I hope you like curried pork, then.'

'I'd eat the leg of the table this second.'

He caught her smile and his shoulders relaxed. He hadn't even been aware that he was hunched up with tension.

As they tucked into the food, he kept one eye on her. A woman alone in the world, with a young upstart of a colleague who seemed to be out to make her life a misery. Amy didn't deserve that. But did *he* deserve her?

He chewed the succulent meat and tried to enjoy the abatement of his hunger, but a feather of unease had floated down to settle on his shoulders. Once again he felt them hunching up. What was it about this woman that did that to him? Unable to come up with an answer to that question, he called for another bottle of wine.

While they were perusing the dessert menu, something she'd said earlier floated up to his consciousness through the haze of food and alcohol swimming around in his brain.

'You said you told a girl at work you had a date. Who is she?'

'Are you going to annoy her like you did Luke?' she said sharply.

He was taken aback, about to apologise, when he saw the twinkle of devilment in her eye.

'I spoke to her on the phone. She was off today. Just a teenager. She called me, really upset. Her neighbour went missing yesterday and was found dead this morning. You might even be on the case.'

His need for something sweet turned sour in his mouth. 'Is it Bianca Tormey?'

'Yes.'

'She was the dead woman's babysitter.'

'Isn't it so sad? Two little mites are now orphans.'

'Did Bianca ever mention a group called Life After Loss? Éilis Lawlor set it up.'

Amy stayed silent for a moment, then turned up her pert nose. 'I've heard of it. Did you see something you'd like?' She indicated the menu in his hand, and he noticed she'd closed hers.

'I'll just have a coffee,' he told the waitress when she appeared.

'Jasmine tea, please,' Amy said. When they were alone again, she said, 'I should have had a glass of milk before all that wine. That's one of the remedies to stop a hangover before it takes hold.'

'Amy, did Bianca tell you anything about Éilis Lawlor that might help us?'

'Really, Larry? Let's not darken our evening by talking about the dead.'

And so he acquiesced and changed the subject.

———

The euphoria from breaking Éilis's bones is long gone. But the scene I set for the guards is class. I am way too clever for them.

I have a choice of victims, but another has made her way into my peripheral vision. I hadn't considered her before, but now... I need to think who will die first. Who has the best eyes to look back at me from their glass cage?

I linger.

But not for long.

I make up my mind.

Someone else will die.

Maybe even tonight.

61

Amy had not intended going to Larry's house, but the effects of the late meal and too much wine had put her in the mood for sex. Afterwards, Larry had called a taxi and she'd been dropped at the head of her road. She had no idea what time of the night it was, and sighed with relief when she reached her house.

Through the glass in the front door the light in the hall shone out. She was immediately grateful for her habit of leaving it on in the morning in case she was home late. It helped her find her keys in her bag. She fished them out, and after trying with the wrong key, she studied the bunch in her hand, trying to work out which was the correct one.

She inserted another in the lock and turned it. As she pushed in the door, a strange smell wafted around her and something gripped her arm. A hand snaked around her shoulder and she was shoved into the hall.

'What the hell?' she gasped, trying to twist.

In her ear she heard a whisper, but she couldn't decipher the words through the fog swirling in her brain. As she struggled to extricate herself, the grip on her arm and around her neck tightened. Her attacker's sleeve was black, but because they were behind her, she couldn't see anything else. She felt the air catch in her throat; she couldn't breathe. She tried to bring her foot back to kick at her attacker's leg, but it was like her body had frozen.

She was unable to move.

No air.

Dark spots danced in front of her eyes, heralding that she was about to pass out. Why hadn't she stayed the night with Larry? Why had she been so damn independent?

Would he miss her? Would he come looking for her when she didn't return his calls? Because she was sure she was in the clutches of the person who had already murdered two women.

If she could have screamed, she would have done, but she couldn't.

As the arm tightened around her throat, Amy was certain she was about to die.

62

The doorbell of Boyd's apartment rang at ten past one in the morning.

He woke up, his back crippled from the couch, and instinctively checked his phone, fearing another body had been found. He had no text or call alerts. The bell shrieked again.

Sergio would wake if he didn't get a move on. He pulled on a pair of joggers and wiping his eyes groggily, opened the door without checking his security camera.

'Surprise!'

'Jackie? What are you doing here? You never phoned or...' Boyd watched as his ex-wife sauntered in past him, shoes clicking on the floor, swinging an oversized leopard-print handbag. She looked even more fake than when he'd briefly seen her in Spain. Her hair was dyed an odd colour, and her skin was leathery from too much sun and not enough sunscreen.

'Where's my boy? I want to see him.'

She sat herself on one of the stools at the kitchenette counter and dropped her bag at her feet. At least she hadn't gone into the bedroom.

'You didn't tell me...' He struggled for words and comprehension. 'You never told me you were coming.'

'Any beer in the fridge?' She hopped off the stool and rummaged through the refrigerator.

He grabbed her arm and hauled her upright. His temper flared and he feared it would tip over. 'You can't just barge in here in the middle of the night.'

'I can see my son any time I want. You have no legal right to him.' She shook him off. 'Ah, you still have the old reliable Heineken. Bottle opener?' She began opening drawers.

'Last one on your left.' Anything to stop her making a noise and messing up his strictly ordered cupboards.

She opened the bottle and swigged from it, then made her way to the couch. Flopping down on top of the duvet, she said, 'I'm glad to see you gave Sergio the bed. Adjusting to fatherhood, are you?'

He sat opposite her, clenching his hands and his jaw.

'What do you want?'

'This place is not ideal for a child, is it? I'd have thought you'd have a house by now.'

'You live in an apartment. I can't see the difference.'

'I have two bedrooms. What do you do when you have lady friends over? Evict my son onto the couch? Or do you send him off to Lottie Parker's house?'

He noticed how she kept referring to Sergio as *her* son. She was up to no good. He was exhausted and needed sleep. He could have done without this hijack.

'I'm tired. I have work in the morning. I'm sorry, there's nowhere for you to stay here. Can you please leave? We'll make arrangements to talk tomorrow.'

'I want to be here when my son wakes up in the morning.' She pointed the bottle at him and stared him down.

Boyd felt adrenaline shoot through his veins. 'You abandoned him in Spain. You'd never have told me about him if it hadn't suited you. Now he's with me, and I don't want to disrupt what we've built together. You made this mess, Jackie, not me. You can't just appear and make demands. I want you to leave.'

She stood and bit her lip as if she was thinking what to say, but he knew she had it all rehearsed. She was a calculating bitch.

'The way I see it, I asked you to look after Sergio for a few weeks in Spain and allowed you to bring him here for a holiday. Now you're refusing to let me see him. I'll get a court order if I have to.'

'I'm not refusing you anything, Jackie. God, but you still twist everything I say. It's the middle of the night. Come back tomorrow evening and we can talk.'

'Okay, I'll go. No matter what you think of me, I don't want to upset Sergio. But I'll be back at seven in the morning. You can go to work and I'll stay here with him for the day. Then we can have an adult conversation when you get home.'

He wasn't letting her get away with it. 'I have arrangements made for his care and I'm in the process of enrolling him into a school for September. You can't upset all that.'

'I can and I will.' She picked up her bag. 'Seven a.m. Be here, or you won't like the consequences.'

Boyd sat on the couch for a long time after she'd left. He picked up the bottle she'd been drinking from. He wanted to hurl it at the wall, but instead he drained the alcohol and got himself another.

DAY THREE

63

Boyd had showered and dressed and Sergio was eating a bowl of cereal at the breakfast bar when Jackie returned. Seven on the dot. She rushed in and swamped the boy in a hug. It was a side of her that hadn't surfaced during their marriage. Then, she'd been cold and calculating. Had Sergio softened her? It could all be an act, so he was on his guard.

When Sergio dragged himself out from her arms, she glanced at Boyd as if to say, *see, he missed me*. She looked tired, and he wondered if she'd sat outside on his step all night. Not that he cared.

'Go to work,' she said. 'We have things to do, don't we, Sergio?'

The boy nodded, and his smile widened.

Boyd hugged his son tightly.

'Can we talk for a minute?' He directed Jackie out to the hall and slipped his jacket on nervously.

She said, 'I know what you're thinking, and you have nothing to worry about.'

That tone. The one that put him on high alert. The one that gave him every reason to worry.

'You can't take him away from me, Jackie. Not now that I know about him and love him.'

'I have no intention of taking him anywhere.' She turned to look back at Sergio. 'We have loads to catch up on, so you need to finish your breakfast.' She moved towards Boyd and walked him to the front door.

He dragged his feet, reluctant to leave his son behind, knowing he might never see him again. But what choice did he have?

'I'm warning you, Jackie. If you so much as—'

'I promise he will be here when you get home.'

Was she messing with him? Back to her old ways, mind games. He wasn't falling for it.

'Yeah, and I know how much to trust your promises.'

'When did you turn into such a cynic?'

He caught the sneer in her words, and the tiny hairs on his neck spiked in warning. She was definitely up to something.

'Listen,' he said, pulling off his jacket, 'I'll take the day off and we can discuss everything.'

'Really?' She raised one eyebrow. 'I doubt your favourite inspector will agree to you taking time off, with two gruesome murders to investigate.'

She was right about that. Was this the kind of daily dilemma Lottie had to face? Having to weigh up her commitment and loyalty to her family against her job? In that instant, his admiration for her grew exponentially.

'Okay,' he conceded, against his better judgement. 'You have my number. Ring me if you need anything. And Jackie?'

'What?'

'Don't do anything stupid, because I'll hunt you down.'

'I don't doubt that for a minute. I've a proposition to put to you. I'm here to talk, that's all.'

With alarm bells ringing a cacophony in his head, he left.

In the car, he patted his pocket, reassuring himself that he had Sergio's passport, then sent a text to Chloe informing her he wouldn't need her today. He hoped Lottie didn't find out about Jackie before he had a chance to talk to her. He loved her too much to lose her because of his interfering ex-wife. And no matter what, he could not lose his son.

He'd sort this out himself.

It was his mess to fix.

64

The boss had asked for an update on whether Orla Keating or Helena McCaul had been sighted since they'd left the council car park yesterday. Kirby, late again, slid in beside Garda Brennan as McKeown spoke up.

'I've trawled CCTV from the surrounding area. The car turned right out of the car park and headed towards the canal area. At the junction, it turned left. We got images from Millie's garage when it stopped at the lights there. Then it went straight on when the lights turned green. After that, I haven't got anything else. Neither of them were home when I checked yesterday evening.'

'Send someone to check again. They can't just disappear into thin air. Any updates on the two murder victims?'

Lynch said, 'We have a lot of data in from the public. Garda Brennan and Lei are coordinating the response and bringing me anything that might give us a clue. So far, not much to report.'

'Keep at it, everyone.'

When Lottie entered her office and closed the door, Kirby rushed out to the yard and lit a cigar. He had texted Amy last night to make sure she'd got home okay, but she must have gone straight to sleep, because she didn't reply. He texted her again now. Still nothing.

'Fuck it.' He phoned her rather than texting. It rang out.

He checked the time, recalling that she'd said she had the early shift this morning, which had been her reason for not staying the night with him. He stubbed out his cigar, but was unable to quench the sudden trickle of fear that shot goosebumps up on his skin. A murderer had targeted two women in the town over the last two days. And now he couldn't contact Amy. Was he right to feel unsettled? Or was he being totally irrational? Amy had known about the Life After Loss group, but she had shot down the conversation. He had to talk to someone.

Back inside, he caught up with Lynch as she came down the stairs.

'There's another woman who knew about the Life After Loss group. Amy Corcoran.' He paused to catch his breath before launching again. 'She mentioned it in conversation, though she didn't say she'd been involved. Bianca Tormey, Éilis Lawlor's babysitter, works with her at Dolan's supermarket. I can't reach Amy this morning.'

'Slow down. What are you talking about?'

So he told her about Amy and their conversation last night.

'She isn't a widow,' Lynch stated.

'No, but she said she went through a messy relationship break up.'

'And what has that to do with our murdered women?'

Kirby watched Lynch lean against the wall, studying him. He wavered under her perceptive gaze.

'I told you. She knew about the group.'

'I'm sure a lot of people know about it.'

'If we're going down the route that women who were in this group are being targeted by the murderer, I think Amy might be in danger.'

'You have no proof she was actually in the group, have you?'

'No, but—'

'You're panicking over nothing.'

'I called her a taxi home late last night. I can't reach her. There's this guy she works with. Luke Bray. He's been harassing her at work. What if he's got her and he's our killer?'

Lynch pulled away from the wall and stepped into his space. He looked down at her hand on his arm. 'Kirby, I've known you for a long time. You are a pain in the arse, but I like you. We get on. We think the same way, most of the time. But this time you are making massive leaps where there's nothing to jump over.'

'I have this weird feeling. Something isn't right.'

'She might be at work and forgot her phone, or something as simple as that.'

'She might not be allowed to use her phone on the tills,' Kirby said. 'Okay, I get that.'

'Tip down to Dolan's and see if she's there. If she's not, come straight back and we'll see what we can do. Deal?'

'Sure,' he said, but he didn't feel sure about anything.

He rushed back to the office, grabbed his jacket and headed out.

Dolan's supermarket was busy, despite the early hour on a Sunday morning. Kirby bundled his way inside, rushing past a group of jeans-clad older ladies who were discussing the joy of having a new young priest saying morning Mass.

He looked around for Amy.

She wasn't at any of the checkouts, but he spied Luke Bray, his eyebrow piercing glinting under the harsh lighting. Skipping past the queue, he leaned over to the black-haired lad. 'Is Amy around today?'

'She didn't turn up. Boss is spitting fire and I've to pull a double shift. She'll be on a warning after this.'

'Where does she live?' Kirby couldn't recall the address she'd given the taxi driver last night.

Luke stood and leaned towards him, ignoring the shuffling line of customers. 'You should know. You're the one fucking her, not me.'

Reaching out, Kirby grabbed a handful of the boy's T-shirt, drawing him in close. Luke didn't resist, but a sneer creased his face, turning his clear skin ugly.

'You better wash your mouth out, pup. When did you last see Amy?'

'Calm down, old man. She was here last night. Wanted to skive off early for a date, but she had shelves to stack. Meeting you, wasn't she? Maybe you were the last person to see her. If you know what I mean.'

Releasing the sweaty polyester, Kirby wiped his hand on his trousers and took a step back. 'What are you trying to say?'

'Women have been murdered around Ragmullin in the last few days. I hope Amy is safe and doesn't turn up like them.'

Feeling his rage bubble past boiling point and not wanting to risk his career by punching Luke Bray, Kirby backed out of the narrow checkout space and rushed towards the door marked *OFFICE*.

He coerced Amy's home address from the accounts clerk and left as quickly as he'd arrived.

Amy lived in a pleasant-looking house in a quiet area out on the old Dublin Road. It reminded him of a house that a child might draw. A perfect square with a door centred between two windows, with three windows above.

The car screeched to a halt in the driveway. No sign of any other car. Amy had left hers outside the restaurant last night. Or had she gone back for it and headed off somewhere this morning? Whatever the scenario, he had a nagging feeling he shouldn't have let her go home. If she wasn't here, he'd check with the taxi company to ensure she was brought to the right address.

At the front door, he leaned heavily on the bell before noticing that the door was ajar.

The trickle of fear he'd been experiencing all morning rose in waves, crashing against the walls of a cracked dam within his chest. He stepped inside.

'Amy? It's Larry. Amy? Are you home?'

Glancing around, he noticed her handbag on the floor in the hall and a bunch of keys on top of it.

'Amy?' He was tentative now, each step slower than the last. He called her name up the stairs. Silence. He was alone in the house. To be sure, he searched the rooms downstairs, then headed up, racing from room to room.

No Amy.

In her room, clothing hung neatly in the wardrobe, a paperback by the bed. The bed didn't look like it had been slept in. He couldn't see the clothes she'd worn last night. Her work uniform of black T-shirt and trousers.

Back downstairs, despite his anxiety, he pulled on a pair of gloves, moved her keys and picked up her bag. Her wallet was still there. Bank cards and cash. And her phone. The screen was like a newsprint of his missed calls and texts.

The images of Jennifer O'Loughlin and Éilis Lawlor's dead bodies flashed before him.

Maybe he was being irrational, but that didn't stop the dam bursting. He rushed outside, where he threw up on the lawn, his body shaking with terror.

65

When Boyd arrived at work with his phone glued to his hand, Lottie called him into her office.

'Shut the door.'

He pocketed the phone and sat.

'Boyd, I need your undivided attention. You might pick up on something I miss, and vice versa. You have to be fully committed to these investigations.'

'Are you giving me the boot?'

'Will you grow up?' She rubbed her eyes wearily. 'What's so engrossing on your phone that you've lost interest in helping me find this killer?'

'I'm sorry, Lottie.'

'I'm all ears.' Concern crept into her tone.

'Jackie turned up last night, and again this morning. She insisted on staying with Sergio today. I'm terrified she'll disappear with him while I'm at work.'

'And staring at your phone is going to help?'

'I've an app linked to my home security. I need to check if she leaves the apartment.'

'Then what? Are you going to go running around town after

her?' She felt her nostrils flare and instantly regretted her lack of empathy. But fuck it, she had two dead women and two other women who appeared to have disappeared off the face of the earth.

'Don't be angry, Lottie. Right now, the welfare of my son is more important to me than finding your killer.'

'*My* killer?'

'The killer. Whoever it is.'

She let out a long breath of frustration. 'Where's Sergio's passport?'

He patted his jacket breast pocket. 'Here.'

'Then you have nothing to worry about. There is no way she can take him out of the country without it.'

'You know Jackie. She has contacts everywhere. She can do whatever she bloody well likes.'

'We can put her name on a watch list. She won't get further than Main Street.'

He smiled with a rueful glint in his eye. 'Thanks. But she won't try to leave via ordinary means. She's buried so far in the criminal underworld, she could get on a private plane and we'd be none the wiser.'

Lottie looked over Boyd's shoulder as the door was shoved inwards and Kirby catapulted himself into her office.

'Where's the fire?' she heard McKeown shout as she and Boyd stood.

'It's Amy, boss. I can't locate her.'

'Who? What are you talking about?'

'Amy, she's a woman I met and I was with her last night and now she isn't at home or at work and I don't know where she is.'

'Sit down.' Boyd shoved Kirby onto his chair. 'Deep breaths.'

Lottie laid a hand on his shoulder. 'From the beginning, Kirby. Who is Amy?'

'I only met her a few nights ago and now she's gone. Something must have happened to her.'

'Why do you think that?'

'I hope I'm not overreacting, but...'

'Tell me.'

'We were out for a meal last night. She came back to mine and after awhile I got her a taxi home. Her car was left outside the restaurant. She wasn't answering her phone this morning and I went to her house. The door was open. Her bag, wallet, keys and phone are all there, but she isn't. She knew about the Life After Loss group, boss. She works with Bianca Tormey, Éilis Lawlor's babysitter. This is similar to how Éilis disappeared, isn't it?' He paused. 'It's just so—'

'Has Amy got any family she might be with today?'

'I... I don't know, to be honest.'

'Try to find out, and once you locate her, I want you concentrating on these murder investigations.'

'Thanks, boss. I'll see what I can do.'

Lottie glanced at Boyd, and he shrugged.

She moved over and knelt down beside Kirby. 'We will find your Amy. I need a description and whatever else you know about her. Can you do that for me?'

'Sure, but we need to take a look at one of her co-workers. Luke Bray. He's been harassing her. The little pup was smirking and mouthing off at the checkout this morning. We need to arrest him and find out what he did.'

'One step at a time. Have you phoned around her friends?'

'I don't know her friends.' His voice rose an octave. 'I only met her two nights ago.'

'So what *do* you know about her?'

She stared at him as he concentrated on a spot on the wall, skin pale and hair on end.

'Nothing. I actually know next to nothing about her.'

66

After Kirby had calmed down enough to start searching for details about Amy Corcoran, Lottie looked up to find Lynch standing in her doorway.

'Have you got an update for me?'

Lynch's eyes narrowed, and Lottie thought she looked worried.

'Garda Brennan handed over a file she was working on for Kirby. Asked me to have a look at it.'

'What file?'

'The Tyler Keating cold case.'

'And?' Lottie snatched up her hair in an elastic band she'd rescued from the midst of the carnage in her drawer.

'Jennifer O'Loughlin gave a statement around a week after Tyler Keating disappeared.'

'Really?' Lottie tried to get a timeline straight in her head. 'Did Kirby not recognise her photo on the board or her name?

'He didn't take her statement.'

'What did she have to say?'

'Not much. She said her husband knew him.'

'Had she any idea where Tyler might have got to?'

'No. She came forward. Must have been after an appeal was made asking for information, but it looks like she didn't actually have much information other than her husband had carried out some work for Tyler. Damien O'Loughlin had died from cancer a year before Tyler went missing. And...'

'So?'

'Jennifer said the last time she met Tyler was three or four weeks prior to his disappearance.'

'She was a dental nurse, not a solicitor. Why did she meet him if her husband was already dead? Was it on a personal basis?'

'He was commissioning her to do a painting,' Lynch said.

Lottie bit her lip, thinking. 'Didn't Damien do work on Tyler's house purchase?'

'Yes. There's a copy of the contract in the box of files that was found in Jennifer's lock-up.'

'We need to figure out *why* those files were in the lock-up, along with Tyler's car.' Lottie tapped her pen idly on the desk. 'When we find Orla, I'll ask her. See if Éilis Lawlor or Helena McCaul had a link to Tyler Keating other than his wife being in the Life After Loss group. We need to get to the bottom of the real reason why it was set up.'

'Do you think it's more than just grieving widows meeting to have a drink?'

'I do, actually. But how can I prove it, with the women being murdered or missing?'

Passing over a printout of Jennifer's statement, Lynch said, 'Orla Keating was interviewed seven times in relation to her husband's disappearance. She had no clear alibi, but nothing was found to point to her being involved.'

'Okay, thanks. Where has Boyd got to?'

'He was on his phone, then he rushed out. Said it was an emergency.'

'And we haven't got an emergency here?' Then she realised

it might have to do with Jackie. 'Fuck, I hope she hasn't taken Sergio.'

'Who?'

'Boyd's ex is back on the scene.'

'Is there anything I can do to help?'

'It's best to let him sort it out himself.'

'Don't you think you should follow him? He might need moral support.'

'I should, but I don't think he'd thank me for interfering. Lynch, we haven't one suspect for either murder. It's unacceptable.'

'I agree.'

'I want you to nail down the connection between the women, Éilis, Jennifer, Orla, Helena, even Amy. It must be more than their widows' social group. Is it Tyler Keating?' She waved the statement in her hand. 'I don't want to imagine what will happen if we don't find the missing women.'

'Jennifer was the first to die,' Lynch said. 'She hadn't been seen for a month before her body was found. Why? Had she been abducted, or was she with the killer voluntarily? Did something shift in his mindset that he killed her?'

'The post-mortem points to her having been kept in a cold-storage room, because of the frostbite. With her broken bones, I believe she had been tortured. Did someone think she might know what had happened to Tyler Keating?'

Lynch raised her hands, animated. 'He could be the key. I'll start there.'

'Notify me as soon as you find anything else. We need something, before another body turns up.'

67

Before he dug into Amy's past, Kirby keyed Luke Bray's name into PULSE, the garda database. Bingo. Bray had been previously arrested for assault, and at the district court he'd been sentenced to community service. He had to talk to him again.

Maybe he should have taken someone with him to keep his temper in check, but it was too late now. Kirby huffed through the supermarket doors for the second time that morning, blowing beads of perspiration from his top lip. He flashed his ID badge as he passed the security guard, and before anyone realised what he was doing, he had grabbed Bray by the collar of his T-shirt and dragged him from behind the checkout. He was barely aware of the queue of open-mouthed customers behind them.

'This is garda brutality,' Luke yelled as Kirby tightened his grip on the collar. Anything to shut up the whining little bollix.

Outside on the footpath, he shoved Bray up against the wall, pressing his arm across his throat. Before he could react, Luke had him on the ground in one swift movement.

'What the...?' Confused, Kirby struggled to put his legs underneath himself.

'Tae kwon do.'

Luke put out a hand to haul him upright, but Kirby turned on his side and with some difficulty stood unaided.

'You'll pay for that,' he wheezed.

'You asked for it.'

He watched as Luke took a crumpled pack of cigarettes from his back pocket and lit one. He then had the audacity to offer the pack to Kirby.

'Stick them up your...' he grumbled. 'I want to know your movements since you finished work yesterday evening until the time you clocked in this morning.'

'Why?'

'Answer the question.'

'I was at home in bed all night.'

'Can anyone vouch for you?'

'You could ask my mother, but she doses herself with sleeping pills and wouldn't hear the house being robbed, let alone if I went out.'

'No corroboration, then?'

'No.'

Kirby wondered why Luke was so calm now. Maybe he was hiding something, or perhaps he didn't want to get in trouble for assaulting a detective. Whatever the reason, Kirby felt the kid was too bloody relaxed. That unnerved him.

'You were arrested for assault a few years ago. I think the judge was particularly lenient with you.'

Luke stomped his cigarette out on the pavement. 'So?'

'You attacked a young woman walking alone by the canal and you only got community service.'

'What are you trying to say, old man?'

'You got a lot of people to provide you with good character assessments. And that's why such a serious crime wasn't suitably punished.'

'So what? It wasn't me anyhow. I was stitched up by you lot.'

'You pleaded guilty.'

'I was eighteen. First offence, though it's none of your business.'

'It is my business, because your colleague Amy Corcoran told me you were harassing her.'

'That's a lie. I wasn't harassing her.'

'Amy thought you were, and now she's missing.'

Luke didn't baulk. 'I never touched Amy, and if she's missing, shouldn't you be looking for her, not *harassing* me?'

Kirby silently acknowledged the point. 'If I find one shred of evidence pointing me in your direction, I'll have you in Mountjoy Jail before you have time to pack a bag. Get it?'

'Sure, old man.'

But Luke's bravado had disappeared, a line of worry furrowing its way between his eyebrows.

Kirby pushed him out of the way and headed back to the station.

He still had no idea where Amy was.

68

Jackie was back at the apartment with Sergio by the time Boyd turned the key in the door.

'Where did you go?' he asked, breathless with relief.

'Ice cream,' Sergio said, taking the lid off a Ben & Jerry's.

Boyd hugged him tightly.

'What is wrong with you?' Jackie said. 'Are you having me followed?'

'No...' His voice trailed off as he realised how stupid it looked. He couldn't tell her about his security system. 'I came back for a clean shirt.'

'Nothing wrong with the one you're wearing.'

'I need it for later. Anyway, I live here.'

'I'm well aware of that.'

'Why did you think I was having you followed?'

Jackie slumped down on his couch and dug a finger into Sergio's ice cream. 'Yesterday, I felt there were eyes on me.'

'I didn't even know you were in Ragmullin yesterday.'

'Yeah, well...'

'You've spent so long mixing with criminals, you're paranoid.' He went to the kitchen, indicating that Jackie should

follow him. He didn't want to have a screaming match in front
of Sergio. He opened a cupboard for a glass and filled it from
the cold tap. He could do with a shower to wash away his
anxiety.

'You have murders to investigate without concerning yourself with me.'

'I have, but...'

'But you can't trust me, is that it?'

'This is my home.'

'It's going to be a bit small for all three of us.'

He slammed the glass on the counter. So this was what
she'd been scheming. 'We are not having this out now. I'll talk to
you later. I'll be home by seven.'

'Do you actually keep to a schedule nowadays?'

'I do when you're around.'

'Pity you didn't keep to one when we were married. We
might not be in this situation.'

'You needn't start, Jackie, we both know who was the wrong
one in our marriage.'

He rinsed the glass, dried it and placed it back in the
cupboard. After folding the tea towel, he fetched a clean shirt
from his wardrobe, hugged Sergio tightly, kissed the top of his
head and left without another word.

———

With no leads whatsoever to locate Orla and Helena, Lottie
decided to talk to some that might count as tentative murder
suspects. Because Smile Brighter was closed on Sundays, she
headed to talk to Owen Dalton. The door to the SunUp studio
was shut tight. She hammered on the glass. No answer. She did
it again, harder and more insistent. Must be closed too.

She was about to walk away when she spied Dalton's tall
figure through the glass.

'Come in.' He stood to one side and she bundled in by him, snagging the strap of her bag on the handle. He undid it for her, then locked the door behind them.

'How can I help you, Inspector?' He sat heavily on one of the reception chairs.

Sitting opposite, Lottie said, 'I need to establish some facts. Namely how well you knew Éilis Lawlor and Jennifer O'Loughlin.'

'I only knew them as clients. Both professional relationships, I can assure you.'

'Really? You weren't tempted to get to know either widow a little better?'

'No, because I'm in a serious relationship. I had nothing to do with either woman.'

'And why should I believe you?'

'Because I'm gay.'

'Right.' Lottie took a moment to consider this. Shit. Was Owen even worth pursuing?

'I can see the cogs whirring in your brain.'

'You can?'

'It's the energy you're emitting. You're wired. And for the most part, it's negative energy.'

'Result of the job I do.' Why was she even sitting here with this man, talking about her mental health, when she had two murders to solve and missing women to find? But his soothing voice was lulling her into a false sense of security. She shook herself and turned towards him abruptly. 'When did you last see Orla Keating?'

'She was booked in for a class Friday morning but didn't turn up.'

'And what about Helena McCaul? You told me that she isn't a member, but do you know her?'

'I think she runs that little herbal shop in town. Is that who you mean?'

'Yes. Do you know her?'

'Only to buy herbal supplements.'

'What time did you finish up here Thursday evening?'

'Around nine p.m. I did another half-hour of meditation.'

'What did you do after that?'

'Hasn't changed since last time you asked, I went home.'

'So you'd have been home by...?'

'Ten.'

'You live on Canal View.'

'Yes.'

'Do you live alone?'

'What has that to do with anything?'

'Probably nothing. I'm just loosening up my mind.'

'If you haven't time for meditation or yoga, work on your breathing. I can do a session with you. Won't even charge you.' He smiled, but she felt it was insincere.

'You told me you could get verification of your whereabouts, so who do you live with?'

'My husband.'

'What's his name?'

'Really? You want to know my husband's name? What type of detective are you?'

'His name, please?'

'He's the love of my life. He brought me to this place and made my life whole.'

'Save me from the violins, Owen.'

'My husband is Frankie Bardon.'

Lottie could feel the cogs he'd mentioned whirring in her brain, but they kept slipping out of sync with each other.

'Do you want me to introduce him to you?'

'No thanks.' Lottie stood and moved to the door. 'I've already met him.'

69

Kirby leaned against the board in the incident room and almost fell over when it wobbled precariously. He righted it on its stand and approached Lynch. She was concentrating on something on a computer.

'Any news about Orla or Helena's whereabouts?' he asked.

'Not a dicky bird. McKeown is going over whatever CCTV he can get his hands on. I reckon if he had any hair he'd be tearing it out right now. Soul-destroying work.'

'Good enough for him.'

Lynch paused her fingers mid-air above the keyboard. 'Have you found Amy?'

Fearing he might cry, Kirby shook his head. 'I don't trust that Luke Bray, but I also don't think he harmed her. He's one of those lads that's all talk.'

'Didn't you discover he had a conviction for assault?'

'It was about four years ago. He's kept his nose clean since, according to PULSE. Except for harassing Amy.'

'Did she report it?'

'No. I've come to the conclusion that he hasn't the intelligence to mastermind two brutal murders and three possible abductions.'

He watched her swivel idly before she stood and arched her back.

'While everyone is losing their heads,' she said, 'at least we can be logical about what's going on. Let's talk this through.'

'Thanks.'

She joined him at the incident board. 'Should we assume one of the missing women is involved with the murders?'

'You think one of them could be the killer?' He stared at her, eyes bulging at the implication. 'Do not include Amy!'

'You hardly know her, Kirby.'

'Yeah, but I'm a good judge of character.' He felt the heat rise in his cheeks. 'Most of the time.'

'Okay, don't get uptight. Let's look at this.' She tapped a photo with her bitten biro top. 'First up we have Orla Keating. You led the investigation into her husband's disappearance. What did you make of her back then?'

Leaning against the desk behind him, Kirby folded his arms to keep his hands from twitching. He wanted to be out searching for Amy, but Lynch was right. He had to approach this logically.

'Orla struck me as having been under Tyler's control,' he said. 'Why did she wait five days to report him missing? That always bugged me. She told me she believed he was at a conference and she had no reason to suspect he was missing. And then when he didn't return home, she reported it.'

'She'd tried to contact him during those five days, hadn't she?'

'She phoned a few times, but the calls went unanswered. She said she assumed he was busy. I really think that marriage was on the rocks.'

'Do you think she did something to her husband?' Lynch queried.

'I honestly don't know. She said that when he didn't return home she made enquiries and discovered he hadn't turned up in Liverpool at all.'

'It's all a bit weird, to use your favourite word.' She chewed the lid of her pen. 'What else struck you about her?'

'She was calm enough in the circumstances.'

'You said she struck you as being under her husband's control. Why did you think that?'

'The house was shining when I visited the first time, but gradually she seemed to be losing her sense of how to keep it tidy. Not that I can talk, if you saw the state of my house. It's just an observation.'

'It might also be because she was struggling without knowing what had happened to him.'

'I don't think it was that.'

'You think he was keeping her stuck at home as his little housewife, but when he was no longer around, she let things go?'

'Maybe she felt a sense of freedom without him around.'

'The statement from Jennifer O'Loughlin in the file, how did that come about?'

'I've been thinking about that. When we went through Tyler's home computer, we found he had a lot of correspondence with Damien O'Loughlin, who worked at Bowen Solicitors. I contacted his office at the time and was told he'd died the year before. They wouldn't give me any information regarding his work with Tyler, so I called Damien's wife to see if she could shed light on things. She agreed to make a statement.'

'Did you not recognise her when we found her body?'

'I didn't take her statement. Never met her.' He looked away, embarrassed. He should have made the connection with her name. Since the night with Amy his mind had not been fully on the job.

'In Jennifer's statement, she says she met Tyler three or four weeks before he disappeared. He commissioned a painting. But what was Damien doing for him other than his house contract?'

'He specialised in conveyancing and wills. That kind of thing. Orla claimed not to know anything about it and Bowen Solicitors wouldn't reveal any specific information. Tyler was missing, not dead.'

'But it's a year later; maybe they'll tell you now.'

'I can try. But I still have those files from the lock-up. I need time to examine them in more detail.'

Lynch sighed. 'I found inconsistencies around timelines in the various interviews that Orla gave. I know she never had an airtight alibi, but first she said she was away the morning he was due to fly out. In another statement, she says she was in bed and didn't hear him leave. Did you notice that?'

Kirby walked to the window and looked down into the yard. 'Yes, and I asked her time and again about her whereabouts. She said she was so distraught that she kept getting confused. I grilled her as best I could, but in the end, I could never find any evidence to point to her having been involved in her husband's disappearance.'

'And now she can't be found.' Lynch sat down, pulling the keyboard close. 'So we can't ask her to explain.'

'Why is Tyler's car in Jennifer O'Loughlin's lock-up? Bleached and cleaned. That's a total mystery.'

'Maybe she was more involved with him than just creating a painting for him.'

'Whatever it was, Jennifer is dead, and because of his car being there, it's possible she was involved in his disappearance.'

'Or his murder,' Lynch said.

'He might still be alive.'

'Do you believe that?'

'Not really, no.'

'Come on, Kirby, we need to find answers. And find a killer.'

'That too.'

70

When Lottie arrived back at the station, Kirby called her to the incident room, where Lynch had updated the board with a bullet-point list of all involved. She added the information she'd just discovered.

- Jennifer O'Loughlin: dental nurse, part-time artist. Body found on waste ground at Ballyglass Business Park. Tyler's car found in her art studio.
- Éilis Lawlor: interior designer. Worked on Jennifer's house. Established Life After Loss widows' group. Body found at Ladystown lake.
- Helena McCaul: Herbal Heaven. Group member. Missing since lunchtime Saturday. Mother claims she's a liar and is not married.
- Orla Keating: accountant. Group member. Missing since Saturday. No clear date of when husband disappeared. Difficult to pin down an alibi.
- Amy Corcoran: Dolan's supermarket. Last seen Saturday night.

- Tyler Keating: accountant/part time lecturer.
  Disappeared twelve months ago. Car (bleached)
  found in Jennifer's lock-up. Five-day window for his
  disappearance. Possible retrieval of GPS data.
- Damien O'Loughlin: solicitor with Bowen's.
  Jennifer's husband. Dead two years – cancer.
  Correspondence on Tyler's computer. Work files in
  Jennifer's lock-up.
- Kathleen Foley: retired nurse. Helena's mother.
  Claims Helena lies.
- Luke Bray: Dolan's supermarket; colleague of Amy
  Corcoran. Harassed Amy? Conviction for assault.
- Bianca Tormey: schoolgirl. Éilis's babysitter, works
  in Dolan's supermarket during holidays.
- Frankie Bardon: dentist. Employed Jennifer as a
  dental nurse. Married to Owen Dalton.
- Owen Dalton: deluxe yoga studio. Éilis, Jennifer
  and Orla members. Married to Frankie Bardon.

Turning away from the board, Lottie asked, 'Did Amy
Corcoran attend SunUp or Smile Brighter?'

'I'll find out,' Kirby said.

'No, you're too close to this.' Lottie patted his arm. He was
shaking.

'With her belongings left behind at her house, she has to
have been taken. It's too similar to Éilis Lawlor's situation. I
need to find her.'

'Was she part of the widows' group?'

'She mentioned that she knew about it,' Kirby said.

'I'm sure a lot of people knew about it.'

'That's what I said.' Lynch capped the marker noisily.

Lottie glanced at the board. 'There are no definite signs that
Orla and Helena have been abducted.'

'Other than we can't find them,' Kirby said grumpily. 'They were last seen driving off together in Helena's car.'

'Maybe they're involved in the killings,' Lynch said. 'Or one of them is, and abducted the other.'

The door shoved inwards as McKeown entered waving a printout. 'I found where Helena's car went.'

Lottie turned with Kirby and Lynch to watch him march up to the board.

'ANPR at the M4 toll caught it travelling to Dublin yesterday evening. And it passed through again this morning at two a.m.'

'And where is it now?'

'Caught it on the bridge at Millie's garage heading downtown this morning. I checked all the traffic cams and figured it had returned to the council car park beside Herbal Heaven. I've just scanned that footage. It's there. Parked by an end wall.'

'And the women?'

'I haven't gone down to look yet.'

'Why are you still here then?'

McKeown flushed up to his scalp. 'Right. I'll go now.'

'I'll go with you.' Lottie grabbed her bag. 'Keep teasing it out on the board. Something will click. And Kirby, do more digging on that Luke Bray. Lynch, see if there's anything in Bardon or Dalton's lives we need to know about. But before you do anything, find bloody Boyd for me.'

Lottie and McKeown approached Helena's car cautiously and tugged on gloves. She had tried calling Boyd on the short drive to the car park, but he hadn't picked up. Reining in her frustration, she peered in through the windscreen with McKeown at her shoulder.

'Empty,' he said.

'I can see that.' She moved to the driver's door. 'Unlocked.'

She leaned inside. The seats were clear, and though the footwell on the passenger side contained some fast-food wrappers, nothing seemed out of place. Not a shred of rubbish in the back. Was it too clean? She pressed the boot lever. Empty. Not even a spare tyre.

'Go back over the security footage.' She pointed to the camera at the entrance. 'I want to see who drove it in and who got out of it.'

'Sure.'

'Let's have a look around Helena's shop.'

The shop was right beside the car park, and she was surprised to find the shutters open. She glanced at McKeown, who shrugged.

Inside, the little bell tinkled and she held a hand to her chest in anticipation. What if the killer had taken Helena and had her displayed grotesquely waiting to be found? She heard a sound like a kettle boiling.

'Wait here,' she told McKeown. She moved forward.

'Be with you in a minute.' The voice came from the door at the back of the little shop, just before a woman stepped out holding a mug. The scent of coffee wafted towards Lottie.

'Oh, Inspector.' Orla Keating slopped her drink on the floor. She stepped over the spillage, her white trainers avoiding it, though Lottie saw a splash land on her pink leggings. 'How can I help you?'

'What are you doing here?'

'Helena asked me to open up. She wasn't feeling well.'

'And when did she ask you to do that?'

'Early this morning.'

'How did you get the keys?'

'She has spares hidden out the back. Told me where to find them.' Orla had moved to the counter and seated herself on the stool at the till. Her voice was calm. 'What is this about?'

'Were you driving Helena's car?'

'When?'

'Orla, it's time to quit the bullshit. You were in Fallon's lunchtime yesterday. I have CCTV images showing Helena's car being driven through the M4 toll yesterday evening and back this morning at two a.m. It's now outside in the car park. Explain.'

Orla remained statuesque, cup raised towards her mouth, but her eyes belied her calmness. The amber flecks had darkened, making them almost black.

'Oh, right. Yes. After our drinks at Fallon's, she didn't want to go home. We decided to get out of this suffocating town for a few hours. I booked us into a hotel in Ballsbridge. We had food and drinks, but she was restless and wanted to go home. I drove back and she rang early this morning asking me to open up the shop, so here I am.'

Lottie huffed. 'There's been a full-scale search on for both of you.'

'Why?'

'You disappeared without letting anyone know where you were going.'

'We're adults.'

'And both of you were friends with two women who were murdered in the last two days.'

'That's why we had to get away. We needed time to think and clear our heads.'

'How long have you known Helena?'

'About a year.'

'How long had you known Jennifer O'Loughlin?'

'What has she got to do with me?' Orla was defensive now, Lottie noted. Good.

'Come on, Orla, you knew her before you joined the Life After Loss group. Didn't your husband, Tyler, commission a painting from her?'

'A painting? I've no idea what you mean.'

Lottie decided to rattle Orla's cage. 'Was Jennifer having an affair with your husband? Maybe you decided to get rid of him, and then her.'

The amber flecks in Orla's eyes flared like fire. The first flicker of anger. 'You are joking me. Tyler was a charmer when it suited him, but he was obsessed with me. He wasn't shagging anyone else.'

'Do you know that for sure?'

She slumped back on the stool and placed her mug on the counter. 'Tyler was hard work, Inspector. He was infatuated with me initially. Then that turned to what I now recognise as coercive control. I couldn't do anything right. He had to be in charge. I was a virtual prisoner in my own home. I had to give up my office in town and work from the attic. I still loved him, and I believe he loved me in his own warped way.'

Lottie leaned both hands on the counter. 'I have two gruesomely murdered women and three... no, two now who are missing. I'm losing ground on this killer, and I think it is the time for the truth.'

'I can't tell you anything other than what I've told you already.'

'Where do you think Tyler is?'

'I assume he's dead.'

'Did you have anything to do with his disappearance?'

Orla shot up off the stool and slapped the counter. 'That is ridiculous.'

'People have died. What do you know, Orla?'

'I can't answer any more questions. If you want to proceed with these preposterous insinuations, I will call my solicitor.'

'Damien O'Loughlin was Tyler's solicitor for his house purchase. What can you tell me about him?'

Orla blew out a sigh. 'Damien did the contracts and related work, but that's it. I don't know where you're going with these questions, but I think you should leave.'

She walked out past Lottie towards the door. McKeown opened it and stepped outside.

Lottie stood into Orla's space. 'I believe these murders have something to do with whatever you were all up to in that group. Was it a front for something sinister?'

'I'm not answering any more of your ridiculous questions, Inspector.'

'Maybe Tyler is alive and is murdering women you knew. Or maybe, just maybe, *you* are killing the women *he* knew. Whatever the answer, you may have been the last person to see Helena. No matter how clever you think you are, I am smarter than you. I will rake over your life as if it were rotting leaves on the ground. Goodbye.'

Outside, she inhaled the warm air. She took one backward glance and saw Orla with her nose pressed to the glass, her mouth open in disbelief. Yes, she had overstepped the mark of professionalism, but sometimes you had to stir the boiling pot vigorously to see what spilled over.

71

Where was Helena? Lottie sent a uniform to check her house, and the report came back that it was empty. She revisited her conversation with Orla but could not figure her out. Was she outright lying, or twisting the truth to suit her own agenda, whatever that might be? They had no clear suspect for the murders. She had already talked to Owen Dalton, and she decided it was time to speak with his husband. She had to be doing something rather than sitting waiting for answers to miraculously appear.

She headed over to Canal View. Frankie and Owen lived in a two-storey sandstone brick apartment block. The grounds were enclosed behind a sliding gate with an intercom. The gate was open. Good.

She inhaled the floral scent from the colourful window boxes. There was a bell, but she lifted the brass knocker, a Buddha depiction, and let it flap down. Instantly the door opened, and she looked up at Frankie Bardon, sunglasses resting on top of his bleached hair. She was reminded of an Australian surfer. She passed in by him when he stepped back to allow her to enter.

Pleasantly surprised by the plump cushions scattered around the floor, she searched for a chair. None. The decor was like a shrine, with golden glittered ornaments lining bookshelves and windowsills.

Frankie pointed to a large cushion. A beanbag, she discovered as she sank into it awkwardly.

'You might want to take off your shoes,' he said.

She noticed he'd removed his flip-flops as he plumped up a cushion.

'I'm sorry. Will I mark your floor?'

'No, but it's more comfortable.'

Thinking of her sweaty feet, she said, 'I'll keep them on, if you don't mind.'

'Not at all. What brings you here?'

What indeed?

'I spoke with Owen earlier today. He told me you two are married.'

'Correct.'

Frankie removed his sunglasses from his head and slowly folded them into the pocket of his creased white linen shirt as he sank down onto a cushion opposite Lottie. She averted her eyes from his long, tanned and shaved legs, and stared at his sculpted face instead.

'I want to know everything about Jennifer O'Loughlin.'

'I've already answered all your questions. What has her death got to do with me?'

'I'm conducting secondary interviews with everyone who knew her.' Trying to wrong-foot him, she said, 'Were you at home last night?'

'Yes, I was. Finished work at five and have been here since.'

'What time did Owen get home?' She was grasping at straws, she knew, as she had no evidence to point her to either man having done anything illegal.

'Why do you want to know?'

'Just answer the question.'

'After ten. And he was here all night until he left at six thirty this morning for his studio.'

'And you were definitely here all night too?'

'I had to be, to know that Owen was here.'

Smart-arse, she thought.

'Did you know Éilis Lawlor?'

'She might have been a client. I'll have to check.'

Lottie tapped her phone and turned the screen towards him. 'Jog any memories?'

'She is a startlingly beautiful woman.'

That wasn't the answer Lottie wanted, and anyway, she didn't really agree. Éilis was pretty, but not startlingly so. 'Did you know her?'

'I gather you know she attended Smile Brighter, hence your questions. But I'm not the only dentist there.'

'You still haven't given me an answer.'

With a half-smile, he said, 'You are persistent, aren't you?'

Lottie glared.

He raised his hands before dropping them to his lap. 'Okay, yes. I think I did some work on her teeth. I can't tell you when I last saw her, though. I'll have to check at the office. Is there anything else?'

'Did you give her any advice like you gave Jennifer?'

'I can't even remember the woman, so how would I know what we might have talked about?'

'Tell me about Orla Keating.'

For the first time, he appeared unsettled. Stretched out his legs and leaned back into his bean bag cushion.

'I just worked on her teeth.' He paused as if considering how much to reveal. 'But I knew her husband, Tyler. Quite a bit of work, he was.'

'Was?'

'He's still missing, isn't he?'

'How did you know him?'

'He was a client of mine.'

'Why did you not like him?'

'Erm, this is awkward.' He looked more unsettled than a moment ago.

'Go on.'

'Tyler Keating was homophobic, if you must know. He heard about my relationship with Owen and asked to see a different dentist, because he didn't want to catch AIDS from me. Like, this is not the 1980s. And in case you're wondering, I am not HIV positive.'

'I wasn't wondering that at all. Times have changed a lot since the phobia of the eighties.'

'The attitude of some people hasn't changed.'

'Were you interviewed when he went missing?'

'No.'

Lottie made a mental note to talk to Kirby. 'Did he succeed in changing dentists?'

'I told him to grow up. It was me or no one.'

'I bet that went down a treat.'

Frankie smiled. 'A joy to behold. He was in agony with an infected molar, otherwise he'd have walked out.'

'Did you see him on more than one occasion?'

'I gave him a script for antibiotics with dates for follow-up appointments. I think I saw him two or three times in total. I can—'

'Check when you get to the office. Do that. Where were you when Tyler disappeared?'

'I don't know for certain, but it was this time last year, so I was probably in India. Yes, that sounds about right.'

'Can you check it now?'

'I keep my diary on my work computer, Inspector.'

'Ring me as soon as you know.' She waved a hand around the room. 'You have a lovely home. Did you decorate it yourself?'

'Owen and I did it together. Why?'

'You didn't hire an interior designer, did you?'

'Owen had some great ideas. I agreed with most of his suggestions.'

'But not all?'

'You really know how to pick words apart.'

'It's my job.'

'To answer your question, we mutually agreed on the decor.'

'Has Owen been to an ashram with you?'

'Yes. He claims I dragged him along.' He laughed.

'And you converted him?'

'That sounds like I shoved him into a cult,' he said with a half-hearted smile. 'No, he came to accept the way of life I proposed.'

'Was he with you in India a year ago?'

'No, I went alone.'

'You say you got him to accept your lifestyle. Was he always a yoga instructor?'

'Not at all. When we first met, he was a college tutor in Athlone.'

Lottie felt her jaw drop. 'Did he know Tyler Keating there?'

'You'd have to ask Owen.'

'I can't believe he gave that job up to teach yoga?'

Frankie rose to his feet like a lithe panther and held out a hand to help her up.

'Inspector, I can't make anyone do something they don't want to do. Owen was in a rut. He was trying to impart his wonderful knowledge to a bunch of uninterested students. He was almost suicidal when I met him. He was open to all I could give. Including my love. I helped him build a state-of-the-art business.'

Lottie paced around the small apartment, lifting elephant and tiger ornaments and replacing them, noticing no dust around them. It made her realise that everything was pristine. Maybe Frankie could have a word with her kids.

'You told me that you know the Herbal Heaven shop in town...'

'Yes. I get all my vitamin supplements there, and the nettle tea is to die for.'

'When did you last see Helena McCaul, the owner?'

His body tensed. 'She isn't dead too, is she?'

'I hope not.'

'I was in there last week. She seemed fine then.'

'Did she talk to you about any problems in her life?'

'I'm not a therapist.'

'But you tried to help Jennifer. Did you try to help Helena also?'

'We only spoke about herbal remedies.'

'When I was talking to you the other day, you mentioned you had lost someone close to you. Do you mind me asking who that was, and when?'

'I do mind, because it has nothing to do with you or who I am now. I've put my grief behind me. I don't think you have put yours behind you, have you, Inspector?'

'Like you said, it has nothing to do with you.'

She tried to read his expression, but failed. Unable to come up with further questions, she took her leave. At the door, she turned as she remembered something.

'Did you know Jennifer was an artist?'

'She never said.'

'You didn't know about her studio?' A lock-up, she thought, not a studio.

'She had a studio? Gosh, if I *had* known, I'd have encouraged her to take up art full-time. Perhaps I was blind to the full picture.'

And Lottie wondered if she was blind too.

72

Lottie picked up Boyd at the station and they drove round to Helena's house again. She marched up to the door with him in tow.

'I still can't understand why you wouldn't text me where you were and why you'd gone home. You can't just disappear like that.'

'It was an emergency.'

'Was it, though?' She knew she was being unreasonable, but feck it, he'd left her high and dry. Another inspector would have him up on orders.

'I thought it was. I can't afford to take any risks or I could lose my son. Do you understand that?'

'I do, but Boyd, we have an active killer out there and we can't find him. Or her. Please give this your all while you're here, and if you have to leave, for God's sake, tell me.'

'I'm sorry, I didn't stop to think.'

SOCOs had completed a quick sweep of the house yesterday, and it was now silent as a graveyard at midnight.

'She's not here,' Boyd said.

'Her mother said she hadn't seen her for over a week, and

she's not at her shop. Orla said she left her at home. Where the hell is she?'

'She might have other friends to bunk in with.'

Lottie yelled up the stairs. 'Helena?'

'We're wasting our time here.'

'There is a back way in.' She made her way to the kitchen, mindful not to walk on the specks of blood. The door was locked. 'Helena could well be our next victim, and Orla Keating was the last person to see her alive.'

She walked into the utility room and scanned her eyes around. Empty wine bottles in a bin. Fresh bottles in a cooler. She tapped the walls.

'What are you doing now?'

'I want to make sure there's no false walls.'

'Lottie, you're losing your shit now. The woman is a pathological liar and could be anywhere.'

'Or maybe someone wants us to think that. She could be in mortal danger.'

'Or she could be a killer.'

'Has the lab come back with a DNA hit on that blood we found?' She pointed to the floor, where the blood had dried brown.

'It's too soon.'

'Get on to them.'

As Boyd slouched off, she had a feeling of dread that Helena could be the next victim. She feared for the woman. It was obvious she was delusional, thinking she had a son and a dog, not to mention a dead husband. Had she become the latest victim of a crazed killer? Try as she might, Lottie could not figure out what the killer was at. She just knew she had to find Helena and Amy before it was too late.

Kirby scanned the file for the names of everyone who had been interviewed with regards to Tyler Keating's disappearance. Frankie Bardon's name was not on the list. But it wasn't a surprise. There had been no reason at the time to talk to his bloody dentist.

And there was still no sign of Amy.

He'd tried to find any friends or family, but hit a brick wall and nothing had turned up on PULSE. He just didn't know enough about her. He phoned the supermarket office and requested her job application form or CV. But he was met with the usual GPD stalling. Get a warrant. He'd just hung up when the phone rang again.

'Is that Detective Kirby?'

'Yes.'

'This is Shauna. I work in Dolan's HR department. I over-heard Mr Cooke talking and I wanted to say I am really scared for Amy.'

'Why so?'

'She's under a lot of pressure. Because of Luke.'

'Do you know Amy well?'

'Just here at work. She's a private person, but I know she tried online dating for a while. And she joined that Life After Loss group after a break-up.'

This was news. 'Do you know who she broke up with?'

'No, she never spoke of him.'

'Shauna, is there any way you could email me her job application and whatever else might help me?'

'I shouldn't, but I'm so worried with all these murders. I'll scan what I have and email it to you.'

Kirby rattled off his email address and said, 'I appreciate this.'

'I just want to help. I sincerely hope Amy doesn't end up like those other poor women.'

He agreed, but felt choked up. 'Before you go, did she say anything else about the Life After Loss group?'

'She only mentioned it briefly. I think she might have gone to one or two meetings. She didn't think much of it, if I recall correctly.'

'Bianca Tormey works with you, doesn't she?'

'Yes, but she isn't in today.'

'What can you tell me about her?'

'She works summer and holiday time. She's still in school. A lovely mannerly girl.'

'And Luke Bray. Anything you can tell me about him?'

'Only that he's a prick and gets away with too much around here.'

'If you think of anything else, phone me straight away. And I'll await your email.'

He hung up and stared at the computer until the email arrived. He opened the attachments and began to read.

73

As Lottie reached the corridor, her phone rang. She sat on a step at the top of the stairs and took the call from the state pathologist.

'Hi, Jane, what have you for me?'

'I've completed Éilis Lawlor's post-mortem. This might be nothing, but I thought it unusual.'

'Go on.' She leaned against the wall, thinking that if she didn't get back running soon, she'd end up wheezing like Kirby.

'Like your first victim, the dress on Éilis is three sizes too big. I'm sure you knew that.'

'I did.'

'And it's evident that the killer washed and dressed both women after he killed them. Plenty of twigs and leaves on Éilis's dress, but I haven't found anything there to link to a killer.'

'Okay. What *have* you found then?' Lottie knew Jane hadn't called for small talk or to arrange to meet for a coffee.

'She was over the alcohol legal limit when I tested her blood. No evidence of drugs. I'll get the lab to do further analysis.'

'Anything else I need to know?'

'Cause of death. Heart attack.'

'What?'

'Probably brought on by shock after her bones were savagely broken. Eyes removed post-mortem.'

'That's one good thing, in this swamp of horror. Any word back on the carpet fibres you found?'

'Nothing yet. I'll follow it up again today.' Jane paused. 'The sculpture where Éilis was placed. It's a depiction of Fionn Mac Cumhaill.' She spelled it for Lottie. 'Pronounced McCool.'

'I know that.'

'I think you might want to dig into Irish mythology, because I did a little research and found that the area where Jennifer's body was dumped is listed on an ancient manuscript as the site of a fairy fort.'

'Really? Isn't it supposed to be bad luck to disturb one of those?' Lottie recalled this from her school days. 'Maybe the carnival being on site pushed someone over the edge.'

'I don't know about that, but it got me thinking about the removal of the women's eyes. I thought of Oedipus from Greek mythology.'

'You've lost me now.'

'He blinded himself with two golden pins as an act of punishment because he was ashamed to realise he had killed his father and married his mother.'

'Ah, Jane, that's gross.'

'I know. But I think the locations where this killer puts the bodies might give you a clue as to the murderer. And that's coming from one who believes in science, not folklore.'

Lottie had to hunch up on the step as two guards came up the stairs.

'Those sites have been plaguing me. You've given me food for thought. Thanks, Jane.'

74

Kirby was well aware that he had no legal right to read Amy's application form. But he was concerned for her welfare, even if she wasn't long enough missing to warrant such an invasion of privacy. Needs must, he thought as he scrolled through the information.

She had filled out the template form, answering standard scenario questions on being a team player, dealing with awkward customers, and what she thought were her best attributes relating to the job. All the usual stuff. He wasn't prepared for the shock when he got down to her employment history.

It was short.

One previous employer. Amy had worked as a legal secretary for Bowen Solicitors, the firm where Jennifer O'Loughlin's husband, Damien, had worked before he died. Why hadn't she told him? Had he even asked? He racked his brain, but their conversations were clouded because on both occasions he'd been drinking.

Was it a coincidence? Unlikely, now that Amy was nowhere to be found. An unexpected gust of wind outside rattled the windows, causing him to jump. What had caused her to leave a steady job eighteen months ago to work in a supermarket? Did her messy break-up account for the change of job?

'All okay over there, Kirby?' Lynch asked.

'Sure, sure.' Biting his lip, he scrolled down line by line on the application once again. He sensed Lynch rising from her chair and coming to stand at his shoulder. He wished she'd feck off. He wanted to do more digging into Amy's life. But he kept getting distracted.

'What have you found?'

'Amy Corcoran, my Amy, worked as a legal secretary for Bowen's, the firm where Damien O'Loughlin worked. She listed one of the partners, Madelene Bowen, for a reference.'

'It's a tenuous link between Amy and Jennifer. It's something, though.'

'Look at her second referee. I don't understand what I'm seeing.'

'Tyler Keating!' Lynch exclaimed, clamping a hand on Kirby's shoulder. 'What the actual fuck?'

'What has he got to do with Amy?'

'I have no idea.'

'You need to talk to Orla Keating.'

'I need a smoke and a pint.'

'No, come on, I'll go with you.'

'Where?'

'The boss said Orla is working in Helena's herbal shop today. We'll catch her there.'

'We need to tread carefully.'

'Kirby? Coming from you, that's a laugh.'

'I'm serious.' He stood and stretched, his knees clicking. 'The boss thought the Life After Loss group and Tyler Keating were key to all of this. But what if it's something to do with Bowen Solicitors?'

'Let's have a word with Orla Keating first and see where that leads us. Okay? I don't want you putting your size twelves in the wrong place, so let me do the talking. And print out that form.'

He hit the print button, and as the copier whirred in the corner, he shrugged on his jacket.

'The boss can't find Helena McCaul,' Lynch said as they got ready to leave, 'and according to her last known sighting, she was with Orla Keating.'

'This should be an interesting conversation, then.'

'Just remember, I'm doing the talking, Kirby.'

'We shall see.'

He pretended that he didn't see Lynch's eye-roll. He had to find Amy, and he hoped the sinking feeling in the pit of his stomach didn't mean he was already too late.

———

It's all getting a little cramped now. That Lottie Parker is no pushover. But I knew she would be a formidable opponent. The thing is, I don't want to be caught. Not yet. I have more work to do. More eyes to collect to help me see the truth of the world. Oh, there was a lot of terror in those eyes just before I took their owners' lives. Jennifer was weak with hunger and had almost given up, but there was a little fight left in her. Then Éilis was setting out to be a challenge until she keeled over and died on me. Shame. In my rush to dispose of her body, I hope I didn't leave any evidence behind. The water from the hose should have helped douse anything incriminating. And then the last one. That was a huge rush and I was almost thwarted. I have to go back and finish the job.

I know every contact leaves a trace, no matter how careful I am. I just hope to be so far ahead of the guards that it won't matter when they do find something.

I have to make ready a new site for the next lot of broken bones.

I move back to stand outside the padded living room. Peering through the hole in the door, I see my latest captive has stopped trying to escape the tight binds. Fruitless. Waste of energy. There's no way they can bite their way through cable ties. And they can't run with broken legs. I grip the piece of timber tighter in my fist. Time to break the arms, and then I'm on to the exquisite part.

75

Lottie was still sitting on the stairs, digesting what Jane had told her, when Kirby and Lynch came bustling out of the office. The information from the pathologist was interesting, but was it really some warped fetish couched in mythology that was driving their killer? Anything was possible.

'Where are you off to?' she asked.

Kirby showed her the printout. 'I found a connection between Amy Corcoran and Tyler Keating.'

'Slow down. In here, and explain.' She took his arm and gently led him back towards the office.

Once seated, Kirby began to speak as Lottie glanced over Amy's job application.

'You mean to tell me that the woman you only met this week has a connection to the husband of our first victim, Jennifer O'Loughlin, and to a man missing for a year?'

'It's not much, but it's something,' Kirby said. 'She worked for Bowen Solicitors, but listing Tyler Keating as a referee gives us a lot more to chew over.'

'How did she know him well enough to ask him for a reference?' Lottie's head thrummed with all the new information coming at her.

'That's why we were on our way to speak with Tyler's wife. Can we head off now?' Kirby stood and turned towards the door.

'Stay right here.' She knew she'd have to be cruel to be kind. She couldn't afford for Kirby to go off half-cocked. 'You have to consider that Amy might be involved in these murders in some way.'

'She can't be. I was with her the night Jennifer's body was dumped.'

'The whole night?'

'Yeah.' He looked doubtful. 'I think so.'

'You think so, eh?'

He rubbed his hands together so hard, Lottie could see flecks of skin flying in the air. 'The thing is, I'd had a fair drop and was a bit out of it, but that's not to say—'

'Enough! You and Lynch stay here. You still haven't thoroughly analysed those files from the lock-up. They must be important. Boyd can come with me to talk to Orla.'

'He was following up with the lab about the blood found in Helena McCaul's house,' Lynch said. 'Then he went to talk to her mother, Kathleen Foley, again.'

'I'll bring Garda Lei or Garda Brennan with me. Let Boyd know about Amy and then contact Bowen Solicitors to find out why she left her job.'

Garda Lei was the only one who was apparently at a loose end, so Lottie nabbed him to accompany her to Herbal Heaven.

At the shop, she pushed in the door, relieved to find it unlocked. She'd been worried Orla might have disappeared again.

The bell tinkled as she stepped inside, Garda Lei following close behind.

'Gosh, the smell is awesome,' he said. 'Look at all those tubs of vitamins. I'd be floating if I took the half of them, and—'

'That's great, but I need you to be quiet.' She moved quickly and immediately realised that the shop was empty.

The door at the rear was slightly ajar. She crept forward. 'Orla? Are you here?'

'Don't think she is,' Lei said.

'I can see that.' She flicked a switch. Light flooded the little shelved room and seemed to heighten the herbal scents.

'That looks like ground-up leaves in that mortar bowl with the pestle.'

'How do you know that?'

'Just do.'

She pulled on gloves, lifted a brown paper bag from one of the shelves and sniffed. It was the overriding scent in the room. She held it under his nose.

He inhaled the scent. 'Lavender. Used as a sleep remedy.'

Returning the bag to the shelf, she noticed a narrow door between two cupboards.

'Another storeroom?' he offered.

'Or an exit.'

She tugged the handle. No movement. She pushed. The door swung open. She stepped into a small alley. Empty, except for two wheelie bins. One for rubbish and the other for recycling. She lifted the lids to find they were both half full of what they were supposed to contain. Dropping the lids, she moved along the side of the building towards the street.

'Anyone could come in this way,' Lei said from behind her.

'Or leave.'

Back in the shop, she looked around to see if there was any evidence of a struggle. Not finding anything unusual, she tried Orla's number. Silence, except for Lei's breathing. She figured he was trying to rein in his need to be constantly saying something.

'Orla didn't leave in a hurry.' She rummaged under the counter. 'Neither her bag nor her phone is here.'

'Where do you think she is?'

'If I knew that, I wouldn't still be standing here, would I?'

'Suppose not.'

She watched as he meandered between the shelves. Had Orla really left the shop voluntarily? Would she have gone without locking up?

Wiping a bead of sweat from the bridge of her nose, she realised that the place was sweltering. Back in the little room, she searched for a thermostat to turn off the heat. On the wall to her right, just inside the door, she found a switch and flicked it. A crash sounded from the shop just as a panel, the size of a narrow door, slid open before her.

'Lei? Are you okay?' She didn't want to see what carnage he'd caused, and the space in front of her looked more interesting.

Without waiting for his reply, she moved into the darkness. She couldn't find a light switch. A knot of fear tightened in her chest.

'Lei! Quick. I need you in here.'

The sound of her own voice muffled any noise behind her.

She didn't see the plank of timber coming down on her shoulder.

She just fell to the floor, into a murky swamp of darkness.

————

Boyd learned nothing he didn't already know from Helena's mother, and was on his second cup of tea when he got Lynch's text about Amy.

'Mrs Foley—'

'Kathleen, please.'

'Do you know anything about an Amy Corcoran?'

'Erm, I'm not sure. Maybe. Is she another dead woman? God Almighty, I hope Helena is okay.'

Boyd stared at her, wondering why Amy's name had caused her to become suddenly flustered.

'We're searching for Helena. Now, about Amy. It seems to me that you do know her.'

'Name rings a bell from somewhere. Does she work with Helena?'

'She works in Dolan's supermarket, but she used to be a legal secretary for Bowen Solicitors in town.'

'I used that firm for my will and to put this house in Helena's name, though she doesn't know about that. I couldn't risk her smothering me with a pillow to get her hands on the house to sell it.' She laughed, but Boyd could see she was only partly joking.

'Any solicitor in particular at the firm?'

'Now that you ask, I think he was called Damien O'Loughlin. Didn't he die of cancer?' She slammed a hand to her mouth. 'Dear God in heaven, was he related to the poor murdered woman, Jennifer?'

'Her husband.'

'Detective Boyd, what is going on?'

'It's safe to say that we're finding connections between all the interested parties, and we just need to pin down what it is that ties them together to make them targets for a killer.'

He knew he had gone too far when her face turned ashen and her hand shook so much that she dropped her cup. It shattered on the floor. She jumped up and fetched a mop and hurriedly attempted to clean up the spilled tea and shards of crockery. The smell of the dirty mop filled the air, and he felt it stick to his skin like glue.

'Here, let me do that. Sit down, Kathleen.'

He took the handle and she grasped his hand tightly.

'Find her, Detective. Find my girl before she suffers like the others.'

A feathery bundle of sorrow settled in his stomach. He thought of the blood they'd found in her home. Would they find Helena in time?

Before he left, he turned to Kathleen. Her lipstick had faded and he could see where some of it was smudged on her teeth. She leaned against the hall table, knocking a set of keys to the floor. She was a broken woman, he concluded.

'Kathleen, Amy Corcoran is also missing.'

Instantly, her hand flew to her mouth.

'Oh no!' Her voice was a whisper, and she doubled over, convulsed in tears.

76

Kirby loitered behind Lynch as she worked. She had pulled up Amy's Facebook page.

'Amy is stunning,' she said.

'You say that like you can't understand why she'd be interested in me.'

He noticed she had the grace to blush. He didn't care what she or anyone else thought, he was sure Amy liked him. Certain she had no ulterior motive. But now that he thought about it, what would such a beautiful woman see in him? An overweight, clotty, cigar-smoking, next-to-useless detective. He leaned against the back of Lynch's chair.

'Do you think she was only with me because of my job?'

She wheeled the chair around so quickly he almost catapulted into the desk behind him.

'I'm sorry, Kirby, but it has crossed my mind.'

'Shit, Lynch, I don't believe it.' He shoved his hands in his trouser pockets and his fingers found a crushed chicken nugget.

'For fuck's sake.' He threw the rancid food into the bin under her desk and went on a little march around the claustrophobic office, coming to a standstill back where he'd started. 'God, Lynch, I hope it's not like that.'

'I found her on a dating site. And you're on it too. Is that how you met her?'

'No, she just happened to be in the same pub as me the other night. We got talking, and one thing led to another.'

'You met her in Fallon's, did you?'

'Yeah. I'd had a few at that stage.' He could add drunkard to his personal CV, he thought.

'She's mixed up in this somehow,' Lynch said. 'I wish the boss would come back with Orla Keating. We need to advance this investigation, and quickly.'

'She's been gone a while. Ring her.'

'She could be interviewing Orla at the shop.'

'Or not.'

Lynch was tapping her phone when Boyd appeared round the door, tugging off his suit jacket.

'I've had the most interesting conversation with Helena McCaul's mother.'

'Has she any idea where her daughter might be?' Kirby asked.

'No, but she knew Amy Corcoran. Broke down in tears. Apparently she'd fostered Amy as a child. Helena was insanely jealous of the girl at the time. Kathleen was sure that jealousy had turned into hate.'

Kirby stood open-mouthed. 'I can't figure out if that's important or not.'

'Kathleen also said she'd used Bowen Solicitors. Damien O'Loughlin worked on her will and the transfer of some property.'

'Boss isn't answering.' Lynch pocketed her phone.

'I'm going there to see what's up,' Kirby said.

'Hold on,' Lynch said. 'Try Lei on the radio.'

'You do that. I want to keep busy and I need the fresh air.'

'I'll go with you.' Boyd shoved his arms into his jacket again.

'Thanks a lot, guys,' Lynch said as the two men disappeared out the door.

———

Her head was thumping like a drummer in a rock band had taken root inside her skull. Lottie brought her hand to the back of her neck and it came away with blood on her fingers. Her shoulder thrummed with pain. Blinking, she looked up into Boyd's concerned eyes.

'What happened?' he asked. Taking her hand, he raised her to her feet. 'Are you okay?'

'No, I'm bloody well not okay.'

'You need stitches.'

'Later. Get me a cloth.'

She watched as he reluctantly left the darkened room. She vaguely remembered a panel sliding back in the wall, and stepping inside. Then... nothing.

'This is all I could find.'

She took the balled-up kitchen paper from him and swiped it at the back of her neck.

'Let me do it for you,' he said.

'I'm fine, stop fussing. Was Lei attacked too?'

'Yeah, he has a bump the size of the Harbour Bridge on his head, but he says he'll be fine. I actually think he's delighted at being in the action.'

'A few more knocks and bangs and he'll change his tune.' She swept her hand around the small enclosure. 'What is this place?'

'Looks like a cold-storage room.'

'That's what I thought. Jennifer had frostbite. Shit, Boyd, do you think she might have been held here?'

'We better call SOCOs. Come on out.'

'Just a minute. I want to take a better look. Is there a light?'

'No.' He switched on the torch on his phone and the room lit up like a Christmas tree. 'Holy fuck.'

'Christ, what is going on, Boyd?'

She tried to ignore the throbbing in her head as she walked down the narrow room, careful not to touch anything but too curious to wait for SOCOs.

The room was designed like a galley kitchen, with cupboards on either side and a narrow stone-slabbed walkway between them. Only they weren't cupboards. They were chest freezers.

At the end of the walkway, she came to yet another door.

'What is this place? This building is like a maze,' Boyd said.

Lottie remained tight-lipped, partly because she had a blinding headache, but mainly because of the large steel bolts screwed to the door with a series of padlocks and a combination lock.

'I don't think Helena was keeping a supply of nettles in there, do you?'

'Doubtful.' She leaned her ear close to the door, but there was no sound. 'What if there's someone in there? Do you think this door is dense enough to block out sound?'

'I don't know what to think.' Boyd lowered the phone and the door became a dark hulk.

'Fetch the big key to get us in there while I check the freezers.'

'Like I said, we need SOCOs. No point in using a battering ram when there could be evidence—'

'Boyd! There could be someone in there. Helena and Amy are missing, and Orla seems to have evaporated into the ether. Any one of them might be inside, hurt or dying, even dead.'

'And any one of them could be a killer.' He raised the phone again and scanned the area with the beam of light. 'It's hard to believe there's this much space. From outside, the shop looks tiny.'

'The shop itself is small, but the building is like a warren.' She raised her hand and hammered the door. 'Ouch. Jesus, Boyd, it's rock solid.'

'Listen.' He moved closer to the door.

'What?'

'I heard something.'

'From inside?'

'Yes. No. I don't know.' He held the phone over his head, the light bumping all over the walls and ceiling. 'Maybe it was from the freezers.'

'Shit.'

She bundled past him and began lifting the lids. Layer upon layer of dried flowers and herbs. Boxes of green tea. So not all made from scratch by Helena with her pestle and mortar.

'Lottie,' Boyd called. He'd opened the lid of the last freezer.

'What? It's empty.'

'I know, but look right at the bottom corner.' He shone the phone torch inside. 'Could be blood.'

'Right. SOCOs will have to confirm it. We found blood in Helena's house too. We just need a sample of her DNA to find out if it's hers.'

'You think she's dead?'

'She could be, or this blood could be from a victim and Helena is our killer.'

'She'd want to be mighty strong to be lugging dead bodies around.'

'Ways and means,' she said. 'Someone was strong enough to knock out both myself and Lei. But you said you heard something. It hasn't come from the freezers, so it has to have come from the locked room. Get the big key.'

'I don't think—'

'That's an order, Boyd. Get the battering ram.'

———

Once Kirby had ensured that Garda Lei wasn't going to die, he went over to listen at the storeroom door. The boss and Boyd were going hammer and tongs. He knew who would win that argument.

Outside, he walked down the alley at the back of the shop and opened a small gate that led to a paved yard surrounded by high walls. Glancing around, he studied the end wall. It had a raised platform, bedded with herbs and plants. A wooden planter, full of peat, which appeared to have been recently disturbed. Why? he wondered. He began to dig in with his fingers, rewarded with little more than dirty hands. Nothing was buried there that he could find at the moment.

Wiping his hands on the legs of his trousers, he stepped back and studied the building directly behind Helena's shop. It looked like offices, but he couldn't get the location straight in his mind. Spatial awareness was not one of his strong points. He took a series of photos on his phone.

As he unlatched the gate to leave, something caught his eye. On the paved ground to his right lay a thick plank of timber with what looked like blood on its tip.

'Fuck me,' he said with a whistle. 'The bastard fled this way.'

He didn't dare touch it, but he examined the herb beds more carefully and was rewarded with two footprints, one deeper than the other, as if someone had launched themselves upwards.

Small feet. Trainers. The Nike symbol imprinted on the peaty earth.

'There you are,' Boyd said.

'Look at this,' Kirby said as he walked carefully around the small yard. 'He came out this way.'

'Someone did.'

Kirby felt like thumping Boyd for not respecting his powers of deduction. 'There's a bloodied plank by the gate. Don't touch it.'

'Did you?'

Now Boyd was really pulling his chain. Kirby pointed to the red-brick building over the wall. 'What's there?'

'Apartments I think. Shops on the ground floor and overcrowded residences above.'

'Reckon the attacker lives in there?'

'Maybe they couldn't risk being seen fleeing onto the street out front. You sure you didn't touch anything?'

He shook his head wearily. Why did no one trust him? 'Just that planter box. The clay had been disturbed and I had a suspicion a weapon might be buried there.'

'Did you find anything?' Boyd wandered over to have a look.

'Nope. I only scraped the top of it, and before you go accusing me of disturbing potential evidence, I didn't touch anything else.'

'We need to be professional, Kirby.'

'Is that a dig at me? Because if it is, you can go fuck yourself.'

'Christ Almighty! What's eating you?'

'In case you've forgotten, my new girlfriend is missing and I'm certain someone took her.' He puffed his cheeks in an effort to keep control of his emotions. 'While we've been farting about, she could already be dead.'

Shouldering his way past Boyd, he was careful to nudge the gate with his sleeve. Shit, he'd opened it without gloves. Maybe Boyd was right to question his ability. But he had no time to waste feeling sorry for himself.

He had to find Amy.

———

It was a close call but I have to put it behind me. I have to keep going.

I stomp up and down the lakeshore, small stones cutting through the soles of my shoes. Fists clench and unclench. Breaths, long and deep. In, out. In, out. I have to calm down if I am to see this through. Will Lottie Parker and her team of misfits succeed in hindering the remainder of my plan? Possibly. The only saving grace is that they have no idea who I am. Luckily, I got to her before she found the locked room. I can breathe a little easier knowing I have removed anything that would have identified me. But the mystery of my identity is close to being solved. I must advance my plans at top speed.

I look at the barrel with the body tightly crushed inside. I had to break the spine as well as the arms and legs to squash it in there. Even now I can see the forehead flush with the rim, loose tendrils of hair flying around in the rising breeze. No way can I drag it to the top of the hill. I'm not that stupid and my muscles are aching.

Tipping the barrel onto its side, I roll it across the stony shore until it rests at the bottom of the hill. I'm glad dark clouds have shadowed this beauty spot, otherwise there could be families picnicking and swimming; teenagers drinking and diving. I checked out the area over the last few weeks, and I know that most people gather at the diving boards a few kilometres away.

I should be undisturbed here in finishing what I set out to do. Those who have attempted to interfere in my life have to suffer. They will learn that there is no life after loss.

I hope you like the present I left for you in the locked room, Lottie Parker, because it was not what I planned. Sometimes I must accept that not everything works out.

77

Lottie knew her face was on fire with the rage boiling within. She'd sent Kirby to check out the apartment block behind the shop, but Boyd was dragging his heels getting the big key and Garda Lei was complaining like he was at death's door. If they wouldn't help her, she'd have to fetch the battering ram herself.

She was about to flip open the car boot, wondering how she was going to lift the heavy piece of equipment, when the technical van pulled up behind her and Grainne Nixon stepped out.

'I really need a break from all this,' she said. 'Is there another body?'

'Not if you discount Garda Lei.'

'What? He's not dead, is he?'

'He thinks he is. Will you give me a hand here?' Lottie opened the boot.

'No way am I lifting that,' Grainne said, stepping around her. 'Not in my job description.'

'For crying out loud, not you too?' Lottie growled. If she could get it to the ground, she'd be able to drag it inside. It was damn heavy, and she nearly let it fall on her foot, which caused Gerry, the SOCO photographer, to come to her rescue.

'Let me help you,' he said.

'One decent person left in the world,' she mumbled, and followed Grainne inside while Gerry laboured behind them.

'Why do you need me here?' Grainne said, tugging the hood of her protective boiler suit up over her voluminous red hair. 'I'm still processing the scene at the lake.'

'Looks like flecks of blood in one of the freezers. Needs to be checked. Whether it's human or animal is anyone's guess at this stage. We found a locked door through there.'

Grainne flicked on a large torch. 'I'll send samples to the lab. Could that door have any more locks?'

Lottie waited for Gerry to get the key in place. 'Boyd thought he heard something inside.'

'I understand the urgency.' Gerry was panting like he'd run a marathon.

'Can you manage it?'

'Sorry. No. You have to be trained how to use this.'

'Give it here.'

She wrestled the heavy ram from him as Boyd joined them in the tight dark space, the door now illuminated by Grainne's torch.

'I got a screwdriver. I think it's best to take off the hinges.'

'And how long will that take?' Lottie felt her shirt sticking to her skin, and if she didn't get a painkiller for her head soon, she was sure she would turn into a serial killer herself. The three people standing around her were in line to be her first victims.

'Okay, let us at it,' Boyd said, abandoning his screwdriver idea.

He and Gerry manoeuvred the battering ram between them, and on the count of three, they had the door in bits, hanging off its hinges.

Inhaling deeply, Lottie stepped over the threshold into the darkness.

———

Detective Sam McKeown studiously ignored Lynch. Their working relationship had been irreparably damaged because of his affair with Martina Brennan. He felt further alienated when he found out the inspector was trying to have him shipped back to Athlone. Fuck the lot of them, he thought, and began to watch another file of security footage. This one was from Dolan's supermarket, a little bit up the road from Herbal Heaven, taken earlier that morning.

There were no cameras in or outside the herbal shop, and he'd already trawled through footage from the council car park without finding anything he could determine as being out of the ordinary. He had seen Orla Keating park Helena's car, and head for the shop. Other than that, it was shoppers in and out of the car park.

Now he concentrated on the camera images captured at the front door of the supermarket. A young lad with piercings, in dark clothing, came out and lit a cigarette. He appeared to be talking to someone just out of the camera angle. He was staring across the road. McKeown glanced at the time on the top corner of the footage. An hour before the boss and Lei had arrived at the herbal shop.

What was the lad so interested in over there? Had he anything to do with whatever horror might lie within the locked room? It was now the talk of the station.

McKeown kept his eyes on him. The lad stubbed out the cigarette underfoot and propelled himself from the wall, making his way out of shot. Not back into his place of work, but down and across the street.

McKeown quickly pulled up Google Maps to see what else

was over there besides the car park and Herbal Heaven. A block of flats to the rear of the shop. His fingers travelled across his keyboard, frantically trying to discover whether the apartments had any cameras. Some at the front, but none at the back where the lad was headed.

Back to the supermarket footage. He fast-forwarded, and within five minutes the lad returned. He was smoking again, and just before he entered the sliding doors, he flicked the cigarette to the ground. That cigarette might have DNA on it. It might be nothing, but it might be everything. Time had passed, and by now there could be a multitude of butts or debris there, but he couldn't take the risk of losing it.

78

The stench hit Lottie first. Human waste. Then she caught the smell of fear and death in the air. She grabbed Grainne's torch and waved it around the small, dank space.

Boyd moved to her shoulder and groaned. 'God, no...'

She was speechless as nausea coursed through her stomach and up her throat. Her saliva dried up and her tongue stuck to the roof of her mouth. She had to force the words out.

'I... I... God, Boyd, what went on in here?'

She moved towards the woman lying naked in a pool of her own blood and waste.

'Inspector, please don't contaminate the crime scene.' Grainne's voice floated over Lottie's head like melting snowflakes as she hunkered down beside the pitiful shape. She could see a bone sticking out from torn flesh. The woman had her arms wrapped around her head. Blue nylon rope bound her hands together. They didn't appear to be broken.

Lottie's nose quickly became accustomed to the rancid odour, and she placed a finger on the woman's throat, leaning down to hear if there was any breath.

A faint pulse.

'She's alive! Ambulance. Paramedics. Quick! Now!'

'Who is it?' Boyd said after he'd shouted back for Garda Lei to radio for the required assistance. The SOCOs had retreated to give them space.

'It's not Helena or Orla. It must be Amy Corcoran. Give me your jacket.'

She took it from him and covered the woman's nakedness. Her intention was to give her heat. She knew she was committing the ultimate sin of contaminating evidence, but her first aim was to save a life.

'Her eyes...?' Boyd whispered.

'No blood there.' She carefully lifted one eyelid. 'Thank God. We need the paramedics! We can't let her die. And keep Kirby out of here.'

'Too late.' Her burly detective seemed to shrink within the beam of light as he dropped to his knees beside her.

'Is it...?' She was unable to continue.

'It's Amy,' he whispered.

'Please leave her to me, Kirby. I'll take care of her, but you need to leave.'

He reached out a gloved hand and touched Amy's brow. Then he raised himself from the floor, leaning on Lottie's shoulder. He squeezed it, and was gone.

'Kirby,' she called after him. 'Don't do anything stupid.'

———

Lynch was pissed off at being left behind while the others got to do active jobs outside. She had to shake off her annoyance, though, because women were missing and women were being murdered. She had to do what she could by trawling through the mounds of information on her desk. If she was diligent, she just might find the needle in the proverbial haystack.

Martina Brennan was busy with Tyler Keating's file but looked up when Lynch banged her keyboard.

'We're missing something vital,' Lynch said, frustration marking each word.

'Tell me, what did Detective Boyd say about Kathleen Foley and Amy Corcoran?'

'Kathleen fostered Amy as a child, and apparently Helena was insanely jealous.'

'Could Helena be behind all this?'

'Well, according to her mother,' Lynch said, 'Helena invented a son and a dog and a dead husband. Kathleen claims she might have been suffering abandonment issues following her biological father's lack of interest and the death of her stepdad.'

'I can't see how having abandonment issues could lead to the murder of innocent women. But let's keep an open mind.'

Lynch began at her keyboard again and documented everything she knew so far about Helena McCaul. She hadn't taken on the Foley name when her mother had married. Kathleen Foley had told Boyd that Helena's stepfather had never formally adopted her.

According to Kathleen, her daughter suffered delusions. But was that actually true? They only had the mother's word for it. Something wasn't sitting right with all this. Something was staring her in the face. Something she just could not see. Damn.

She went to the incident room and stared at the photos of the dead and missing women, plus Tyler Keating. Then she looked at the photos they'd added that morning of the main people of interest. Frankie Bardon, Owen Dalton, Luke Bray. Kirby had added the last guy because he worked with Amy and had allegedly harassed her at work.

That caused her to remember that she still had to follow up with Bowen Solicitors about the reason Amy had left the firm.

And what about this Luke guy? She searched through her pile of notes to see if he had been interviewed. She knew Kirby had spoken to him but she couldn't find his name anywhere. Maybe she'd missed it. But it was more likely that Kirby had failed to write it up.

79

McKeown didn't waste any time faffing about with introductions.

'I want a word, Mr Bray. Outside. Now.'

His tone worked, because Luke dropped the oranges he was stacking and walked with McKeown out the back door.

He shoved the lad up against the wall and held him there, his forearm tight to his chest.

'If you don't tell me what I want to know, I will personally extract each one of your piercings with pliers, and then I'll start on your teeth, braces or no braces.'

'Wha... What are you doing, man? Is it not enough one geek manhandles me, he has to send another one?'

Tightening his grip, McKeown said, 'Only speak when I tell you to speak. Got it?'

Eyes wide, Luke remained silent.

'You went out front earlier today to have a smoke. Nod if that's true.'

Luke nodded.

'You met someone there.'

Another nod.

'You went across the road to Herbal Heaven.'

A hesitant nod.

'Who did you speak with?'

An imperceptible shrug.

McKeown loosened his hold slightly. 'You can talk.'

After a few gulps, Luke said, 'I can't say.'

'If you don't want to end up in jail for murder, you better tell me.'

'M-murder? Hey, no way, man. I didn't kill anyone.'

'Who did you speak with?'

'I could end up dead.'

'That's a risk you have to take.' McKeown breathed deeply. He knew that what he was doing was intimidation, but he'd heard that Amy Corcoran was fighting for her life.

Luke shook his head, and his eyes sprouted tears. 'Man, you're giving me a death sentence.'

'Who the fuck did you meet?'

'She said it was nothing. She gave me fifty euro. Said to tell no one.'

'Who did?'

'I don't know who she was. Fifty euro is fifty euro when you haven't got it.'

'What did you have to do for your measly fifty quid?'

'I had to walk into the shop and unlock the back door. That's all.'

'Who was there when you went in?'

'No one. It was empty. She could have done it herself.'

'Did you wear gloves?'

Luke's jaw dropped, and McKeown saw the realisation dawning on the lad's face of what he had walked himself into.

'No! Shit. Whatever happened there, my prints will be all over the gaff. Fuck.'

'Not so clever after all, are you?'

'Shit, fuck.'

'I want a description of the woman.'

'No way, man. She said that if I talked, I'd end up in the bottom of Lough Cullion. Said her boss would break my legs and then my arms, and gouge my eyes out. Gruesome shit.'

Now it was the turn of McKeown's jaw to drop. The lad had described how the two murder victims had been found. Information that had been withheld from the media. He stepped back, releasing him. 'She said all that?'

'Yeah. Fucking headcase, if you ask me.'

'And still you did it.'

'Fifty quid is—'

'Fifty quid, I know. You're coming with me to make a statement and to look over some photographs.'

'What about my shift?'

'Should have thought of that when you took blood money.'

'Blood money? What are you talking about? I only opened a fucking door.'

'You let in a killer, and now a young woman is taking her last breath in this world because of you.'

Luke had the sense to keep his mouth shut.

'Your good friend Amy Corcoran is almost dead, and you set her up to be murdered.'

He wasn't prepared for the lad to take flight, and the kick to his shin hurt bad, but McKeown was bigger and faster despite the shock. He caught Luke, and this time he handcuffed him.

'Now I have you for evading arrest.'

'You never said you were going to arrest me.'

'You must be deaf as well as stupid. Come on.'

And just for spite, because he was pissed off, McKeown marched Luke back through the crowded supermarket and out to the car.

The air around Ragmullin was stagnant. The relentless heat, following the torrential rain a few days ago, had lost its initial appeal, and it was now just overbearing.

Kirby dragged off his jacket and bundled it up under his arm. Found his cigar. Lit it and inhaled deeply. He nearly let it fall, his hands were shaking so badly.

Why had Amy become a target for the killer? Was it something to do with her previous job at Bowen's? Was it because she'd been fostered by Helena's mother? Was it even because of Luke Bray? No, that dimwit hadn't the wherewithal to plan and carry out the abductions and brutal murders. If not Luke, then who?

He rounded a corner and was surprised to find he was back at the station. Garda Martina Brennan was coming out the door with Lynch. Both women took him by the arm and hugged him. So, they had heard.

'Don't do anything stupid, Kirby,' Lynch said.

'That's the second time that's been said to me in the last half-hour. Did you know that Amy called me Larry? Had me looking around to see who Larry was.'

Martine smiled sadly. 'Can't wait to meet her and fill her in on a few home truths about you. She might run a mile.'

He remembered the scene on the floor in the room at the back of Herbal Heaven. Amy wouldn't be able to walk, let alone run, for quite some time. His heart almost broke at the image. He tried to distract himself by making conversation.

'You both seemed like you were in a hurry. Have you found out something?'

Martina looked sheepish. Lynch straightened her shoulders and said, 'Boyd called. Said the boss told us to find you and sit on you.'

Kirby sat down heavily on the step, reluctant to go inside. He couldn't face any jibes from McKeown. Not today.

'I saw her, you know. Lying there. She looked like a broken doll. So damaged. How can someone do that to another human being?'

'Because they're pure evil, that's how.' Martina sat beside him and gave his arm a squeeze.

He resisted the urge to put his head on her shoulder and cry.

'Come up to the office,' Lynch said. 'We need to work every hour in the day.'

'Why are we still out here then? Come on.' He shook himself and stood. He took Lynch's outstretched hand, clasped it firmly.

As they reached the corridor to the office, McKeown came towards them, his face pumped.

'I have someone in the interview room who may have met the killer.'

Kirby stalled; then, before Lynch could stop him, he hurried along with McKeown. 'Let me at them.'

Luke was sitting in interview room two.

Kirby had asked McKeown why he hadn't put him in the newer interview room.

His tall, shaven-headed colleague had smirked. 'The little shit doesn't deserve any comfort.'

Kirby squeezed in beside McKeown while Luke sat on the chair with the burst leather seat and protruding springs. He hoped they tore another arsehole for the young prick. Unable to hide his distaste, he said, 'I knew you were a bad one when I first heard about you.'

'You know nothing.'

'I know you've committed a crime, and it won't be community service this time, young pup.'

McKeown butted in before Kirby lost it. 'We will find your fingerprints on the door of the building where a vicious assault took place. You better take a look at the photographs we're about to show you and—'

Kirby interrupted. 'And if you don't come up with an answer, then I'm not sorry to tell you that you'll be locked up and I will personally throw the key in the canal.'

'All talk, fat man. I know my rights. I'm entitled to a solicitor.'

Kirby turned to McKeown. 'Aren't all the duty solicitors busy for the entire day?' Rhetorical question. He glared at Luke. 'You'll have to spend a night in the cell waiting for one.'

'Okay, okay. Show me the photos.'

McKeown opened the slim folder and proceeded to place six photographs in front of Luke, whose braces clicked as he ran his tongue around his teeth.

Keeping his eyes firmly locked on the young man's expression as each photo landed on the desk, Kirby was certain one image had evoked an even louder click.

'No. Sorry. Don't know any of them. Can I go now?'

Liar.

'Look very carefully. You're already an accessory to attempted murder.'

'I'm what? Go on, you're making an eejit out of me. I never did anything.'

'You opened a door to let in a killer. That's accessory in my book. Is it in yours, Detective McKeown?' Kirby was relieved when McKeown played along.

'All the way.'

'Hey, piss off, the pair of you.' Luke jumped up.

'Sit down, before I make you.' McKeown dropped the smile

'You assaulted me outside the supermarket.' Luke pointed from one to the other. 'That's garda brutality.'

'And that's a lie. Indicate the photograph that shows the person who gave you the precious fifty quid. If there even was fifty quid at all. Maybe that's another lie and you're mixed up in this way more than we first thought.'

'You took my wallet. You know the money's in it.'

'Could have had it all along.' The notes were being forensically examined as they spoke. 'Do you recognise anyone in these photographs?'

'No.'

'What about this one?' Kirby knew he was leading the witness, as he pointed to the photo he was sure had evoked a reaction.

'That's Helena,' Luke said at last. 'She owns the herbal shop where I buy magnesium for my mam. It wasn't her.'

Shit. Kirby pointed to Orla.

Luke shook his head emphatically. Too emphatically? Kirby wondered.

'No. I told you, it's not any of them. I swear on the Bible.'

McKeown snorted and placed another six photos on the table. Kirby studied Luke. The lad was trying hard to keep his face neutral, and failing miserably. Something on the table had caused his pallor. His hands trembled before he let them drop to his knees.

The six photos had a few wild cards, but the rest were people they had interviewed so far, and McKeown had thrown in Tyler Keating as well.

'I think I'll wait for that solicitor.'

'You haven't been charged with anything. You're just helping with our enquiries.'

'Well, I'm done here.'

'Luke, this isn't a Netflix crime show,' Kirby said. 'This is real life. Amy is lying in hospital, critically injured. I believe you met the person who assaulted her. Tell me.'

But Luke kept his now pale lips firmly sealed.

And Kirby knew they would eventually have to let him go.

81

In the incident room, Kirby drew out a chair and sat between Martina and Lynch.

'Want to talk it through?' he said to Lynch after telling them Luke had refused to say another word.

'I'm now thinking could Helena McCaul be the key to what's going on? It's even possible she is the killer.'

Martina said, 'It was her shop where Amy was locked up. It has to be her.'

'But Orla was running the shop earlier in the day when the boss called there.'

'We'll come to her in a minute,' Lynch said. 'The Life After Loss group was for widows, but not all the women were widows. Separated and divorced women were involved too. Éilis Lawlor set it up. Jennifer O'Loughlin was a member. Amy Corcoran? We don't know yet, but you said she went through a messy relationship, so maybe she was.'

'The girl in the supermarket office said Amy joined the group and may have gone to one or two meetings.' Kirby tried to force concentration while his mind kept flicking back to Amy. Her photo pinned on the board reminded him that she was perilously close to death. And of course that twit Luke had opened the door to let in a killer or give them an exit.

'We still can't figure out a motive for the murders and attempted murder,' Martina said.

'If we forget about Life After Loss and concentrate on the women,' Lynch said, 'we might find something else.'

'Like what?' Kirby asked wearily.

'First let's look at Helena McCaul.'

'Go on.'

'Her mother, Kathleen Foley, says she's delusional. Kathleen fostered Amy as a child. Helena was jealous. Helena made up an imaginary husband, then invented a child and a dog. We haven't found a marriage cert for her yet, so we could assume Kathleen is correct.'

'Why did she pretend to be a widow?'

'To gain access to the group?'

'But why? She's a herbalist. She has her own business, kept afloat by her mother. Why would she set about killing other women?'

'To hide the murder of the woman she really wanted to kill, namely Amy.'

'That seems a bit extreme.'

'Maybe. But we need to look at other motives.'

'Like what?' Kirby was tiring of talk. He craved the opportunity to get going to find the killer and throttle them.

'Before that, another question,' Lynch said. 'Why take the eyes? Jane, the pathologist, mentioned Oedipus to the boss.'

Kirby looked at her blankly, and she explained about the Greek mythology.

'So now you think Helena killed her father or something?'

'Don't know what to think. Look, I collated all the intersecting characters and cross-referenced their statements. Some are just notes but three interesting characters come to the fore. Orla Keating, obviously, because her husband disappeared mysteriously a year ago, plus she has a connection to most of the women. Amy named Orla's husband Tyler as a referee on her CV and she used to work for Bowen Solicitors, the same firm that employed Damien O'Loughlin, Jennifer's husband. Orla knew Éilis and Helena through the group; she has the tightest links to all the women. Plus she attended SunUp yoga studio.'

'Loads of people do yoga, but I don't recall that Helena or Amy did.'

'That brings me to the next character. Owen Dalton, the yoga instructor. He said he bought vitamins in Herbal Heaven.'

'Not a crime.' Kirby tapped his shirt pocket. He needed a cigar.

'The next person of interest is Owen's husband Frankie Bardon; he is top of my list after Orla. He's the head dentist at Smile Brighter, where Jennifer worked. He's released his client list. All the women attended his clinic and—'

'Listen, we still haven't a shred of evidence to tie anyone to the murders.' Kirby felt his head going round in a perpetual circle.

'I know that, but if we can find a likely suspect, we can work backwards with the evidence we have.'

'What evidence?'

'Tyler Keating's car was in Jennifer O'Loughlin's lock-up. Why? Who put it there? Has it been there a year? I don't know yet. We're still waiting to see if anything can be got from the GPS. Did you finish going through the files from the lock-up?'

'I had one look through. Seems to be property transfers. I haven't had time today to go over them in any more detail.'

'It's important, Kirby,' Lynch said. 'Delegate it. I phoned Bowen Solicitors to find out why Amy left.'

'What did they have to say for themselves?' Kirby ran his finger inside the collar of his shirt and loosened the button. He wanted to go to the hospital. He wanted news on Amy, but at the same time, the longer he heard nothing, he wasn't hearing bad news.

'I spoke with Madelene Bowen. She sounded distraught. She agreed to meet me.'

Kirby was at the door in a second. 'Let's go talk to her.'

Lynch stalled. 'I don't think you should come. You and Amy—'

'I'm going to meet this woman whether you like it or not.'

'Fine. You know you're nothing but a big bully.'

Kirby stared, but his shoulders dropped with relief when he saw the smile appear on Lynch's face.

82

Madelene Bowen was waiting for them in the tight reception area of her legal practice. She shook their hands warmly before leading them along a threadbare carpet to her office. Bowen Solicitors was located in a Victorian-style house that had been haphazardly converted into small offices. It was situated down a side street not far from Dolan's supermarket. Kirby had googled it on the way over and found that the exterior was protected by some heritage order, and now he wondered if the interior was similarly protected.

They took seats in the small, square office, which had an even older-looking carpet than the corridor. They declined the offer of tea or coffee.

Madelene appeared tall behind a desk that was too large for the room. Her black leather chair gave the impression that she had sprouted dark wings. She wore her platinum hair tugged back severely, and Kirby felt she would be a match for any foe across a courtroom.

'We appreciate you meeting with us, Ms Bowen,' he said.

'Madelene, please. Talking to you is the least I can do after hearing about Jennifer and poor Amy. Is she going to survive? This world never ceases to amaze me.'

Without answering her question, Kirby said, 'How long did Amy work for you?'

'Six or seven years, I think. She came to us straight from college, and I have to say, she was the best legal secretary we ever had.'

'Why did she leave?'

'She gave no explanation. One day she was here and the next she wasn't. Posted in her resignation and took her annual leave in place of her notice. It was very odd.'

Kirby looked at Lynch, who raised an eyebrow. 'She didn't email or tell you in person?'

'It was unusual. We are a tight-knit firm and I view my staff as friends. I was shocked, to tell the truth.'

'Did you notice anything different about her in the weeks leading up to her resignation?'

Madelene closed her eyes. 'I certainly did. Her personality changed.'

Opening her eyes quickly, she stared at Kirby, and he knew he definitely wouldn't like to stand in a witness box being cross-examined by her.

'In what way did she change?' he asked.

'She had always been quiet and diligent; then suddenly she was loud and her work slipped. She made a few mistakes. Nothing major, but I noticed them. I had a chat with her and I found her... how can I put this... floaty, maybe? Like she was a little vacant. Then the next minute she was yelling at me. So unlike the Amy I'd come to know.'

'Did you find out the reason?'

'In the months leading up to her resignation, she had been dealing with an awkward client. I can't divulge the details because of confidentiality, but she had been working with Damien before his death on an acrimonious probate. My firm deals with everything, but Damien's speciality was wills and conveyancing. That's the transfer of property title. There was some dispute over rights to ownership of a house, if my memory serves me correctly and she was dealing with the paperwork in the months after his death. Then she quit.'

'What was Amy's exact role here?'

'She was Damien's legal secretary. She kept his diary, sat in on meetings, took notes, located title deeds, liaised with the land registry office. That type of work.'

'Can you tell me the name of this awkward client?'

'No I can't. And I don't know how our client could have anything to do with her attack this morning.'

'We don't either, but we are investigating some brutal murders. I believe Amy was another intended victim. Luckily we found her in time. At least, I hope we were in time—'

Lynch cut in. 'Madelene, we are trying to find a link between the women that might lead us to their murderer.'

'I don't know how I can help you.'

'You knew Jennifer O'Loughlin?'

'Yes, of course. Damien was an excellent solicitor and was a huge loss to our business. Poor Jennifer. She was devastated when he died.'

'Did you call on her at all?'

'At the beginning, I called a couple of times. She came to the office and cleared out her husband's personal items. I hadn't seen her in months.'

'What did she take from the office?'

Madelene looked from one to the other, an eyebrow raised. 'What do you mean?'

'Do you know exactly what she removed?'

'I didn't oversee what she did. Damien had some photographs and things like that, so I imagine she took those.'

'What about copies of files?'

'Dear God, no. Why would she? She had nothing to do with my firm. She was a dental nurse, for heaven's sake.'

Kirby debated telling Madelene about the boxes he'd found in the lock-up, but Lynch kicked him on the ankle, so he stayed quiet.

'Do you know any of Jennifer or Damien's relatives?'

'Damien's mother and brother live in Donegal. I don't know about Jennifer.'

'And Éilis Lawlor, do you know her?'

'No. I'm sorry.'

'What about Helena McCaul?'

A blink of the eyes, before she said, 'We did some work for her mother.'

'And Orla Keating?'

He knew immediately that Madelene recognised the name. But hadn't it been all over the media when Tyler went missing?

'I can't comment, as I believe she and her husband are our clients.'

'Tyler Keating has been missing a year. Amy named him as a referee on her CV.'

'Is there a question there, Detective?'

'I'm thinking aloud now, Madelene, and I'm thinking maybe Damien O'Loughlin was working on something for Tyler Keating and Amy met him here.'

'Still not a question.'

'Why would Amy list Tyler Keating for a reference?'

Madeline remained silent.

'That was a question,' he added, sounding more peevish than he intended. But fuck it, Amy had almost died – could yet die – and this woman had information that could be crucial to their investigations.

'Perhaps she knew him outside of the firm. Why does it matter, Detective?'

'It matters to me, because—'

He stopped as Lynch dug her foot down on top of his to shut him up.

Madelene looked from one to the other. 'It sounds like you have a personal interest in the case, Detective. To me, that's a conflict of interest.'

Kirby expected her to smile like she'd won the battle, but she remained expressionless.

'Life is a conflict of interest, Madelene,' he said.

Lynch made to stand, then sat. 'You said Kathleen Foley is a client here. Did you know that she once fostered Amy?'

That was when Kirby saw Madelene's expression change. Her mouth drooped and her eyes darkened.

'What is it?'

'I can't say anything further. I think you should leave.'

His hands were now sweating profusely. This woman had information to help them, he was sure of it. 'Madelene, too many women have already died. You have to help us.'

'I have said all I can say. I'm sorry.'

Kirby knew he was beaten. He stood with Lynch and reluctantly left Madelene to her thoughts. What he would give to read them.

83

The wounds on Lottie's neck and shoulder had been stitched up quickly in A&E, and armed with a prescription for strong painkillers, she left the hospital with Boyd.

'If I never see the inside of a hospital again, I'll be happy.'

'Me too.'

'Where is Garda Lei?'

'He got a couple of stitches too. I sent him home to rest.'

'Any update on Amy?'

'She's in theatre for work on her leg. No internal injuries on her scans. She should make a full recovery.'

'Physically maybe, but what about mentally?'

'That, I cannot answer.' He pulled the car out of the tight space where another vehicle had almost blocked him in. 'I'm tempted to stick a note on the windscreen. You know that one... *next time leave a tin-opener.*'

'I'm trying to get the timeline right in my head.'

'I was there first, and then that arsehole parked—'

'I'm talking about Amy and whoever abducted her. Kirby thinks she was taken last night. Orla was in the shop this morning. Then she wasn't. Then we found Amy. Where is Orla? Where is Helena? Could they both be involved?'

'Anything is possible,' he said, 'but there are so many similarities between the victims' injuries that I believe it's one highly organised killer. And he, or she, is escalating.'

'We don't even have a viable suspect yet.'

'Watch where you're going!' Boyd yelled out the window at a driver who had cut across him.

'Will you ever calm down? I haven't seen you this animated in a long time.'

'Maybe it has something to do with the fact that my ex-wife has returned and is making all sorts of threats.' He clamped his mouth shut and Lottie knew he was holding out on her.

'What threats?'

'It's not for now, Lottie. We have too much at stake to talk personal problems. You told me to focus and I'm trying. We need to find Helena and Orla. One of them could be next on the killer's list.'

'Or one of them *is* our killer.'

Her phone vibrated in her pocket and she checked it.

'We need to head to Lough Cullion, Boyd. Turn around.'

He glanced at her, almost rear-ending the car in front. 'And how do you expect me to do that?'

'Siren and lights.'

A group of teenagers, lathered in something like baby oil, stood congregated beside a squad car. Garda Thornton was leaning against the car, notebook in hand. Lottie walked gingerly towards them, still feeling the effects of being whacked across her shoulders and neck.

Thornton straightened his back.

'These kids,' he said, sweeping his hand at the four lads,

who looked pale beneath their sunburn, 'saw a car drive away at speed. Then they noticed that on the shore.'

She looked to where he pointed. A blue plastic barrel was bobbing on the little waves. On its side.

'There long?'

'Not too long, or it would have floated out.'

'Anyone try to pull it ashore?'

One lad, no more than fifteen, skinny with red hair, raised his hand.

'Go on.'

'We were over by the boathouse. Swimming and messing. Heard the wheels of a car plough up the stones and then it screeched off. Then we saw that.'

'Did you attempt to bring it in?'

He bit his lip and nodded.

'Why didn't you get it ashore?' She glanced at Thornton. Why hadn't he helped?

The kid said, 'There's something in it.'

'Do you know what?'

He looked anxiously at his pals. They were staring at their feet.

'Erm, I don't know exactly, but it looked like hair.'

She followed Boyd to the shore. He kicked off his shoes and socks and waded into the shallow water, attempting to haul the barrel in.

'Thornton!' he yelled. 'A hand, please.'

Without waiting for the guard to wake the hell up, Lottie kicked off her shoes and joined Boyd. They gripped the heavy barrel and between them succeeded in getting it to dry land, upright. A hole close to the bottom spewed out water. Glancing in, she saw what the kids had seen.

She shivered beneath the bright sunshine.

This was bad. Very bad.

———

The woman is a frightful sight. Even I am shocked at her demeanour. I knew she was damaged, but I didn't think she'd be a snivelling mess. I hate that carry-on.

'I want you to shut up and listen.'

She cried even harder.

Did I bind her too tightly?

I inspect my handiwork. The nylon rope is biting into her flesh. A little blood. Not too much. Not enough to kill her. I don't want her keeling over dead like her friend Éilis. I have a routine and I want to complete it. I need to act even faster than before.

I tighten the zip on my new overalls, then pull the mask tight on my mouth and nose and tug up the hood. I am careful. I don't want any evidence left on her. At least the lake water will have contaminated anything that may have been left on the other one. I was too annoyed to be careful. Maybe I shouldn't have been so cocky, leaving Amy before she died. I thought she was too far gone to survive. My miscalculation, because reports say she is alive, in a serious condition with life-threatening injuries. I do hope she dies. She would be the ultimate loose thread that could string me up and hang me. And I don't want that to happen until I have completed what I set out to do.

I turn my attention to my latest captive. When I finish with her, I have one more to deal with, then I can rest.

'Now, crybaby, I need you to cooperate.'

I pick up the bloodied plank and walk towards her. Her crying turns to a strangled scream as she sees what I'm holding.

I can't help the smirk unfolding behind my mask.

'Don't worry. You won't see anything at all after I'm finished with you.'

84

In the incident room, Lynch wrote up her notes on the meeting with Madelene Bowen, occasionally glancing at the photos on the board.

'Busy?'

'Jesus, Lei, don't do that.' She hadn't even felt the presence at her shoulder until he spoke.

'What?'

'Creep up on people. I thought you went home to rest.'

'To stare at four walls? Might as well help out here. Who is that guy?'

'Owen Dalton. He owns a yoga studio. Healthy living and meditation shite.'

'He doesn't look very healthy.'

Lynch noted Dalton's thin face shrouded by a mane of dark curls, and those eyes. God, they were like glass marbles, an extraordinary pale blue. She dragged a strand of hair out of her own tired eyes. They knew so little about any of their potential suspects.

'We need to do a thorough search on his life, his studio, and Frankie Bardon, his husband.'

'Sure.'

She tapped open the studio's website. After a few minutes, she'd gathered little information. Everything seemed to be window-dressing. That made her think of Éilis Lawlor. Interior designer. She opened Éilis's website and scrolled to the testimonials. Sure enough, Owen Dalton had written a glowing review for how she had transformed the studio space. She had also worked on Jennifer's house. And Tyler Keating's car had been found in Jennifer's lock-up.

'There are too many crossover threads with little to solidify them into a motive,' she muttered.

'Look at this,' Lei said from the corner of the room.

Lynch gladly rose from her chair to join him.

'Dalton set up a company, so his accounts are public. I just thought I'd have a look at how he financed it.'

Leaning over his shoulder, she peered at the screen. 'Good work.'

'What does it mean?'

'It's another thread, but eventually they'll all come together.'

Back at her desk, she wondered why Tyler Keating had been one of Owen Dalton's initial investors.

———

The soft ripples on the lake were making Lottie's head swim. The body was still in the barrel. Grainne insisted they had to wait for the state pathologist before removing it. A tent had been erected around it.

'This is ridiculous, Boyd,' she said, shivering with her wet jeans sticking to her legs. 'We have to get the body out.'

Garda Thornton had found him a pair of uniform trousers in the boot of the squad car, and navy fleece jackets for both of them. The trousers were halfway up his legs, showing off bare ankles. At least he was dry, Lottie thought with another shiver.

'I suppose so,' he said. 'We need to know who it is.'

'Right. Let's do it.' She marched towards Grainne, fighting the growing vertigo in her head and the crushing ache across her shoulder blades. 'Grainne, we need to release the body from the barrel.'

'I still say wait for the state pathologist. Maybe you should call Superintendent Farrell first.'

'My decision,' Lottie said, hoping it was the right one.

She suited up with Boyd and instructed two SOCOs to remove the body. It wasn't easy. They had to cut off part of the upper rim to allow it to be dragged out.

Standing to one side, half afraid to look, Lottie watched as the naked form slid into view.

The curls were long and dark. The face deathly pale.

She'd been full sure it was going to be either Helena or Orla.

It was neither.

'What the hell?'

85

McKeown had just about finished up with his report on the Luke Bray interview when an email shot up on his screen. He read it and looked around for someone to tell. His eyes landed on Kirby.

'Tech have succeeded in restoring some of the GPS data. Tyler Keating's car was moved to the lock-up only four weeks ago.'

'Really? Where was it before then?' Kirby asked.

'I'm checking it on Google Maps. It's a location very close to where Helena McCaul's mother lives.'

'Kathleen Foley?'

'Yep.' McKeown rubbed his head and creaked his neck. 'What do we have on Mrs Foley?'

'Not much,' Lynch piped up. 'Retired nurse. She fostered Amy Corcoran as a child for a time. Not much else.'

'Give me a minute to check PULSE.' Kirby typed furiously. 'No, she hasn't come to our attention for anything.'

'If Helena had something to do with Tyler's disappearance, she could have hidden his car at her mother's house before moving it to the lock-up,' Lynch said.

'Why, though? I can't see how it fits in.' Kirby leaned back in his chair. 'Nothing fits at the moment.'

'Want to do a brainstorm?' Lynch suggested.

'Wait until the boss gets back,' McKeown said. 'She's out at Lough Cullion with Boyd. Another body.'

'Foul play?' Lynch and Kirby asked together.

'If you mean is a body stuffed in a barrel and shoved into the lake foul play, then yes.'

'Same killer?' Kirby felt a shiver down his spine thinking of Amy's close call. He slammed his fist on the desk. 'Each one of these sites is different, even his methods of killing are different. We need to catch this fucker.'

'I second that.' Lynch went back to what she was doing. Namely, following up on the list of the SunUp investors after Lei's discovery. It might be a dead end, but she couldn't leave the job unfinished.

Frankie Bardon's name was there too, but that was to be expected, as the dentist was married to Owen. Why wouldn't he invest in his husband's business? After fifteen minutes, she shouted at McKeown, 'I found something. SunUp might have been about to go under. The studio has been making a loss for the last three years. Dalton had paid back some of the investors, but three remain.'

'Who's still to be paid?'

'Well, the husband, Frankie Bardon. Tyler Keating. Opportune that he disappeared, isn't it?'

'And the third?'

'Kathleen Foley.'

———

Kathleen picked up the ornaments one by one. Ignoring the heavy bronze figurine, a gift from Madelene, she held one of the Lladró statues in her hand. She opened her fingers and watched as it slipped away and smashed on the floor. She picked up another and did the same. When the floor was littered with broken porcelain, she stomped down on each of the larger pieces until they were nothing more than tiny fragments.

'Just like my life,' she said to the empty room. 'Fragmented.'

She knew exactly when it had all started going wrong. The day she'd met Madelene. The day Amy had arrived, her little hand in that of a social worker.

Money had been tight back then and fostering meant a weekly income. But there was a price to be paid. The change in Helena had been instant. She couldn't understand why she was no longer the centre of her mother's universe. Because of that, Kathleen had changed too. Her whole damn life had changed. No matter what she did over the years, she could not bring back the beautiful balance she'd once enjoyed with her daughter. It was like living on a set of scales. Up one day, down the next, and the next and the next. Now that she thought about it, there were very few ups in her life after Amy arrived. She thought she was doing right by sending the girl back to the care system. That hadn't turned out too well either.

She found the sweeping brush and dustpan in amongst the clutter of her utility room and began the task of clearing up the crushed porcelain.

She was about to put the pieces in the bin when the door-bell shrilled.

———

The meditation wasn't working at all. Too much unwanted information floating around in his head. He needed a shower and he needed to eat, but he didn't want to do anything.

His energy was off today. He knew why, but he didn't want to go there. He abandoned the meditation. There were just some things he could not allow to invade his mind. Things he had pushed so far down that you'd need a deep-sea diver to extract them. But he knew they were uncontrollably extricating themselves from their burial site to bring him to his knees.

Maybe a few weeks on a retreat would do the job. Get a sense of balance back into his life. Idly he wandered around the apartment picking up Owen's discarded clothing. He was so untidy. Usually it didn't bother Frankie, but today it did. Everything bothered him. As he was shoving the clothes into the washing machine, the doorbell shrieked. All his energy lopped to one side and he almost keeled over.

Whoever was at the door was not here to bring him good news.

86

Standing on the doorstep, Lottie studied Frankie Bardon's demeanour.

'Can we come in?' she asked.

'If you must,' he said, his oversized T-shirt clinging to his body.

She noticed the wariness in his expression as he stepped back. She figured he'd been working out and hadn't yet had a shower.

'Anywhere we can sit other than the floor?'

'It is what it is. You can stand if you find it too uncomfortable to sit down,' he said tetchily.

Gone was the glittering smile, and his tan seemed to have faded. Maybe it was fake. Maybe Frankie Bardon was all fake too.

'Suit yourself,' she muttered, wishing there was a chair to rest her bones. Even with a change of clothes from her locker, she felt damp and grubby. 'Can I start by asking what your movements were since I spoke with you earlier this morning?'

'I went to Centra for a few bits and pieces. My turn to make dinner. And talking of dinner, time is getting on. I'm making idli and I need to soak the lentils. Hopefully Owen is late home again, or he'll be crying at me for a takeaway.'

Boyd nudged Lottie. He got it too. Frankie referred to his husband like he was a child.

'What time did you go to the shop and what time did you return here?'

'I don't know exactly.'

'Do you have a till receipt? That will show when you made your purchases.'

'What is this about?'

'Can you answer the question?'

'Not until you stop this game.'

'Did you walk or drive?' She wasn't giving in that quickly.

'I refuse to answer.' He leaned against the wall and folded his arms. She could see the outline of his abs beneath the damp white T-shirt.

'Maybe what I have to say will make you more cooperative.' She paused, watching him closely but he seemed to be back in control of his emotions. Even his pallor had improved. Why? Did he feel no longer under threat? Did he relish being the dominant party in the room? Let's see how you digest this then, she thought. 'We found a body about an hour ago. Out at Lough Cullion.'

He cocked his head to one side, diminishing his six-foot-two height a little. 'Is that why you're quizzing me? I'm sorry to disappoint you, but I didn't harm anyone.'

'The person we found was brutally murdered and the body stuffed in a barrel and set afloat. A hole in the bottom of the barrel ensured it got no further than shallow water on the shore-line.' She let that sink in. Hopefully Grainne would be able to rescue some evidence.

'And?' His eyes darted between her and Boyd. She figured he was working hard to keep his emotions under control. 'What has that got to do with me?'

'I'm sorry, Frankie, but we believe the body is that of Owen Dalton. Your husband.'

The effect of her words was instantaneous. His arms unfolded as if by remote control and he slid down the wall to the floor.

'No! It can't be Owen.' A distinct quiver in his voice. 'You're wrong.' He looked up, pleading, his lips trembling.

'There is no mistake. It is him.'

'But why?'

'I thought you might be able to tell me that.' She felt awkward standing while he was on the floor. But she knew if she squatted down to his level she might not be able to get back up.

Boyd must have noticed how ill at ease she felt. He leaned towards the distraught man and offered his hand. 'Here, bud, you need to stand up.'

Frankie took the hand and Boyd hauled him upright.

'I need a drink, and I want to know what happened.'

He moved out of the room and Lottie followed him into a narrow kitchen. The decor reminded her of Éilis Lawlor's kitchen.

As he ran water from the tap into a silver goblet, she said, 'Did Éilis Lawlor advise on your kitchen design?'

'I don't know. Owen organised all that. I can't believe it. He can't be dead.'

She waited while he refilled the goblet and gulped down the water with much the same speed as the first glass. Pulling out one of the two stools at the counter, she indicated for him to sit. She felt instantaneous relief as at last she took the weight off her feet.

'What can you tell me about Owen that might have caused someone to kill him?'

'Did you stop to think you are dealing with a psychopath? There is no reason for anyone to kill Owen.'

'I need to understand the victim to find his killer.'

'I don't believe... I can't believe he's dead. Not until I see his body. It makes no sense. Owen was everything to me. This is just bizarre.'

'Any confrontations recently? Upset clients? Money troubles?'

'None that I know of. Why is this happening to me? First Jennifer, now Owen.'

'You worked with her and have a kitchen that seems to have been designed by Éilis Lawlor. Both are now dead. We have another injured woman and two missing.'

'Who?'

'Orla Keating is one. She is also a member at SunUp. You treated her and her husband, Tyler. Then there's Helena McCaul, who runs the herbal shop where you buy your vitamins. Everything leads back to you and Owen.'

'And now Owen is dead. Did I do something to cause this to happen?'

'You tell me.'

Lottie wondered at his self-absorption. His husband was dead. Was Frankie Bardon the killer? She shivered and looked around for Boyd, who was conspicuous by his absence. She heard him on the phone in the other room. At least he was close by.

'I see that look on your face, Inspector. That's why you asked where I was earlier. You think I'm a murderer.'

'Everyone is a suspect until they're not.'

'Yeah. Tell that to the innocent guys on death row. I think I better stop talking to you now. I want to call Madelene Bowen, my solicitor.'

Lottie felt her eyebrow rise in surprise, but hoped he didn't notice it. 'Make the call. Then you're coming to the station with us to answer a few more questions. Formally.'

'I need to shower and change. Can I meet you there?'

'We'll wait here.'

She watched him amble off, bowing his head under the low lintel. Glancing around the kitchen, she noticed no sign of newly purchased groceries on the worktop. Hadn't he said he was about to prepare dinner? She had no idea what idli was. She opened the refrigerator. It was sparse. On the counter, she saw his phone. She tapped the screen and exhaled as it opened without the need for a PIN or finger ID. The notes app. A grocery list. She looked around again and noticed a plastic shopping bag bulging with fresh supplies. Shit.

87

Lynch decided McKeown might be too intimidating to face Mrs Foley, and Kirby was wired, ready to snap, so she dragged Garda Lei along with her. She was half sorry after the five-minute drive, because he talked non-stop about being assaulted in Herbal Heaven. God, you'd think no one had ever been injured in the line of duty, the way he went on about it. Did he think he was some sort of hero? Was she being too harsh? He was young and inexperienced and more used to being on his bicycle patrols. She should be more charitable.

He was still talking. 'I could have concussion, though I hope not. Could I apply for compensation, do you think?'

'Lei, *I'll* be applying for compo if you don't quit moaning.'

'I wasn't moaning... Oh, was I? Sorry. Didn't mean to. You know the way it is.'

'I don't, but I want you to observe in silence as I do the talking with Mrs Foley.'

'Sure. No problem at all. I'm not one to talk too much normally. Am I?'

Instead of answering him, Lynch hid an eye-roll and rang the doorbell.

'Wonder where Tyler Keating's car was stored, seeing as the GPS placed it somewhere close by,' she said.

'God only knows,' Lei said. 'Garden could do with the run of a lawnmower.'

Did he not know when to shut up? The lime-green door opened after she pressed the bell a second time.

'Mrs Foley? I'm Detective Maria Lynch and this is Garda Lei. Can we come in for a moment?'

'Have you located Helena? I can't stop worrying about her. Come in.'

In the living room, Lynch found the lack of space over-whelming. She glanced at Garda Lei, silently urging him with her eyes not to mention the mess.

'Nice room,' he said.

Kathleen lifted a basket of laundry from the couch. 'It's hard to keep on top of things in a large house. Too big for me. I'm thinking of selling it.'

'Really?' Lei said. 'It's gorgeous.'

Lynch elbowed him in the ribs as they sat on the couch. 'We have no word of Helena's whereabouts, Mrs Foley. Are you certain you've no idea where she might be?'

The woman shrugged, her face seemingly a lot older than her fifty-odd years. The worry of having a liar for a daughter? Or was it the result of hearing about the assault on a woman she'd once fostered as a child?

'I don't know where she is. I'm sorry.'

'When was the last time she was in contact with you?'

'Two mornings ago, I think it was. She rang in a bit of a stupor. I reckoned she was in the midst of a roaring hangover. I regret to say, I hung up on her.'

'And you haven't seen or heard from her since?'

'I haven't.'

'Can I ask you about SunUp?'

'What?'

'It's that fancy yoga studio in town.'

'Oh, right. That place.'

'Do you know Owen Dalton?'

'Who?'

'He's the owner of the studio.'

'Okay.'

'How do you know him?'

'I don't.'

Lynch shifted to the edge of the uncomfortable couch. 'Mrs Foley... may I call you Kathleen?'

'Sure.'

'Kathleen, we know you invested in Owen Dalton's studio.'

'Invested? You must be mistaken.'

'We know you haven't been paid back.'

Foley bit the inside of her cheek. Lynch could see her tongue running around her teeth. 'That's none of your business.'

'It is, actually. We're investigating murders, not petty theft. Everything is our business until we find the murderer.'

'Well,' Kathleen said huffily, 'my financial affairs have nothing to do with you or your investigations. You should be out searching for my daughter.'

'What would you say if we told you Owen Dalton has just been found murdered?'

Kathleen's face hardened, accentuating the sharp lines around her mouth. 'I'd say good riddance.'

'I thought you didn't know him?'

'I know he's a money-guzzling rat.'

'Why did you invest in his business?'

A look of defeat shadowed Kathleen's expression. Or it could have been a cloud blotting out the sun outside the window. Lynch waited and hoped Lei had the sense to wait also.

'Amy asked me to invest.'

'Amy? Why would she come to you?'

'You're aware that I fostered her for a year when she was a child. I kept in contact. I couldn't say no to her.'

Lynch was wondering about the bond with a girl who'd only been in Kathleen's life for a short time about thirty years ago.

'What was her connection to SunUp?' Lei said.

'I-I don't know. Talk to Amy about it. I could tell she was afraid. I guessed she might have been intimidated. I don't know, because I didn't press her. You have to realise that I felt guilty for abandoning her. I felt I owed her. She wasn't the problem in this house. Helena was. I couldn't turf out my own daughter, so Amy had to go back into care.'

'Did she hold that over you by playing the guilt card?' Lynch asked.

Kathleen bit her lip silently.

Lynch felt the woman had drawn a line under it. 'Did you ask for your money back?'

Kathleen sighed heavily 'I did.'

'And what answer did you get?'

'Owen said I'd get it when he was good and ready.'

'How did you take that?'

Her lips flatlined. She stood and ran her finger along the mahogany mantelpiece.

'I don't blame Owen, Detective. It was Tyler Keating who made the mess. He's the one to blame for all this. I'm sure of it.'

Lynch wondered if she had heard right. 'What has Keating got to do with anything?'

'He was a swindler. He knew Owen from their college days. I'd say he made off with money belonging to Owen. That's why he disappeared and no one can find him.'

'A thorough investigation was carried out at the time,' Lynch said, though she now wondered whether Kirby had fucked up.

'Obviously it wasn't thorough enough or you'd have learned what type of man he was.'

'We believe his car was hidden near here for some time. Can you explain that?'

Kathleen's bottom lip dropped and her eyes widened. 'Where did you get that information? It's totally untrue, I might add.'

'I'm confident it's correct.'

'Well, I didn't hide any car. Feel free to look around outside.'

'We know where it is now. Did you move it four weeks ago?'

Kathleen's eyebrows linked in a thin line. 'Detective, Tyler Keating and his car have nothing to do with me.'

'Why did you move the car?'

'Like I said, it has—'

'Nothing to do with you. Right.' Lei folded his arms.

Lynch changed direction. 'Kathleen, how did you know Jennifer O'Loughlin?'

'I didn't know her. I told your colleague, Detective Boyd, that her husband drew up my will and transferred ownership of this house into Helena's name, but I didn't know Jennifer.'

'Are you certain?'

'Of course.'

Lynch eyed the painting over the mantel. 'Why do you have one of her paintings on your wall then?'

Kathleen twisted to look up at the abstract splashes. 'Oh, that thing. Helena gave it to me ages ago. Said it didn't go with her colour scheme. I hate modern art, but she was in one of her moods so I let her hang it up.'

She seemed to have an answer for every question she deemed fit to engage with. But Lynch couldn't help feeling that Kathleen Foley was still holding back information.

'One last thing, Kathleen. Amy said she'd been in a bad,

long-term relationship. As a point of interest, do you know who she was with before they broke up? And don't tell me to ask her myself. Amy is seriously ill.' There was something between Kathleen and Amy that had her ask the question. Something about the intimidation that had brought Amy to Kathleen for investment in SunUp.

Kathleen stood and gripped the back of the chair, her hands alabaster white.

———

After Lynch had left for Kathleen Foley's with Garda Lei, Kirby abandoned McKeown, who was being so nice to him it was suspicious, and headed to see Amy.

A call to the hospital confirmed she was out of surgery and the operation on her leg had been successful. They were hopeful that with physio and rehab, she would walk normally in the future.

He was relieved when the ward nurse allowed him in to see her. Her butterfly lips were almost transparent, her eyes shut tightly. A tube led to her nose and a series of machines gave off intermittent beeps. Pulling over a chair, he sat by her bed and took her hand in his.

'Amy, can you hear me?'

Her eyes flew open and a frightened tremor started in her hand. He stared at her face, trying to read the silent message written there, but failed.

'You don't have to talk if it's too difficult.'

'Sorry,' she said in a weak voice. 'Should have... told you... truth.'

He tried to unravel the knot of anxiety before it took root in his chest. Was she more involved than he could imagine? Surely not.

'I'm so sorry this has happened to you.'

'Not your fault.'

'You don't have to talk now, Amy, but Orla Keating and Helena McCaul are missing. I need your help.'

She remained silent.

'I think whoever abducted you might have taken one or other of them. Can you tell me anything about the person who took you?'

She shook her head slowly and a loud beep emanated from the machine by the bed. 'I didn't see... anything.'

'Were you brought to the shop straight away?'

Her eyes drooped, lids heavy. 'What shop?'

'Herbal Heaven. That's where you were found.'

'Don't remember. Sorry.'

He noticed tears gathering at the corners of her eyes.

'I don't want to upset you, Amy. You've been through such a horrific time. But I need to find those two women. Did one of them do this to you?'

'Can't help. Don't understand... what happened.' Now one of the machines beeped more loudly than the others and he noticed her blood pressure stats rising.

'It's okay. Don't stress. You need to get better.'

'Thanks, Larry.'

He said nothing for some minutes, lulled by the machines. He remembered reading her CV and that he'd been about to dig deeper into her past but had got distracted.

'Can I ask you a personal question?'

'Sure.'

'Because you joined the Life after Loss group, I'm wondering if you'll tell me the name of your ex? The one who caused you so much heartache?'

'Why?'

He shrugged. He just wanted to know, because there was so

much about Amy Corcoran that he *didn't* know. Because there was a possibility that her previous messy relationship might have something to do with what had happened to her.

She spoke then, her voice low and trembling.

And some of the puzzle pieces began to click into place.

88

Lottie left Frankie in the interview room waiting for his solicitor, and went to see if someone could find a green tea for him. Garda Brennan drew the short straw and headed out to the Bean Café in hope rather than confidence.

Lynch filled her in about her visit to Kathleen Foley, and she wondered why a disappeared man, Tyler Keating, kept popping up in their investigation into the murders.

She stood with Lynch in the incident room as the detective updated the board.

'Can we corroborate any of what Mrs Foley told you?'

'Amy might be able to. Kirby's gone to visit her. Kathleen thinks she was intimidated. When I find out who Owen Dalton's accountant was, we might get to shed some light on his current financial status and why some investors were left unpaid. Could be a motive there.'

'You could search his finances yourself.'

'Boss, we're working every hour in the day. I've barely seen my children or husband in days.'

'Okay. I'm sorry, Lynch. But seeing as Tyler is involved, what about Orla? She's an accountant.'

'If we ever find her, we can ask her,' Lynch said, her tone irritable. 'We need to follow the money.'

'How do we do that?'

McKeown picked that moment to walk in. 'What was Owen Dalton's cause of death?' he said. 'Did he drown in that barrel?'

'According to the pathologist at the scene, he was already dead.'

'How could she tell without a post-mortem?'

'A ligature around his neck. Blue nylon rope.'

'Similar to what bound Jennifer O'Loughlin and Éilis Lawlor,' Lynch said.

'And his eyes were removed. His legs and arms were broken. Maybe to fit him in the barrel, but—'

'Why, though?' Boyd said as he joined them. 'None of this brutality makes sense.'

'It does if we're dealing with a psychopath.' Lottie wondered about those words. Frankie Bardon had uttered them not an hour ago.

'Kathleen told me Amy Corcoran was once in a volatile relationship with Bardon,' Lynch said.

'What?' Boyd said.

'Yeah,' Lottie said. 'Another intersection on our diagram. None of these people were random victims. They all interacted with each other over time, in one way or another.'

Boyd walked along the boards, where the bullet points documented their investigation.

'Tyler Keating is the common denominator in a lot of them. And he's either dead or in the wind.'

'Kathleen Foley had no time for him,' Lynch said. 'She called him a swindler but wouldn't elaborate. That's why I say we need to follow the money. She also gave no explanation as to why his car might have been stored close to her home until four weeks ago.'

Boyd said, 'Orla Keating is an accountant. If she worked on Owen Dalton's accounts, maybe she found out her husband had invested—'

'Give me a minute. I'll find out if she was Dalton's accountant.' McKeown walked to the end of the room, on the phone to his source in Revenue. He gave a thumbs-up and continued his conversation out on the corridor.

'So,' Boyd continued, 'Orla had to know her husband had invested in the yoga studio.'

'What amounts are we talking about?' Lottie asked.

'Twenty grand each.' Lynch said. 'And Kathleen doesn't look like she has two grand, let alone twenty.'

'But what would make people invest in a pissy little studio?' Boyd said.

'It's marketed as high-end, deluxe,' Lynch said. 'Kathleen mentioned intimidation.'

'Okay, we can get back to that, but let's concentrate on Orla,' Lottie said. 'Did she find out what else her husband was up to? Was Damien O'Loughlin involved? Why were copies of his work files in the lock-up? And where the hell is Kirby with his report on those files?' She took a breath, and spoke as she paced. 'If Tyler was a swindler, he could have left a lot of unhappy people in his wake, especially if some sort of intimidation was involved. Is Orla killing off those who could point to her husband for fraud or embezzlement? Was she complicit in whatever he was up to?'

'We have no evidence of embezzlement,' Boyd said. 'Just a few investors who didn't get their money back. Not a cause for murder in my book.'

'People have been killed for less.'

'Who wants this slop?' Garda Brennan appeared holding a cardboard cup of steaming liquid.

'I'll take it,' Lottie said. 'Frankie Bardon must know more than he's already told us.'

. . .

Frankie had been crying. Lottie could see the tear stains on his cheeks.

'I'm trying to contact your solicitor, but we need to go over a few questions now. I know you want space to grieve for your loss, but time is slipping away and I have to find Orla Keating and Helena McCaul.'

'I can't help you. I have nothing to do with them. I barely know them.'

'Did you ever meet Orla Keating outside of your clinic?'

'A couple of times. At Owen's studio. She did his accounts.'

'What was your impression of her?'

'Nothing stood out other than she was a bit on edge.'

'Did you ever talk to her on a personal level?'

'Suppose I did, when I first met her at the clinic. I can't help interfering, can I? I have faith in my beliefs and maybe I try too hard to convert others.'

'Did you try with Orla?'

'I advised her to start yoga. And then I had a conversation with her at the SunUp desk one day. She was supposed to be going over the books with Aileen, the PA, but I overheard her crying. Asked if she wanted to get some fresh air or a coffee. She agreed. She talked about her unhappy marriage. I have a way with people. They open up to me.'

'Go on.' He suddenly knew a hell of a lot about Orla, Lottie thought.

'There's nothing else. I told her about my meditation. She said she had no intention of sitting cross-legged on the floor with her eyes closed and hands in the air letting her mind wander. I had to laugh at that. But she didn't want to listen to any more advice. Said she was fine. She'd just had a minor hiccup when she was going over something with Aileen. I walked her back to the studio, and Owen and I headed out for dinner. But then she did take up yoga.'

'Did she explain *how* her marriage was unhappy?'

'No. We talked about her, not her husband.'

'Was she a patient at Smile Brighter for long?'

He shrugged and sipped his green tea. 'I can't believe I've lost my husband to a murderer.'

'You told me you'd lost someone else too. Who was that?'

After a long sigh, he said, 'Before I admitted to myself that I was gay, I dated a woman. I thought she was the love of my life, but she had so many secrets, I couldn't cope with her.'

'Who was she?' Come on, arsehole, Lottie thought, say her name, it won't kill you.

'She's not relevant to anything that's happening now. We finished a few years ago. It was messy. It's over. That's it.'

'You want to find out who killed Owen, don't you?'

'Yes.'

'Frankie, I know about you and Amy Corcoran. She's in hospital, badly injured. What do you know about that?'

'I never touched her.' His face paled. 'Not recently, anyway. We didn't work out. I went away to India to recuperate. I really don't want to talk about Amy.'

'Did you intimidate her into asking Kathleen Foley to invest twenty grand in your husband's studio?

'I haven't spoken to her in years. We didn't last long together. She found out the hard way that I was struggling with my sexuality. I was in denial. I'm afraid to say I wasn't the nicest person back then. And she wasn't particularly nice either, under all her faux sweetness and light.' Tears spilled uncontrollably from Frankie's eyes. 'I loved her in my own way. But then I found Owen and realised who I needed in my life. Amy couldn't understand it. I don't blame her. And the worst thing is, I think I still love her. God, I'm pathetic.'

And are you also a murderer? Lottie wondered.

———

She couldn't see anything such was the depth of darkness. She realised it had been some time since she'd sensed anyone in the room.

She tried deep-breathing in an attempt to ward off the pain in her legs. One was broken, she was certain, but somehow the other was more painful. Was her captor the one who had killed Jennifer and Éilis? She couldn't let that image invade her brain or she would give up there and then.

To picture where she was being held, she tried to use her other senses. The room smelled old and fusty. Mouldy. She knew she was lying on plastic sheeting, but a bristly carpet lay underneath, pricking her through the plastic. She couldn't use her hands because they were bound tightly, but she could listen. The tick of a clock. In the room? Probably. She had the feeling she was in a room in an old house. Where was it?

She fell back against the sheeting and gritted her teeth. She wasn't gagged. Did that mean there was no one to hear her? She must be somewhere remote, then. Somewhere far from other human beings. She wept with frustration, terror and pain. A feeling of despair washed over her. No one would hear her. No one would find her. Because – and this caused her the greatest grief – no one would look for her.

No, she was not going to die. She could fight back again. Her desolation was not total.

Despite the horrific pain in her legs, and a growing thirst, she had to work to keep her focus.

If she was to get out alive, she could not lose hope.

89

Frankie Bardon had shut up then, and Lottie had to leave him to await his solicitor.

Kirby bustled into the incident room and flung himself onto a chair.

'How is Amy doing?' Boyd asked.

'She'll survive, but she's so damaged. I found out something crucial to all this.' He pointed to the board with a sweep of his trembling hand. 'He did it. He killed them all. I'm absolutely certain.'

'Frankie Bardon?' Lottie asked.

'We have to bring him in. I'll go once I get my breath back.'

'You're in no state to bring anyone in.'

'Frankie Bardon was in a relationship with Amy. He beat her. She said he used to hit her with a piece of timber. Chair legs and that.' Kirby was close to tears.

'Christ Almighty. That's awful. How is she doing?' Boyd asked as his phone beeped in his pocket.

Lottie wondered if it was Jackie, and hoped he wasn't going to disappear again. 'Does she know who abducted her?'

'Nope,' Kirby said, 'but I'd bet my pension it was that prick

Frankie Bardon.'

'He says Amy was violent towards him. His husband, Owen Dalton, is dead and Frankie is distraught. We're waiting for his solicitor before a formal interview.'

'He's here?' Kirby jumped up and rushed to the door.

Boyd grabbed his sleeve and led him back to the chair.

'This is insane,' Kirby yelled. 'Amy nearly died, and you're pissing about without charging the chief suspect.'

'You either stay in here or head home.' Lottie gritted her teeth. 'But you do not go anywhere near Frankie Bardon. You got that?'

She understood his anger, but she had to figure out whether it was Frankie or Amy who was lying and if so, why. And had it even got anything to do with the murders?

There was still no sign of Madelene Bowen, and Frankie was refusing to talk further until she arrived, so Lottie began an impromptu brainstorming with the team.

'I say we lean hard on Bardon,' Kirby said.

'I thought I told you to stay out of it.' Lottie glared at him, then realised she sounded childish. She relaxed her shoulders and slid onto a chair. 'Sorry. I know we've had a hectic few days, but we need to keep going. We have three murder victims, an attempted murder, and we still can't locate Orla and Helena.'

'One of them could be the killer and is keeping the other one captive,' Boyd said.

'Agreed, but we have to treat them as victims until we know more,' Lottie said wearily. 'They might not even be alive at this stage, but let's remain positive.'

Lynch said, 'Earlier today, I was certain Owen Dalton was the murderer. He owed so much money and his investors must have been screaming for their share to be returned.'

'That's unlikely now that he's dead.' McKeown kept his

eyes down and tapped his iPad.

'You always have to state the obvious,' Lynch retorted.

'Sometimes it has to be said aloud.' He raised one eyebrow without looking up.

'God, but you're a dose,' Lynch muttered.

'Enough,' Lottie said. 'We're tired, but we need to concentrate our energies on finding the two women.'

'We need to pin down the killer's motive,' Boyd said.

'It's someone who loves causing pain.' Kirby kept tapping his pocket as if he could light a cigar. 'It has to be Frankie. What if we let him go then follow him. He could lead us to the women.'

'He's going nowhere until I talk to him again,' Lottie said. 'What is keeping his solicitor?'

'She was in her office earlier today,' Lynch said. 'Very cagey, and shut up fairly quickly when we mentioned that Amy had once been fostered by Kathleen Foley.'

Kirby said, 'She was definitely spooked by that.'

'I wonder why?' Lottie mused. 'See if there's anything worth looking at about Amy and Kathleen Foley, and their links to Madelene Bowen.'

'Damien O'Loughlin drew up Kathleen Foley's will,' Lynch said, 'and the transfer of title on her home at Ballinisky to Helena. Kathleen claims that she didn't tell Helena about it.'

'But what does it all mean?' Lottie threw her arms upwards before letting them fall, twisting her hands into fists.

'We don't know yet, but we must consider Tyler Keating's role,' Lynch said.

McKeown said, 'His car was found in Jennifer's lock-up, having been moved there four weeks ago. The GPS shows it had been located prior to that in the Ballinisky area, close enough to Kathleen Foley's house.'

Lottie said, 'Did we find out anything further about the widows' group?'

Lynch stood and walked along the photos on the board. 'We initially thought the group was exclusive to widows. Then we discovered that wasn't the case.'

'But all the female victims, and those who are missing, were members of the group at some stage. Was it more than just a social outlet? Was it a front to hide something? Did Gary find anything when he dug into it online?'

Lynch said, 'He says it's like any other closed Facebook group. Éilis Lawlor was the administrator, and to join you just sent her a request. He couldn't find anything in the DMs or comments that looked suspicious. It was set up by Éilis, and Jennifer was the first to join. We have no way of knowing who actually met in person, though.'

'Okay,' Lottie said. 'Maybe Amy can give us more of an insight. Kirby, I know this could be viewed as a conflict of interest, but she might talk to you about it.'

'I'll go back to her later and see what she says.'

Lynch continued. 'We tried following the money, and Owen Dalton's murder kind of puts the kibosh on that. Like I said, he owed back the initial investments of Kathleen Foley, Tyler Keating and Frankie Bardon.'

'Gives Frankie a motive to kill him.'

'It gives *someone* a motive to take out Tyler Keating, but Frankie and Kathleen haven't been targeted.' Lottie stood. 'Frankie and Amy had a previous relationship. She's been badly injured. He is currently married to Owen, our latest victim. Can we trace a definite link where the other women have had an interaction with him?'

'They all attended Smile Brighter,' Boyd said.

'So did half the town,' Kirby pointed out.

McKeown said, 'Just because he once might have beaten your new girlfriend doesn't mean he murdered three people.'

Garda Martina Brennan coughed. 'Can I say something?'

'Open forum,' Lottie said.

'I did a deeper background check on Frankie Bardon. He went to college in Athlone. He was originally studying Irish mythology, but after year one, he changed college to study dentistry.'

'Tyler Keating lectured part time in Athlone,' Kirby said.

'And Owen Dalton lectured there too before giving it up,' Lynch said.

Lottie joined her team as they formed a curve at the board. 'Jane Dore had a theory about the locations where the bodies were left. She mentioned mythology. Not enough to pin down Bardon for murder, though.'

'Okay. What about the missing women?' Boyd said.

'Have you found anything in Helena's background check, Martina?' Lottie asked.

'Yes! Just a few minutes ago I got confirmation that she was once married. In Las Vegas, if you don't be minding. It was never registered here.'

Boyd swirled round. 'Her mother said she didn't have a husband. That she was a pathological liar. That she invented imaginary friends and hated Amy.'

'Maybe Kathleen Foley is the liar and not her daughter.' Lottie paused. 'Bring in Mrs Foley. I want to talk to her here and see how she performs under stress. Martina, work with Detective McKeown and do a thorough background search on Kathleen and her family.'

'Sounds good to me,' McKeown said.

'And Kirby, those files from the lock-up...'

'I did an initial read-through, but—'

'Make the time,' she said, pre-empting his excuse.

Garda Lei entered the room. 'Inspector, Madelene Bowen is asking to see you.'

'Good. Hopefully Frankie Bardon won't invoke the no-comment mantra now that his solicitor is here.'

'No, boss, she's here with Kathleen Foley.'

90

Boyd had pleaded to be allowed to go home. Jackie had been ringing him, and when he tried to call back, there was no answer. Always drama. With her team knee deep in work, and against her better judgement, Lottie brought Kirby to the interview room.

Madelene Bowen seemed very well put together, sitting beside a nervous-looking Kathleen Foley.

'I thought you were Frankie Bardon's legal representative,' Lottie began without preamble.

'I've informed him that I can't represent him, but I've agreed to meet him later to advise him,' Madelene said. 'Kathleen – Mrs Foley – phoned me in a distressed state after two of your officers upset her. She is here for an apology and an explanation as to why you have failed to locate her daughter. Let's get on with it.' Determined voice and harsh intonation. She jutted out her chin and nodded at Kathleen to speak.

'My daughter is still missing and I've told you everything. Why can't you find her?'

'Kathleen, we are doing everything in our power to locate

her.' Lottie forced a sweet smile. 'I need you to be totally honest with me.'

'I-I have been honest.'

'Economical with the truth, more like,' Kirby said. Would he ever learn to reel it in? Lottie wondered.

'That's a preposterous statement, Detective,' Madelene said.

'I apologise.' Kirby spoke quickly. Lottie knew he was far from sorry.

'It's okay,' Kathleen said. 'Your detective is correct. I have not been totally honest with you.'

'I'm listening.' Lottie folded her arms.

'Helena *was* married, when she was twenty-one. She was pregnant. She lost the baby six months into her pregnancy. A little boy. Noah, she called him. She went into a kind of psychosis. Wouldn't accept his death. Her husband, Gerald, left her. He's living in New York now. She never fully recovered.'

'Why didn't you tell me this originally? You specifically told me that she was delusional, a liar even, and imagining a son and husband.'

'I'm sorry. I panicked. I was afraid of what she might say to you. But it's been a long time and she's still living in some sort of fantasy land. I tried to get her to move on from that part of her life, but she struggled.'

'Your daughter is suffering from a type of depression.' Lottie couldn't believe the insensitivity of the woman in front of her. 'She needs professional help.'

'Don't you think I haven't tried? I've worked hard all my life and paid for the best in the country. And still she's getting worse, not better.'

'Kathleen, do you think Helena might be a danger to herself or others?'

'God forgive me, I believe so.'

'Was she ever violent towards you?'

Kathleen shook her head. 'No, but she has succeeded in alienating me. Even after all I've done for her, supporting her and her business.'

Madelene leaned forward. 'I think that's enough, Inspector. My client is distressed.'

'I'm just getting started.' Lottie checked Lynch's notes before her next question. 'Why was Tyler Keating's car parked close to your home for the last year?'

'That's enough,' Madelene repeated.

'I know nothing about it,' Kathleen said. 'That's the truth.'

'We will find where it was kept.'

'I hope you do, but it's nothing to do with me.'

'Did you know Jennifer O'Loughlin? I believe you have one of her paintings on your living room wall.'

'I never met her! Helena gave it to me. How many times do I have to—'

'We're done,' Madelene said, rising, her formidable voice matched by her physique.

'I'm not.' Lottie glared. 'Kathleen, you said that Amy asked you to invest in Owen Dalton's yoga studio. You've also said Helena drained your finances, so my question is, why did you put money into a venture you knew nothing about?'

Kathleen's eyes softened. 'I loved Amy. I let her down. I suppose it was partly guilt, but she practically begged me to invest. I had to borrow the money.'

'Twenty thousand is a lot of money to pump into something because of a girl you fostered thirty years ago.'

'I did my research on it. It was to be a state-of-the-art luxury venture.'

'Was Frankie Bardon threatening Amy?' Kirby asked, shuffling forward, shoving his belly into the table.

The change in Kathleen was subtle, but Lottie caught it. A wariness had crept into her eyes.

'I believe so.'

'Amy left her job with you, Madelene,' Lottie said, 'a few months before Tyler Keating went missing. Kathleen, his car was found close to where you live. What do you know about him?'

'Nothing. Only that he took money that wasn't his.'

'How do you know that?'

Kathleen's lips puckered and the little lines beneath her nose deepened into an ugly sneer. 'I know because he swindled me out of my previous home after my husband died.'

'How did he come to target you?'

'Kathleen,' Madelene said, 'let's go. You don't have to say anything further.'

Lottie wasn't giving up. 'Is that why you killed him and hid his car near your property?'

Madelene said, 'Inspector, as far as I can see, you are on a digging mission. You have no evidence that Tyler Keating is dead. And there is nothing to connect my client to any criminal activity, including murder. Mrs Foley came here to find out what you're doing to locate her daughter, but you've badgered and insulted her. Come, Kathleen.'

Lottie had nothing on which to hold the woman. And that frustrated her greatly, because in her gut, she knew Kathleen was still hiding something. Was she covering for her daughter? Why had she lied about Helena? Was it even relevant?

She watched the two women leave and listened to Kirby wheeze out of his chair.

'Frankie next, boss?'

91

His apartment was small enough to have no hiding places, and Boyd knew it was empty the second he stepped over the threshold. There was no point in shouting out their names. Jackie and Sergio were not there.

He slumped onto the couch and picked up a piece of Lego that his son had been playing with, anger quickly replacing his frustration.

Why couldn't she have waited and talked it out? Perhaps she knew he'd never agree to her ridiculous idea of them living together. And now he had lost the son who had only come into his life a few months ago. The hollowness inside him was all-consuming. Was this what Lottie had felt like when Adam died? Because Boyd knew he was going to go through a grieving process for his son.

Wallowing in self-pity wasn't going to help, though. He had to do something. He had to get his son back. He needed Lottie's help, but first they had to solve the murders. Then he could go after Jackie and bring his son home.

He wanted to thrash the place.

Instead, he went into the bedroom. He lay on the sheets and inhaled his young son's scent. Tears came hard and fast.

Drained of emotion, he fell into a troubled sleep.

———

After a hasty meeting between Frankie Bardon and a junior solicitor, Lottie knew she was beaten for the day. She watched them leave together not a half-hour after Kathleen Foley had walked out with Madelene Bowen.

Outside, the media scrum had increased in size as the days passed. Superintendent Farrell was holding them at bay with press releases and briefings, but the headlines were critical of the lack of progress. The fact was, her team had made progress over the last few days, but more people were dying. Despite that, she felt in her gut that they were closer to a conclusion, even without substantial evidence. Her gut, yes, that again. Still, she could do with forensics giving her something on a plate. A DNA hit or a fingerprint. Anything to bolster a suspicion. So far it was an unravelling thread. That thread had a beginning and an end. She just had to find her way through the tangled middle.

But before she could do another thing, she had to go home, to eat and to sleep.

92

She scoffed down a chicken breast with two roast potatoes, compliments of Chloe, before checking on her mother.

Rose was lying on the bed they'd set up in the sitting room for her, staring at the ceiling, her eyes fixed, unseeing. Lottie stood by her side. Her mother's stare never wavered. Frightened now, she reached down and tapped Rose's shoulder. The woman shuddered, startled, moving her head from side to side as if to refocus.

'Why did you wake me up like that?'

'I didn't think you were asleep. Did you eat?'

Rose struggled to sit upright, and Lottie placed her hands under her arms and shimmied her up on the makeshift bed. Why couldn't she have been reasonable and taken Lottie's bedroom? She was quickly learning there was nothing reasonable about dementia. The tall woman with her short, sharp silver hair was no more. It broke Lottie's heart to see her like this, and despite the lies and revelations of a few years ago, she wanted to help her mother. But how?

'I had my dinner,' Rose said. 'I think. What day or time is it?

I feel like I'm living a groundhog day. If I went back to my own house, I would get better.'

These lucid periods were what gave Lottie hope.

'I've applied for a carer for you. When that's approved, you can go home.'

'I don't need anyone. I'm perfectly capable of living on my own, of minding myself.'

But Lottie could see that her mother knew somewhere deep down in her clouded brain that the words were a lie. And that made it all the sadder.

Without thinking, she blurted out, 'What if Chloe lived with you? Then we could see how you manage at your own house.' Her daughter would go apeshit for not discussing it with her first, but Lottie didn't expect Rose to accept the offer anyway.

'Would she? Do you think it's possible? I really miss my house, Lottie. Everything is familiar there. It might help my brain recover.'

'I'll talk to Chloe. I'm sure she'd be delighted.' She crossed her fingers behind her back. She didn't have much confidence in a positive outcome from that conversation, but if push came to shove, she'd go live with Rose herself for a while. And bring a pair of Sean's noise-cancelling headphones with her! There would be fewer rows that way.

'I feel better already.' Rose lay back and pulled the sheet to her chin. 'Think I'll take a nap now. Even though we never saw eye to eye, you are a good little girl. Send your father in to me when he gets home.'

Lottie left her mother to rest.

And braced herself for an awkward conversation with her middle child.

. . .

'You can't be serious!' Chloe flapped around the kitchen in her bare feet. 'And where are my shoes? If Katie took them again, I swear to God I won't be responsible for—'

'It was just a suggestion. A way to help out your granny.' Lottie tapped the table with a spoon, counting in her head to keep her nerves from snapping.

Chloe paused, having found one shoe beside the basement door. 'Resorting to emotional blackmail now, are you? I have to get to work and I only have one shoe.'

'I saw the other one in the sitting room.'

'How on earth did... Oh, forget it. I'm going to be late, not that you care. After I cooked a roast dinner and all.'

Lottie hunched her shoulders, waiting for the door to slam, but Chloe let it swing shut slowly as she exited.

She needed to lie down. If she stayed up any longer, she wouldn't be able to function in the morning.

A strong smell of perfume preceded Katie into the kitchen. 'Louis is asleep. If he wakes, just give him juice and he'll fall back asleep immediately.'

'Where are you off to?'

'I told you when I asked if you could watch Louis for me. I've another date.' Katie feathered Lottie's head with a kiss and picked up her bag from a chair. 'See you in the morning.'

'Hey, you're not staying over somewhere, are you?'

With a wink, Katie said, 'One can only wish.'

In the silence of the kitchen, Lottie tried to recall when she had agreed to babysitting, without success. The investigation was swamping her brain; things were going a mile a minute on that front, still with no resolution.

She needed sleep.

As she climbed the stairs, she hoped Louis wouldn't wake.

Of course, he did. She brought him into her bed, where he settled into an easy slumber. She lay staring at his closed eyes and long lashes far into the night, going over what Foley and

Bardon had said and trying to make sense of what was behind the murders and abductions. Was it as simple as the age-old motive? Money?

If so, what was all the drama with broken bones and taking the eyes from the victims? It had to hinge on something much more devious than money. If she discovered what that was, then she would have the murdering bastard.

93

She was too weak to move when the door creaked open. If he wanted to kill her now, she would gladly agree to be taken out of her misery.

Silence. No talk. Just the rustle of paper clothing. The crackle of the plastic underfoot.

She didn't feel pain any more. Her body was numb. She knew she couldn't allow her mind to freeze. She had to think of a way out of this. Appeal to his better nature. Ha, she thought, someone who has murdered people won't have any goodness in their soul. No, she couldn't allow that thought to derail her determination.

'If you let me go, I won't say anything to anyone. I'll say I fell down the stairs at home and I'll go to the hospital to get fixed up. Please let me out of here. I want to leave.'

'Of course you'll be leaving. As soon as I'm finished with you. You won't walk out, though, unfortunately for you.'

Her chair was righted and she no longer lay on the floor.

'What do you want from me?'

'I want you to admit your role in everything you've done. How you planned my downfall. How you wanted to shame me.'

'I don't understand.'

'I think you do. I really think you do.'

The voice. She knew it.

In that instant, she realised she had been wrong about absolutely everything. That was her last thought before something hard smashed into her leg. Even the numbness didn't dim the pain. She lost her last grasp on reality and began to sink quickly into the realms of darkness.

———

I am exhausted.

I didn't think all this would take so much out of me, all this planning and execution. This running around from place to place. The physical drain on my strength. The mental strain. It's difficult being good on the outside while a demon crawls around like a black eel inside my stomach.

I thought I had mastered the art of deception, but with the authorities closer to the truth, I feel a bit lost. Floundering now. No, I cannot allow any doubt to derail my end goal. They all have to pay, some more quickly than others. Having two here at the one time is hard work, but I have to make them suffer before my time runs out.

After I'm done, I have one more to target. She will have to acknowledge my role in all of this. I can't let her live.

I keep thinking I made a mistake. Somewhere I left some trace behind. The plank of wood, perhaps. I stashed it in the small yard at the rear of the shop. Is that it? I wore gloves. I should be okay. But I feel an unusual tug of sadness.

Owen.

He preyed on the wrong person, so he had to go. I hope that by throwing his death into the mix, I will have wrong-footed the detectives so that I can continue with my mission.

I cannot rest until then.

DAY FOUR

94

Boyd sat in Lottie's office and told her that Jackie and Sergio were gone.

'Jesus, Boyd, you can't deal with this in isolation. Why didn't you call me?'

'It totally wiped me out. I'm trying to process it. I'm devastated. Sergio...'

'You need to look after yourself. Still no answer from her phone, then?'

'It's dead now. She probably dumped it and bought a new one. Jackie knows how to disappear.'

'Feck that. Together we'll find her and your little boy. You must be going through hell.'

'I am, but thanks. We will find them, but first we need to track down this murderer.'

She filled him in on the two interviews that had taken place after he'd left yesterday evening.

'My money is on either Kathleen Foley or her daughter,' he said. 'Helena hasn't been sighted at all since Orla drove off in her car with her.'

'Since I talked to Orla yesterday morning at Herbal

Heaven, she hasn't been seen either. And then we found Amy battered and broken there. Either Orla or Helena could be the killer. Or perhaps even Frankie Bardon. He isn't off the hook, though the time on his till receipt means he couldn't have been at the lake when his husband's body was dumped. I agree with you, we have to consider Kathleen Foley.'

'You think she'd hurt her own daughter?'

'I'm not sure. Who knows what she's capable of.'

'Motive?'

'Money? Helena was losing it like she kept it in a sieve. Maybe Kathleen had had enough of bailing her out. Owen Dalton owed her money too. She had to borrow to invest. Now he's dead.'

'Maybe,' Boyd said doubtfully, 'but that doesn't account for the other deaths. Jennifer and Éilis haven't popped up on any financials that we've gone through so far. I'm thinking someone knew something they shouldn't. Maybe they told the wrong person and had to be silenced.'

'Complicated, but it's another possibility.' Lottie thought for a moment. 'We need to draw up a search warrant for Kathleen's house.'

'On what grounds?'

'The GPS on Tyler Keating's car shows it was moved from somewhere close to her property to Jennifer O'Loughlin's lock-up four weeks ago. And she was kept in a cold-storage room at some stage, because her body had evidence of frostbite.'

Boyd seemed to be considering that. 'There were freezers in Herbal Heaven, but I didn't see anything like that when I was at Kathleen's house.'

'Didn't she say something about Tyler swindling her out of her home before she moved to where she is now? Could be another lie. She might still own it.'

'That's a long-drawn-out *might*.'

'Tell me something I don't know, Boyd. And tell Kirby I

want a detailed report on what's in those files found in the lock-up. I know he said at first glance they didn't appear to be suspicious, but why were they hidden?'

'I'll lend him a hand.'

'Do you think Tyler Keating is somehow involved in it all?'

Boyd shook his head. 'He must be dead, otherwise he'd have surfaced by now.'

'It's simple enough to change your identity and disappear if you have the resources and know the kind of people who can help you arrange it. As you found with Jackie.'

'Yeah, but his bank accounts haven't been touched except for normal spending by his wife. Kirby checked that.'

'Those are the accounts we know about. According to Kathleen Foley, he swindled a lot of people. He might have accounts in... the Cayman Islands... even a shell company. Get McKeown to check for those.'

'Will do.'

'Kathleen also said she thought Amy might have been intimidated by Frankie Bardon into asking her for the money for the investment. Frankie intimated that Amy was abusive, but if Amy is to be believed, *he* was the abuser. But is he our murderer?'

'You just said he couldn't have—'

'Dumped Owen's body? I know.'

'Where is he now? Do we have eyes on him?'

'We had nothing to charge him with. No evidence to link him to any of the murders or sites where the bodies were left. God, we have nothing to charge anyone, and we're now into the fourth day since the discovery of Jennifer's body.' Lottie felt exhausted thinking of all they didn't know. 'We need something soon. The killer is escalating.'

Her phone rang and she checked the caller ID. She glanced up at Boyd.

'It's Jane. Please, if there is a God in heaven, let her have some evidence for me.'

———

Sitting behind the old desk, Madelene Bowen faced a dilemma. Her conscience was divided. She owed it to her clients to keep their business confidential. Damien O'Loughlin, the one person she'd always trusted to help in her decision-making, was dead.

The time had come for her to make a stand. She had to decide on what was right and what was wrong. She'd been doing that for some time, but it was not straightforward. Yet she had always believed that everything she did was for the greater good, whatever that might be in a corrupted world.

Rubbing her eyes, she leaned back in her chair and tried to think of a legal way out of her dilemma. But of course she knew it would come down to morality, not legality.

She stood up, massaging her arms, bemoaning the fact that it had been necessary to skip her morning gym routine. She paced over and back on her worn carpet. She had to come up with a logical course of action. She owed Kathleen Foley that much.

95

Lottie hung up and read over her scribbled notes as Lynch and Kirby joined them.

'Jane has completed the preliminary post-mortem on Owen Dalton's body. And she has some evidence for us.'

'How? He was in water,' Kirby said.

'His bones were broken like the other victims,' Lottie continued without answering. 'And the eyes were removed by a surgical implement. We can conclude that the three victims were killed by the same person.'

'Frankie Bardon would know his way around a surgical implement,' Kirby growled.

'And Kathleen Foley is a retired nurse,' Lynch said. 'What did the lab say?'

'The blue nylon rope used to bind the victims was standard. Readily available.'

'What has you excited? Tell us,' Boyd urged.

'Jane has received some lab results. Jennifer's dress was sent for forensic analysis. A fibre was found nestled within the hem.'

'Okay.'

'The piece of timber Kirby found behind Helena's shop had

blood on it.'

'Amy's?' Kirby asked.

'Yes.'

'So it was used to break her bones,' Boyd said. 'What about the blood in the freezers?'

'Not human. Helena may have stored meat there.'

'Go on.'

'There was an unidentified fibre caught in a splinter.'

'I gather it is no longer unidentified.' Boyd breathed out in relief.

Lottie nodded. 'That fibre is a match for the fibre discovered on Jennifer's dress. It also matches another one that Jane extracted from deep inside Éilis Lawlor's leg wound.'

'What type of fibre is it?' Lynch asked, excitement coating her tone.

'Carpet fibre. Orange in colour, according to Jane. A lab technician researched it and matched it to a 1970s Axminster design.'

'That's nothing to get excited about,' Boyd said, his shoulders slumped.

'The carpet fibre places all three victims in the same location at some time. If we can trace that old orange carpet, we might find out where that was.'

Lynch moved forward. 'Wait a minute. I was somewhere recently that had old carpet throughout the building. Let me think.'

Lottie glanced at the photos on the incident board. 'Was it one of the victims' houses?'

'I remember!' Lynch cried, her eyes wide with excitement. 'Shit, boss, you're not going to believe this.'

The Victorian building leaned crookedly like it was bowing and scraping towards them. Lottie ignored its ramshackle exterior and launched in through the front door.

'We need to speak with Madelene Bowen.' She slammed her ID on the table.

The flustered receptionist picked up the phone.

'Feck that,' Lynch said. 'I know the way.'

Lottie followed her detective down the narrow corridor towards the open door at the end. She looked down at the carpet she suspected Lynch had been referring to. A knot of memory in the back of her mind told her she'd seen it somewhere else recently. A knot that refused to untie. Not yet, anyway.

'I wasn't expecting a visit,' Madelene said, rising, tall and regal.

'This is not a social call,' Lottie said, and for a moment she felt dispirited. If it was proved the carpet fibre came from this building, how could this woman have carried out the brutal murders and transported the bodies to the various locations? Stuffing a grown man's broken body in a barrel took strength. Then again, if you had a will to kill, you were capable of anything. However, the building was accessed by many other people, including, she supposed, some of the victims and people of interest.

'Sit down, please,' Madelene said authoritatively. Used to commanding a room, Lottie thought. 'I was about to call you with some information.'

'You were?' Leaning her hands on the back of a chair, Lottie eyeballed the solicitor, forcing the other woman to speak.

'First, I want to know why you barged into my office.'

She toyed with the idea of forcing Madelene to reveal her hand, but she hadn't time for games. She toed the floor. 'That's an old carpet. Axminster, is it?'

'I'm sure you aren't here to discuss the aged decor.'

'As a matter of fact, we are.'

Her statement elicited a raised eyebrow from Madelene. 'Is

it linked to evidence?'

'I can't divulge anything related to an ongoing investigation.'

'You found something on the bodies?'

'I want your permission for SOCOs to take a sample of your floor covering for comparison purposes.'

'I'm not the only one with access to this building.'

'I can get a warrant.' Lottie wasn't confident this request would be successful with a judge.

'Then get one.'

Shit. She'd gone about this all wrong. 'What did you want to talk to me about, Madelene?'

'Following your unceremonious entry into my office, I am reconsidering. You seem to think I'm a murder suspect.'

'Not yet, but I'm inclined to think you know who we are looking for.'

Madelene was quiet for such a long time, it reminded Lottie of how Rose had slept with her eyes open. She gave the solicitor a verbal nudge.

'Two women are missing and are in danger of being murdered, if they're not already dead.'

The woman focused her eyes on Lynch, then moved them to Lottie. 'I want to speak to you alone, Inspector.'

Lottie nodded to Lynch, who left and shut the door behind her.

'You may sit,' Madelene said.

Lottie resigned herself to a long-winded explanation couched in legal speak. She was surprised, then, when Madelene leaned forward, her tone low and conspiratorial.

'I must make it clear that I had absolutely nothing to do with these murders.'

'Go on.'

'I believe everything started with Tyler Keating.'

'I gathered that much.'

'I'm deeply ashamed that my firm could be linked to this

debacle, and I'd like it if you could keep my name out of it.'

'I can't guarantee anything of the sort, as well you know.' Lottie wondered how anyone could refer to murder as a debacle.

Madelene sighed. 'Tyler's wife had worked on some of our client accounts for a short time years ago, and he engaged our services for the purchase of his house. Damien compiled the contracts and registry for the purchase. Amy was Damien's legal secretary. Then last year, Tyler went missing.'

'What are you trying to tell me?'

'I couldn't prove anything, but I now believe Tyler was corrupt. And it has absolutely nothing to do with Bowen Solicitors.'

'How can you make such a statement? Have you evidence?'

'I found copies of files in Damien's office after he died. I boxed them and meant to destroy them, but I never had time. Jennifer arrived to clear out his things. I was in court that day. I now believe she took the files. Did you find them?'

Lottie was going to choke Kirby when she got back. 'Are we talking about fraud? Theft?'

The platinum-haired woman nodded. 'I don't believe Damien did anything criminal, but perhaps he was unprofessional. My belief is that Tyler used him. He was such a charmer when it suited him. From what I have ascertained so far, grieving widows were his target.'

'So, you're confirming Tyler stole from widows?'

'Those who had property and money? It's possible.'

'And Orla Keating would have had access to these clients' financials?'

'She may have been the accountant for the people Tyler targeted and defrauded.'

'Why didn't you do something about it?'

'I didn't know. I left the property clients to Damien.'

'I've met Orla. I don't understand how she would be

involved in—'

'Inspector, Tyler Keating might have been a charmer in public, but from what I saw, he was a control freak. He controlled his wife like everything else in his life. But I believe he crossed one person too many, and that person fought back. That's why you can't find him.'

'So if it's not Tyler who's murdering innocent people...'

'That is your job, Inspector. I have no idea.'

Lottie mentally scanned what they'd learned since Jennifer's body had been discovered. Who benefited from these murders? A widow wronged? One person stood out as being more damaged than others.

'Kathleen Foley's daughter has issues, problems. Kathleen is a widow. Was she one of Tyler's victims?'

'Kathleen is a dear friend. She recently told me that she was fragile at the time she was duped by the swindling charmer. Both she and Helena suffered greatly following that experience.'

'Do you think Helena is capable of murder?' Even as she asked the question, Lottie couldn't understand what the young woman's motive might be. But the fact remained, she had maintained the pretence of having a son, and now she could not be found.

'I can't answer that, Inspector. You arrived here talking about the carpet under our feet. Tyler took ownership of a lot of old properties, some of which he didn't get to offload before his disappearing act. Maybe it came from any one of those.'

'I don't have enough evidence to get warrants to begin ripping apart properties that might have nothing to do with my investigation.'

Madelene sat erect, her hair like a halo on her shoulders. She dragged her briefcase onto her knee and was about to open it when Lynch stuck her head back around the door.

'Boss? You're needed. Another body has been found.'

96

'The car bothered me from the time it was found,' Kirby said to Garda Lei as they walked around the area specified by the GPS from Tyler Keating's Hyundai. He glanced down at his phone. He had scanned a page from one of the files in the lock-up boxes.

'Did you carry out all the searches at the time of Keating's disappearance?' Garda Lei asked. 'I know it wasn't a murder investigation, but there are certain protocols to be—'

'Don't tell me how to do my job.'

'I was only saying... Do you think we need to crack Tyler Keating's disappearance to figure out why people are being killed and abducted and beaten? Why was the car left near Kathleen Foley's house? Was she interviewed in connection with Tyler's disappearance?'

'Lei? Shut up.'

'Perhaps the connection is her daughter.'

'Helena?' Kirby scratched his head and a flutter of dandruff floated before his eyes. 'Maybe I'm looking at this the wrong way round. What if the GPS was manipulated to lead us here?'

Lei pulled up short, and Kirby watched as the young garda turned around. 'Can that be done?'

'How would I know?' He checked the image on his phone. 'Kathleen Foley once owned a house close to here. These are the coordinates from the land registry map. It's around here somewhere.'

'She didn't move far then.'

'Seems like it.'

'So the GPS wasn't tampered with?'

'Doesn't matter for now. Come on.'

His phone rang with an incoming call. Garda Brennan.

'Shit, Lei,' Kirby said. 'Another body.'

———

McKeown was determined to be the hero on this case. The back-breaking work of trawling through CCTV had yielded little, so when Boyd asked him to check into Tyler Keating's finances, he rose to the challenge. He was sure Tyler Keating's disappearance had led to the current murders. But how? And more importantly, why?

He searched everywhere for the man's financial footprint. Made phone calls. Scoured the internet. As a last resort, he put in a call to his friend in Revenue. She put him on to the Criminal Assets Bureau. That was when he learned something he knew was important.

Two months ago, based on a call from an anonymous source that they believed was credible, CAB had begun an investigation into Tyler Keating's financial affairs. It was early days, they said, but they'd discovered that he'd set up a company fifteen years previously. McKeown calculated that Keating was still a student then and already thinking years ahead.

He waited patiently for the information to be securely emailed over.

———

Boyd took the call from Garda Brennan just as McKeown walked in.

'Come on, Sam, you're with me.'

Boyd drove, so that he had something to concentrate on other than McKeown moaning about his wife.

'I have no idea why the killer would have chosen the Loman area of Ragmullin to leave another body for us to find,' McKeown said, once he'd finished his tirade on the state of his marriage. 'There are a lot of businesses and residential areas around here.'

'Martina said the body is located by an old mill close to the new bridge.'

'It's also a well-lit area at night,' McKeown said. 'I found out something interesting about Tyler Keating. CAB have started investigating him. He set up this company years ago, a shell company, and—'

'Later.' Boyd parked behind the squad car with its door open and lights on.

Martina had called in reinforcements, and the bridge was blocked on either side, with no traffic, foot or vehicular, allowed.

'Who found the body?' Boyd asked.

'That guy over there.' Martina pointed to a thin youth kitted out in jogging gear. 'He was out for a run. Saw something yellow fluttering in the breeze. He's a wreck.'

'Not a suspect, then?'

'I doubt it. The guy is a total mess.'

'Lead the way.'

They walked down the side of the bridge onto the field. The ground underfoot was soft, despite there having been little rain in the last three days. Boyd glanced at the sky, with its ominous bulging clouds. He was glad he had his tough shoes on, because McKeown's smart leather loafers were soon covered with mud.

Under the bridge trusses and buttresses, he saw for himself the yellow material fluttering in the breeze on the body dangling, barely off the ground.

'We need SOCOs and the state pathologist,' McKeown said.

'I've made the calls,' Martina said sharply.

Boyd moved forward, conscious that they hadn't suited up to preserve potential evidence. But he had to see who it was. The yellow dress swirled around obviously broken limbs. Short blonde hair fluttered in the wind. The face was eyeless.

'Ah, no! Fuck. What the hell does this mean?'

The three of them stared at the figure, mouths open and hands hanging loose by their sides. There was nothing any of them could do for the victim.

Lottie and Lynch joined them then, slipping and sliding down the embankment.

'Christ Almighty,' Lottie swore. 'I was terrified it might be Orla or Helena.'

'It's neither of them,' Martina said.

'Not unless they sprouted a penis,' McKeown said.

Boyd fought the urge to punch him.

Lottie turned and pressed a finger into McKeown's chest. 'Get out of my sight. Now!'

'Don't you dare touch me!'

That was when Boyd did attempt to punch him, his fist glancing off the detective's chin. Lottie sighed loudly.

The murders had got to all of them. And they were still going round in bloody circles.

Just like Frankie Bardon's body, hanging from a rope, his feet trailing the ground, beneath the newest and longest bridge in Ragmullin.

97

With Lei by his side, Kirby studied the map on his phone. He was glad Boyd had said he wasn't required at the latest crime scene, because now his bones tingled with anticipation. He felt they were close to the conclusion of this murderous episode.

Following the map, they made their way on foot across a field until they came to a two-storey house, a dilapidated garage to one side. It was situated just over a kilometre from Kathleen Foley's present abode. The GPS had placed Tyler Keating's car close by. Unseen from the main road, the house would have been hard to find without the map. An old railway goods carriage stood some distance away. Was that where the car had been located all along?

'House looks derelict,' Lei said.

'Master of the understatement.' Kirby kept walking. 'Stay quiet and keep your head down. Someone could be in there, watching our approach.'

'We should have put on the Kevlar. Do you have your weapon?'

'I'm not stupid.' But he was. He hadn't given a thought to personal protection.

Lei must have seen the worry cross his face. 'It looks deserted, anyway.'

'Clever lad. Who would even think to investigate this place?'

'Us?'

Kirby sighed. From the outside, it was obvious that the house was in serious need of repair. Trails of ivy tracked up the drainpipes and along the gutter. A shrub sprouted out of the chimney. He made his way forward carefully, telling Lei to stay well back. He peered through a ground-floor window, but it was as if years of grime had congealed into black.

He took a step backwards, surprised to find Lei standing right behind him. 'The windows are covered with something on the inside.'

'To keep nosy people from looking in?'

'Maybe. Or if someone was being held inside against their will, it could be there to disorientate them.' He looked at the young garda, still bruised from the encounter at Herbal Heaven. 'Radio for backup and wait up on the road.'

'You aren't going in there alone, are you? It's suicide. It's... stupid.'

'Whatever it is, there could be someone injured or dead in there. Maybe Helena or Orla. I need to look.'

'Can't I call it in from here?'

'Go back to the road, Lei.'

There was no way he could put the rookie in danger. He watched as Lei cut a lonely figure trekking through the long grass, and then made his way to the rear of the dwelling, to see if there was any way in besides the front door.

98

Frankie Bardon had not been dead long, according to Jane Dore. Six hours maximum. Early hours of the morning, then, Lottie estimated. He had to have been killed and hung up just before dawn, when no one would have been about. The ground was marshy and now trampled; footprints would be useless. However, Grainne did point out the tracks of two wheels. Some sort of small trolley, she thought.

They tried to trace Frankie's movements from the time he'd left the station yesterday evening, but it was proving difficult. No one in the Canal View area where he lived could remember seeing him.

'You do know you shouldn't have hit McKeown,' Lottie said.

'He had it coming and it made me feel good. After Jackie and Sergio... I don't know... I have this anger simmering and—'

'And it was good to let fly? I get that, but despite you barely making contact, he'll report you to the super.'

'I don't care, to be honest.'

'Don't say that. It could damage your career. You'll need this job to support your son when you get him back.'

Boyd shrugged and walked on ahead in silence. Her heart crumbled for him.

In the incident room, she concentrated on the carpet fibres. It was the only lead she had. She knew she'd seen the carpet somewhere other than in Madelene's office this morning. Think! Pressing her fingers into her temple, she visualised every house she'd been in over the last few days. Then she twigged. Éilis Lawlor's office. The samples pinned to her wall.

She rushed to the incident board to study the photos taken in the garden office. There among swatches of material was the orange Axminster carpet. Did it come from a house Éilis had worked on? She recalled that the woman had used an office in town before moving it to her home. Was the carpet from there? Pulling up files, she searched for all she could find on the address. The building had been owned by Éilis and Oisín Lawlor. A year after his death, it was in the ownership of a company called Widow Island.

What the hell did that mean?

Her brain was a riot of information and she was unable to see her way through it. And squarely in the centre of the riot was the image of Frankie's body beneath the bridge, grotesquely damaged and naked beneath a yellow dress.

She shook herself to keep alert and went over all the notes about Éilis.

'Boyd, hear me out.'

'Okay.'

'Éilis worked on Jennifer O'Loughlin's house. She also designed Owen's deluxe studio. I suspect she worked on his and Frankie's kitchen; it's a similar design to her own house and—'

'Is this about the Axminster carpet?'

'Yeah. What if she had taken samples from some other property but never got to do the work? I didn't find anything in her notes to identify such a place. Did she inadvertently come across something that led to her being killed? And why is her old office building now in this Widow Island company name?'

'McKeown found out about a company Tyler Keating set up ...'

'It looks like Damien O'Loughlin and Tyler Keating were involved in illegal property dealings. Maybe Éilis sold her office in town to this company under duress.'

Boyd sighed. 'This is all speculation. We need evidence.'

'There has to be something in those files Kirby was going through.'

'He was looking at them before he headed off with Lei. Left in a hurry. Never said where they were going.'

'If he found a lead, hopefully it will help us.'

It bloody better, because she was clean out of ideas.

99

The overgrown grass rustled as Kirby walked. But the old Foley house was shrouded in a deathly silence. At the rear of the house, he put his hand on the latch of the back door, and held his breath as he depressed it. The door opened.

Taking a step across the threshold, he quickly put the crook of his elbow across his nose and mouth. Too late. The stench of faeces and blood filled his airways and he dry-retched into his sleeve.

Was this where Amy had been held captive for a few dark hours while some deranged bastard beat her to within an inch of her life before being moved and left to die in Helena McCaul's shop? Anger bubbled in his chest.

There had to be a reason for Amy being left at the shop. Had the murdering deviant wanted her to be discovered? Was the intention to shift the blame to Helena? Or was Helena their killer?

He made his way through the kitchen. There was evidence that it had been used recently. A box of cereal on its side, corn-flakes attracting an army of ants across the scratched wooden table. Unwashed cutlery and crockery filled the sink and another colony of insects crowded around food-stained plates. He lifted the lid of a garbage bin. His heart almost stopped. Blood-soaked crime scene protective clothing.

'Christ Almighty! Fuck,' he swore.

He stepped into a large utility room. Cold air caught in his throat. It was like an ice box. He backed out and made his way from the kitchen to the hallway. Finding a pair of gloves in his pocket, he blew to expand them and shoved in his sweaty, awkward fingers.

Pausing, he listened.

Not a sound, save for the creak of old floorboards and a rising wind outside. A sliver of sweat tracked from his hair down his neck to pool along his shirt collar. A sudden blast of fear crashed through his chest and he wondered if he'd been stupid to come in alone. Maybe he should fetch Lei? No, he needed him on lookout. Someone could return.

The door to his right was padlocked. He'd need a bolt cutter. Then a thought occurred to him and he ran his hand along the top of the lintel.

A key.

He placed it in the lock. Turned it. The door opened inwards, sticking as if something was caught beneath it. He looked down. Thick plastic sheeting with holes or cuts in places. Call it in? Get Lei to witness this? Whatever *this* might be. But the image of Amy's injuries propelled him into the room without further thought for procedure.

'Holy Mother of God.' His voice was a whisper of disbelief.

The floor was covered in bloodstained plastic. The walls were lined with cushions and some sort of packing. Soundproofing? To keep noise contained inside? His darting eyes were drawn to the slumped figure tied to a chair in the corner of the room.

Broken. Bloodied. Silent.

He made for the figure. It was difficult to determine if it was male or female, such was the amount of blood and protruding broken bones. The hair was damp and matted.

Falling to his knees, he listened. A soft, slow breath feathered his face. Alive. A woman. His fingers fumbled with the knots on the thick blue nylon rope. He dared not look at the bloodied face, detaching himself momentarily from the reality of the devastating injuries she had suffered.

A sound reverberated. A door banging. A shout.

He stalled, hands in the midst of the blood-soaked knots.

Garda Lei stumbled into the room.

'I called it in and... Oh my God,' Lei exclaimed. 'What... Oh God. What is this place?'

'The killer might come back. Keep watch and call an ambulance.'

'Sure. Sure. Yes. Oh God. What the...' Lei fumbled with the radio and backed out of the room.

Kirby returned to the knots. He was afraid to look too closely to see if her eyes had yet been removed. He no longer felt her breath. Was she dead?

'Concentrate,' he warned himself, his voice quivering.

As he released the knot at the damaged ankles, bones jutting out, the woman groaned, and Kirby held his breath and looked up into the severely battered face.

Orla Keating keeled over, her head cracking against his shoulder.

———

It is near the end. They are close. I can smell them as if their investigation was leaving a burning smoke trail. I thought I'd have my work completed before they arrived. But all this running around, trying to be in two places at once, has exhausted me.

But do they know who I am? Why I am doing all this? Will I have to make it crystal clear for them? No, they'll figure it out. Eventually.

And then realisation dawns on me as I hear the sirens, and cars and ambulances appear on the brow of the hill. It is already too late.

I've always been ahead of them. I need to keep it that way.

The one I had to abandon in the house won't survive, but I mourn the fact of missing out on that death. I glance at my rucksack with the other treacherous eyes swimming in their glass jars. I should have got hers, but time closed in on me. I did what I had to do. And now I have one remaining task. A final person to meet. To tell them that this was all for them.

Then I am done.

I will disappear into the ether, never to be found.

Just like the man that was Tyler Keating.

100

Orla Keating was rushed to hospital with life-threatening injuries and would not be providing information any time soon. So, Lottie divided Damien's files from Jennifer's lock-up among the team. There had to be some sort of proof of a killer and their motive within the buff manila folders.

Helena was still missing. Could the sad, damaged young woman be the killer?

McKeown arrived, looking none the worse for Boyd's punch. She decided to deal with the fallout later.

'What did you find out about the company established by Tyler Keating?'

'CAB set up an investigation after a recent tip-off. They discovered the company called Widow Island. It's linked to a foundation helping children who have lost a parent. Based on what we now know, that's a crock of shit.'

Flicking through pages in the file open before her, Lottie wondered how Tyler Keating had convinced Damien O'Loughlin to get involved in the corruption. Money and greed, she supposed. Tyler was a part-time lecturer, well able to get his point across. Combining what they'd learned from CAB with what Madelene had said, it seemed the pair had used the foundation to extort funds in the form of property from unsuspecting grieving widows.

'Everything I've looked at so far,' she said, 'and what Kirby discovered, involves bereaved women signing over part of their estates to Tyler Keating's company. Damien O'Loughlin was the solicitor in each case.'

'And I'm sure Orla Keating was able to doctor the accounts,' said Kirby.

'Her name doesn't appear on these files,' Lottie said, 'but we know Tyler was also an accountant. We can follow it up when we arrest the murderer.'

'The file that led me to where Orla was being held contained a deed of transfer showing that Kathleen had signed the house over to this Widow Island.'

'Okay. Let's recap.' Lottie paced. 'Could Jennifer have found out what her husband was up to from something she overheard in the clinic? Or did she discover it when she took the files from Damien's office?'

Boyd said, 'Doesn't matter how she made the discovery. The fact that all these dealings affected grieving widows must have inspired Éilis and Jennifer to form the Life After Loss group.'

'Why allow Orla into the group,' McKeown said, 'if she was involved in the scheme?'

'She mightn't have been a willing participant in the fraud,' Lottie said. 'I think the widows' group was set up to gain enough support and information to unmask the corrupt dealings.'

Kirby scratched his chin. 'Maybe Orla joined them in order to help, after her husband disappeared.'

Lottie folded her arms in determination. 'Or she wanted to keep an eye on what they were up to. The women who have been killed or physically abused this week may have been working towards exposing the fraud, but they then became targets of someone who didn't want it to be exposed.'

Boyd agreed. 'So who had so much to lose that they resorted to gruesome murder?'

Lottie was as bewildered as her team. 'I can't figure out why Frankie and Owen were murdered if that scenario is true.'

'I don't like it, but I think the killer has to be Helena McCaul,' Lynch said. 'She's still unaccounted for, and it's possible she had access to her mother's old property, where Orla was found.'

Lottie said, 'But if it's her, why would she want to keep the fraud secret? It could even be her mother.'

Garda Lei entered with a sharp knock on the door. 'Luke Bray is downstairs. He seems agitated. Asking for Detective Kirby. He wants to see those photos again.'

Kirby stood up and Lottie nodded for him to go.

'You okay now, Garda Lei?' she asked.

'Right as rain, thanks. That house was such an awful blood-letting den. Those poor victims. How are you able to sleep after witnessing such horrors, Inspector?'

'Not very well,' Lottie said.

———

Luke Bray was dressed in his work clothes and sweat bubbled in pools around his eyebrow piercing.

'I should have told you before but I was scared. After I thought about what happened to Amy, I phoned her in the hospital.'

'Yeah, pull the other one,' Kirby said. He tried to sneer but was too exhausted to get it right.

'You can think what you like about me. I don't care. I want to tell you who gave me the money to open the back door of Herbal Heaven.'

Kirby opened the folder of photos, updated with all the people of interest in the case. He laid them out on the desk.

'Her.' Luke pointed to one image as soon as it appeared.

Kirby leaned over and stared at it with surprise. 'Are you sure?'

'One hundred per cent. I know her.'

This was going to throw a spanner into the discussion they'd just had in the incident room. They'd been totally wrong.

101

Clouds shifted over the evening sun with a sense of foreboding. The sky faded as the weather broke with a streak of lightning and a deafening clap of thunder. A persistent deluge followed.

After fruitlessly waiting for the rain to subside, Lottie decided to proceed. She jumped out of the car, tightened the Velcro on her Kevlar vest, pulled up her hood and tugged her jacket zip up as far as it would go over the bulk. She whispered instructions to the team before heading towards the house.

It was in darkness save for light escaping from a gap in the curtains of a downstairs window. Lottie closed her eyes to get a mental picture of the layout. She put her finger to her lips and beckoned her team to their stations before marching up to the door and knocking loudly. They'd already been to the house of the person identified by Luke, but no one was there. The friend's house was her last hope.

The door remained closed. The silence was once again shattered by a clap of thunder and the downpour continued. She knocked again, then pressed her hand on the bell.

'Kathleen? Open up. We need to talk.'

Still no reply. She stood to one side as two uniforms

slammed into the door with the big key. The timber shattered, the old hinges snapping.

Boyd was at her shoulder as she stepped over the splintered wood. Torch beams gleaming behind her lit the hallway. She headed to the door to her left just as Kirby and McKeown arrived from the kitchen, having broken in through the back. She nodded, acknowledging them, and opened the living room door.

'Stop!' came a voice from inside. 'Don't come in.'

Lottie blinked, eyes adjusting to the dimness of the room, lit only by a standard lamp by the window. Three people were there. A woman lay on the couch, listless.

'She's unwell,' Lottie said. 'She needs to go to the hospital.'

'She's going nowhere.' The voice was sharp but weary.

That worried Lottie. People at the end of their tether were unpredictable, at their most dangerous.

'Can we talk? I think I know what went on. Jennifer and Éilis were working towards exposing a fraud that could bring your business down. Honestly, I don't blame you. I'd be mad myself.' Wrong word, she realised too late.

'How dare you! I am not mad. I have never been more lucid in my life. I can see the wrongs in this world. The naked greed that led to corruption. They were the ones who were mad. All of them tried to implicate me and my life's work and drove me to seek revenge.'

'Will you sit down and talk it out with me?' Lottie chanced.

'I'm done talking. Time for my last action. Come in and you can bear witness.'

Taking a deep breath, Lottie moved forward. She felt a tug on her jacket: Boyd, behind her, trying to prevent her from walking into the viper's nest. She shrugged him off.

'Only you, Inspector,' screamed the voice. 'You may leave, Detective. Close the door behind you.'

'It's okay, Boyd,' Lottie said, quickly assessing the situation.

The house was surrounded. She was safe, wasn't she? The woman stood regimentally tall, her back to the empty fireplace, holding a short blade, like a scalpel, in one of her hands. She would be able to disarm her, wouldn't she? Kathleen sat in an armchair, and on the couch, Helena lay motionless, eyes closed, skin pale, breathing shallow. Lottie didn't notice any blood and hoped the young woman was only drugged, not beaten.

Hearing the door click shut behind her, she waited.

The woman at the fireplace stared, her platinum hair faded in the dim light. 'Sit, Inspector.'

'I'd rather stand. Why, Madelene? Why all these deaths? What have you accomplished?'

'Would you like some tea? Kathleen made a pot for me earlier.'

Lottie glanced at Kathleen Foley. A silver teapot and china cups were laid out on a small table in front of her. She held an old biscuit tin on her knee, a photo in her hand. She was shaking, her eyes darting between her daughter and Madelene. Was she trying to tell Lottie something? Or was she just terrified?

'No tea, thank you, Madelene,' Lottie said, trying to keep her tone neutral. 'I want to know what your intentions are here.'

Madelene turned towards Kathleen and spoke directly to her.

'My love, I succeeded in keeping our relationship secret for so long, and I knew I would be vilified if those bitches revealed it. You received photos that proved someone knew about us. You should have told me, because I was sent them too. So maybe I'm at fault for not confiding in you.'

'What's a few photos got to do with anything?' Lottie asked, blinking with confusion.

Madelene continued to address Kathleen, slapping the blade's flat side against her trouser leg. 'I couldn't live with the shame of it becoming known. You know how I feel. Maybe I'm old fashioned in that respect, but to be outed... it would destroy me.'

Lottie fought hard to understand Madelene's reasoning. There was no shame in being gay. How could that idea lead the woman to murder?

Madelene continued, her voice monotone. 'And they threatened to blame me for the corruption of others. You were my friend, Kathleen. You fell victim to Damien and Tyler's greedy plans. Defrauding grieving widows. I promise you, I did not know what was going on, but when Jennifer came to me after Keating disappeared, she told me she had evidence of the scheme and wanted to make amends for her husband's actions. Silly girl. I panicked at first. Told her to wait, I had to think about it.'

'What did you do, Madelene?' Lottie interjected softly.

The woman dragged her eyes away from Kathleen and her black pupils rested on Lottie.

'I thought Jennifer had seen it my way; obviously I was wrong. I weighed up all my options, and I knew I could not let any of it become known. She wanted to report it. That would have destroyed my firm. People would have put two and two together and made ten.' She swivelled back to Kathleen. 'Then I got the photos. Someone knew about us. I suspected that Jennifer had found them among Damien's belongings. The bastard had been spying. Arming himself for blackmail if I ever discovered his wrongdoing. If those photos went public, people would have known about our relationship. How could I live with the shame of it? I had to consider you too, Kathleen.'

There was that word again. Shame. Ice slithered down Lottie's spine.

'How did Jennifer find out about the scheme?' She kicked herself for not surreptitiously switching on her phone to record.

'The bitch claimed she'd overheard Tyler discussing it with Frankie Bardon at the clinic. Said she talked to Damien but he denied it all. But then he died and she told Éilis Lawlor. They set up that silly little widows' group. I suspect they used it to work out how to damage me and my reputation.'

Lottie waited as Madelene drew breath. Was telling her story a delaying tactic? The vicious glint in the woman's eyes told her something else was going on behind them. But what? She kept one eye glued to the blade and the silence was so long that she asked, 'What did you do?'

'Nothing at first. That Tyler creep had disappeared. Not my doing, unfortunately. Then a month ago Jennifer appeared on my doorstep again. Mouthing off about her little group. Saying that Helena was struggling because her mother had sunk money into that damn studio and could no longer fund her shop. I was incensed. You should have told me at the time, Kathleen. I would never have allowed things to get so out of control.'

A sly smirk crossed Madelene's face as she glanced at Lottie. 'My dear friend and her daughter had suffered loss after loss. Even before our relationship developed beyond friendship, I owed her, Inspector. I owed her big-time.'

'Owed her for what?'

'Sweet little Amy, of course. My firm had dealt with her case. She had suffered a brutal childhood. Abandoned to the care system. Lost and anonymous. I pulled some strings, but I was single and childless, not allowed to foster back then. I desperately wanted to. I talked to Kathleen, and she agreed to foster her. She helped form that child into the woman she became. I secretly funded many placements for Amy over the years and hired her straight out of college, which I had paid for. I loved that girl.'

Madelene didn't know the meaning of the word, Lottie thought. 'If you loved her, why did you try to kill her?'

'She'd resigned her job without explanation. She'd joined that silly group. I feared she could corroborate what Jennifer knew. She never once came to me. I waited. All I got was a stony silence. I would have done anything for that girl, but in the end she let me down.'

Twisted love? Lottie wondered. No, not love, control.

'You took the eyes from your victims. You broke their bones. You killed them and displayed their bodies in obscure locations. Why did you let Amy live?'

'I wanted to kill her, but it got complicated.'

I know all about complicated! Lottie thought. Her head was buzzing.

Madelene continued. 'You arrived.'

'You assaulted me and a young guard.'

'I tried to muddy the waters.'

'Luke Bray?'

'I had represented him on his assault case when he was eighteen. He got community service, that's how good a solicitor I am. I saw him smoking outside Dolan's and paid him to unlock the back door of the shop so that his prints would be on it. In a way, I was glad you got to Amy before I could go back to her.'

'Is Amy related to you?'

'God, no. Her parents were crack addicts who used and abused her. I rescued her when she was three. Then she betrayed me when she left without explanation.'

'Tell me why Owen and Frankie had to die.'

'Simple. Owen wouldn't pay back Kathleen's investment. His state-of-the-art idea was anything but. He squandered the money Kathleen had borrowed at Amy's insistence. I believe Frankie knew about Tyler and Damien. If he talked, my firm's reputation would be in ribbons. I would be humiliated. In the end, my loyalty to my firm and to Kathleen outweighed any value their lives might have had. They deserved their fate.'

'And Tyler? Where is he?'

'I imagine he's where people think he is the salt of the earth.'

'Why all the mythological hints in the places where you left the bodies?'

'Frankie Bardon once attempted to study a course in mythology. I wanted to give you a riddle to solve. One of the few things I was wrong about.'

'What else were you wrong about?'

'You, Inspector. I thought I'd finish my mission before you unmasked me.'

Lottie feared what the final act of that mission might be. She glanced over at Helena. Her breathing was laboured. 'Can I ask the reason for the yellow dresses?'

'Don't you get it? Yellow signifies cowardice. They were all yellow-bellied cowards. Some preying on defenceless widows, and others wanted to shame me and destroy all I'd worked for. My brilliant mind was far superior to any scheme they might come up with.'

Lottie was about to ask why she'd targeted Orla, but she now knew how Madelene's brain worked. She'd have seen Orla as being instrumental in Tyler and Damien's swindling scheme and being part of the group.

Madelene stood straighter, flexing her arm muscles. 'What are you going to do now, Inspector?'

'I will arrest you and get Helena to a doctor.'

'You're as delusional as she is. You can't use anything I've just said.'

'I have evidence, including DNA from the house where we found Orla.' Lottie watched a dark shadow slip down Madelene's face. 'What did you give Helena?'

'Plenty of alcohol, which she willingly administered to herself.'

'And what was your plan for Kathleen?'

Madelene's fingers tightened around the scalpel. 'If you don't mind, I'll have some tea. I'm parched from talking.'

They'd been right about one thing, Lottie thought. This killer was arrogant.

As Madelene bent forward, either to pick up her teacup or to use her weapon, Lottie noticed a line of jars on the mantel behind her. Jars with pairs of eyes floating in some sort of liquid. Bearing witness after death. She realised now why Kathleen's face had been masked in horror.

Lottie hadn't time to be shocked by the jars. Kathleen burst out of her stupor. The biscuit tin fell, scattering the photos. In her hand she held a small bronze ornament. She whacked it hard into the solicitor's face. The scalpel flew into the air as Madelene fell, upending the table. Crockery smashed across the floor. The noise brought Boyd and Kirby bursting into the room.

Leaving them to deal with the two older women, Lottie moved towards the couch.

'Helena? I'm taking you to the hospital. Can you sit up?'

The young woman opened her eyes and nodded weakly. Lottie put one hand behind her head and the other around her back, up under her arm, and raised her to a sitting position.

'You're safe now.'

Helena glanced at her mother. Kathleen nodded silently as she was led out of the room by Kirby. Boyd had Madelene sitting up, her hands in cuffs. A trickle of blood seeped from her temple.

'Why?' Helena whispered.

'Life After Loss,' Madelene groaned. Then her voice sharpened. 'A hiding ground for secrets. Revealing those secrets would destroy me, my firm, and my relationship with your mother. And the fraudulent schemes could never become visible to the world. I had to stop them. Can't you see that?'

Helena shook her head.

Lottie's gaze rested on the jars of eyes.

She had no words.

102

It was late and the hospital was quiet by the time Kirby stepped out of the lift onto Level 3. Amy was sleeping, so he sat by her bed. He was nodding off when she awoke.

'You came back, Larry.'

'I did.'

'I'm so sorry.'

'For what?' He felt his stomach muscles clench. This was it. The confession. How she had used him for information. He really liked her, and now she was about to destroy that little bit of happiness she'd brought into his life.

'For not being honest with you from the start.'

'About Frankie Bardon being your ex?'

'I didn't think that was relevant to us. No, it's the rest...'

Kirby scratched his chin nervously. 'You don't have to talk about it now.'

'I do, if we are to have any chance...'

'Chance of what?' Maybe all would not be lost.

'Us. A relationship.'

'Okay, fine. Did you only meet up with me to get information?'

Her eyes never left his. She was one strong lady.

'Not really. I didn't stalk you or anything like that, but I knew you were a detective. I knew you from the television appeal you put out for Tyler Keating a year ago. It was coming up to the one-year anniversary and I decided to get close to you to see if I could be brave enough to tell you what I'd learned.'

'And what was that?' His voice wavered. Had she been more involved than Madelene had admitted? Was sweet Amy the reason Tyler was still missing?

'I knew some of what he'd been involved in before he went missing. I resigned a good job because of him. I was terrified to open my mouth about the property he'd hoodwinked from grieving widows. Orla claimed he coerced her, and swore the group to secrecy. I was a little scared of her, so perhaps she really was complicit in his deeds all along.'

'Why didn't you come forward at the time of Tyler's disappearance?'

'I was terrified. I thought that if I spoke up, he'd come after me.'

'Did you not suspect that he was dead, or had absconded abroad?'

'I didn't know what to think. Then when I was ready to talk to you, the murders started.'

'You thought he might have returned to commit them?'

'That, or he was dead and someone else was out for revenge.'

'Revenge on those who'd kept quiet at the time?'

'Or someone who wanted the truth to remain hidden.'

'You should have talked to me.'

'I'm sorry. I took the easy way out when I left Bowen's. I was already damaged from Frankie... and from before, as a child. Look, I'm not trying to get sympathy.'

'Kathleen Foley says you asked her to invest in Owen's studio. Why did you do that?'

'Frankie knew Kathleen had fostered me as a child. He thought she was loaded. Somehow he knew she had owned two properties, despite Tyler having stolen one from her. He said if I didn't convince her, he would make me pay. I knew what he meant by that, so I begged her. I'm sorry, Larry. I should have spoken up sooner.'

'That's okay.' He leaned back in the chair.

'When Jennifer was murdered, I truly believed Tyler was back. She knew all about the fraud. When she was clearing out her husband's desk at Bowen's, she found the boxes of files, copies of his and Tyler's deceitful corruption. She believed that the stress of what he was involved in caused Damien's cancer.'

'You really should have told me all this.' He didn't add that it might have helped save lives. He could see in her bloodshot eyes that she knew that already.

'Do you hate me?'

'No, Amy.'

'Have you lost respect for me?'

'Not that, either. In the back of my mind, I suspected it was too good to be true.'

He saw her eyes fill up and a little piece of his heart shattered.

'I'm so very sorry, Larry. For hurting you, and for being a sneaky bitch.'

He squeezed her hand and stood to leave.

'Do you think we could start over?' she asked.

He paused. Could they? Could he put her duplicity behind him? What the hell? Of course he could. Everyone had secrets at some stage in a relationship. Look at Madelene and Kathleen. Nothing was ever straightforward. No one was good all the time. He was certain Orla Keating could testify to that. He himself carried enough baggage to tip the largest scales.

'I can if you can,' he said softly. 'Do you really want to start over with me?' Had he actually said that? He must have done, because a wide smile broke out on her face.

'Oh God, yes, Larry. I do.'

'Once you get out of here, we're going away for a week to a nice secluded hotel. We'll get to know each other properly, and from now on we'll be honest with each other. Deal?'

She smiled crookedly, her face bearing the scars of her beating. 'Deal.'

He had no idea how he could afford a hotel for one night, let alone a week, but he wasn't about to allow lack of money to dim the dream. Money and greed had caused enough heartache, horror and death for one week. But could he truly trust Amy again? He was willing to give her a chance.

She grabbed his hand and pulled him down towards her, and every last doubt vanished.

103

The night had closed in around the lake, casting shadows over Farranstown House, by the time Lottie arrived home with Boyd in tow. He didn't want to go to his empty apartment with the evidence of the months he'd spent with his son scattered around. Once they had the case tied up, she would help him track down his bitch of an ex-wife and get Sergio back. Witnessing his heartbreak was unbearable.

The kitchen smelled of cooked food, and in the oven, a Pyrex dish held the remains of a stew. First, though, she needed tea. She flicked on the kettle.

Boyd unscrewed the cap of the Merlot he'd brought and searched for a clean wine glass.

'It's very quiet,' Lottie said, a worried furrow creasing her brow. 'Make the tea and I'll check on my mother.'

In the sitting room, she found Rose and Chloe folding clothes into an old suitcase.

'What's going on?'

'Ah, Lottie, there you are. Darling Chloe said she will come live with me for a while. Just until you realise I'm capable of being on my own again.'

Chloe rolled her eyes behind her grandmother's back. 'Gran is a hard taskmaster. She worked on me all day. I even swapped my shift tonight to help her pack. Isn't that right, Gran?'

'You're a good child,' Rose said. 'Unlike your mother, standing there with her mouth open. The image of her father, she is. Did you see my slippers?'

'On your feet,' Lottie said when her mouth eventually ceased flapping like a goldfish. 'You can't leave tonight. It's late, and your house will need to be aired before you go home.'

'I may be getting old and have a bit of that dementia yoke, but I'm not totally senile yet,' Rose said sternly. 'We're going tomorrow, aren't we, Chloe? Now be a good girl, Lottie, and make us a cup of tea. I'm parched. A slice of brown bread with plenty of jam on it would be nice. What would you like, pet?' She turned to Chloe.

'I'll have the same, Mam.' Chloe winked, and this time Lottie rolled her eyes before she returned to Boyd in the kitchen.

'You won't believe this.' She took the mug of tea from him, inhaling the grape aroma from the glass in his other hand.

'Try me.'

She told him about Rose and Chloe.

'Isn't that what you wanted?' he said, sipping his drink, leaving a red stain on his lips.

'Yeah. No. I don't know. Shit, Boyd, I don't want to ruin Chloe's life. Rose isn't easy.'

'I think Chloe is independent enough to make her own decisions. Like her mother.' He winked.

'I kind of backed her into it, didn't I?'

'Chloe Parker won't do anything she doesn't want to do, so quit fretting. If it doesn't work out, it doesn't work out. You have no control over it.'

'Thank you, wise old owl.'

'Less of the old, please.'

She poured more milk into her tea to cool it, and they sat side by side at the table, shoulders touching.

'I really miss him,' Boyd said, and bit back a sob.

'Come here.' She held his hand in hers. 'Jackie is a scheming bitch. She uses people. Including your son. If we have to turn the world upside down, we will get him back.'

'She has more of a right to him than I do.'

'Not if we use what we know about her. Just keep thinking of the great months you've had together and plan for his future with you.'

He gently kissed the top of her head.

'There are still a few things I don't understand,' she said. 'How did Madelene Bowen come to have access to the old house that Kathleen used to own?'

'She probably had keys because of their long relationship. Or she took them from Tyler before she killed him.'

'She hasn't admitted to doing anything to him. She confessed to the murders and abductions, but is resolute in her denial about his disappearance.'

'Maybe he really did skip town and is living it up somewhere with a new identity.'

'Wouldn't surprise me,' Lottie said. 'And why did she move his car to the lock-up?'

'Once Jennifer's body was discovered, she wanted us to suspect that Jennifer had killed him, perhaps.' Boyd drained his glass and reached for the bottle.

'Maybe.' But she wasn't convinced. 'That file from Madelene's briefcase has a list of Damien's clients cross referenced with those Orla Keating did accounts for. I'll hand it over to CAB to help their investigation into Tyler's fraudulent dealings.'

'Orla was more involved than she'd like us to believe,' Boyd said, and sipped his wine.

'For sure. Are you staying the night?'

'Is that an invitation?'

'Yes, old owl, I would love your company.'

'Do you just want to talk, Mrs Parker?'

She leaned up and kissed his wine-covered lips. 'Who said anything about talking?'

EPILOGUE

TWO WEEKS LATER

Jimmy Grennan was so late bringing in the turf from the bog this year, he wasn't sure it was even worth the hassle. He walked along the muddy trail, dragging the trolley of fertiliser bags behind him as he wended his way towards his plot. He'd had to leave the tractor and trailer up on the lane because the ground was still soft after the storm two weeks ago. He despaired of rescuing any of his turf. Still, he was thankful that the sun was beaming through the clouds today.

'Goddammit to hell,' he grumbled as his wellington boot stuck in a bog hole. He dragged his leg out of the murky brown water and promised himself there and then that he'd have a nice creamy pint of Guinness in Cafferty's later. That thought should keep him going over the next few hours.

He made his way slowly over the churned earth to the turf stacks. The sods on the outer edge of the stacks were wet, but underneath he discovered they were dry.

'Thank you, Lord,' he proclaimed, and got to work.

He hauled the first lot of bags onto the trolley and wheeled it to the trailer. He was on his way back to the plot when something caught his eye close to where he'd got his leg stuck earlier.

A piece of cloth? No, it was more like leather. People were always burying rubbish in the bog since the price of refuse collection had gone through the roof.

Bending over, he tugged at it, trying to dislodge it from the earth. He dropped the roll of fertiliser bags. It was the sleeve of a jacket, and within it he saw a bony hand with brown leathery skin.

An ancient bog body? he wondered. No, it couldn't be. They didn't have leather jackets, did they?

He got down on his haunches, careful not to fall into the stagnant water, and stared with his rheumy eyes. A ring on one of the fingers. Silver. He dragged away more of the turf, realising that the recent rain had unearthed this poor soul from his boggy grave. As he jostled his memory, he thought he knew who it was.

A curlew sounded across the bog. A breeze chilled the air.

As he brushed away the soggy soil with his fingers, Jimmy uncovered more of the jacket. Then a shirt collar. A leathery neck. Skin turned tan from the bog.

He *had* found a bog body. But it wasn't centuries old. It had only been buried for twelve months.

Jimmy Grennan knew he was slow on the uptake at times, especially after a few pints, but he was right about this. He recalled the appeals he'd seen a year ago. The man's photo on lamp posts. The dry-eyed wife in front of clicking cameras, pleading for information about her missing husband.

He rummaged in his trouser pocket for his phone and dialled 999.

Then he slowly made the sign of the cross and waited.

Jimmy wasn't in a hurry to go anywhere, and he knew Tyler Keating wasn't either.

———

The hospital smells too much like a hospital, Orla thinks. The air is too clean, following the stench of the place where she was held. Her eyes are bandaged to protect them from the light. Scar tissue on her retinas from the beating she'd sustained, the consultant said.

The news on the television is too loud. She wishes someone would turn it off. She could call out to the guard outside her door. He's posted there to ensure she doesn't escape. As if she could, with two broken legs. They want to interview her when she is able. She is aware of what they know. But they don't know it all. They have no idea of her biggest and most daring crime. Complicit in stealing from a few widows? No, it's something far worse. A crime that will never be discovered. She is totally confident of that.

The newsreader mentions something about a bog body.

Orla tries to straighten up. She's unable to move. Confined. The sound of trolleys out on the corridor is too loud. The television not loud enough, now that she wants to listen.

'Shush,' she says.

The newsreader tells the world about the male body in a leather jacket found by a man cutting his turf.

'Local gardaí are on the scene. Our reporter Sinead Healy is there. What can you tell us this evening, Sinead?'

'I spoke with Superintendent Farrell from Ragmullin garda station earlier. She confirmed the deceased is not an ancient bog body. An incident room has been set up and they will be investigating it as a suspicious death. Local people are saying this could be the body of Tyler Keating, who went missing just over a year ago. His wife is currently in hospital recovering from serious injuries sustained in an alleged attack by the suspected serial killer Madelene Bowen. Back to you in the studio.'

Orla sighed heavily, thinking back over her mistakes. One of the more critical mistakes was moving his car. Panic set in once Jennifer had disappeared, and she thought she could lay the blame at her door by leaving it in her lock-up. Stupid GPS. She hadn't thought of that. She should have left it where it was, in the old goods carriage close to where Kathleen Foley used to live. That would have thrown suspicion on Kathleen and Madelene, who she'd targeted with explicit photos. She'd stolen them from Jennifer after Tyler *disappeared*. Even the most recent one she'd left at Kathleen's door hadn't brought a result. Such a shame, really.

It's all been for nothing, she thinks wearily. CAB are investigating Tyler. It had to be Jennifer or stupid Éilis who contacted them. Orla's role in the schemes will soon be discovered. And, she is powerless to convince anyone that she had been coerced by Tyler.

She clenches her eyes behind their bandages.

Curls her hands into fists.

He couldn't even stay buried.

She feels his hand reach out for her, dragging her with him down to the murky darkness.

A LETTER FROM PATRICIA

Hello, dear reader,

I am delighted that you have read *Three Widows*, book twelve in the Lottie Parker series. If you want to keep up to date with all my latest releases, just sign up at the following link.

www.bookouture.com/patricia-gibney

Your email address will never be shared, and you can unsubscribe at any time.

I hope you enjoyed *Three Widows*. If you did, I'd be absolutely delighted if you could post a review on Amazon or on the site where you purchased the eBook, paperback or audiobook. It means a lot to me and I'm grateful for the reviews received so far.

To those of you who have already read the other eleven Lottie Parker books, *The Missing Ones, The Stolen Girls, The Lost Child, No Safe Place, Tell Nobody, Final Betrayal, Broken Souls, Buried Angels, Silent Voices, Little Bones* and *The Guilty Girl*, I thank you for your support and reviews. If *Three Widows* is your first encounter with Lottie, you are in for a treat when you read the previous eleven books in the series.

You can connect with me on my Facebook author page, Instagram or Twitter.

Thanks again for reading *Three Widows*.
    I hope you will join me again for book thirteen in the series.

Love,

Patricia

facebook.com/trisha460

twitter.com/trisha460

instagram.com/patricia_gibney_author

ACKNOWLEDGEMENTS

I want to thank you for reading *Three Widows* and for joining Lottie on this journey. Thank you to one of my readers, Orla Machin (née Keating), who had the highest bid in the Everyday Kindness auction in aid of Shelter charity to have her name used in this book.

Many people have been involved in bringing *Three Widows* to you, and I wish to take this opportunity to thank them. As ever, special thanks to my agent Ger Nichol of The Book Bureau, who works tirelessly for me. Thanks to Hannah Whitaker at The Rights People, for sourcing foreign translation publishers for my books.

Thank you to my editor, Lydia Vassar-Smith, whose editorial expertise enhances my books. To Kim Nash, I am grateful for your friendship, advice and work on my behalf and congratulations on your promotion to Digital Publicity Director at Bookouture. Thanks also to Sarah Hardy, Jess Readett and Noelle Holten for their promotional work, and to Mark Walsh of Plunkett PR in conjunction with Hachette Ireland.

Special thanks to those who work directly on my books at Bookouture: Alex Holmes (production), Alex Crow, Mel Price, Occy Carr and Ciara Rosney (marketing). Thanks to Tom Feltham for proofreading.

I'm forever grateful to Jane Selley for her excellent copy-editing skills and being able to see things I totally missed.

Sphere Books and Hachette Ireland publish my books in trade paperback, and I'm thankful for their support. Thanks also to all my foreign translation publishers for producing my books in their native languages. And thanks to all the translators for their tremendous work.

Michele Moran brings my books to life in the English-language audio format and has narrated all my books to date. Thanks to Michele and the team at 2020 Recordings.

My sister, Marie Brennan, helps me with the editing process and proofreading, and I am so thankful to her for this work.

Bookshops and libraries are essential in the heart of every town, and I am grateful to booksellers and librarians everywhere.

As an author, I know how important reviews are for my books, and to each reader who takes the time to post a review, thank you. A massive thank you to the book bloggers and reviewers who read and review my books. I appreciate the time and effort this entails. I am so grateful for your time.

I wouldn't be able to write these books without the support and encouragement of my family. My children, Aisling, Orla and Cathal, are the strongest, most hard-working and loving young people I know. My children and grandchildren fill me with love and gratitude.

I dedicate this book to my Uncle Louis who sadly passed away on 1st November 2022. A golfer, an artist and a family man. He will be missed.

On a final note, you, dear reader, make my writing worthwhile. I'm currently writing the next book in the series (book thirteen), so you shouldn't have too long to wait to see what happens in the world of Lottie, Boyd and, of course, Kirby! Sincere thanks for accompanying me on this journey.

Note: I fictionalise a lot of the police procedures to add pace to the story. Inaccuracies are all my own.

Made in United States
North Haven, CT
02 October 2024

58193913R00281